POSSUM HO

DIRTY

ERIN RUSSELL

By Erin Russell

Copyright © 2024 by Erin Russell
Cover by Erin Russell

All rights reserved.

ISBN 979-8-9899256-1-2

STUPID
DIRTY

ERIN RUSSELL

CONTENTS

A Note on Content

Possum Hollow is a fictional small town in rural Missouri. All the roads and surrounding towns mentioned are also fictional, so don't look for them on a map. The world was inspired by real places where I spent some of my childhood.

X

The backdrop for the series is one of rural poverty. Across the series, you'll find common themes of drug & alcohol abuse, family violence, parental neglect, toxic masculinity & violence, cultural homophobia and untreated mental illness.

X

This book features plotlines regarding depression & suicide (off-page or ideation), on-page family violence & neglect, disordered/controlled eating, and postpartum mental health issues that some readers may find triggering.

For each book in the series, I list the most significant triggers at the front, but if you'd prefer to read a comprehensive list that may contain spoilers for the story, please check my website.

www.erinrussell.com/content-warnings

The American Motor League is also a fictional institution, because I didn't want to besmirch the real organization. I've tried to keep true to the reality of professional motocross as much as possible, but a few liberties had to be taken for the sake of telling a good story.

We're all here for the dicks and feels anyway, not a term paper on professional motorsport operations.

CHAPTER ONE

CADE

I know I should be used to this, but I'm still so fucking pissed that I nearly rip the door off its hinges when I open it.

Which would be perfect. Because this trailer is falling apart as it is, and I'll be the one who has to fix it.

"Mom! Get your ass out here!"

I slam the plywood door behind me, but the crappy bolt doesn't catch, and it swings open again, letting more of the oppressive August heat in. Anger squeezes my chest and creeps up my throat until I have to stop in the doorway to take a deep breath, reining in the urge to cause as much destruction as possible.

I will not turn into my father.

Blowing a breath out slowly, I turn around and grab the cracked, ill-fitting door, closing it firmly but not slamming it. My heart is still hammering in my chest, but I feel under control enough not to cause property damage. I'm still holding on to my sister's hunting bow, and my fingers are clenched so tightly that it's hard to let go. I have to relax them one by one before I can set it down on the kitchen counter and move deeper into the house.

'House'. Trailer.

Whatever.

My shithead father, as his last act before abandoning this family for good, scavenged up two half-rotten double-wides, cut out the usable parts and basically glued them together. So the layout doesn't make any sense, and it looks like Frankenstein fucked a Winnebago and this is their spawn, but it's better than nothing.

The front door opens directly into the little corner that functions as a kitchen, and then a narrow hallway covered in uneven, water-stained linoleum leads me past the bedrooms and bathroom. I've spent every one of my twenty-two years living in this ugly beast, and each dip in the floorboards or sag in the ceiling feels like it's mapped out in my DNA. The hallway takes me to the open space at the back, which has a couch and a TV and everything else a living room should have, but because there aren't enough rooms for everyone, it's also where my mom sleeps.

Or, in this case, passes out.

"Mom!"

Thank fuck the girls are at school, so there's no reason to tamp down on my anger. I'm bellowing, but she doesn't flinch. The trace of white powder on the coffee table tells me everything I need to know. Mom has been doing well lately. She's stuck to her softer vices like booze and nicotine, but it looks like now we're back to theft and oxy and all that progress is in the past.

Judging from the peaceful expression on her face, she's still high enough to be blissfully numb to the guilt of her shitty actions.

Not on my watch.

It seems harsh, but this is about the thousandth time this has happened, and I'm over it. My job pays the bills around here because she's burned bridges with nearly everyone in this town. And now the prize money I won from the race last weekend is in the pocket of the pawnshop owner instead of buying groceries, because Maddi woke me up this morning sobbing when she realized her bow was missing, along with our mother.

Most people would think thirteen is young for a hunting bow to be your prized possession. Hunting is still a way of life in rural areas like ours, though. Not to mention, she's kicking ass in the archery competitions at school.

Our trailer is set on the back corner of a plot of woodland that used to belong to my nana. When she sold it to move into a nursing home, her only requirement was that the rancher who bought it keep renting the space to us for pennies on the dollar. Which makes it affordable, thank fuck, but also means we're miles from anywhere and my sisters have grown up with a lot more bow hunting and wood chopping than other kids their age.

Either way, thirteen years old is definitely too young for her first assumption to be that her mom stole from her, and for that assumption to be correct. I remember the feeling, and it's something I've spent my entire life trying to protect my little sisters from.

Sitting on the table, there's an old gallon jug of water, still two-thirds full. Without stopping to second-guess myself, I pick it up, flip off the cap and turn it upside down over her head.

It doesn't take long before she's awake and sputtering under the stream, scrabbling away from me until her ass hits the floor. "Mother of fuck!" she shrieks, pushing wet, dark hair out of her face and shooting me a glare.

I'd be more inclined to feel bad about it if my dad hadn't been the one to teach me that little trick. Before he skipped town, he used to love waking me up with a bucket of water to the face while he filmed it on their shitty digital camera and laughed his ass off. Mom was always too high to stop him, I guess. At least the water I used wasn't ice cold.

I point at her, looking her in the eye so she knows I am absolutely not fucking around right now.

"Get up. Get dressed, and go beg for your shifts back at the Dollar Tree. I just spent my entire prize from last weekend getting back Maddi's bow, and you're paying me back this time. She saved all year to get that bow, and she doesn't have much longer to practice if she wants to qualify for state finals this year. Do you want your daughters to have a better life than you? Or do you want them to be stuck here with you and me in this shitty trailer, rotting away?"

She groans and rubs her hand over her face. It takes her a while to pull herself back up onto the sagging couch that's such an ugly shade of brown it could only have been made in the seventies. A lifetime of poor choices and worse nutrition has left her body much smaller than her personality, but she still looks tough: all short, sharp lines with sun-damaged skin drawn tightly over bony edges. But today, something about her looks frail.

For a second, I'm about to cave, and let her off the hook again. But I can't. She's got kids to feed.

"Get. Up."

My arms are crossed over my chest as I take a deep breath. I'm waiting for the screaming to start, because my mother has never been one to back down from a fight. Yelling is our primary form of communication around here, and normally I don't care. But sometimes when shit gets serious like this, she has a way of making me feel like I'm eight years old and four feet tall again, and I can't afford to back down right now.

Of course, then she starts to cry.

Not big, dramatic sobs, like I've seen her do when she's trying to get her way. This is the quiet crying, when she actually feels like shit.

"I'm sorry, Cade." Her voice cracks, and she sniffs and sobs between the words. "I wanted to get the girls some stuff for the new school year, and I thought I had enough to cover it, but then the check bounced and they were going to take me back to County if I didn't pay them back. I didn't know what else to do. I was gonna find the money to get it back before it got sold, I swear."

There's nothing I can do but sigh. Today wasn't supposed to be a real feelings day.

Anger is like an old friend that always has my back. I can do anger in my sleep. Anger keeps me safe. Other emotions are dangerous, and I don't have the bandwidth for them right now. But my mother is the one person who's been consistent in my life, even if it's consistently shitty, and she always knows how to get under my skin.

Crouching down in front of her, the last of my rage dissipates and leaves a profound sense of exhaustion in its wake. I put myself at eye level with her where she's huddled on the couch, before reaching out to touch her face and wipe away some of the snot and tears.

I swear, sometimes the moments where she tries to be a mom, but does it in the most chaotic way possible, are harder than all the other shit. It's too much of a tease.

"We've talked about this. You have to tell me first, and I'll figure something out. You can't keep taking away the girls' stuff, even if you are getting it back. They're too young to get it. Tell me first, okay? No more breaking into the girls' room. Promise me."

I hate how soft my voice is right now. But she's my mom. She'll never win any parenting awards, but she protected me from a lot when my dad was still around, fiercely, when she could. And no matter how much of a wreck things were, she always made me feel loved.

That counts for something.

She nods at me, still looking kind of pitiful.

"I promise. I just wanted to take care of it myself, for once."

Sighing one more time, I release the last of my anger. "And spare change goes on food, not fucking oxy, okay?"

Suddenly, the carpet is really interesting to her. I decide that's enough fighting for one day, so I kiss her on the forehead and let her go back to sleep.

My mom had just about the shittiest childhood a person can have. The kind of childhood that gets written about in *Time* magazine articles or made into *Lifetime* movies so the middle class can get their vicarious thrills over the woes of American poverty. And my dad didn't keep us all chained in the basement or anything, but he was no prize, either.

She's been through a lot, and she's never stopped trying to take care of us. I owe her for that, in spite of all this shit.

I wander back into the kitchen, running my hand through my hair and taking deep, slow breaths to get my frustration under control. My hair is thick, dark and curly enough to always look messy, so I shave the sides to keep it at least a little under control, but it's too long right now and falling in my eyes. My best friend Wish calls it my "fuckboy haircut", which annoys the shit out of me. I'm tempted to shave it all off for the thousandth time.

But I know I won't. I like it when girls tell me I look like a model. It's not like I'm even getting them into bed, it's just a nice little ego boost once in a while. I have almost no worldly possessions apart from this trailer, my decrepit old truck, and my dirt bike, so I let myself cling to my vanity more than I should. Sue me.

A quick survey of the kitchen shows a depressing lack of food in the fridge, and it's almost the end of the month, which means bills. EMTs in this county get a paycheck every other week because we're on hourly. I got paid three days ago, so I won't get anything else for a week and a half, and my prize money is already drained.

One day, I'll be able to race because I want to, and not have to care about the win. I love everything about it, from the smell of fresh earth mixed with gasoline to the punch of an engine starting up beneath me. I love feeling like I'm flying. But until the girls grow up or mom gets her act together, the money is always going to come first.

There's another race this weekend. I hadn't been planning on going, because Jasper County is four hours away, which means I'll need to crash with someone and come back the next day. I already leave the girls alone with Mom overnight when I go to my actual job. I try not to add to it for motocross. But it looks like this time I don't have a choice.

I'll have to enter, and winning that prize money isn't going to be optional.

CHAPTER TWO

SILAS

The water stain on the ceiling over my bed looks exactly like a possum. At least, I thought it did when I was a kid. I remember lying here, staring at it for hours when I couldn't sleep, tracing all the little whorls and patterns in the flaking paint, convinced that it was a magical manifestation of the town's namesake.

It's been six years since we left this house, and it's still here. I'm kind of surprised that the ceiling hasn't collapsed yet, to be honest. The house was already sagging with neglect when Dad sold all our furniture and boarded up the front door, and neither of us had set foot in it until last week, when we both showed up with our tails between our legs. My motocross career was supposed to be our ticket out of this town, but it didn't take much for that to collapse like a house of cards.

My childhood home, which was his childhood home before that, is a two-story clapboard house, sitting on a small lot of weeds that are trying to strangle the last drop of life from it, on a street of other decrepit clapboard houses on weed-choked lots, running along the edge of town.

Dad insists he didn't sell it for sentimental reasons, but I suspect that's bullshit. It's because the property value has only gone down since we left. He's hoping that one day the meth dealers will move on and it'll be worth something to sell. I sincerely doubt it, but good for him for being optimistic.

Possum Hollow is a decaying town built around agricultural products that are becoming obsolete. It has a population of less than 2,000 and the tallest man-made structure is the Dairy Queen sign. If you want a job that's not in a store or on a farm, you're shit out of luck.

People aren't exactly flocking here to buy real estate.

Personally, I think we should have taken the loss to get rid of the house and all its ghosts as soon as we left the first time. Dad never wanted to come back here, and neither did I. The air has been suffocating since the moment we stepped inside.

But here we are. It's not like we have any other options. Dad's fondness for 'investment opportunities' means we've never been able to keep savings for long. As soon as my license was suspended, I lost the ability to enter national races. No races means no prize money, and definitely no sponsorships. Not that I was rolling in those to begin with. That's a cold, hard guillotine on all my sources of income, all in a matter of hours.

Now I'm a grown-ass man, sleeping on an old mattress on the floor in my childhood bedroom because we haven't bought new furniture yet, staring at the same damn stain. Feeling the same weird, elusive numbness that I did back then. Trying to avoid thinking about anything in particular, and especially the fact that I have to race today.

"Silas! Get up or we're going to be late! It's a four-hour drive to the track!"

My dad's voice booming up the stairwell jolts me into action on instinct. No thought required.

I can shower, get dressed, and then "yes, sir, no sir, three bags full, sir," my way through breakfast, also no thought required. I know he's going to be in a pissy mood today, so I don't want to give him any excuse to spend the entire drive bitching at me.

He's been in a pissy mood since we moved back. As if it's not his fault that we had to. But today is the first time I'll be missing a race in the American Motorsports League Pro Tour. We're supposed to be in Florida right now, but instead we're back home in Missouri: broke, humiliated and facing an uncertain future. All because of my father's stupid, reckless actions.

Of course, he's going to find a way to take it out on me. I just hope it can wait until after the race. I need to focus, and we need the lousy excuse for prize money that I'll get from winning the 450 class pro race of the shithole-something county fair.

When I get downstairs, my dad is leaning against the kitchen counter with a cup of coffee in his hand, watching me with cold blue eyes. My spine straightens on instinct. For the millionth time, I'm glad I got my looks from my mom's side. I spend enough time with those eyes boring into me. I can't imagine if I had to see them staring back at me in the mirror as well.

Dad always seems to think he has a sixth sense for whether I'm 'ready' for a race or not, whatever that means. He claims it's from all his experience as a pro racer back in the day. But the truth is, I've heard the stories. Things were a little looser in the nineties, and he and his buddies spent their glory days of racing so fucked up I'd be amazed if he could remember half of it.

He just loves any excuse to talk about his legacy.

There's a plate on the counter of the same meal I've eaten before every race for the past five years. Steamed chicken, scrambled eggs and kale, boiled oats, all meticulously measured and planned out to the last calorie. I choke it down as quickly as possible while he watches me, like always. It sits in my stomach like lead, making my body sluggish as I drag myself to the next step of our routine.

A distant part of me wonders what it would be like to spend a day without having my calorie intake kept on a tight leash, also like always. Motocross riders need to maintain the maximum amount of physical strength to the least amount of bulk. The lighter you are, the faster you'll ride. Dad was made for it. He's average height and built like a greyhound; all wiry, coiled power.

I am not. I'm 6'1" and broad-shouldered, with a body that desperately wants to put on muscle or fat or both. I'm meant to be thick. Dad wasn't going to let that get in the way of me living his dream though, so I've been on a strict diet since before I was old enough to know what one was, and it's kept me lean. *Ish.*

That, the lifetime of training, and a fuck ton of grit was enough to go pro, but I was never going to be one of the greats. Which is fine. I've been happy kicking around at the bottom of the professional pack. I like staying out of the spotlight.

And whenever Dad told me that this season was going to be the season I made it big, I just nodded and pretended that I believed it as much as he did.

Or that I even wanted it.

Once breakfast is done and we're in the truck with my bike and gear securely loaded in the back, I can relax a little. For the next four hours, I don't have to do anything but sit here and hydrate. Dad will be too irritable to make conversation, if there is a god.

It's so early that the sun has barely risen, the night sky lingering like a faded bruise. I lean my head against the window and watch the scenery pass by. We haven't been back to Missouri much since we left, so it all feels somehow foreign and familiar at the same time.

We're right by the border with Arkansas, and the countryside here looks exactly the same. It's all trees and hills and farmland, as far as you can see. Everything is green. But not a lush, verdant green like farms in pictures. It's all brown-tinged. As if the heat or poverty or some combination of them are siphoning the life from everything, everywhere I look. The cracks running through the two-lane blacktop seem like they're trying to tear it apart, and every plant we pass looks brittle.

Or maybe I'm just projecting.

Shifting in my seat, I try to snap out of my myopic daze and look down at my phone. I've been scrolling through names of local racers to see if there's anyone I recognize that might give me competition. I've been racing at a national level for years, so to be pulled back down to the county fairs and local tracks I can access without an AML license means I should be punching well below my weight.

A lot of guys I've met would hate that. They'd say without the thrill of the competition, there's no point. But not me. I don't care about getting the edge on anyone; I don't get any kind of juice out of passing someone at the last possible second. I just want to win races, collect my prize and keep my dad happy.

I'm scrolling absently, not really thinking about anything, when I see a name I do recognize.

Cade Waters.

Fuck. I remember him. We went to school together before I started getting enough wins under my belt for my dad to be my manager/coach/jailer first, parent second, and take me across state lines for races.

Cade was an excellent rider. As soon as he got on his bike, he had this intense focus. Like riding was all he was.

But off the track, he was the total opposite. All smiles, he was always getting in trouble at school for goofing around. I think his home life was a mess, but for a farm town in this area, that's not unusual. He had friends; he had a life. He always seemed totally unstoppable.

I was so jealous of him.

I've spent every day of my life with some invisible storm cloud hanging over me, but Cade seems to walk around with sunshine permanently on his face. I'd slit my wrists to have a little taste of that.

Okay—that was the worst possible way for my brain to frame that thought.

Reeling in my melancholy, I do my best to shake the thought from my head. Actually, I try to shake all the thoughts from my head. Cade probably won't be racing today, considering it's a long-ass drive for not a great pay-off. But I wonder what it would be like to see him.

I wonder if he still has that big, easy smile that always made all the girls go goofy for him. I wonder if life has beaten that out of him yet.

The rumble of the truck is enough to lull me into an uneasy sleep, with my face pressed against the window and the rising sun warming my cheek.

I don't really dream, but my brain throws up more flashes of memories from when we lived here. And Cade's stupid smile is one of them.

Dad makes the last few checks and adjustments on my bike, even though I already looked everything over, while I start my pre-race routine, double-checking that all my gear is in place.

I don't know why I get paranoid before a race, but I do, every single time. I put all my gear on in the same order, and everything goes left to right. Every zip and cuff and clasp gets checked and checked again.

Ever since I was little, my brain has been convinced that if I do things out of order, or forget to double-check something, it'll end up coming loose during the race. I'm haunted by the mental image of a piece of my knee brace or the hem of my jersey getting tangled in the chain, ripping me off the bike mid-ride and throwing me to the ground so I can be mowed down by the other riders.

Which is ridiculous, because it's literally designed not to do that. It's the least likely thing to go wrong during a race. Also, coming off your bike is a totally normal part of racing, and happens every time. Nobody gets run over, everyone just goes around you until you can get out of the way and remount.

But knowing that doesn't get my brain to shut up. Images of getting my skull popped under a rogue front tire can't be kicked out of there by logic.

The shittiest, most life-defining thing that's ever happened to me had a 0.00004% chance of happening. That's less than a one in a million chance, and my family got to win that miserable lottery. I actually sat down and did the math once.

Anything can happen to anyone.

I normally run through this pre-race ritual with a laser focus, but this time, something distracts me for a second. A rider pulls up his bike a few gates down, and there's something in the way he moves that's so familiar. He's a lot taller and broader than the gangly teenager I used to race against, but I don't need to look at his face to know it's him.

Fucking Cade. So he is here, after all. The shock of seeing such a familiar face when I wasn't expecting it makes my breath catch in my chest, and I end up staring at him for longer than I should.

He looks good. I was always jealous of his delicate, pretty features, and they look even better now that the rest of him has filled out. He's got a fashionable haircut that's letting dark curls fall in his face in a way that makes me want to push them back, and also makes me feel like my high and tight is boring as hell. But I guess I'm boring as hell, so that works.

His gear is all worn and none of it matches, which makes sense for a weekend warrior. No sense wasting your money on matching gear for what can be a very expensive hobby. The only thing it all has in common is that it's all fucking pink. White, black, bubblegum pink and hot pink, to be exact, making him stand out like a flamingo, even in the flurry of bright colors that make up the line of riders.

All dirt bike gear is brightly colored, but leave it to Cade to take it the extra mile and make sure he's still the center of attention. I watch him tip his head back to laugh at something, revealing a tattoo of a bird or something on the side of his neck, rippling over the tendons of his throat as he moves.

My attention is drawn to the person standing next to him and making him laugh. It's a girl, at least half a foot shorter than him, and petite. She's about the same age as us, and I might recognize her from high school. But she has a short, ice-blue mohawk and multiple tattoos covering her neck, crawling up under the dark fade on each side of her head, so I'm guessing she's changed her appearance in the past few years. I can't quite place her.

There's an easy familiarity to the way they're laughing and smiling with each other, and I feel a pang of jealousy as she reaches out and chucks him on the chin.

Of course, Cade is goofing around right before we ride instead of focusing on preparing. His intensity will snap into place the second he gets on that bike. In the meantime, he's enjoying the company of the people around him, like always. She's probably his girlfriend.

Or wife, I guess. We're old enough now, which is a sobering thought. Maybe one of her tattoos matches Cade's bird.

Either way. They look happy.

She's dressed like a rider as well, with a rumpled jersey and dirt smudged over the bridge of her nose, so I guess she rode in a different class earlier and is here to watch him now.

It's so cute I could puke all over my bike.

Good for Cade. If anyone was going to end up happy despite everything, it was going to be him. He had that quality. I wasn't even friends with him, and I could see that.

I wasn't friends with anyone, to be fair. My rigorous training regimen didn't leave a lot of time for socializing. Between that and what people have described as my "off-putting personality"...

Yeah, someone like Cade would never have been buddies with someone like me.

Looking back down at my gloves, I realize I've completely lost my place in what I was checking, and it makes my stomach twist. Everyone's bikes are at the starting gates now and their helmets are on. The countdown to the gates dropping is about to begin. We're running out of time.

"Silas!"

By the tone of Dad's voice, I'm guessing this isn't the first time he's said my name.

"Thirty seconds, son, move your ass!"

He's a little wide-eyed, and I realize I'm not on my bike yet. Fuck. I didn't finish checking anything. Fuck. There's no time left, and the strands of what little control I have over my life are slipping right through my fingers.

Fuck.

I swing my leg over and get into position, trying to let the familiarity of it all counter the gnawing sense of wrongness in my gut.

Just focus on the win. These are a bunch of amateurs. Just ride until you win. If you lose here, you really will be useless. Just win.

I ignore the fact that the voice in my head sounds more like my dad's than mine.

When the gate snaps down, I hesitate, and by the time my bike jumps forward, I'm already in the middle of the pack.

Fuck.

CHAPTER THREE

CADE

This never gets old. All the other shit in my life fades away and gets drowned out by the thrum of adrenaline through my veins. All I see is dirt. All I smell is fuel. I move with the bike, constantly adjusting my body to counterbalance so I can keep leaning around every corner and flying over every jump as fast as I can.

Nothing will ever compare to the pure joy of breaking out into the lead and then tearing through the course, lap after lap, leaving everyone else in your dust.

I was apprehensive when Wish told me that Silas Rush would be racing today. Well, first I was fucking flabbergasted, then I was apprehensive.

Apparently, I live under a rock and am the only person in the state that didn't know about him and his dad moving back to town. No one knows why Silas quit in the middle of the AML season. Only an idiot would give up a fancy-ass pro career to come back here and ride kiddie league with us. But Wish assured me that the rumors range from cheating scandals to injury rumors to alien abductions.

Sure.

I've watched him race since he joined the national circuit at sixteen, and he's never become a superstar, but he's a solid rider. Just like when we were kids, he was always reliable and consistent. If there was a textbook for motocross, he would have followed it. Hell, he would have written it. He was picture-perfect technique. He never had heart, though, even when we were little. From day one, he was like a dirt bike robot.

Nothing ever got to him, and he barely acknowledged that the rest of us existed. He just showed up, rode well, didn't talk to anybody and then went home. Over and over and over.

He obviously thought he was too good for us, just because he had a former pro for a dad and lived in a house that didn't have wheels. I wasn't going to waste time and energy trying to talk to some rich asshole with a superiority complex.

It's a lot easier to go pro when you have all the equipment you need and all the time in the world to train, instead of worrying about putting food on the table.

He had everything handed to him on a platter, and now he's giving it up? To come back to Nowhere, USA and compete for prize money that I desperately need, but probably means nothing to someone like him.

It pisses me off.

I wasn't prepared to face him today. Especially on a day when I need this prize money so badly.

He looked just like he does on TV. Dark blond hair cut short and neat. Impassive face. Everything about him is uniform and neat, and he's wearing the same boring-ass gray and black gear he always wears. I caught him staring at me while we were at the gates, with the same weird, blank expression he used to have. The one I assume he uses to cover up his disdain, or whatever.

Which I'm used to, especially from him. There's not one inch of me that doesn't scream *white trash,* and I've made my peace with it. But when I saw him eyeing Wish with the same judgy robot stare, I felt anger trying to claw its way to the forefront of my attention.

17

Times have changed, even in places like the back ass of Missouri. But Wish has always been unapologetically herself, from her tattoos and punky haircuts to coming out as bi when we were teenagers, and she still gets shit for it sometimes from the more conservative side of the community. She doesn't need my protection, but that doesn't mean I'm going to stop being protective of her, ever.

Especially from straight, cis, rich, white boys who've spent their entire lives thinking the world revolves around them. I never heard him say anything bigoted back in school, mostly because he never condescended to talk to any of us, but I've heard his father say plenty of shit and I'm sure the apple doesn't fall far from the very privileged tree.

All of that bled away as soon as I left the gate. The second the moto started, it was just me and my bike, and as soon as I got the holeshot—being the first rider to hit that initial corner—I knew I was in for a good ride. I'd expected to be neck and neck with robot boy, if not trailing behind him, so the fact that I couldn't see him anywhere in my periphery took the pressure off and let me focus on myself.

The 450 class is grueling. It's thirty minutes on the track, around and around, but I've always kind of liked that about it. You can get lost in it. Nothing else matters, it's just you, your bike and the dirt. And it's dry as hell today, making every turn and landing take that much more muscle power to keep myself stable on the loose grit.

By the final lap, I know I have it in the bag. No one has gotten near me in a while, and I haven't seen Silas, so I assume he must have wiped out somewhere or gotten bogged down at the start and never made up the time. The profound sense of peace that I associate with a win is already settling over me as I go into one of the last turns of the track.

Which is when I finally catch sight of him. And he is *flying*. I see him out of the corner of my eye, shredding through the track, moving way faster than he should be for a track this dry and going for too much distance on every jump.

His head is down, and I recognize that same grim, soulless determination that's been keeping him on the national stage. In all those years, though, I've never seen him ride recklessly before.

And this is reckless. He's a hair's breadth from washing out in the loose dirt. We slip on the track all the time. It's part of the race, but at the speed he's going, he could really get fucked up.

I can see him gaining on me, and it splits my focus as I go into the final turn. My inside leg is out for balance, and I realize I fucked up and left him way too much space on the inside. If he's close enough, he can easily pass me.

The roar of his engine in my ears tells me he's definitely close enough.

But, instead of passing me in the eight-freaking-foot gap I stupidly left for him, he slides in so close to me that my inside leg knocks against his leg, which is scary enough. It's not hard to catch your heel on something and tear an ACL when you're sticking your foot in the fucking air half the ride.

And instead of pulling straight away and into the lead, that reckless dipshit lets his back wheel fishtail. Just a little. Not enough to make him lose his balance, but enough to knock into my front wheel and send my bike careening into the berm lining the track.

My left side explodes in pain as I end up in the dirt with my bike half on top of me. I've been moving forward relentlessly for half an hour, and now that I'm suddenly still and lying in the dirt, the world telescopes in front of me like I'm still moving. All I can hear is the sound of my own ragged breathing and the blood pounding in my ears.

That fucking asshole. He just ripped the prize money out of my hands and nearly killed me in the process. I want to snap his fucking neck.

That's my first concrete thought.

I've seen him ride a thousand times. Just because we weren't friends doesn't mean I don't know what kind of rider he is, and the one thing he's always had is absolutely perfect control. Too much control. I honestly think he was born to do some other fancy-ass sport, like fencing, and was cursed to slum it in motocross with us rednecks because of his heritage.

There's no way in hell that was an accident. By the time somebody gets to me to see if I need a medic, I'm already trying to get up. I'm ready to kick his perfect robot ass.

"You got lucky."

Tristan doesn't bother to be gentle as he scrubs the graze on my forearm before flushing it with saline again, determined to get out the last of the grit that was embedded into it during my skidding stop. He also doesn't bother to mince his words.

We're both medics working out of the Possum Hollow ambulance station for our day jobs. While I moonlight as a rider for extra money, he picks up shifts doing first aid for events. Both of them involve dragging our asses all over the state on our days off for extra cash, and it's how we became friends in the first place. He was busting my ass for being hot-headed long before we ended up working together. Tristan used to be an army medic, and he's damn good at his job, but he's not exactly known for being a soft touch.

Which means he isn't going to waste his limited supply of bedside manner on me.

"If you ate shit any harder, you could've broken your wrist. And how long would that put you on PTO? That bruising by your eye is going to swell like a bitch, by the way." He grabs my chin, tilting it to examine my face one last time. He still speaks with a Boston accent, even though he's been gone for who-knows-how long, and something about it makes him more intimidating than he would be, anyway. Which is pretty intimidating. "I'm not picking up the slack for you on Monday because you enjoy spending your weekends playing speed racer. Maybe you should think about joining my side of the track. The girls are cute out here and there's a minimal chance of getting a concussion."

Yanking my head out of his grasp, I snort. I can see Wish walking towards us, thank God, so I can escape this conversation. "Pass, thanks. Forty hours a week of playing doctor to the self-destructive is enough for me."

Tristan is apparently satisfied that my arm is clean, because he slaps a dressing on it harder than he needs to and gives me a grin that's anything but comforting. Sadist.

"No, you'd rather be one of them."

"Hey, I was fine. If that self-righteous, condescending, stuck up little prick hadn't-"

"Jeeeeeez, who lit the fuse on your tampon?" My best friend sidles up next to me and takes my freshly bandaged forearm out of Tristan's hands to examine everywhere that the graze intersects with the large, intricate design that she inked there last year.

That's a weird and confusing mental image which stops me mid-rant. "Gross."

"Please. Menstruation is natural. What's gross is you sitting here pretending to be all alpha male about Silas beating you. It was weird enough when you got all pissy because he dared to look at you before the race. Did you two even speak in high school? You're being extra."

"Maybe I don't appreciate being sandbagged by the rich and famous when some of us actually need the prize money. Can you stop that?" I pull my arm away from where she's still staring at it because I'm beginning to feel like a piece of meat. "It's just a graze. I'm sure your precious ink will heal up fine. I'm still your walking artistic advertisement. Don't worry."

21

I don't get a response right away, and the silence only amps up the tension. Tristan looks between the two of us, holding up his hands in the universal sign for *I'm out*, and then walking back to his ambulance.

"Are you going to be a grumpy asshole all night because you lost?"

Wish is looking at me with an arched eyebrow, and I realize I'm standing with my shoulders hunched and my arms crossed, already giving off *angry toddler hissy fit* vibes.

I sigh, forcing myself to uncross my arms and my body to relax.

"No."

I do not pout as I say it. I don't.

Wish clearly disagrees, because she reaches up and pinches my bottom lip in a way that she knows I hate, until I slap her hand away.

"Come on, dollface, I know you were born with those pouty lips, but that doesn't mean you have to literally pout. You won last week. You lost this week. Life goes on. Can you please act like an adult? We're all going to a party at Braydon's house, and I shotgunned the last spare bedroom for you to sleep in so you can loosen up, have some fun, and not spend the rest of the day sulking and driving back to Possum Hollow."

She sways her body back and forth, smiling up at me like she knows she's already won.

"Pleeeeeeeeease. Your mother can babysit her own daughters for one night. You don't have work until Monday, Tristan just told me. You have no excuse. And we haven't partied together in forever. I refuse to take no for an answer."

I huff, but she's right. It would be nice to let loose.

"Fine. You win, devil woman."

Clapping, Wish squeals and does a little spin, because she might like to dress butch, but she also loves to act girly as fuck sometimes, and loves it even more when people get confused by that.

"Excellent! And you'll be happy Cade, not asshole Cade?"

I grin at her in the most creepy, emotionless way possible, and it makes her cackle.

"Perfect." She rolls her eyes at me. "Besides, when was the last time you got laid? Maybe that's what's putting the itch in your jock, not Silas."

"Again, ew. Please stop worrying about anything to do with what goes on in my jock, thank you."

Wish threads her arm through mine, and we head over towards the cars, squinting against the glare of the sunset. I hauled Wish's bike here as well as mine, because they both fit in the bed of my truck and it's easier, which means she did me the solid of loading it up for me while I got lectured by Tristan.

So we can get the fuck out of here, asap. I don't see Silas anywhere, which suits me fine. I'm sure everyone was kissing his ass like they used to, and he probably took off right after the race, also like he used to.

"I'll take that to mean it's been a long time."

I don't dignify that with a response. Yes, it's been a long time.

"I have sisters who are basically my kids, a mom who needs constant supervision and two jobs. Excuse me for not having more free time to spend hanging out at honky-tonk bars, trying to get laid. I don't need an STD on top of everything else."

Not to mention, whenever I've tried to hang out with a girl lately, the lurking fear of potentially knocking her up and ending up like all of my cousins has been so crippling, I've ended up bailing before the topic of sex even came up.

But Wish doesn't need to know that, because she'd point out how stupid it is. And I already get that it's stupid.

"Fine. Then let's go get drunk."

She squeezes my arm a little tighter, and I take comfort in the intimacy. Platonic intimacy is wildly underrated. Anyone who says otherwise can't separate women from sex dolls and men from threats to their masculinity. Which is ridiculous. Affectionate physical touch, without expecting anything in return, does everyone a world of good.

I'm right, and I will die on this hill. I lean into her tiny body and try to release the remaining aggression from the race.

Fuck Silas Rush. With any luck, he'll get bored with slumming it soon and go back to the pro tour. Then I'll never have to see his stupid perfect robot face, ever again.

CHAPTER FOUR

SILAS

The world is spinning something fierce.

It was kind of spinning before the race, when I didn't get to finish my routine and everything started off wrong. And then I spent so much of the ride behind, desperate to catch up to the leader, that I pushed myself way too hard.

By the last lap I was so hot and breathless and scared I could barely see straight, and it felt like the muscles in my arms were going to seize up and betray me at any moment. I'm amazed I didn't wipe out. The whole track looked like a blur, and I still don't know how I made it to the front. I just turned my mind off and moved as fast as I could.

Once I wrapped my head around the fact that I wouldn't have to face my dad's disappointment tonight, I expected the spinning to get better. But it only got worse.

People were getting in my face, congratulating me, shaking my hand, welcoming me back home and taking pictures with me. Dad thrives on this shit. He was in the thick of it, grinning away, posing for pictures with his arm hanging too heavy around my neck.

I have a very camera-ready smile. When Dad pulled me out of high school, he told me I had to get over the whole quiet and awkward thing to make it in the pros. Along with all the actual motocross training we did, there were a whole host of things Dad made me work on to become more presentable to the public. I lost my Ozarks accent. I learned how to do small talk and firm handshakes and bro-hugs. I stared at myself in the mirror until I figured out how to smile on command.

Each thing made me appear smoother and calmer on the outside, while each thing seemed to ratchet up my internal anxiety. I never understood how it came so naturally to everyone else. Sure, after six years of this, I know how to look like I'm moving through a crowd easily. I can say the right words and my face can make the right shapes. But no one knows how many hours and hours of studying it took to get me here. And no one knows how much I fucking hate the chaos of it.

All the people pressing in on me, talking at the same time and wanting things, it's always too much. The noise creates a buzz that settles into my bones, making my entire body vibrate with discomfort. A buzz that insists that everyone else is normal, and I'm the one that doesn't belong.

Dad was watching me with a critical eye, of course. When he finally came over to me, my knees almost buckled with relief that we could go home.

Until I saw the look on his face that said no.

He told me he was going to hang out with some of his old crew, and we would drive back in the morning. But not to worry. One of his buddy's kids is a rider. He throws a party after the race every year out on his property, and I would be welcome to go. He didn't say I had to go, but the implication was there.

Thanks, Dad. Because spontaneous socializing is clearly my thing.

I tried to bury my nerves as I showered and changed at the track, then Dad gave me a ride to a modest farmhouse sitting on several acres of land in the back ass of nowhere. I gave him one last imploring look before I got out of the truck, but he just slapped me on the back and gave me one of those tight smiles of his.

I've never known exactly what those smiles mean. But I think it's something along the lines of *How is this the son I ended up with?*

Or maybe thinking about what he could have had instead.

There's never any point in responding to it.

Since then, the spinning has gotten worse and worse. I was welcomed into the party with a lot of back slaps and congratulations, but I was already people'd out and looking awkward, I could tell.

Now, I'm wandering around, trying to avoid making eye contact with anyone or lingering in one spot long enough to be drawn into conversation. People keep handing me beers though, so I drink them. Partly out of politeness, and partly as a fuck you to Dad, who isn't here to gripe about empty calories while he pounds one double Jim Beam after another.

I don't know if anyone cares that I'm not actually socializing. Maybe they just like having what passes for a local celebrity at their party. Maybe no one cares if I'm here, one way or the other.

That's a freeing thought, so I cling to it. I'm not sure how many drinks I've had, but they're starting to do their job. I feel numb and tingly, and every passing minute leaves me less worried about whether people think I look weird as I wander from room to room, looking at whatever piece of decor or motorcycle magazine seems halfway interesting.

The whole thing seems like a weird preview of what life will be like if we end up staying here in Missouri.

A hollow voice in my head wonders what the point is, if this is all that's left. I can keep obeying Dad forever, but if there's no more pro career, what's it all for? I'm too drunk and tired to put any real emotion behind the thought, but it is distracting.

Which is why it completely blindsides me when a hard body barrels into mine and pins me against the wall.

Cade.

His face, which is usually so full of joy, is currently radiating fury and barely an inch away from mine.

"You reckless fucking asshole! What the fuck are you doing here? Didn't fuck me up enough on the track so you came here to finish the job?"

His fingers are fisting my shirt and his entire body is leaning into me, pressing me into the wall. I was right, earlier. He really did get bigger. Now that he's only in a t-shirt—which is also bright pink, I notice—I can see the thick, sculpted muscle of his arms, covered in tattoos, and all that muscle is being used to hold me up.

I'm not a small guy. And as much as he's grown, I've grown more. Even though we're about the same height, I'm a lot broader. I'm intimidated by a lot of social situations, but not physically intimidated by people very often.

Anger is pouring off Cade like smoke and there's fire behind his eyes. This. I forgot he had this temper. It didn't happen often, but when he snapped, he was ferocious.

It makes my stomach swoop in the weirdest way. I can't tell if I'm more intimidated or impressed.

He's waiting, breathing hard, and I eventually realize he asked me a question that I don't understand.

"What?"

Nice, Silas.

He frowns briefly, then shoves me harder into the wall with a growl.

"Don't play dumb, robot boy. You took me out when you passed me and it was totally unnecessary! You could have easily made a clean pass, instead you took out my front wheel and sent me face-first into the dirt."

I look at his face, and briefly get lost in the slate gray of his eyes. For the first time, I notice some bruising around his left eye, and guilt hits me like a brick wall. I don't remember doing it to him, but he doesn't deserve to be hurt like that. My hand comes up of its own volition and I touch his face, my fingers gently tracing over the bruise, which confuses both him and me equally.

28

I might be a little drunk.

"What the—"

I stop, and my fingers hover awkwardly in the air in front of his face. He stares at them and then looks at me, flicking his eyes back and forth like he's trying to crack a code.

"How drunk are you, Silas?"

Moving my thumb and forefinger until they're about an inch apart, I make a face. *Just a little.*

"Fuck," he practically groans, but still doesn't let me go. I don't really care, though. This is the most physical contact I've had in months, and every time his fingertips brush my chest through my t-shirt, it makes me shiver. It's not quite as good as a hug from a loving parent or something, but maybe picking fights with strangers is as close as I can get.

"Caden Michael Elizabeth Waters!"

A female voice carries through the room and now Cade does groan, dropping his head forward and looking resigned.

"That's not my middle name, Wish. I don't even have a middle name."

He's grumbling, and she probably doesn't hear him, but it doesn't seem like that's the point.

The cute, punky-looking girl I saw him with earlier—*girlfriend? wife?*—stomps across the room, drawing our attention. I'm scared, and I'm not the one in trouble. Cade immediately looks like he's about to get sent to the doghouse. I almost feel sorry for him, except he's still pinning me against the wall with his warm body in a way that's pulling my focus.

Being threatened is distracting.

"Let him go, asshole!"

She shoves him as she says it, and Cade unclenches his fingers from my t-shirt and takes a big step back, his hands in the air. The room suddenly feels too cold.

"Jesus, Cade. I thought you were past doing shit like this. How many times have you told me you were never gonna turn into your father?"

The look that she's giving him is so honest and heartbroken. I feel like I'm intruding on something intensely private. I don't know what to do, and it's clear from the awkward silence that everyone else feels the same way.

Two guys getting physical in an argument? No one bats an eye.

This kind of naked emotional honesty? Everyone freezes.

Cade looks so hurt she might as well have slapped him. When she turns around and stomps back out of the room, he doesn't bother to go after her. He just keeps standing there, hanging his head. I can see the tension running through him and I wish I could help, but comforting people isn't where I excel.

Eventually, he looks back up at me. He's still pissed, but the fire is gone and instead he looks tired. This time, when he speaks to me, he doesn't touch me and he keeps his voice low, but there's no concealing the amount of venom in his voice.

"You're not riding with the other millionaires anymore, okay? We all have day jobs. I have a fucking family to provide for, and they can't eat if I break my arm because you felt like showing off and threw me off my bike. Ride clean, or next time I really will kick your pampered ass, whether Wish likes it or not."

He storms out of the room in the same direction as his girlfriend, and the world spins worse than before.

After the incident with Cade, it's like there's a weight on my chest. It doesn't help that before I could wander around, mostly ignored, but now everyone is watching me, whispering to each other. Clearly, Cade and I have just become the hottest new rivalry in town, and I don't even remember my part in starting it.

I'm more pissed than ever at my dad for stranding me here. I'm pissed that he won't let me drive myself to races. I'm pissed that he won't let me have my own fucking truck. Most of all, I'm pissed that I'm twenty-two years old, yet somehow all my problems seem to boil down to letting my dad control every aspect of my life.

I owe him my life, sure, but at what point can I consider that debt paid? If we're allocating value to people's lives, mine isn't exactly at the top of the list.

A few more drinks find their way into my system, but they're not doing their job anymore and jack shit feels numb right now. If anything, all the emotions I wanted to ignore are getting louder and more insistent, which is the opposite of my comfort zone.

People are still staring, so at some point I wander outside and away from the crowd.

It's a nice house. All dark wood, set back into the trees on a little parcel of land. I'd say whoever owns it must be pretty wealthy, but if there's anything around here that's cheap, it's land. Even my house is on a chunk of land and we are currently broke as shit.

Well, $600 richer after today. Minus gas money and whatever my dad blows while he's partying tonight.

Was it worth it? If my American Motor League suspension ends up being as permanent as I expect it to be, this could be the rest of my life. Driving all over the state and scraping by on whatever prizes I can get until I injury out; no endorsements, no future, just living from one $600 check to the next until the well dries up.

My dad's had me training to ride since I was four years old. It's not like I know how to do anything else.

These are the morose thoughts that claw at me as I wander through the trees, no destination in mind, propelled only by the overwhelming desire to be as far away from those people as possible. The trees are thick though, and it's dark in that way it only gets in the countryside, so I only have to walk for ten minutes to feel like I'm finally alone. It's just me, the silence and the few tendrils of moonlight that penetrate the cloud cover.

Normally, that would be enough to make the weight lift from my chest. But today it stays lodged where it is. The cup of cheap whiskey in my hand is going down like water, and I keep drinking, even though it's not making me feel any different.

The ground underfoot changes from dirt to rock so abruptly I almost don't notice it in time to see the quarry ahead of me.

Fuck, that's a long way down.

It's a rock wall that's nearly a straight drop, maybe forty feet down to still, dark water at the bottom. The water is black, but it glitters in the moonlight, mesmerizing me for a long time.

Staring into the water, I let myself get lost in it. The endless loop of loud, terrifying thoughts that chased me out here from the house is still going, but the beauty of the water makes it a little quieter. My shoes scuff over the edge and the sound of gravel echoing down to splash in the water is satisfying in the most basic, visceral way.

I want to hear it again and again, so I kick more rocks, and the sound continues to soothe me more than anything else has tonight. The weight in my chest isn't gone, but that sound makes it lift just a little.

I wonder what it would feel like to fly.

Maybe Cade should be angry at me. I'm completely wasting my life.

Maybe I'm angry at me.

Looking out over the water, I focus on the glittering. At least the world is still beautiful, even if I'm not. Swaying with the breeze, I let out a sigh and try to let go of all this melancholy that's threatening to drown me.

The weight is finally dissipating from my chest, and I feel like I can breathe again.

My trance is broken when I hear someone barreling towards me.

"Silas, what the fuck are you doing?"

Chapter Five

CADE

The quarry is my favorite thing about Braydon's house. It's a long drive to get all the way out here to Jasper, so I don't see him as much as I'd like, but he's a decent guy and his place is nice. Modest, tranquil, plenty of green surrounding it. Exactly the kind of thing I'd love for my sisters to grow up and have one day.

The most peaceful part of it is the quarry. Braydon's parties are legendary. Every rider in this part of the state hangs out here, but most people avoid the quarry because we're all country kids who know that darkness, alcohol and steep drops don't mix. Not to mention that there are mountain lions around here sometimes.

I'm the only one who tends to slip away and spend some time looking at the water. I've never had company before, so I was surprised when I saw a figure framed by the moonlight.

I was more surprised when I saw it was Silas, and the annoyance that unfurled in me at the sight of his stupid face almost made me turn around and march back to the house. But then I saw how close he was standing—no, swaying—to the edge.

"Silas, what the fuck are you doing?"

Dumb, drunk fuck.

I run towards him before he slips and dies. If he dies, everyone will say that I pushed him, and I'll go to jail, and my mom will end up turning Maddi and Sky into little oxy addicts, just like her. These are the images that bubble through my brain as I move, my legs eating up the distance between us as fast as I can.

"Cade?"

He looks confused when he turns around and it makes him lean back, swaying more precariously over the edge. I swear he looks like he's about to take a step back into nothingness.

Thank fuck I have long arms. I reach towards him, snatching his wrist as I dig my heels in to reverse my momentum. It works, but it's so abrupt that I fall ass-backwards into the gravel and bring him down on top of me, sending all the air whooshing out of my lungs.

Which hurts, but is worth it. Because I'm a little drunk too, but I know I was right. His dumb ass would definitely have fallen. And there's water down there, but definitely not enough to avoid grievous bodily harm.

I know that and everyone at the house knows that, but obviously Mr. First Place doesn't.

I'm stuck on my back and Silas is on top of me, staring at my face with the widest eyes I've ever seen. In fact, it's probably the closest thing to a facial expression I've ever seen him have. Unless *serious* is a facial expression. The plastic cup he was holding landed somewhere nearby and the smell of cheap whiskey is hanging around us like a cloud.

"What did I do?"

Goddammit. Between the wide-eyed confusion and the innocent voice, he practically looks like Sky when she's worried I'm about to yell at her for something. Why am I such a pushover?

I elbow myself up to a half-seated position, hauling him with me because he seems too shocked to do it himself. We end up sitting in the gravel facing each other. I've got one leg straight out in front of me while the other is bent and resting against him, because I wasn't expecting to run like that and I'm still trying to catch my breath.

"You were about to fall off the edge, you asshole."

"Oh."

Oh. Sweet Christ on a cracker. I don't remember him being this infuriating in high school. Although I think we've now officially exchanged more words today than in our entire high school experience.

"What the hell are you doing out here, anyway?"

"Nothing." He doesn't look me in the eye, staring at the edge of the quarry instead and making some hand-wavey motion that I don't understand. "Everyone was staring. Their faces were too loud. I wanted to be by myself."

His words come out with the loose slur of the truly hammered, and his normally sharp movements have become sludgy. Who even let him leave the house alone when he's this drunk?

"There are plenty of places to be alone that don't involve a rock face. If you fall down there, you're not coming back up, you feel me? Not to mention how many snakes your drunk ass could have tripped on in the dark."

No response. He's still staring straight ahead like the secrets of the universe are about to crawl out of that quarry and land in his lap. The silence is so thick it feels like a living thing, sitting between us.

"Did you hear they suspended my AML license, Cade? Do people know that's why I'm back?"

That's a sharp segue, but he's clearly pretty faded, so I'll roll with it.

"No, I didn't know that," I say. Silas runs a hand through his hair, tugging at the short strands like he's frustrated, but doesn't respond. "Do you want to talk about what happened?"

Another dismissive hand wave. The rest of his words come out in a crashing wave, tumbling over each other so quickly I have to concentrate to make sense of it.

"Doesn't matter. Pending investigation. Whatever. But I came out here, and I was thinking that maybe this is my life now. Forever, if they suspend me for good. I can spend the rest of my life being awkward and friendless at terrifying parties. Or I can end up like my mom."

He shrugs, and his face is completely blank.

A pang of concern hits me, but he keeps talking.

"It doesn't matter. It's fine. Dad'll tell me what to do next, unless he leaves me for good. All he ever let me do was ride, so who the fuck knows what he's gonna let me do now? I have nothing left to pay him back with. But the water was pretty, and looking at it made me feel better."

Pulling his knees into his chest, Silas wraps his arms around them like a little kid, folding his big, powerful body up until it seems small and fragile and then burying his face in his arms. The sight is making something in my gut twist. The resentment I felt towards him before is receding as the piteous sight of him trips the switch in my brain that puts me into caretaker mode.

I don't want to feel responsible for Silas' safety. I want to keep sulking about the race and being pissed at him. But it looks like it's a little late for that. Duct-taping broken people back together is all I do, really.

If his career really is falling apart, then getting shit-canned and wandering around feeling sorry for himself is understandable. But there's something about the words he's saying and the set of his shoulders that's making me nervous. He doesn't seem upset about it so much as...resigned. I wish he'd look at me, so I could get a better read on him, but he's still doggedly staring at the stupid quarry.

I've spent a lifetime watching people tear themselves apart. There's a fine line between being reckless and self-destructive—something I'm guilty of from time to time—and feeling so much like your life is already over that the basic concept of your safety doesn't even exist.

I need to figure out which side of the line Silas is on, because right now, he's setting off every internal alarm bell I have. All my anger from earlier seems petty in the face of this black hole of human misery. The only thing I care about right now is figuring out how much danger Silas is actually in.

"Cade?"

"Mhmm?" I stay still and quiet, letting him come to me. A long time passes before he turns his head. It's still nestled in the crook of his arms, but now he's facing me, looking me in the eye for the first time since we started this conversation.

"Have you ever wondered what it would feel like to fly?"

And that's it. Five-alarm-fire bells are ringing in my chest and I'm practically vibrating with the need to get him inside and the fuck away from this drop.

I shove that feeling down and force a smile onto my face. The calm, EMT smile that tells people they can trust me, and everything is going to be okay.

"Silas, do you wanna see who's better at Mario Kart?"

He snorts and pulls a face so derisive I'd laugh, if I weren't caught up in the thousand other things I'm thinking right now, one of which is *Fuck, has he ever played a video game?*

"Come on, let's go inside."

Pushing myself to my feet, I stay close enough to him that I can help him stand up as well, because the boy is swaying worse than before, if that's possible. I think the booze he was chugging finally hit him. The walk back to the house takes forever, because he's tripping over his own feet like a big, drunk puppy, but at least he lets me keep an arm around his waist to steady him.

He doesn't just let me, actually. He leans into me, all warm and bulky, hanging off my side like I'm his tether to something. He smells like motor oil and cheap whiskey. Guilt at how I lost my temper at him is already working its way through my limbs like cold sand, weighing me down.

38

The noise of the party tells me we're almost at the house when Silas stops, turning to look at me.

"Why are you helping me? You hate me." He looks dumbfounded, swaying forward a little until his face is only an inch or two away from mine. The drunken honesty makes me smile, despite everything.

"Nah, I don't hate you. I was just pissed about the race. Never forget, I was raised by drug addicts. Anger is basically my love language." That makes him laugh, a deep, rich laugh that seems to light him up from the inside, and the fear that's been clenching my heart relaxes its grip a little.

"Oh." He smiles, and it looks out of place on his robot face, but in a way that's kind of endearing.

It's impossible to tell whether the sudden lurch forward is deliberate, but I find myself with an armful of very sad, very drunk Silas, giving me an awkward approximation of a hug. I hug him back, waiting for some of the stiffness to leave his body, but he hugs like he does everything else: as if he's following instructions he read in a manual but never practiced before.

Eventually, his weight sags into me.

"Come on, buddy. Let's get you inside."

I shrug him off my shoulder, but now he seems about two-thirds on his way to passed out, so I don't bother waiting for an answer.

Dragging his ass inside gets more difficult with every step, and by the time I'm at the bottom of the stairs I'm thankful that Wish sees me and runs over to help. All everyone else wants to do is stare, apparently.

She's too short to prop him up completely, but she's strong as hell, and between the two of us and what remains of his consciousness, we muscle him upstairs and into the spare room that I'm supposed to be sleeping in tonight. I know he's not my responsibility, but I also know myself. If I shove him in a corner somewhere, I'll spend the rest of the night worrying about him finding his way back out to that drop.

It's just easier to keep him where I can watch him. Until he snaps out of this funk.

Thankfully, Wish waits until we've got him in bed, lying on his side before she pulls me outside to harangue me with questions.

"Did you poison him? Because I thought you were supposed to be letting go of this stupid feud."

I'm so drained, I can't stop myself from rolling my eyes at her.

"No. Mr. First Place got hammered and wandered into the woods by himself. I brought him back so he wouldn't die of exposure, come back as a ghost and end up haunting my bike, making me wipe out in races for the rest of my life."

I shrug like it's no big deal. Like he didn't just spill a simmering cauldron of repressed human misery at my feet after flirting with the boundaries of self-destruction. Wish gets to know all of *my* secrets, but I wouldn't betray someone else's privacy like that. Even Silas.

"So?" She looks at me expectantly.

"So?"

"So, are you going to tell me what your deal is with him? You've been batshit angry at him for no reason all day and now you're fishing him out of the woods. I don't get it. Why did you hate him in the first place?"

I shift my weight from side to side, wishing the adrenaline hadn't burned all the alcohol out of my system and forced me to be mostly sober for this conversation. Admitting insecurities, even to Wish, always feels like I'm inviting someone in to see all my weaknesses and use them against me.

"There's no big, dramatic story, I swear. He just pisses me off. You didn't come to the track back then, but he was so fucking stuck up. He always thought he was better than us because he was fucking rich. He bounced straight after every race, like the great Silas Rush was too good to be seen mingling with all the trailer trash."

I've believed this for nearly a decade. But as I say it, something inside of me crumbles with guilt and shame.

I can spend the rest of my life being awkward and friendless at terrifying parties.

Shit.

Maybe he didn't avoid us because he thought he was better than us, and I'm a presumptuous asshole.

Wish's voice pulls me out of my epiphany.

"You know he wasn't actually rich, right? I get that you grew up thinking that everyone who didn't have to shoplift Wonder Bread was a millionaire, but his family was just as broke and miserable as the rest of us. And I'm pretty sure his dad's an even bigger asshole than yours. Cut him some slack."

"I am! Did you not see me carrying him in from the woods, cutting him reels and reels of endless slack? He is currently lying on a bed that I'm supposed to be sleeping in, comfortably swaddled in all the slack that I am giving him."

She studies me too hard for a minute.

"Okay, good. You know I hate it when you go back to the old ragey Cade. Or, as he's also known, pre-Wish's-positive-influence-Cade. I prefer baby bird caretaker Cade."

"Yeah, well, he could use it." There are so many thoughts swimming around in my head right now, but none of them are forming into anything coherent. "I don't know if he's ever had a real friend, Wish."

Leaning up on her tiptoes, Wish kisses me on the cheek before she turns to head back down to the party, leaving me with Silas. "Well, it's a good thing that baby bird caretaker Cade is on the case."

Before she walks away, I snag her arm to ask one more question.

"Hey, do you remember what happened to his mom? He said something about her, but I don't know the story. My parents didn't exactly subscribe to the PTA newsletter back then."

Wish almost laughs at that. "Sorry, I never knew him. He was already gone before I started riding. I always thought it was just him and his dad. Maybe she left them?"

Based on the conversation we just had, my money's on something darker, but Wish doesn't need to hear that.

"Okay, no worries."

Chapter Six

SILAS

Why is it so bright in here? I never open my curtains, ever. I fucking hate the sunlight. What monster would come into my room and open the curtains? Even Dad shows me that basic courtesy.

I peel apart my eyelids and it quickly becomes obvious that this isn't my room. That's why the curtains are open. I have no idea whose room this is. My stomach lurches, and between that and the dead possum/cotton ball situation going on in my mouth, I think it's safe to say I got very, very drunk last night. It also feels like I'm shirtless and wearing what must be someone else's sweatpants.

When I roll over to take in my surroundings, ignoring the screaming protest of my entire body, it looks like I'm in a normal bed in a normal room. I can handle this. It doesn't seem that bad until I realize there's someone else in the bed with me.

That's enough to make me freeze.

I don't do the hook up thing. Ever. Literally ever. Between how awkward I am and how overbearing my dad is, no girl has seemed worth the hassle, and I've made my peace with that. So I have absolutely no frame of reference for what I'm supposed to do now, if that's what this is.

Then the person moves more, and the blanket shifts enough to reveal a broad, muscular back, covered in tattoos. Most are normal, but there's some shit that's like nothing I've ever seen before. Scattered all over his back and arms, there are designs that make it look like the skin is torn, revealing something mechanical underneath. It's incredibly detailed and intricate, and I find myself staring without meaning to.

The contrast with the more normal designs actually works. I think I can see the top of a butterfly wrapping around his ribs, but that seems like a weird tattoo for a dude. I wish the blanket would shift lower so I could see the rest of it.

It takes a minute for me to snap myself out of that distraction. Either way, it's a guy.

Phew.

Not a hookup.

I still don't know why I'm sharing a bed with a dude, but the reasons are all less awkward, so I'm fucking relieved until the guy rolls over and happens to be wearing Cade Waters' face.

Didn't Cade yell at me last night? My memory is fuzzy as hell, but I'm pretty sure I remember him leaning his weight into me and pinning me between him and a wall hard enough to send a tingling sensation through my body. Unless I dreamed that.

"Cade?"

The word slips out of my mouth before I remember that it's rude to wake up someone who's probably also hungover, and potentially wants to murder me.

It takes him a few seconds to wake up. He rubs at his eyes, and I'm kind of surprised by how slender his fingers are. His hands are elegant, like a pianist or something, not a dirt bike rider. He blinks a few times, just as sluggish to orient himself as I was, but that pulls my focus away from his hands.

When his gaze lands on me, he doesn't look angry anymore.

"Mornin'," he mumbles. His voice is raspy with sleep, and his stupid Ozarks accent, the one my dad made me work to shed, is thick. It makes me feel more like I'm at home than I have all week.

"What happened?"

I should probably get up, but I don't want to. The world feels a little wobbly, and I'm content to lie here for a minute and get my bearings. I'm on my side facing Cade and he mirrors my position, only a foot of space between us. The sheets are warm everywhere I touch them.

"You," he looks at me pointedly with slate-gray eyes, "got wasted, ya light-weight. And then you wandered out to the quarry and nearly slipped off the edge, until I saved you, because I am a damn hero."

He closes his eyes as he says this, smiling that big, *Cade* grin to himself and snuggling down further into the covers. He looks so content, it almost distracts me from what he's talking about, until his voice turns serious. Cade keeps his eyes closed as he speaks, and I don't let myself consider that it's to preserve my dignity, because that would be the kindest thing anyone's done for me in a very long time and I'm not sure if I could process it right now.

"Then we talked, and you said some stuff. Y'know how it is sometimes. I didn't want you to be alone. I was planning on crashing in Braydon's guest room anyway, so I dragged you in here where I could keep an eye on you and make sure you didn't do anything stupid."

He cracks one eye open and peers at me, just a sliver of gray shining through.

"So no more stupid shit, okay? Because I have a job, and I'm only available for heroics part-time."

I nod my agreement, probably looking a little dumbstruck. It seems to satisfy him though, because he closes that eye again and settles down to go back to sleep.

There's no way I'm getting back to sleep. As soon as he started talking, the memories trickled back in.

Fuck.

He did yell at me. Something about the race, although I can't remember what. Everyone was staring at me and whispering, and I felt so fucking worthless I wanted to crawl under a rock and never come out.

I remember touching his eye, because somehow I bruised it, and guilt twists in my gut. The bruise is still there, purple and ugly in the soft morning light.

I remember running away from everyone and finding the little quarry, and being mesmerized by the moonlight glittering in the water and the sound of the gravel falling. Then Cade was there, pulling me back from the edge.

And then I told him about all my stupid, humiliating shit. I think I even mentioned my mom, which is not something I've ever talked about to a stranger.

All the blood rushes to my face at the thought, although I have no idea if it's from embarrassment or shame or sadness or all of the above, and there's a pressure behind my eyes. I force myself to swallow back some bile at the memory of word-vomiting my self-pity on Cade, who probably has enough shit of his own to deal with. I feel like my body is desperately trying to produce tears, but I'm so dehydrated there's nothing to draw from.

I'm so fucking selfish, just like Dad says.

Getting a lungful of air feels like I'm trying to suck it in through a straw, and when I exhale, it comes out with a sad, choked noise.

Cade's eyes fly open, and all his lightheartedness is gone. His total focus is on me and I'm pinned by it.

I'm waiting for him to ask me what's wrong. The words to apologize need to come to me quickly so I can get up and get out of here and stop burdening him with my shit, but something about his stare holds me still. Instead, I focus on trying to pull in a normal breath and stop sounding like a wounded animal when I do it.

Cade sighs, low and soft. "Oh, Silas. I'm sorry, bud. Come here."

Reaching out for me like it's the easiest, most natural thing in the world, Cade wraps his arms around me and pulls my face towards his shoulder. The same hard body that was threatening me yesterday, and then pulling me back from the edge, now seems like something soft that I can burrow into and hide.

I have no idea what to do. I didn't think guys even hugged like this. He's not wearing a shirt, and I can feel an expanse of smooth skin under my hands, indescribably warm and soft. No one's held me since my mom died, and I'm pretty sure I'm as stiff and awkward as a corpse, but he doesn't seem to care. He just rubs his hand up and down my back and murmurs nonsense in my ear. At some point, my body finds enough water to produce some tears, and now they're streaming down my face to smear over his chest.

One raw, ugly sob rips its way out of my chest and gets muffled in his neck.

Eventually, I pull myself together. I have no idea where that came from. I never fucking cry like that. I never cry, period. I would feel embarrassed, but after the last twelve hours, I think I've actually maxed out my capacity for it.

Leaning back, I put enough distance between us so I can wipe the tears and snot off my face, and Cade lets me go, but he keeps one warm hand on my arm like an anchor. He nods a little as he watches me, with the tiniest hint of a smile tugging at the corner of his mouth.

"Better?"

I don't know why, but that makes me snort out a wet, undignified laugh. Which makes him fully smile, and wow.

His smile was always spectacular. No matter what, he could light up the room with it. I could see that, even from miles outside of his social circle. But having it directed at you is something else. Years of rust and stiffness are being carved away from my insides, allowing his warmth to seep in and settle in my bones.

Although his sunshiney face only seems to highlight my own twisted, awkward behavior from the last twelve hours, making me squirm with embarrassment. "Yeah, I guess. I'm sorry. That was so weird. I'm being so weird."

My voice cracks a little, but it's the first time I feel remotely human since before the moto yesterday.

"Nah, man, don't push it aside. Ignoring how you feel and letting it build up is how you end up becoming an alcoholic and turning into my dad. Or your dad. Or standing at the edge of a quarry. It's no good. It's a whole new fucking millennium. We're allowed to feel our feelings and shit. Get it out."

There's so much sincerity in his eyes I want to believe him. Fuck, I want to believe him.

"Okay. Then... Thank you. For saving me."

There's a really long pause, because actually being honest and saying things out loud goes against everything I've ever learned. It's tripping every warning I have. My lips are dry and my throat feels too thick to get words out of. My brain is screaming at me not to say it.

If you say it, that makes it real. That makes you weak. And everyone will know.

But I say it anyway.

"I, uh," my voice cracks again, and I clear my throat. Cade is still staring at me with the same lightning focus he gets on the track, and it's enough to push me that last inch. "I think you really might have saved my life."

Swallow. Breathe. Keep looking at Cade.

"I didn't mean to end up there. But I did. And you saved me. So...thank you."

One more tear squeezes out, but I ignore it.

Cade smiles again, something softer this time, but no less brilliant. Reaching for me just like before, he pulls me in for another hug and pats me on the back in some weird, intimate version of a bro-hug. For once, I allow myself to sink into the touch. To let him comfort me and trust that he actually wants to.

"I've got you now, buddy. You're stuck with me," he murmurs in my ear.

Something in my chest cracks open so my guts and my heart and everything else can spill out onto the floor.

"Okay."

Chapter Seven

CADE

"Why are we doing this?"

Silas looks at me with the most plaintive expression he can pull, and I almost cave. Honestly, I don't know how someone who is built like an action figure can look so tough and so pathetic at the same time, but Silas manages it. Seriously. He's better at the puppy-dog eyes thing than my little sisters, and that's saying something.

He's looking at me with those whiskey-brown eyes all sparkling and shit, silently begging me not to make him socialize. But I won't give in. Because as much as I've loved becoming his first and only real friend over the past couple of weeks, everyone needs more than one person in their corner.

I still don't know that much about him. In the past few weeks, I've made the effort to draw him out of his shell as much as possible. Mostly revolving around going enduro riding in the woods near my place, because dirt bikes are the one thing we have in common. Which isn't a talk-heavy activity, but I've managed to drag a few bits and pieces out of him and figure out a couple of key things.

He looks serious all the time, except when the camera's on him, when he has a plastic, pre-packaged smile. It's the reason I thought he was stuck up in school, and most people who meet him now assume he's an asshole. But it's really because he has the whole awkward, social anxiety thing going on. I still haven't totally figured it out. It's like he has no idea how he's supposed to act around other people, or maybe he just hates having to try, so he shuts down instead. This serious mask snaps into place, and he goes dead behind the eyes.

Hence, robot Silas.

Underneath all that awkwardness, he's like, the sweetest guy I've ever met. All soft-spoken and always trying to be considerate of other people, even if it comes out in a garbled heap of mumbled words. Maybe if he'd been allowed to do anything other than train and ride for his entire life, he'd have developed the social skills to cope with whatever mental health stuff is going on, but that's clearly not the way his dad saw it.

That's the other thing. I am never, ever, going to let myself be alone in a room with his dad. Because I do a lot better keeping my temper in check these days, but after just a glimpse into the isolation and manipulation that he's put Silas through for the last two decades... Yeah, even my willpower will snap.

I learned a long time ago that you can't do anything about the shitty hand you were dealt. So, I'm focusing on introducing some positive human contact into his life, outside of a moto track.

Which is why I dragged him to a party. Plus, it's Wish's party, and she hates it when I bail.

"We are doing this because you are my friend," I throw my arm around his shoulder as I say this and he only flinches a little before he settles into the contact. He's getting better at that. "And you need to get out more. Plus, my mom is sober enough to be left alone with my sisters, which almost never happens, so I'm taking this as a sign from the gods. We're going."

Silas doesn't say anything, he just sighs and starts walking towards the house. We're slipping into winter now, and as soon as the sun goes down it gets cold as fuck outside. Like right now. The air is crisp, the breeze snapping at me like it's trying to snatch what little warmth I have left, and dry twigs crack underneath our feet with every step. Silas was sensible, as usual, and is wearing a brown Carhartt jacket over a red flannel. It makes him look like what people with a lumberjack fetish who have never met a real lumberjack think they look like.

I've exercised extreme restraint in not making fun of him, I think. Partly because I don't want to make him any more uncomfortable than he already is, and partly because the son of a bitch pulls it off and looks pretty damn good.

I, obviously, am a dumbass, so I only threw on a ratty black hoodie over my t-shirt and ripped jeans. We just got out of the car and I'm already shivering. On the upside, Wish lives in town in the numbered streets, not buried in the backwoods. Her driveway is driveway-length, instead of the half-mile monstrosity that leads up to my place, so there's less than twenty feet to cover while I shiver and regret my life choices.

Which is still enough time to make Silas frown. He has this way of looking at me like he's trying to pull me apart, or something. Maybe figure out all my secrets; not that I have any. I assume it's part of him needing a little more conscious thought than most people for social interactions, and it doesn't bother me, so I don't say anything. In fact, it's almost kind of nice. I spend a lot of time watching everybody else in my life; it feels good to have someone looking at me once in a while.

"You're cold."

To the point, as always. He doesn't talk much when he's sober, but what he does say is about as subtle as a starting gun. Something about his inability to bullshit always makes me smile, though. I've been lied to enough for one lifetime. I'll take a little blunt honesty.

"It's winter, big guy."

Thank fuck we're getting closer to the house. I'm worried I'm about to lose a testicle to exposure. And I like my testicles where they are, thank you.

Silas frowns again. My arm is still hanging loosely over his shoulder, but I feel him snake his own arm out and wrap it around my waist, pulling me into his side.

It's kind of weird. Most guys wouldn't do that, but I don't buy into that toxic masculinity, homophobic bullshit. And the more time I spend with Silas, the more I suspect that he's not always awkward. It's more that he doesn't always have an appropriate frame of reference for things that most people consider normal. Like all the basic rules of friendship and platonic physical affection that we learned growing up are just a black hole of question marks in his brain.

He wasn't raised by wolves, but when it comes to social stuff that's outside of a racetrack, I'm beginning to suspect he might as well have been.

And more importantly, he's super fucking warm. I let him pull me tight against his body and siphon off some of the heat that always seems to roll off him. I'm a big guy, but I'm lean. I look like a dirt bike racer. If Silas wants to use his bulk to block out the wind and warm me up, I'm not going to argue with it.

Especially when I know how big a deal it's been to get used to touching anyone in the first place. From the first time he hugged me in a drunken haze, I realized it was not something he had a lot of practice with.

I do reluctantly peel us apart when we get to the door, though. I don't want anyone to crack a joke and hurt his feelings. They don't get how big a deal it is for him to just be here in the first place, and I don't want any asshole behavior setting back the progress he's made.

He watches me silently as I put a few inches of distance between us, but he doesn't say anything as he slips his hands into his pockets. Maybe I should explain? It's possible that drawing attention to it would only make things more awkward.

The window of opportunity closes before I get the chance to say anything when the door swings open.

"Oh my God you actually caaaaaaaaaaaaaaaame."

If the way Wish launches herself into my arms is any indicator, she's already having a good time. Her mohawk is slightly askew and there's a smear of dark lipstick at the corner of her mouth.

I wipe it away with my thumb, making her giggle. Silas watches the movement intently.

"I told you, you're supposed to warn me if it's a sex party, Wish. I'm not sure Silas is ready for that. And I know I'm not. Your friends are terrifying."

Even Silas laughs at that, although he sounds a little uncertain, and Wish punches me in the arm for my troubles.

"Dick. Don't be biphobic. We're not all sluts."

"I never said that. My aunt Jaz is bi and I don't think she's had sex since the Bush administration. Bush Senior. That woman fucking loves quilting. You, though, light of my life, are a slut. And I love you for it. It's important that someone in this relationship is getting laid. Now let us in, woman. I'm freezing my nuts off out here."

She tries to scowl at me, but I keep grinning at her in the most charming way I know how and eventually she relents. Stepping back from the door, we finally cross the threshold and get into the fucking warmth.

It's loud and hectic inside, in a way that always settles me. Which seems counterintuitive, but I blame my childhood. Silas, however, looks like he's trying to become one with the wall.

It probably doesn't help that Wish is giving him the once over. This is the first time they've really met since the time she dragged me off him at Braydon's house.

Not my finest moment, I'll admit.

Her face is intense, which makes her next question for him seem more ominous than I think she intended.

"So, Silas, what's your deal? Girls? Guys? Threesomes? Pet play? You have but to name it, and I shall try to acquire it for you."

She ends this kind but incredibly invasive offer with a slightly wobbly curtsey, and Silas gives me his *help me* face. Drunk Wish is not good at boundaries.

"Ignore her. She doesn't know how to mind her own business."

Grabbing Silas' hand, I pull him away from the bisexual inquisition and towards the other side of the room for a drink.

I've lived here for my entire life, so I know everyone in the room and I've partied here a hundred times before. Which is nice, because it means I can ignore these knuckleheads and focus on making sure Silas isn't secretly having a meltdown. There's a table with a bunch of half-drunk liquor bottles scattered over it and I pour us both a drink out of habit.

He's already taking a sip from the jack and coke I handed him before I realize it might not have been a good idea.

It's only been a few weeks since the quarry. Every time we've hung out, I've either been on my way to work, or we've been riding together. There weren't any situations where alcohol came up, so I hadn't given it any thought.

But he was fucking wasted at that party. And I have no idea whether that was more of a root cause or an unfortunate coincidence.

Tread lightly here, Cade.

"So, do you drink a lot?"

Smooth.

He looks perplexed for a minute, but then shakes his head. There's a long pause while he finds his words.

"My dad, he drinks. I've seen what it's like. Plus, he never liked anything that interfered with training. Parties, girls, whatever. If I wanted something other than training, I had to fight for it. And twice as hard if it was something that directly impacted training, like 'empty calories'." He air quotes and it's so dumb it's almost endearing. But the idea that his dad kept track of his calorie intake puts a queasy feeling in my gut. He keeps going, though. "The party at Brayden's was probably the first time I got truly shit-faced. Booze never seemed worth fighting for, especially if it was just going to make me more like him."

If only I'd had that kind of foresight when it came to booze. For a guy that doesn't talk a lot, he has a way of dropping these little observations that are so on point it's scary. I lean in close to his face and squint like I'm suspicious.

"Silas, are you secretly super smart and insightful? Is that what's going on? Did someone put a nerd's brain in a motorcycle meathead's body? Blink twice if you need me to smuggle you back into the secret government facility that spawned you."

He blushes crimson, and it's stupid cute. I notice for the first time that he's got freckles dusting the bridge of his nose, and it makes him look younger.

I take a long pull of my drink. I can relax now that I'm less concerned that Silas has a secret drinking problem. Not that I wouldn't have supported him, but y'know. It would have hit a little close to home.

Silas is watching me swallow, the blush fading from his cheeks as a crease forms between his eyebrows and I can tell he wants to ask me something. When I finally drain my cup, I raise an eyebrow at him, waiting for him to speak.

"What? Spit it out."

He's staring at my mouth, which makes me realize I have jack and coke smeared there, so I wipe it on the back of my sleeve. Eventually, his eyes flick back up and he looks at me.

"Why did you call your girlfriend a slut?"

Chapter Eight

SILAS

Cade looks confused. Then he burps, because he just chugged his entire drink like he's in a frat, and then he bursts out laughing so hard I think he's going to fall over.

"What did I say?"

He's still doubled-over at the waist and wheezing, but this makes him start laughing all over again. He takes what feels like hours to stop, and when he finally straightens up, he punches me in the arm, just like Wish did to him a few minutes ago.

"Silas, you sweet summer child. *No.* Why the fuck did you think that Wish was my girlfriend?"

I feel my cheeks warming, and I'm pretty sure I'm blushing harder than I did a minute ago when he made that joke about me being smart. I can never tell when he's being serious and when he's making fun of me. He might never be making fun of me, I don't even know. But he's always smiling that megawatt smile at me while he does it, which is good enough for me.

His laughter is infectious, and I crack a smile as well.

"I don't know, man. You're always together, you seem really happy around each other... Normal people have girlfriends! I don't know!"

His grin downshifts to something smaller but more warm. Something just for me. I have to fight the urge to bask in it.

"First of all, please don't lump me in with the normies when you're assuming shit; I worked long and hard to become the white trash wackadoo you see before you. Second of all, I get that the whole friend thing is new to you, but I'm gonna let you in on a secret. Not only can you have friends, but you can have friends that are *girls*. You don't even sleep with them. It's like they're whole people with their own thoughts and personalities and shit. It's magical, honestly."

"That's not what I meant." I cross my arms over my chest, trying not to look like I'm sulking. I'm awkward, not an incel.

Cade tilts his head at me and keeps smiling. He bumps my shoulder with his playfully, but it's not enough to move me.

"Come on, I'm only teasing. I know you didn't mean it like that."

There's a pause, and his tone gets more somber.

"Wish is awesome. She's been my best friend since junior year and she's been there for me through a lot of shit. But this is back-ass-rural America, and she's Wish, so she still gets shit from small-minded assholes sometimes. We both do. A lot of people still don't think straight guys can have female friends. I'm a little protective of her, is all."

"I bet. I would be too." I can picture the kind of snide bullshit my dad would say if I was friends with a girl, let alone one who looked like her. "And you don't mind that people give you shit?"

"What, homophobic shit? Nah. Fuck 'em. If they're so insecure they have to pick on other people's friendships or sexualities or whatever to get off, they're not worth my time. I have actual, real-life problems to deal with. I don't have time to care about what people think I do to get my dick wet." His brow furrows for a second. "Or not *wet,* I guess. Does the phrase still apply if the wetness is synthetic? I guess there're fluids involved no matter what junk everyone has. But anyway, you get what I mean."

"Hardly ever." I smile at him so he knows I'm teasing.

He always goes off on tangents like this, and it's kind of nice. It can be hard to follow the logic sometimes, but I'm always happy to let the constant, reassuring sound of his voice wash over me.

It's nice not to feel alone, for once.

It's already becoming a crutch. I don't know how I'm going to cope with it whenever this comes to an end.

Cade claps his hands together, startling me out of my spiraling thoughts.

"Okay, well, now that we got that cleared up, I'm going to say hi to some people and you're going to try socializing. I have faith in you. Technically, you know a lot of these people from high school, even if you never talked to them before. If you get stuck for conversation, just talk about bikes. Remember, this is Possum Hollow. Everyone fucking loves dirt bikes. I'll come rescue you in a little while."

This is fine. I can do this. I'm not scared.

Cade moves like he's about to walk away, and I resist the urge to snag his shirt and pull him back so he stays by my side. But, at the last second, he turns back and leans in to whisper in my ear.

"You can do this, robot boy."

And I can. I mean, I'm capable of making polite conversation, like Dad trained me.

But it's fucking exhausting. Every word, every expression, every shift in body language has to be analyzed and then I have to figure out how I'm supposed to respond. The worst part is, I'm not allowed to be honest about the fact that I don't know what to say to these people and don't really want to spend time with them.

I have to pretend that it all comes naturally to me. As if it isn't the single most draining activity a person can do.

There's a flurry of movement out of the corner of my eye, and I catch sight of Cade. He's standing with some of his friends in a corner and telling a story that seems to require an excessive amount of hand gestures, but is making everyone laugh. Cade is definitely someone that all this comes naturally to. People flock to him. It's warm in here, so he's slipped off his hoodie and is wearing nothing but his ripped jeans and a t-shirt that says "Trailer Park Barbie" in pink glitter. Somehow, he manages to make it look cool.

There's a flush to his cheeks from how animated he is, and everyone around him is totally enraptured. It's like his superpower; the ability to draw people in. I'll never know how he does it, but I'm not jealous.

It's almost a relief when Wish slides her compact body in beside me. I don't really know her, and the piercing way she looks at me is terrifying, but at least I don't feel like I have to be *on* with her.

Not if she's Cade's best friend.

"So tell me, new bestie-in-law," she says as she slings an arm over my shoulder. It's almost exactly like what Cade did earlier, except she's so short I have to kind of stoop so she can reach me, and she feels foreign next to me, soft in all the places he's hard. "Cade seems to think that you grew up under a rock and need to learn to play nicely with others, but I've been watching you do the rounds, and you seem fine."

"Um, it's not so much that I can't talk to people, it's more that I—"

She cuts me off.

"I've also watched him watching you. All concerned and protective. It's very cute, I'm not gonna lie."

I don't know what to say to that.

"And I've watched you watching him. Watching you. The whole thing is giving off some real *Wuthering Heights* vibes."

She's slurring a little and apparently likes to ramble as much as her BFF does.

"Um—"

"So what's the deal?"

"The deal?"

She leans forward to poke me in the chest. Not hard enough to move me, but she does sway a little as she leans back, staring me down.

"What's your deal? With him? Because I love him and it's my job to protect him, because no one else does."

That sounds too familiar, and my heart gives an uncomfortable squeeze. I still don't know what answer she's looking for, so I say the only thing I do know.

"He's my friend. He looked out for me when no one else was there. I would never do anything to hurt him."

She's still staring at me with that piercing, if slightly alcohol-glazed, look in her eyes.

"I promise."

That seems to satisfy her.

"Then go find him and tell him to take you home, because you obviously hate it here."

I let out a long sigh. "That's the first thing anyone's said all night that makes sense. But he's having fun. I'm fine to hang out for a while."

Wish nods, giving me an indecipherable smirk before wandering back into the crowd. I know I could follow her, but there's a five-foot bubble of emptiness around me right now and it feels like a relief. I'm going to take advantage of the peace and quiet, leaning against the wall and letting my gaze trail over the room.

They all move around so smoothly, leaving one small group to join another without causing so much as a ripple of friction in the air. I guess that's what happens when you hang out with the same group of people for your entire lives. These would be my friends if I hadn't left, I guess.

Not that we were friends before I left.

Dad had a general ban on anything that didn't involve training. He also specifically warned me against partying, although his warnings were always vague and stiff, but in that tone that told me follow-up questions would not be tolerated.

"Your mother was quite the party animal when I met her, Silas. You take after her too much already. Stay away from all that, or it'll sink its claws into you and you'll end up just like her. And stay away from pit bunnies, or you'll end up just like me. Riding is what matters. Winning. Getting out of this shithole."

I snuck out once. Only once. I was sixteen, staring down the barrel of a long, lonely career on the road, and I wanted my chance at a normal high school experience before we left.

It didn't take long to learn there was a reason I was never invited to those parties.

A bunch of people were having a bonfire out in the woods. I figured it would be open enough that I could sneak in without drawing too much attention to myself. By the time Dad was passed out enough for me to slip out of the house unnoticed, and then get to the party on foot, it was late.

I expected everyone there to be shit-faced by then. I was not expecting everyone to be sucking face. My naivete crashed into me like a tsunami and I nearly choked on embarrassment as I wandered around people who were almost entirely coupled off, trying to decide whether it was more obvious to turn around and go straight home, or pretend like I had been here the whole time. There were still a few people drinking and having quiet conversations around the fire. Maybe it wasn't too late to have at least one normal human interaction before I abandoned my life for good.

After I helped myself to a lukewarm beer I found lodged in the dirt, I looked around for anyone that seemed approachable. Instead, I saw Cade. He had a girl wrapped around him who I vaguely recognized from my AP American History class, but couldn't name in that moment. She was giggling and whispering something in his ear while he traced his fingertip down the line of her jaw.

They were both cast in flickers of orange and black by the bonfire in front of them. Every movement was slow and syrupy sweet, and I was totally entranced by the gentle way that Cade was touching her. I saw him ride every week; I knew the level of fierce intensity and passion that he had in him. I wouldn't have thought he also contained this kind of softness, too.

At the same time, I'd noticed a bruise around his eye, dark and sallow-looking. I wondered who had put it there, and how anyone could hurt someone as charismatic as Cade. Everyone always wanted to be closer to him. Even me, and he never spoke to me.

That was as far as I got before he noticed me looking. Cold, steel-gray eyes took me in, tension hanging between us for a long time before he finally broke it.

"This isn't a peep show, Rush. If you want to get your rocks off, I'm sure your dad has plenty of hookers on speed-dial." There was enough slur to his words to tell me was half-wasted, and when the girl in his lap giggled at his comment, he gave her a sloppy smile in response.

For whatever reason, the sight of it made loneliness grip my heart and squeeze so tightly I thought it might burst. Tighter than it had in years. The feeling kept me frozen in place, staring at Cade like I had something—anything—to say in response.

But I didn't. The only noise inside my head was the white noise of panic and fear. I tried to pull myself together enough to leave, but it was too slow for normal people, apparently.

"What the fuck are you still standing there for? Fucking go. Get out of my face." Cade didn't move from his spot by the fire, but there was an edge of threat to his voice that made my feet finally pick up and move. I turned around and stepped away, but I wasn't far enough away to miss the conversation they had as I left.

"What's wrong with that kid, anyway?" Cade's girl asked, also slurring and still giggling through her words.

"I don't know. He's always like that. Why do you think we don't invite him? He's fucking weird. His mom must have dropped him on his head as a baby or something." Cade's tone was light. He was joking around with her, and I'm sure the memory of the confrontation was already fading from his mind.

That didn't stop his words from cutting through me like a hot knife through butter. I made it fifty feet into the woods before I kneeled down in the leaf litter and puked.

It wasn't fair. That's all I could think, the whole way home. Other kids got to have parties and make-out sessions and tease each other. I got to have a prison-guard instead of a father, and a trauma hair-trigger that wouldn't let me ignore a stupid joke.

My stomach clenches at the memory. It takes some effort, but I drag my mind out of the past and back to the present. Wish's party, where I am very welcome. Watching Cade laugh, and not make out with anyone, secure in the knowledge that he won't tell me to fuck off at any point. The rest of the memory will continue to fade until it feels like a bad dream, as long as I let it.

I blink until the world comes fully into focus and swallow past the lump in my throat. It's all just a memory. It doesn't mean anything now. Move past it.

When I see someone wander close to where I'm leaning, I take advantage of the moment to say hello. I've been wallowing in my isolation for long enough.

CHAPTER NINE

CADE

I t's nice to catch up with people and be in charge of fuck-all for once. I'm pretty relaxed. But I'm keeping a close eye on Silas all the same, which is why I clock the moment his social battery hits the red zone.

Watching him tonight has been a series of contradictions. Honestly, I'm starting to feel like I want to put this guy under glass and study him like a bug.

When we were on our way, he was like a little kid being forced to eat his vegetables. And I could tell he was genuinely nervous. I left him alone to see how he would do, and a part of me was convinced he would have some sort of meltdown. But he didn't.

Instead, it was like a switch got flipped.

He was still Silas. Strong, quiet, serious Silas. But he acted like a normal person. He shook people's hands and smiled and moved around the room like he wanted to be there. He made conversation and never once looked like he was about to panic or dissolve into the wallpaper.

Has my compulsive caretaker complex gotten so bad that I made this whole thing up? Maybe the quarry thing was an isolated incident, and he's really a normal, quiet guy who doesn't need my help. Meanwhile, I've fabricated this little scenario where I befriend him out of kindness so I can feel good about myself and absolve my guilt about being kind of an asshole to him in high school.

Ever since that night at the quarry, I've been turning over my old memories of Silas. Before, they were always fogged by all my irrational jealousy and resentment, but now that I have some perspective, I feel like an idiot for not noticing sooner that something was wrong.

Sure, I was just a kid. But if there's anything I knew about, it was what it looks like to cover up a shitty home life. All the things I saw as pretentiousness, I now see as him being awkward and trying to reach out, but with the shadow of his dad always lurking. Instead of noticing, I made fun of him behind his back. And to his face once or twice, if my very fuzzy memory serves.

It's all too clouded with anger to remember clearly. There were a few years where everything at home seemed so violent and hopeless; I remember carrying around this rage with me every day like a second skin. I would try to laugh it off and pretend it wasn't there, but it always was. I'm mind-numbingly grateful that I've gotten a lot more control of it since then, but that doesn't undo whatever collateral damage I must have done along the way.

All I can do is try to make up for it now. And tonight is going better than I expected. I even see him have what looks like a serious conversation with Wish and walk away unscathed.

Maybe he doesn't need me at all. Maybe this is all in my head.

Then I see the cracks start to show.

He's having a conversation with Matteo, who is enthusiastically talking about one of the things he loves, which means it's some kind of team sport. Which Silas knows nothing about. I know from experience that Matteo can talk for hours when he really gets going. Silas' responses get fewer and farther between, and every time Matteo asks him something, Silas seems to slow-blink at him for a while before any words come out. He looks like a computer that has too many windows open and its processing speed is for shit.

I know I'm not imagining it when I see relief all over his face as I walk over. The smile he gives me is small and genuine, unlike the stiff, plastic one he's been flashing all night.

"Can I steal my mortal enemy away from you for a minute?"

Matteo laughs, and I take advantage of the opening to put my arm around Silas' shoulders and walk him away to an empty corner of the room.

He sags into me as soon as we're out of earshot.

"Thank you. I was trying to be nice, but he would not stop talking about college lacrosse. I can pretend to be interested in a lot of stuff for at least a couple minutes, but I don't know anyone who can pretend to care about fucking lacrosse."

"But you did so gooooooood." I ruffle his hair until he jerks back and scowls at me. It makes him look a little like an angry teddy bear. "You almost looked like a real boy, talking to people and shit. Are you sure you're not making up this whole social anxiety thing to get my attention? Because throwing me off my bike into a dirt wall already did the trick. You had my attention."

"You know I'm sorry about—"

"Yeah, yeah, that's not what I meant," I cut him off. He's apologized way too much already. Really, I was out of line for getting so mad. It's all part of the race.

Sighing, Silas stares into space with a vacant expression. It reminds me too much of how he looked out at the water that first night, and anxiety churns in my gut. But my arm is still around him, and he's not pulling away. If anything, he's softening enough that I can pull him closer.

Every inch of me is screaming that whatever I do in my life, I cannot let him go. Like as soon as I do, all the broken pieces of him will fly apart.

Maybe that's arrogant of me, but I'm not taking the risk. I know how it feels to be raised by parents who can barely keep themselves alive, let alone someone else. Having my sisters to take care of has been the only thing that helps me keep my shit together most days. Without them, I don't know where I'd be. Silas' rootlessness hits a little too close to home for me to just ignore it. I'm invested now, whether he likes it or not.

"It just takes so much work," he says in the end. "Dad always drilled into me to act 'normal', whatever that means. Shit like this is supposed to be fun. But it's like everyone's speaking a different language, and I'm the only one without the dictionary. Every time someone says something, I have to go through my brain like a Rolodex to figure out what to say back. It's like…" There's a pause while he searches for his words, and it takes all my self-control not to fill the silence. "It's like algebra. Yeah. I can do it if you ask me. But it's not my idea of a good time."

Silas blows out a big breath, turning to shoot me a wary look. I think he's trying to gauge how weird what he just said was based on my reaction.

"Wait, you can do algebra?"

From his expression, that's not the reaction he was expecting. I can only hold a straight face for a few seconds before a grin takes over, and I light up inside when he finally laughs.

Everyone else might be tiring for him, but somehow, I know how to make him laugh. It's like I was born with the cheat codes. Power like that can't go to waste.

"Come on, robot boy." I ruffle his hair again, which he pretends to hate, but doesn't duck away from this time. "Let's go home so you can plug your social battery back in to charge."

I spend the whole walk out and drive home pestering him about his math skills. Maddi is thirteen and about to lap me in academics, so this could come in handy. I need somebody on deck to help with homework shit soon. So, I poke and prod and make more robot jokes, and Silas keeps that small smile on his face all the way.

When I pull up in front of Silas' house to drop him off, the lights are all off, even though it's still pretty early.

"Your old man asleep?"

He sighs and looks at his lap.

"Nah, he'll be out for a while. We got some bad news today."

"What the fuck? You didn't say anything earlier. What happened?"

I ditch my seatbelt so I can turn around fully in the seat to look at him, but he's totally focused on his hands and it's too dark out here for me to make out his expression. He's still not saying anything.

"Silas?"

"They made a final decision today. The motocross league. About the thing."

Just when I think the suspense is going to make me physically explode, Silas looks up at me with an inscrutable expression, and his voice is totally emotionless when he speaks.

"I am banned for life. I will never ride in any event the AML hosts, in any state, ever again. Which means my pro career is officially done."

He turns back to stare at the dark house.

"Silas..." I don't know what I'm going to say, but he cuts me off, anyway.

"Dad's probably on a bender. I don't think he'll come home anytime soon."

"I'm sorry, Silas. Really. That's not fair."

"Yeah, well, it is what it is." He shrugs to himself and keeps staring blankly forward. He still hasn't spilled the details on how this all happened in the first place, and I want to ask, but I figured he'd tell me if he wanted to talk about it. All I know from the news is that it was something about illegal fuel additives.

Which is definitely a thing that happens. There are a bunch of regulations about what you can and can't put in your fuel tank and bikes are regularly tested before races. Sometimes all it takes is a little drop of something to set off the sensors and cause a shit storm.

But it's normally handled with fines. It's not something guys get their licenses pulled over.

There has to be more to the story, but I don't want to push. It takes a monumental effort to swallow down my curiosity and keep my voice level.

"How do you feel about it?"

That pulls his attention back to me, but he turns his head slowly, like he's moving through syrup, and takes a long time to choose his answer. One hand comes up to run through his hair in a shaky motion.

"Pass. Next question."

I snort. He's dry as hell, but funny when you actually listen to him. Everybody who doesn't see that is missing out.

"Okay. What are you going to do now?"

"Pass."

"Nope, you only get one pass. And you need money to live, which I don't see Travis fucking Rush helping with if he already drank and 'invested' away the money you made before. What are you qualified to do other than ride a motorcycle in circles over really bumpy dirt?"

That earns me a scowl, so at least he's not totally shut down. Then he thinks about the question.

"Ummm..."

The whites of his eyes are practically glowing in the moonlight now, which tells me he hadn't considered that part yet.

His hand is still in his hair, almost scratching his scalp in a repetitive motion. His fingers are trying to grab his hair and tug, but the strands are too short to get a grip, and the whole thing seems unconscious and anxiety-driven in a way that makes me queasy. When he does get a grip on his hair, he's pulling at it hard enough that it must hurt.

Well, his future is scary, but he's gonna have to face it, eventually. At least right now I can help.

I grab his hand and pull it away from his head, holding it for a second until he realizes what he was doing. Our eyes meet over his fingers, and the vulnerability shining out of him makes something in me crack open.

The decision about what to do now practically makes itself. Letting his hand drop, I throw the truck into reverse and pull back down the driveway.

"Cade, where are we going? This is my house."

"You're staying with me tonight."

"I am?"

"Yeah, well, you're all stressed out and I don't wanna leave you alone. I'd stay here, but I also don't wanna leave my sisters alone for that long. Which leaves us with one option. I realize it's not exactly the Ritz, but it's better than freaking out in a dark house by yourself. Cool?"

Silas watches me for a while before he answers with a quiet voice.

"Cool."

"Cade!"

The second I open the door to the trailer, light and noise spills out and Sky launches herself into my arms like a distressed monkey. I can already tell Silas is getting the all-circus version of the Waters family introduction.

"It's a little late for you to be out here screaming instead of in bed, isn't it, Sky?"

Pulling her face out of my neck just enough to look at me, I can see from her stormy expression that she's not having a good night. Sky is the baby of the family. Maddi is the middle child and also the only calm, even-keeled person in this entire household.

Sky is an agent of chaos, like me.

"Maddi won't let me go to bed until I've cleaned my side of the room. I need you to tell her to fuck off!"

And there it is.

Silas isn't some wilting flower, but the sight of a nine-year-old screaming "fuck off" down the hallway will make anyone at least a little shook.

"Fuck, Sky, I brought a friend home. Can you please try to act like you haven't been raised by a biker gang?" I set her back on the ground, but she completely ignores both me and Silas in favor of storming down the hallway and banging on her and Maddi's bedroom door.

"Let me in, ass wipe!"

I try not to, but a laugh slips out of me. She's like four feet tall and wearing a pink t-shirt with a cartoon frog on it! But she swears like a trucker. It's kind of adorable, if you think about it.

Silas still looks more wide-eyed than amused, but I shake my head at him. "Ignore them."

"You can come in when you get rid of your disgusting laundry that's so gross it grew legs and invaded my side of the room." Maddi's voice is as calm as ever through the closed door.

I have no idea how she does it. There's a line dividing the room in half—literally, I painted one a couple years ago because I couldn't take all the fighting—and the two sides always look like the before and after shots from an episode of *Hoarders*. But Sky doesn't always keep her shit to her side, and Maddi's patience for her little sister can only go so far.

"Fuck off!" Sky's getting louder and banging on the door with her tiny fists, which makes me think all the cursing is more of a bid for attention than her actually being angry.

Which I get. It's easy to slip through the cracks and not get babied as much as you need. But pissing off everybody around you to get attention is a page out of mom's playbook that I don't really want her sticking with.

"Yo, Tarantino, will you please stop fucking cursing?" She squints at me like she doesn't get the reference, so at least I haven't fucked up that much.

We can save *Reservoir Dogs* for her thirteenth birthday, or something.

"But—"

"But nothing." I cut her off. "Go in there, pick up your shit, apologize to your sister. *Nicely*. And once you're ready for bed, I'll come in and we can read for a while. But only if everyone chills the fuck out. Deal?"

I can see the wheels spinning like she wants to kick off again, but she really does look tired. Mollified by the promise of actual, positive attention, she nods.

Mom chooses that moment to emerge from her cave, moving down the hallway towards the bathroom. She's wearing an oversized AC/DC t-shirt that's seen better days. It reaches down past her ass, thank God, because she's not wearing pants. There's a lit cigarette in her mouth and she doesn't seem to notice Silas standing behind me. When she jars her hip against the doorframe, walking into the bathroom, that's all the confirmation I need that she's too drunk to be worth dealing with.

It pisses me off anyway.

"Thanks for your support, Mom. You clearly did a lot of active parenting while I was out. Have you considered a career as a mommy blogger?"

I don't think she even hears me until she sticks her arm back out of the bathroom long enough to give me the finger. Letting out a soft snort, I can only shake my head.

"And I thought we agreed you were going to start smoking outside!"

I take a deep breath, in and out. Goading her into a fight would normally be a nice way to blow off some steam. But not while we have an audience. She can pass out in peace tonight.

Turning to Silas, there's a set to his jaw that tells me he wants to say something, but he's holding back. I imagine it's something judgy, which is fine, because there's plenty to judge. Even beyond the inter-sibling curse-a-thon, there's the trailer itself. Remnants of what looks like box mac 'n cheese sit on the counter from the dinner that Maddi must have made for them. And the whole place is—I do my best—clean-ish, but not exactly tidy.

"Go ahead." I make an over-the-top wincing face to break the tension. "You can say it, I can take it." I close my eyes, but when he doesn't say anything, I let myself squint one open to peer at him.

He looks more contemplative than anything, though. Not disgusted, which would be the worst-case scenario, or the awkward, shuffling pity that I get from most people and hate.

Eventually he speaks.

"You're like, an actual dad. That's pretty cool." I must look confused, because he babbles a little as he backtracks. "I mean, I know you're not actually their dad. But it's like you are. And you're taking care of them, not just yelling." He shrugs, and a hint of a blush colors his cheeks. "It's nice, is all I meant to say. That you take care of them like that."

Well. I'm not exactly known for being quiet, but for once, someone's rendered me speechless.

"Uh, thanks." Very cool, Cade. "They deserve to have someone look out for them. Even if it's a twenty-two-year-old fuck-up who teaches them to curse like grease monkeys."

That makes him smile, and the awkwardness that had settled between us dissipates.

"Come on." I tug at his sleeve. "Let's grab a beer and go sit out back while the girls get ready for bed." Moving towards the fridge, a thought occurs to me and I pause long enough to yell toward the bathroom one more time. "Mother, if you drank all of my beers, I swear to God, I will put arsenic in your smokes!"

There's a click as the door unlocks and Mom wanders out, lit cigarette still dangling from her chapped lips. Her eyes are glazed, but she's smiling at me, so she must be in the sweet spot of her buzz.

Lucky her.

"Go fuck yourself. I didn't touch your pisswater. I got my own money."

Shuffling the rest of the way down the hallway towards me and Silas, she pauses to look him up and down while he freezes under her gaze, looking more uncomfortable than I've ever seen him. She gives him an up-nod, but he doesn't seem to know how to respond to that, so she ignores him.

She removes her cigarette from her mouth long enough to kiss me on the cheek before going to the fridge and pulling out a mostly empty bottle of some acidic-looking wine. I can see past her that my off-brand Mexican lagers are untouched, thank fuck.

"I suppose you can remain unpoisoned another day then, woman. But I'm watching you." That only makes her laugh as she turns around and goes back to her room, her mouth full of cold mac 'n cheese from the foil container on the counter. "And next time, make the girls eat a vegetable!"

Silence.

Silas looks way more disturbed by my love-hate banter with my mom than the potty-mouthed nine-year-old, for whatever reason. Who hasn't seen a middle-aged lush before? I ignore him, swipe two beers and then get us settled on some plastic lawn chairs I keep out back. They're so sun-scorched and brittle they kind of look like lizards trying to shed their skin, but they're still holding up. Even when I lean my weight back to push the whole thing onto two legs and stare up at the stars.

"So. Skills, other than dirt bikes. Whatcha got?"

Silas shakes his head, staring into his open beer bottle like a genie's about to pop out and give him a lap dance.

"Nothing. I got nothing. I wake up, I eat my stupid, healthy food, I train, I work on my bike, I train on my bike, I race on my bike, I sleep. That's it. That's all I do. A monkey could do it, as long as it had proper pull-up technique and knew how to do an oil change."

My mind spins, trying to come up with a solution to this problem. Realistically, I know he doesn't need to decide right now. But I'm a fixer, and he feels like the ground is coming out from under him.

He needs something to hang on to. Anything. At least for a little while.

"Did you ever get your GED after you dropped out to go race?"

"Hm? I didn't need to. I almost had enough credits. I was able to finish the rest on the road. Dad would sign me up for online classes, but I could usually test out of them and get the credits. Dad liked it. He said it made me look well-rounded, or whatever." Silas shrugs, like giving yourself a high school education in a motel room is no big deal. Fuck, he really must be smart.

"What about getting a job with me? You can get certified as an EMT in a couple of months, if you do the course full-time. And the work is gross sometimes, but at least it's interesting. The first time Tristan suggested it to me, I thought he was crazy, but he wouldn't stop pushing. He ended up loaning me the money for school himself. I've almost paid him back, and once I have, me and the girls are gonna be, like, rolling in singles. Or at least dimes. Beats the hell out of working at Sonic for minimum wage."

Eventually I cut myself off, realizing I've descended into the beginnings of a ramble, and see that Silas is making a face and shaking his head.

"I hate small talk at the best of times. I can't see myself being able to talk to people about their medical problems. Sorry." He looks a little sheepish about it.

"No problem." *Think, brain.* "You work out all the time. What about becoming a personal trainer? I think you can get qualified for that shit online."

Silas squints at me. "Are there are a lot of people paying for personal training around here, Cade?"

True. Damn.

"Okay, point. Um..." Taking a swig of my not-cold-enough beer, I let my mind keep wandering through everything dirt bike adjacent that might have a paycheck attached. And then it hits me.

"Oh! Oh! Fuck yeah! Silas, I am so smart. If we weren't already besties, this would cement it. Hell, you might want to marry me for it."

The flat look I get in response tells me I'm not as cute as I think I am, but I disagree. Still grinning, I explain.

"I know a guy who has an auto shop just outside of town. It was his dad's, but his dad passed last year and he's been running it by himself ever since. I don't think he's planning on hiring anyone because he's the textbook definition of a loner, but he has a soft spot for me. I bet I could convince him to take you on as an apprentice, or something. Mostly cars, obviously, which you'd have to learn, but most people take their bikes to him as well if it's not too complicated, because the nearest specialist is halfway across the state. Mechanic, that might be a sweet gig for you? Lots of engines, not too many people. Zero facial expressions required."

Silas eyes me with suspicion. I get it, this kind of sounds too good to be true. And I have no way of knowing if I can convince Ford to hire him. But it's worth a shot, at least.

Plus, Ford and I aren't super close, but I'm not crazy about him being out there all alone now that his dad's gone. He and Silas might be good company for each other. Even if neither of them would ever admit it.

"I don't know, Cade. If he needed help, I'm sure he'd have hired someone already, right?"

"Ah, see, that's the thing. I'm pretty sure Ford would rather be crushed to death under an engine block than go through the process of finding, interviewing, and hiring someone. But if I present you to him, gift-wrapped and ready to go, that's a lot harder to say no to."

Silas continues to be a brick wall of incredulity.

"He's really that much of a loner? Then why does he tolerate you?"

76

"Because I'm charming as fuck, robot boy. I won you over, didn't I?" I laugh and start ripping the label off my beer in little shreds, so I have something to do with my fingers. "No, seriously. He was in some kind of accident when he was a kid, and he lost the use of his voice. After that, he pretty much only spent time with his dad. He got in a lot of fights when he was younger, ended up with a bad rep. I know a lot of people are weird around him, and I think he likes that I don't act like I'm scared of him. Come on, you barely talk, he doesn't talk at all, you're both huge fans of brooding like the lead in a tacky vampire novel... It's a match made in heaven! I'm doing it."

I pull out my phone and start texting Ford without waiting for an answer.

Silas shrugs, which is more enthusiasm than I expected, honestly.

"Okay, it's worth a shot. Thanks, Cade."

He keeps watching me, and for whatever reason, his gaze feels heavier than usual. But not in a bad way. It's almost grounding. It feels like this conversation is important, and something about that makes me feel more solid in return.

By the time we flesh out all the details, we have a solid plan to work on and Silas seems less adrift in the face of his impending future. But it's also late as hell, and we've had a few beers. We're both too tired to give a shit about how cramped and shitty my bed is when we collapse into it.

Silas knocks out the second his head hits the pillow. Good. I bet this has been eating at him more than he'll admit.

I close my eyes and let myself drift off, comforted by the rhythmic sound of his breathing. He deserves some rest, at last, and for whatever reason, it feels damn good to be the person who gets to give it to him.

CHAPTER TEN

SILAS

When Cade initially told me he was adopting me as his friend, I kind of thought he was joking.

Then, I assumed it was some sort of pity-project that he would eventually lose interest in.

But it's been nearly a month now, and he's never wavered. Then last night, the way he saw through me and gave me exactly what I didn't realize I needed—to not be alone in that stupid empty house—was incredible.

If this is what having a best friend is like, I get what I've been missing all this time.

I got to see his life, and it only sucked me further into his world. Sure, it's not what most people would picture as an ideal family life. 'Chaotic' was the first word that came to mind when we walked inside.

Although that's also one of the first words that comes to mind when I think about Cade, so...

Even though it's loud and messy and his mom is kind of a lot, he was so in his element. It was incredible to watch. He handled his sisters easily and with this kind of raw, naked affection that I've never seen in anyone before, let alone someone who's not even their actual parent.

Cade and his mom—Kris, he told me her name later—have this weird bitchy relationship that made me uncomfortable at first, but even that turned out to be super affectionate, once I got used to it.

He's like the Energizer Bunny of compassion. He never stops. First, he settled down the house. Then, he solved my job problem, getting more excited in the process than anyone has ever been to help me with anything, I think. Then we went inside, where he made sure his mom was as okay as she could be.

His sisters were still awake, and he never forgot his promise to Sky that he would read with her. I occupied myself by cleaning up the messy kitchen while I listened to all three of them read together in the bedroom, constantly interrupted by bouts of laughter. Even from the older sister.

Most thirteen-year-olds would probably think they were too cool to read a kid's book out loud, but I know from experience that Cade has a way of sucking you into stuff and making anything seem fun.

We had to squeeze to fit both of us on his not-quite-a-double bed to sleep after that. That small space felt crammed to the brim with people and life, which should have been suffocating. Especially since I'd never experienced anything like it before.

Instead, I slept better than I had in a very long time, squished against Cade's warm body with the sound of the *Home Shopping Network* seeping in from the living room. I hope he knows what he got himself into when he invited me into his world, because he's not going to be able to pry me off him anytime soon.

It's too late. There's no way I'm giving this up now.

When Cade came up with the mechanic idea, he was buzzing with excitement. It was kind of cool to see someone get that excited about my future. I didn't have to believe it would work out.

I also half-figured Cade would forget about it by the next day, because he can be flaky like that. But no.

As soon as we woke up this morning, his buddy had replied to his text, and now it's less than twenty-four hours since he had his eureka moment and we're pulling up to a modest little shop sitting by itself, just off Rt 140.

There's a small hook-and-chain tow truck parked out front, an office building attached to the garage, and what looks like a house sitting on the land behind it. Everything is clean and well-kept. The roll door on the garage is still open, even though it's late, and inside I can see several cars in varying states of repair, as well as a couple of bikes.

"Some people drive to Mission Flats to go to Jiffy Lube or whatever because it's cheaper, but Ford's dad really knew his shit. He did restoration stuff on the side that I think brought in a lot of money. I don't know if Ford's into that or if it was just his old man, though." Cade keeps up his chatter as we park up and he leads me into the building.

Most auto shops I've been to are loud. There are a lot of machines, and also a lot of people shouting and swearing, a radio on, customers coming in and out, etc. It's a cliche, but it's true. This place is still. I kind of like it.

There's more space than I thought at first glance, with some good-quality equipment. Whatever this guy's doing, he's obviously making enough money to run a tight operation, which makes me feel less guilty about Cade trying to strong-arm him into hiring me.

Now that I've seen the place, I can feel myself getting invested in the idea. My fingers are already itching to work on an engine. It feels peaceful out here.

"Yo, bitch! Where you at?" Cade shouts into the ether, chewing gum casually like it's not obnoxious to call people 'bitch'.

The guy that walks out of the office entrance is not what I was expecting. For one thing, he's fucking scary. Built like a brick shithouse, with hands that could probably crush my skull. Long, dark hair that's tied up in a sort of messy man-bun situation, which I also didn't expect, and a scowl on his face that seems pretty permanent. There's a gnarly-looking scar running down his cheek, but a dark beard covers enough of it that I can't tell what it might be from.

He's wearing dark coveralls, but the sleeves are rolled up, revealing tattoos covering both his arms. But where Cade's tats are intricate, almost delicate, Ford's are dark. It's black on black, covering every inch of his skin like it's not meant to be a picture *of* anything.

He raises an eyebrow at Cade, which would be enough to cow most people, but Cade keeps grinning.

"Ford, this is Silas. I'm sure you two will immediately hit it off over your mutual distaste for social interactions. Once you hire him, I'll be taking bets on just how long you can go without speaking to each other. I'm thinking at least six months."

Ford nods, his expression softening like this sounds good to him. Slipping his phone out of his pocket, he types something out with a lot more dexterity than I'd expect from hands that big. As soon as he's done, he holds up the screen to show me what he wrote.

Cade's been blowing up my phone all day. Normally I wouldn't want to encourage him being such a prima donna, but tbh I could use some help. You have experience?

I give him a quick rundown of what I can and can't do, as well as the shit I'd like to learn if this is potentially going to be my career. With every word, the idea of it becomes more real and more appealing. I can actually see myself here, having a future, which is not something I thought I'd ever say.

Ford nods along as I talk. His expression is still severe, and I can see why Cade says people find him terrifying. But I'm getting the feeling that might just be his face. I can relate.

**Sounds good. I can show you
some info later if you want to get
your license. You're hired, as long
as you swear you're not as talk-
ative as your buddy. I'll work on
his bike, but I am not spending a
whole day with Nicki Minaj over
here.**

"Okay, rude," Cade protests next to me, but I ignore him.

"That's it?" Technically, I've never had a job interview before, but I'm pretty sure they're supposed to be harder than this.

Ford sighs, pointing to his message again. Oh.

"Yes, I promise I'm not chatty. Cade calls me 'robot boy'."

"It's true." Cade grins again. "He's incredibly dull. You'll love him."

A loud exhale of breath through his nose is the only response that gets from Ford. He pulls his phone back and types out one more message to show me before dismissing us and turning back to his work.

**Be here Monday at 8. Leave the
brat at home.**

But Cade is laughing as we head back to the truck.

"Thank you! Love you!" he calls back into the garage, getting silence in response.

I guess I have a job now.

Working for Ford isn't exactly easy, but so far the benefits easily outweigh the downsides. The steady paycheck, meager though it is, is only the start of it. I definitely know a lot more about bike engines than cars, but Ford is a much more patient teacher than I would have expected, and it's really interesting to learn. It comes naturally to me in the way most things don't.

Not to mention, doing something every day without my dad looking over my shoulder and harping at me has been more of a relief than I could have imagined. I never realized how much of a constant presence his criticism was until it disappeared.

Silas, you're never going to compensate for your weight if you keep slacking on your runs.

Silas, personality is as big a part of it as riding. You have to charm these fuckers. That's what I always did. I swear you cost us the Honda contract with your shitty attitude.

Silas, never forget that I gave up my career because of you. You owe me this. Now focus and get the win.

It was such an intrinsic part of the soundtrack of my life I'd gotten used to it, but now, whenever I'm at the shop, I feel ten pounds lighter.

Not that Dad is that easy to deter. A week into me working here, he'd dragged himself off the couch to come down and start throwing his weight around. He walked in and sucked up all the oxygen from the room, like always. Initially, he claimed he was there to take me to lunch. But it was barely five minutes before he was leaning over where I was doing a very simple car battery installation and telling me everything I was doing wrong in that low, raspy voice that makes the back of my neck prickle.

The problem with getting a little distance from him was that it had also weakened my defenses, and the sound of his criticisms suddenly made my stomach cramp so abruptly I was worried I might hurl.

I couldn't say anything. I couldn't even look at him. All I could do was keep working, pretending those words in that tone were being said to someone else and weren't infecting my nice, shiny new workplace that didn't think I was a waste of space yet.

Not that it would take them long if he kept showing up to point it out.

But then something completely unprecedented happened. Ford, the most terrifying-looking man I've ever met, came skulking out of the corner to loom over my father and growl at him. He actually, honest-to-God growled. It is still the only noise I've heard him make.

Dad had looked at me with wide eyes, half in disbelief but half in genuine fear. Ford didn't give me the space to answer before growling again and pointing at the open door.

It was the fastest I've ever seen my dad take a hint, and he hasn't been back since. So, now it looks like I owe Ford for more than just the job. Since then, this quaint little shop has become my sanctuary. After the warmth and controlled chaos of Cade's trailer, this is my second favorite place in Possum Hollow.

Hell, probably the world.

That's a little sad, but I'll take it.

It's even better right now, because my second favorite place is filled with just me and my favorite person. Ford closed up already, but when I asked him if Cade and I could use the space to work on our bikes after hours, he shrugged and tossed me a set of keys.

I was sure I was getting off easy until right before leaving, he turned around to look at me one more time. Pointing with two fingers at his own eyes, then mine, then the shop before making a throat slicing gesture got his point across pretty clearly: *Take care of the shop or you're dead.*

Fair.

A death threat or two between employer-employee is totally worth it for me and Cade to have a space of our own to relax. Right now, he looks happier than I think I've ever seen him. He's bent over his bike, trying to grease his cables but constantly getting distracted, finding new scratches to buff or meticulously picking through his tire tread for gravel. I want to help him, but he's clearly having a good time doing it his own way. I don't have the heart to interrupt.

He's barely been here for twenty minutes and there's already grease smudged over the arc of his cheekbone. It's cold enough to snow outside, but the roller door does a good job of keeping heat in. Between that and the space heater chugging away behind us, the air is thick and muggy, so Cade pauses his anarchic attempt at repairs to strip off his sweatshirt.

I watch the way his muscles flex and bunch as he gets back to work, now just in a worn-out t-shirt. He's worrying his bottom lip between his teeth while he concentrates, making it look swollen and even poutier than usual.

Just as I realize how far my thoughts have drifted, Cade's voice snaps me back to reality.

"Hey, I know what we should do right now." The impish look on his face tells me his plan is going to piss me off, get me in trouble, or both.

I raise an eyebrow and wait, knowing I'm going to agree to whatever it is, anyway.

"We need to celebrate your new job!" Cade stands up abruptly enough to make tools clatter to the ground. "And it seems criminal for a mechanic to not have his own wheels."

"But, Dad..." I trail off, not sure where I'm going with that, and Cade's face tells me exactly how much he doesn't give a shit about my dad's opinion on the subject.

Reaching down, Cade grabs my hand and yanks me to my feet. A thrill goes through me as I think about defying my dad so casually. He keeps my hand in his warm grip, using it to hold me close to him while he leans in, inches from my face, and whispers, "Come on, bitch. We're going shopping."

85

CHAPTER ELEVEN

CADE

I didn't mean to derail our bike maintenance time with the spontaneous shopping trip. But Silas needed his own wheels. It was non-negotiable. Oil changes could wait.

Not forever, though. Which is why it's only a few days later that I'm back at Ford's after hours, sitting on my ass on the concrete, pretending to know what I'm doing.

When I hooked Silas up with the job, I swear I wasn't thinking about any potential perks for myself. But I have to admit, it's pretty cool that Ford lets us both use the space. Beats the hell out of working behind the trailer, patching my bike up with duct tape and optimism.

Okay, that's an exaggeration. I'll shell out to get it tuned up properly when I have to, because that bike is my secondary source of income and I'm a shitty fucking mechanic. But only when I have to.

It'll be a lot easier to keep up with the maintenance myself if I can do it indoors, with actual tools and paddock stands, under Silas' watchful eye.

He may hate talking to people, but Silas speaks fluent machine. All of my robot boy jokes have clearly been on point. What he lacks in formal training he makes up for in instinct, and watching him run his gaze over an engine with absolute focus, calculating and sharp, is a thing of beauty. Everything about him that's so often uncertain becomes calm and sure. His hands are steady, working over every piece of metal like it's instinctual.

Watching him work is only a fraction of it. The past couple of weeks, he's fucking blossomed. I've never used the word 'blossomed' in my life, but it's the only way I can describe it. All this time away from his dad is showing how much of his old behavior wasn't the real him. It's like he was a shadow-version of himself.

The real Silas—*my Silas,* my brain prompts me, which is a weird way of looking at it but not technically untrue—is so much brighter than the old version. He smiles more: still small, shy smiles that are mostly for me, but they're so genuine. He laughs and talks more easily with me and the open, unguarded way he gives affection to Maddi and Sky makes me want to beam at him and never stop.

He even looks different. Before, he had this way of holding himself, like he was trying to take up as little space as possible. Now, he's more relaxed. And with his dad too busy drinking himself into a stupor in the wake of the AML suspension, he hasn't had time to police Silas' calorie consumption like a drill sergeant, and I can already see the difference.

Silas is thick-set. He's built. He's stacked. There's a solidity to him that meant he never seemed lean, let alone too lean. He just had great muscle definition. The eight percent body fat kind that most people would kill for, with individually defined obliques that popped and that sexy V that girls are obsessed with. I'm not un-ripped myself, but I was pretty jealous until I realized he hadn't eaten a carbohydrate since the eighth grade.

As soon as I got him to break out of his dad's ridiculous 'high-performance' diet, he started to fill in, and he looks so fucking healthy. Yeah, his muscle is a little less defined, but it looks better that way. Dips and curves of muscle that look firm but warm, not the cold, hard definition of a statue. He's bright and full of life. And even though it's winter, his normally pale skin has picked up a hint of tan, because he's going outside for things that don't require him to wear full moto gear.

Right now, he's bent over a bike, wearing grease-stained coveralls and a look of intense concentration on his face. The sleeves are rolled up, revealing forearms that are thick from all that riding, but are now also covered in a surprising amount of freckles from the extra sunshine and a dusting of hair that's been sun-bleached. He's covered in a thin sheen of sweat despite the cold. I watch his throat work as he swallows, still concentrating, and his skin seems to gleam in the light as his muscles flex and move.

He looks like some kind of *Magic Mike* mechanic pin-up shit. I'm not typically the kind of person who gets jealous over other guys' looks, so I don't know why I'm fixated on this. I just can't get over what a difference a few weeks of real food and distance from his dad has made in him.

He's fucking glowing. If I took a picture of him right now and he threw up a Tinder profile, his phone would blow the fuck up. Which makes my stomach twist with envy a little, which is also unlike me. I don't know what's going on in my head right now.

"Do I have oil on my face or something?" Silas' voice breaks me out of my stupor. I realize I have no idea how long I've been staring at him, drifting on my own intrusive thoughts and not doing a damn thing to my bike.

"No, sorry. I mean, yeah. You do. But that's not why I was staring."

Way to sound composed, Waters.

Silas squints at me and paws at his cheek with one large, equally dirty hand, but he only makes it worse.

"Better?"

"Not even close."

Forcing a smile, I try to shove the weird, flitting jealousy out of my brain. I hardly ever hook up with the chicks around here. He's welcome to them. Hell, a little physical affection would be good for him. I'd be a shitty friend not to encourage him to get out there, if that's what he wants?

"You look like you just walked out of a sexy mechanic calendar photoshoot. You must've been beating off pit bunnies with a stick the last few years, I swear."

Silas blushes. It makes all the freckles on his face even darker, crimson spreading across his cheeks before he turns his attention back to his bike. It's so fucking pure I want to wrap him up in bubble wrap and keep him away from the rest of the world forever.

Despite that, the tone of this conversation is taking a turn towards offensive locker room stereotypes. That's not my jam. It feels gross as hell, but I can't seem to stop my mouth from spewing shit even as my stomach continues to churn with uncertainty.

"How come I never saw you on Instagram or something with a girlfriend? Too busy to settle down?"

Silas clears his throat, still not looking at me. I've made him uncomfortable, and now I feel like a dick, because I am a dick. But I didn't mean to be on this particular occasion.

Silence hangs between us for a while, punctuated by the scrape of metal on metal as he continues to unscrew the drain bolt on his radiator. I hate silence. It makes my brain feel like it's going to eat itself. But I've already said enough stupid shit for one afternoon, so I do my best to exercise self-control.

Eventually, Silas speaks. He still doesn't look at me.

"There's an old military joke that goes 'If the army wanted you to have a wife, they would have issued you one'. I kinda feel that way about my dad. If a girlfriend had been important for my career, he would have arranged for me to have one. But he never did, and he kept me too busy to find one on my own, so it didn't seem like something worth fighting about."

But what about what you wanted?

The thought floats through my brain, but I don't voice it. He already knows how I feel about his dad's dictatorial approach to parenting. We don't need to rehash it.

"When Dad wants me to get married or whatever, he'll tell me. I can wait."

I try not to let my eyes bug out of my head. That's old Silas speaking, not my new, independent version.

"Bullshit, dude. Your dad isn't in control of shit anymore. You can do whatever you want. Don't wait around for him to green-light your dating life. It's not like he's a fucking role model in that department."

The words are out of my mouth before I can stop them. If I could pluck them out of the air and shove them back into my big, fat trap, I would. I would swallow them whole. But I said the dumb, insensitive thing, and now I have to watch as he winces at the oblique, unintentional reminder of his father's relationship history.

I know Travis had a reputation before he got married, like a lot of guys back then. I still don't know what happened to Silas' mother. I asked my mom a while ago, and all she knows is that Travis' wife died when Silas was little. But she spent a lot of my elementary school years experiencing the finer points of domestic violence, so she didn't pay a lot of attention to town gossip.

And all I know from Silas is that it seems to be a pain that he holds on to more tightly than any other.

I blow out a breath, feeling myself sag in defeat at my own stupidity.

"Silas, I'm so-"

"What about you?" He cuts me off before I can get out an apology.

"'What about me' what?"

"It doesn't seem like you hang out with a lot of girls, except for Wish. What's keeping you from dating?"

Silas turns to look at me for the first time in this conversation. His brown eyes are warm as always, but his expression is guarded. I still feel shitty for bringing up his mom. I hate talking about this stuff with anyone, but honesty is the least I owe him at this point.

Blowing out a breath, I drop my ass back onto the cold concrete floor, abandoning the pretense that I'm still doing anything with my bike. The hex key I wasn't really using hangs from my hand, and I twirl it in my fingers to keep myself occupied.

"I mean, it's not like I'm against dating. It's more the kid thing. Most of the girls around here are pretty traditional. They want to get married one day and have babies. Which is fine, but I've been raising kids since I was one myself. I can't even think about starting a new family when mine still needs me. I know that sounds presumptuous as hell to act like all girls are trying to trap me or whatever, and I don't mean it like that. I just don't want to lead anyone on, y'know?

"I used to do the casual hook-up thing a lot, but as I watched my cousins get knocked up one by one, it felt like this constant looming threat, until hooking up wasn't even fun anymore. And then what was the point? It's fine, though. I have an entire lifetime to do that shit. In the meantime, I am in a committed relationship with my left hand, and we're very happy together, thank you. We're thinking of making a wedding registry, if you'd like to buy us a gift. Astroglide ain't cheap."

I hold up the hand in question, wiggling my fingers at him and wiggling my eyebrows at the same time.

Silas actually laughs at that, which makes me laugh, and thank fuck, the tension is lifting from the room. He's stopped working as well and takes a seat on the ground, his posture a mirror of mine a few feet away, both of us grinning at each other like a couple of idiots.

Shaking his head, Silas looks down at his own hands and flexes his fingers.

"Yeah, well, I can commiserate. I mean, I'm right-handed, but still."

Hesitantly, he holds up his right hand to show me, and I laugh again. When it dies off, I turn to look at him, feeling too intensely not to say what I want to say.

"Your dad never should have controlled you the way he did, but he definitely doesn't control you now. You can do anything you want. I still think you need to move out the second you can afford it. You're a goddamn adult. If you wanna date, you can date."

He's still giving me that *does-not-compute* face, but I don't know how I can put it more bluntly.

"So, do you want to date?"

CHAPTER TWELVE

SILAS

I don't know why this feels like the most difficult question anyone's ever asked me. It should be easy, right? Everybody wants to date. The only reason I didn't before was because it wasn't worth the hassle of fighting with my dad to find the time, and then fighting through my own awkwardness to actually get a girl to like me. Especially one who wasn't a pit bunny.

Not that there's anything wrong with that, but I already have one person in my life who only cares about me because of my skills on the track.

Cade is still staring at me because he asked me what should be a simple question, and instead I blue-screened like a moron holding a torque wrench.

The truth is, this stuff never bothered me as much as it should have. Dad kept me too busy to dwell on it and my sex drive has never been out of control. Jerking off occasionally was enough to keep me satisfied. For the most part.

But lately, things have felt different.

Everything in my life has changed so dramatically, it feels like tectonic plates shifting beneath my feet. No matter how still and quiet I stand, all the other pieces of me are getting sucked down and shifted with the rest of it, whether that's a good or a bad thing. Whether I want it to change or not.

I have no idea if the fact that I'm constantly horny now is a good thing or not. But it is annoying. If this is how most people feel all the time, then I have no idea how Cade managed to give up hook-ups as a conscious choice.

It's not like it could have been hard for him to get girls' attention. He was always popular in high school, and since then he's only gotten more attractive. The sharp edges of his face pair well with his pouty lips, and his hair is just curly enough that it constantly looks messy. Like he just got out of bed and doesn't own a brush. It's infuriating, and the neat, orderly part of my personality is always itching to run my fingers through it to tame it.

And those tattoos. Fuck. I'd never cared about tattoos before, but something about the intricate tendrils of black creeping over every dip and curve of muscle is breathtaking. I can see now why people consider them a work of art. Girls must go crazy for them, wanting to trace every inch, study all the intricacies of where his muscles have been made to look like a machine. How they travel down his back and then sweep over his lats like wings, almost inviting someone to grab on.

Heat prickles in my neck and my groin, and when my pants start to feel uncomfortably tight, I realize that even the thought of Cade's hypothetical anonymous hook-ups is turning me on. If constant humiliation is what a high sex drive buys you, I'll pass. I can't stop myself from blushing at the realization, and it fucking sucks.

This extra embarrassment means my answer to Cade's question comes out even more flustered than it would have, anyway.

"I don't know, man. I wouldn't know where to start. I don't... I've never..."

I rub the back of my neck, avoiding Cade's eyes and trying to will my face to return to its normal color.

Staring at the floor doesn't stop me from noticing Cade watch me though, and I can see him trying to pull the subtext out of my babble. I can't decide if I want him to figure it out on his own so I don't have to say the words out loud and we can be done with this humiliating conversation, or if I want him to stay clueless so we can stop talking about it and never talk about it again.

Of course, Cade is like a dog with a bone once he gets an idea. The fact that we're friends is proof of that.

"You've never dated? It's not a big deal, Silas. I can help, if that's what you want."

He's so earnest it makes my heart crumble a little.

Taking a deep breath, I decide I might as well tell him. It's not like he isn't already aware that I'm a freak.

"I've never done any of it."

"Oh." Cade's eyes go comically wide. "*Oh*. You're a virgin?"

This is mortifying. Groaning, I shove my face in between my knees so I don't have to watch him stare at me wide-eyed anymore.

"Any of it, Cade. Dating, sex. I've kissed like…two girls in my entire life. Do you remember seeing me at any parties back in school? Because it didn't get any better when dad made me drop out to go on the road with him. Not a lot of girls want to come back to a shitty motel room you share with your drunk, snoring father."

My voice is muffled by how deeply I've curled into my own body, but even though I can't see Cade, I can feel him moving closer to me. I'm always aware of where he is. As if his presence is too big for my body not to notice.

Strong arms wrap around my shoulders, and then Cade is pressing his forehead into the back of my neck, which is probably the only piece of me he can get to. His chest is against my back, warm and solid, and I'm surrounded by the familiar *Cade* smell of wood smoke and pine trees that shouldn't be comforting, but is.

The tension slips from my body in a way that I could really get used to.

Cade is like a puppy, all boundless energy and wanting to be in your space. It was weird going from never touching anyone to having him constantly around.

He's such a tactile person. Grabbing my arm, tapping me on the shoulder, hugging me, high-fiving me, tugging on my sleeve to get my attention like a toddler, poking at my face when he's bored, also like a hyperactive toddler. It doesn't matter. It took me a minute to adjust to it after a lifetime of nothing more than the occasional handshake, but I'm here for all of it.

It's more Cade, at the end of it all. I'll take what I can get.

"I'm sorry. I didn't mean to embarrass you. I'm an insensitive asshole."

He's still hugging me as he speaks, so the words are mumbled into the back of my neck. I can feel his lips brush against my skin and even though his breath is warm, it leaves goosebumps in its wake.

Pulling my face out of the knee-cave, I turn to look at him, folding my arms so I can rest my head on them and still stay hunched in on myself. Cade leans back enough to meet my gaze, but keeps his arms around me. He's sitting with his long legs stretched out on either side of me and I have to resist the urge to turn around, burrow into his chest and never come out.

Nothing has ever felt as solid or safe as the arms of this guy I barely know, but I'm not going to question it. It's a fucking gift.

"Nah, I'm sorry. I'm just being melodramatic. It's embarrassing, but it's not the end of the world."

Cade frowns. "You're like the least melodramatic person I've ever met. You're allowed to have a fucking feeling. I was—"

"It's fine." I cut him off, because I can sense him ramping up for a rant, and I don't think I have the energy for it right now. He still looks concerned, so I try to sell it with a smile.

"Fine," he says begrudgingly. Which means a lecture about being honest about my feelings or whatever is being filed away for me for later. For a few seconds, Cade squeezes me so tightly I can't breathe, then he presses a noisy kiss to the side of my head, ruffles my hair the way I hate, and stands up, offering me a hand to do the same.

My body feels too light without him wrapped around me. Like I might float away. But there's no way to say that without sounding crazy, so I stay quiet.

"You don't have to do anything you don't want to do. Ever. Let's go for a drink on Friday and feel it out, if you want to see what you've been missing. Life sucks enough all on its own. We should savor the shit that feels good."

His grin is infectious, and I don't have the heart to point out his hypocrisy. Besides, maybe I really have been missing out.

"Sure, Cade."

He's still holding the hand he used to help me up, so he claps me on the shoulder with the other and we lock eyes for a moment. His tongue slips out to wet his lips, and I find myself watching it for no reason.

Somewhere deep inside my lizard brain, a warning bell goes off. But I don't know what the warning is, and I'm pretty sure I won't until it's too late.

Today was probably the most time I've spent talking about sex with another human being in my entire life, which I'm blaming for why I'm unbearably aroused right now.

I can't sleep. I've been tossing and turning, willing this fucking hard-on to go away, but it's persistent. I don't know why I didn't just rub one out before trying to sleep, but for whatever reason, that felt like giving in.

There is no reason that a fifteen-minute conversation with my best friend about the fact that I'm a fucking virgin should be making me horny. No. Reason.

This is all so fucking confusing.

Punching the pillow and rolling over for the millionth time, I wince when my very stiff, over-sensitive cock jabs into the mattress. Ouch.

I give up.

With my face buried in the pillow, I roll my hips, dragging my length along the mattress. It's impossible not to moan at the relief that floods through me. Every inch of my body feels lit up and at attention. My muscles are all tense as I keep moving, grinding slow and dirty.

I feel like a desperate, horny teenager. Even more than when I actually was a teenager. I know this can't be how adults are supposed to jerk off. Normally if I need to get myself off, I'll do it in the shower for easy clean-up. Quick and to the point. I've never had the urge to spend a lot of time building up to it or pulling out elaborate fantasies.

But right now, the slow build of pressure and anticipation almost feels better than it would to just give in and stroke myself, even if my dick is crying out for it.

In the quiet dark of my room, I wonder how Cade jerks off.

Is he quick and efficient? Doubtful. That boy can't make a fucking sandwich without taking a detour. Plus, he gets too much enjoyment from the little things.

Savor the shit that feels good.

I can picture him in his room, tucked away when everyone else is asleep, taking the time to tease himself and draw it out. I bet he strokes himself slowly until his cock is practically purple and he feels like he's going to explode.

Groaning, I bite the pillow and drag my swollen cock along the sheets again, but that's not cutting it anymore. I need my hand. Reaching down, I shove at the waistband of my boxer-briefs and then kick them down until my cock is free, wrapping my hand around it and giving a long, slow pump.

I bet Cade would be relaxed while he jerks off, because he's always fucking relaxed. He'd sprawl out on his back, just miles of muscle covered in ink, bunching and flexing as he moves his arm. I can picture him spreading his legs wider as he gets into it. Maybe he likes to tug on his balls.

Maybe he likes to do other stuff.

I've heard of guys liking their prostate stimulated while they jerk off, and if anyone is secure enough in their masculinity to try shoving a finger up his own ass for the sake of an orgasm, it's Cade.

It's got to be hard to reach that far down, though. I picture him pulling back his thigh before stretching out one long arm and spreading himself open.

Would he use one finger? Two? How deep would he have to fuck them into himself to feel whatever pleasure he's looking for? As soon as the idea pops into my head, it's all I can think about.

I stop stroking my cock, instead making a tunnel with my fist that I can fuck into. It's slick with precum and if I keep my face pushed deep enough into the pillow with my eyes closed, I can pretend I'm fucking into an actual human being instead of dry-humping my mattress into oblivion, all alone.

I wonder how hard it is for Cade to keep quiet as he fucks himself on his fingers. He's loud in every single thing he does. He must be loud during sex. I can picture him splitting himself open, fucking into himself with one hand while he strokes himself with the other, biting his lip, a flush covering his face and chest from the effort of not moaning and whining as he writhes in pleasure.

He's loud when he does anything else. If he didn't have to keep quiet, how loud would he be when he came?

"Fuck." I almost choke on the word as my balls draw up without warning and I spill hot cum into my fist. I'm still rocking my hips as my cock pulses, and the orgasm seems to draw out forever, until my muscles are trembling and the pillow is about to suffocate me.

Rolling over, I collapse on my back away from the wet patch, struggling to catch my breath. Small, tremoring aftershocks are still making my spent cock twitch, and there's cum smeared across my thigh.

That was weird.

I don't know exactly what that just meant, but I feel like the ground isn't finished shifting underneath me yet.

CHAPTER THIRTEEN

CADE

Silas is a fucking mess.

I've told him a thousand times that this is low-key. We're at The Feral Possum, a brewery that sits out on Rt 20 about halfway between Possum Hollow and Mission Flats, and is one of the few businesses around here that could pass for cool.

The vibe skews more hipster than honky-tonk. Classic rock soundtrack, trendy local drafts on tap, and inclusive signage like BLM and pride flags scattered around behind the bar. There's even an honest-to-God gender neutral bathroom.

The sign is a picture of a unicorn farting and the word 'Whatever'.

But it's still not too far that I can't haul ass home if an emergency beckons. Which makes it my preferred hang out on the rare occasions Wish convinces me to lighten up and go out.

It's super chill. I've tried to convince Silas that it's super chill, but he's not listening. We're just here for a drink with Wish and a few of her friends, some of whom may or may not be female and single. There's no pressure.

This isn't some test he has to perform on. But that hasn't stopped him from spending the night alternating between lurking behind me like a nervous toddler, and avoiding me, making awkward conversation with people while throwing me these inscrutable looks whenever he thinks I'm not watching him.

"I swear, if you stare at him any harder, I'll think you're trying to make his head burst open like an overripe melon left out in the sun."

I frown at Wish as she takes the stool next to me at the bar, a few seats down from where Silas is intensely listening to some girl explain something that apparently requires a lot of touching his arm.

"Thank you for that vivid and not at all terrifying image. But I am not staring, I'm observing. There's a difference."

"Uh huh. Well, I don't think he needs your supervision to have a conversation with Cassidy."

Wish gets in my face, forcing me to lean further over the bar so I can keep watching Silas and Cassidy and make sure she's not making him too uncomfortable. She shouldn't be touching him this much. I bet he's itching out of his skin, but doesn't know how to say no.

All because I embarrassed him about being a virgin and then pressured him into this, like an asshole. Maybe this was a bad idea.

"Earth to Cade!" Grabbing my jaw less gently than I would have liked, Wish jerks me over until I'm looking at her bright blue eyes instead of at Silas. "What the fuck is wrong with you?"

"What?" My words come out garbled because she's still holding the bottom half of my face like a disobedient child. "I just want to make sure he's okay after I dragged him here."

The eye roll I get in return is so hard I'm sure she sees the back of her skull.

"Dude. He's your friend. He doesn't know anyone here, and he hasn't had time to date until now. You asked me to organize a casual bar thing, so I did, and I brought my absolute nicest, least-intimidating friends, by the way. Cassidy is the sweetest. He's hot and shy. Nice girls are going to want to talk to him. It's not fucking rocket science, so you need to cut the damn apron strings."

Her eyes are wide as she keeps staring at me, and I feel like there's other information she wants to shove into my head by eye contact alone.

"That was a lot of mixed metaphors, Wish." My brow furrows as I realize why Cassidy looks so familiar. "Wait, didn't she used to go out with Mason Boyd after he got expelled for dealing in the tenth grade? That's one of your nicest friends?"

"Ugh. Who cares who she dated half a decade ago? Now she's a dental hygienist. It doesn't get more boring than that. You weren't exactly a prize yourself back then, I should point out." Finally letting go of my face, she wipes her hand on her ripped jeans in mock disgust.

A sound catches my attention, and I look up to see Silas laughing at something Cassidy said. Actual human non-robot laughter. It's a goddamn miracle.

Now her hand is on his arm. Just resting there.

I have no idea why this is making me so uncomfortable. Maybe I'd feel better if I knew he wasn't forcing himself to do it just to impress me, or something.

That's it.

My head feels noisy at the best of times, but this is worse than usual. Drumming my fingers on the bar, I look around the room, trying to look at anything other than Silas having a good time or Wish's weird, judgy face.

Fuck it. I wasn't planning on drinking tonight, but I need something to take the edge off all of this...something. This fuzzy, anxious feeling that's creeping in at the edges of my brain. Just far enough to let me know it's there, but not enough to see the shape of it.

Catching the bartender's eye, I order a draft and a shot. The bourbon is cheap, but I didn't buy it for the taste, so I swallow it quickly and chase it with the equally cheap draft. It's already doing its job of dulling my anxiety until I dare to look back at Wish.

She doesn't look judgy anymore. Now she looks sympathetic, which is so much worse.

"What? Silas drove me here and I'm not working tomorrow. I'm allowed to have a drink. You drink all the time. One shot on a Friday night does not mean I'm following in my parents' footsteps."

"I know." She's being uncharacteristically quiet, and it's freaking me out even more.

"Then tell your face. What's wrong?"

Instead of answering, she gives me a weird half-hug as she stands up from the stool.

"I think this is one of those things you have to figure out for yourself. I'm gonna leave you to it, but maybe Silas isn't the only person here who could stand to make some new friends. Or get laid."

She doesn't give me the chance to answer before turning around and heading over to talk to someone on the other side of the bar.

Ugh. Getting laid sounds like so much effort. Even the idea of it is exhausting.

Instead, I sit by myself, powering through the first beer in about four minutes, and then two more, all while watching Silas and Cassidy out of the corner of my eye. While trying not to look like a crazy stalker.

I'm protective. It's not my worst quality. And Silas has been dicked over enough for one lifetime.

But the night drags on, and he never shows any signs of being uncomfortable around her. In fact, he seems to really relax. He and Cassidy talk, with other people drifting in and out of the conversation. Silas is laughing and smiling, Cassidy is throwing back cocktails as quickly as I'm throwing back shots, and the whole thing is making me uneasy.

I turn back to order another beer, but the woman who was serving me has been replaced by a guy. I feel like I should recognize him from the times I've been here before. He's one of those guys that could be almost any age. Handsome, with olive skin, thick dark hair and a neat dark beard with a little salt and pepper in it.

Also well put-together enough that words like 'distinguished' come to mind, especially in a town named after a trash-eating marsupial. He's wearing neatly pressed slacks, a white button-down and a waistcoat that makes him stand out in the sea of jeans and ball caps that surround him. If a guy like this is from around here, I should know who he is. Even if he's a decade or two older.

I suddenly feel very young, and very disheveled, just by sitting near him. But I still need a drink, so I smile up at him and try not to look as drunk as I feel. "Hi."

The bartender smiles back. There's a warmth to his expression, like he can definitely tell that I'm drunk, but finds it more adorable than offensive.

Which is my wheelhouse. Getting away with shit by being adorable. My smile gets bigger and a little sloppier.

"Hey," he says. "What can I get you?"

"Can I get another Bud Light and...." The world is tilting slightly on its axis as I'm watching the man smile at me, and it makes me reevaluate what I was about to say next. "And a water. A giant glass of water, please."

He snorts, and the naked disdain on his face as he reaches to pull my Bud pushes his whole vibe from classy to pretentious.

"What? It's cheap, and I'm not a snob."

His cool gaze returns to mine as he slides over my beer and fills a second glass with water. "I didn't say anything. But a word of warning: if you're determined to keep getting shit-faced, the hangover will be a lot easier tomorrow if you stick with a higher-quality booze. Although my actual advice is that you switch to water altogether for the night. But that's your choice."

I shrug, but I keep leaning towards him, even though our interaction is technically over. Something about his face is drawing me in. Plus, it feels nice to have something to look at other than stupid Silas and Cassidy flirting all night.

"Do they teach you that in bartender school?" I do my best to keep a charming expression on my face, because the last thing I need is this guy cutting me off and making a scene.

He chuckles, holding eye contact as he speaks to me and casually wiping the bar down like we're in an old western.

"No, that one comes from extensive life experience. You should learn from your elders, kid."

Now it's my turn to snort. "I'm not a kid. And you're not that old. Trust me, I have plenty of life experience."

I can't help but look over my shoulder and check on Silas. He's in the same spot as before, and Cassidy is still hanging off his arm. My stomach churns a little from the cheap beer, but I'll be damned if I let Pretentious Bartender know he was right, so I take an obnoxiously large gulp and lean back in towards him.

"What do you do for fun when you're not dispensing life advice, oh wise one?"

"Gunnar," he introduces himself. But then there's a pause, and he studies me for a minute, making me feel more exposed than I like. "And you're cute and everything, but you really are too young for me. Sorry."

It takes a minute for my bourbon-soaked brain to process the words. Did he think I was hitting on him?

I mean, he's a good-looking guy. But I hadn't been flirting with him.

Right?

"Sorry, I didn't..."

I was about to explain that I wasn't hitting on him, but Silas and Cassidy are still in my eyeline, so I have an unobstructed view of the moment she stands up on her tiptoes to whisper something in his ear. I don't know what it was, but I can see how her arm snakes out around his waist as she does it, and how he grabs her hip with one large hand to hold her steady, and it distracts me from whatever I was saying.

Whatever question she asked him, when she leans back, he's nodding yes.

I feel sick. Maybe I went too hard on the shots.

When I turn back around, the bartender—Gunnar—is giving me an unnecessarily sympathetic expression. Moving my half-drunk beer out of my reach and the water directly in front of me, he leans forward until his warm, sensible face fills my vision.

"Well, here's some more unsolicited advice, kid. Stop drinking, go home, get some sleep. Maybe talk to your friend in the morning. It won't seem so bad with a little perspective."

There's no chance for me to ask him what the hell he means before he turns away to answer another customer down the bar.

I'm trying to evaluate if I need to go to the bathroom and hurl when the two of them walk over to me, and I have to peel my eyes from where Cassidy is holding on to Silas' beefy arm to zone in on what he's saying to me.

"—been drinking, so I said I'd give her a ride home. Okay?"

What's he talking about? I must look spaced out, because he repeats himself.

"I said that Cassidy's been drinking, so I'm gonna drive her home." Ah. So all my hard work to get him laid was a success. Yay, me. "Do you wanna come with us?"

The thought makes me snort. My drunk ass cramping his style is the last thing he needs. Shaking my head vigorously turns out to be a bad idea though, because I slip off the stool, and Silas has to grab me and prop me up.

His hands are warm and sure, holding me upright. The familiar smell of his aftershave fills my nose, all citrusy, and settles the churning in my gut.

"I'm fine, man. Go ahead. You two have fun." I really hope I'm not slurring, but Silas' sudden concern tells me otherwise.

"Cade, are you okay? How much have you had to drink?"

"I'm fine," I say, peeling his hands off my arm and pushing him towards Cassidy. "Get out of here." Then I grin, so they know I mean it in the nice way, but the expression feels weird and vacant.

"Cade, you seem not good. Let me take you home." Silas is reaching towards me again, making Cassidy's hands fall away from where she was holding his arm. She looks up at him with a hurt expression, but he doesn't notice, and I feel even more shitty than I did before.

Why am I being so weird? This is exactly what was supposed to happen. I just need him to leave so I can make the world stop spinning and clear my head.

"I told you I'm fine. I don't need a fucking babysitter." I jerk my body out of his reach, and now he's the one who looks hurt. Awesome.

"I'll take him home. Come on, dollface."

I've never been so relieved to see Wish in my life, and my whole body sags.

"See? I'm fine. You guys should go." I gesture at the two of them and try to smile again, but it feels pained. "Enjoy."

Slinging my arm around Wish's tiny shoulders, I lean as much of my weight into her as I can and try not to look completely obliterated as we head for the exit.

I can feel Silas' frown follow me the entire way out. But once I'm sitting in the passenger seat of Wish's Wrangler, I catch sight of Silas walking Cassidy over to his F150 on the other side of the parking lot.

She's hanging off his arm again, and he holds out his hand to help her step up into the cab.

That's the truck we got last week on our spontaneous shopping trip, to celebrate him getting the job at Ford's. I joked that it had to be a Ford, but the truth was it was dirt cheap, but still ran well enough to drag his bike to and from races. I even managed to sweet talk Ford into co-signing the loan. I think he might secretly be loaded since his dad died, and I know for a fact he already likes Silas more than me.

Maybe I shouldn't have pushed Silas right away, but I felt like he needed it. He'd never had his own truck before. His dad had never seen the point in them having two vehicles, Silas said.

The way his fucking face lit up when he drove it home was insane. He looked so free.

There's no way for Cassidy to get how fucking cool that truck is, even though she gets to ride in it, probably flirting with him on the way back. Maybe they'll fool around in the truck once they get to her place.

Maybe they'll fuck in the back seat, and then Silas will always associate it with losing his virginity instead of getting a piece of hard-won freedom from his shitty dad.

Whatever. It shouldn't matter to me.

This is supposed to be exactly what I wanted.

Leaning my head against the window, I close my eyes and let the cool glass soothe my throbbing head as Wish pulls out of the parking lot. I don't want to watch Silas drive away.

I don't want to think about this anymore.

And God bless that woman, but Wish says nothing the entire drive home. She just puts a soft hand on my knee and leaves it there, like an anchor.

At least I can take comfort in that. It's the only thing that makes sense to me right now.

Maybe the rest of my jumbled thoughts will sort themselves out in the morning when I'm sober.

CHAPTER FOURTEEN

SILAS

I hope it's not too early to be here. I'm sure Cade is nursing a killer hangover after last night, and he'll want to sleep in, but I spent the entire morning pacing around my house until my (also hungover) father yelled at me to get out before he duct-taped me to an armchair. I couldn't wait any longer.

The cold air wraps around me as I step out of the truck, and I nestle deeper into my Carhartt. It really feels like winter now. The light is thin and blue-tinged; the earth is hard-packed under my feet and there's almost an inch of snow covering all the old, rusted-out farm equipment that lies abandoned around the trailer.

It would almost be peaceful if there wasn't something slick and oily swirling in my chest, dragging me down.

Things are not right between me and Cade.

At first, I thought my possessiveness and neediness towards him was because he was my only friend. Or some sort of pathetic kicked puppy-syndrome—offer me a family and I'll follow you around with heart eyes for the rest of my life.

The idea of Cade was wrapped up in everything else that was changing: getting distance from my dad, getting a real life, spending time with a real family, no matter how fucked up they might be. It made sense that I would feel intense about all of it.

But after the road my brain took me down during my jerk-off session the other day, I think my weird feelings are also about Cade, specifically.

For someone who's never been super interested in sex, my entire fucking body lit up like a Christmas tree when I started picturing him finger-fucking himself and jerking off. I'm not an expert, but I'm pretty sure that crosses the boundary of being just good bros.

Last night only confirmed that I need to sack up and talk to him about it.

Cassidy was great. I'd walked into that bar with one foot in a panic attack, but once I started talking to her, things got easier. She was sweet and funny, and didn't make conversations into the insurmountable challenge that most people do. I should have wanted to keep talking to her all night.

But the only person I wanted to be with was Cade.

I told myself I was watching him out of the corner of my eye because he seemed to be in a funk, and I was concerned. Then it was because I saw him getting pretty sloshed. But the truth is, I would have been watching him, anyway.

Even once I knew he was safe with Wish taking him home, I was still thinking about him. Cassidy wanted me to kiss her in the truck, but it didn't matter that she was beautiful and kind and I could talk to her. The idea of it left me cold.

I don't know what any of this means.

I don't know if it had been Cade trying to kiss me in the cab of my truck, I would have wanted it any more than I did with Cassidy. Maybe I don't want to hook up with anyone, and the jerk-off fantasy was just wires getting crossed.

Shaking the thought out of my head, I pull into the circle of flattened grass in front of the trailer that passes for a driveway, parking my truck off to the side and hopping out. Cade's rig and bike are here, so he's still home, at least. And his mom's beat up old SUV is sitting under the old awning, like usual.

But there's also a car I don't recognize, and it isn't snow-covered like the others. A Supra that was probably a thing of beauty in the nineties, but is currently so rust-eaten and weather-damaged I'm surprised it even survived the drive up the long, rocky driveway.

That's the only thing I have time to think before I hear the noise coming from the house.

At first, it sounds like indistinct yelling. But Cade says he and his mom can get into the occasional shouting match and they never go too far, so I'm not that worried.

Then I hear a crash, and I cover the remaining twenty-five-ish feet to the house at a sprint.

"Where's the money?" A man's voice—not Cade—is loud enough for me to hear before I throw open the door, followed by another crash.

Inside, I see exactly what I was expecting, but still hoping not to.

Kris is standing in the far corner of the kitchen with Maddi and Sky huddled behind her. Her stance is so strong and protective, but her face is totally blank. She's smoking a cigarette, and even though it looks like she's been crying, she's devoid of expression. She isn't saying anything or looking at anyone.

The girls both have red-rimmed eyes but aren't crying either, and it makes me wonder how many times they've been through this to be able to keep quiet for it.

The owner of the Supra and source of all the yelling is standing in the middle of the room, looking unhinged. He's tall, even taller than me and Cade, as well as older and filled out like someone who used to be really fucking strong. He has dark hair that looks exactly like Cade's would if he grew it out long and then stopped showering. His face gives me the fucking creeps.

The resemblance is so strong. I don't think I ever saw Cade's dad when we were kids, but I'd know they were blood relatives without question.

It must really suck for Cade to have to look at this vicious, violent, funhouse mirror version of himself. He has the edge of a seasoned meth addict that we all got used to seeing growing up. Everything about his jerky, violent movement and crazed expression is screaming to me that he's high as fuck right now.

I can see why Cade doesn't like to talk about him.

He's going through the room, turning everything upside down with a feral intensity, ripping open anything he can get his hands on and throwing the pieces aside when it doesn't have whatever he's looking for.

And in between this threatening man and the girls is nothing but a dingy Formica countertop and Cade.

His dad doesn't notice when I burst into the trailer, still focused on his manic search. But Cade turns and looks at me with wide eyes.

He's in nothing but his boxers, like he was still sleeping when this chaos descended, and there's already a nasty bruise forming on his ribs, as well as some redness and swelling around his eye.

He looks scared, and so incredibly young.

I feel fucking enraged. I've never been a violent person, but it's taking all my self-control not to go completely apeshit right now, and it's only because I don't want to escalate whatever situation I just walked into.

"Get the fuck out before I call the cops, Dad." I can hear how much effort Cade is putting into keeping his voice steady. "Aren't you still on parole in Arkansas? I bet not crossing state lines is a condition of that parole, asshole. Whatever money I have got spent on bills or Mom smoked it. There's nothing left." He bites off the last few words like it physically hurts. "Now. Get. The fuck. Out."

His dad stills, and it's so much scarier than the frantic destruction of a few seconds ago. The backpack that he'd been rifling through, sending sheets of one of the girl's homework all over the floor in the process, falls from his hands as he points at Cade.

113

"This is my house. I built it. I'll show up whenever I want." His chest is heaving as he breathes, rage clinging to every movement. "As soon as I got to town, I heard about how many races you've been winning. There's no way you've spent it all. I know you. You've got something squirreled away somewhere, and I need it. I bought you the damn bike. Any money you make with it is mine."

Tension crackles through the room like an electric current, but Cade holds his ground.

"Fuck you, Nana paid for that bike and let you take credit for it. She told me that years ago. You didn't give me shit. I'm the one paying to keep the lights on and raising your children, since you're too fucked up to do it yourself. Get the fuck out of my house."

He tilts his chin up just a little, and I swell with pride watching him stand up to this shitbag. For a few seconds, the only sound in the room is Cade's heavy breathing and Sky's quiet, muffled crying in the corner.

Until his dad fucking explodes.

He moves faster than I expected, crossing the distance to Cade in two large strides. I see Cade flinch away and curl in to make himself a smaller target, although I can't tell whether it's out of instinct or experience.

Either way, seeing him so scared snaps any last reservations I had left.

He's got his meaty hand wrapped around Cade's throat when I charge into him. I never played football in high school, but there's not a lot of finesse in the movement. Bending low, I throw every ounce of strength I have into my shoulder and then throw that shoulder into the man's body.

He hits the Formica hard enough to crack it.

Cade is trying to get up from the floor where he fell, coughing and reaching for his throat. His voice is raspy when he yells at his mom to take the girls to his room and lock the door.

I think I knocked the wind clean out of his dad, because the man is gasping for air when I pull him up from the broken countertop and start hauling him towards the front door. He puts up a fight, but he's disoriented now.

As soon as the girls disappear down the hallway, Cade turns to help me. It's a flail of limbs and everyone's fucking cursing, but between the two of us, we're able to shove him out of the door and drop him, sprawling on his ass in the snow.

Cade looks down at him, pretty fucking intimidating for someone who's beat up and still in their underwear. The way his tattoos cover his arms and chest almost looks like armor. For a second, I wonder if that's why he has them.

"If you show up here again, I'll fucking kill you."

The coldness in his voice makes me think he means it.

Pulling me back inside, Cade slams the door shut so hard the whole wall rattles and then he flips the crusty old deadbolt. As if someone who wanted in badly enough couldn't rip the whole door off its hinges.

Inside, Cade puts his back to the door and slides down until he's sitting on the floor, then throws his head back into it with a thunk.

The sounds of crashing drifts through the door, as all the rusted crap outside gets thrown around in anger. There's more yelling about how he wants his damn money. I'm buzzing with so much adrenaline it's like I've got fire in my veins, but all the fight has already drained out of Cade.

His eyes are just as vacant now as Kris' when I walked in.

"Sit." He plucks weakly at the sleeve of my hoodie. "He'll tire himself out and leave soon. He knows if he comes back in here, I'll actually call the cops and it's not worth it to him."

I sit beside him, with my knees up and my back against the door.

"Maybe you should call the cops. Does he do this a lot?"

Cade snorts.

"And risk getting on CPS' radar so the girls can end up in some fucking foster home? No, thank you. Mom spent half her childhood in foster homes. I know exactly what goes on there. Not fucking happening. Cops are useless anyway. They can't even tell him to leave because this is technically still his house."

The sigh that he lets out seems to last a lifetime, and his eyes close like they're suddenly too heavy to keep open.

A particularly loud crash from outside makes Cade flinch, but he quickly settles again. I feel completely adrift here, but I'd do anything to make him look less exhausted.

Cade shivers beside me, and I realize it's fucking winter, and he's still half-naked.

"Dude, you must be freezing. Go get dressed."

He shakes his head with his eyes still closed, even though his teeth are chattering now.

"Not until he leaves. Just in case. This door won't stop him if he really wants to get in."

Fuck. Pulling my hoody over my head I shove it into his hands, but by the time he's putting it on he's shaking violently enough that he needs my help to get his arms through the sleeves and tug it down over his head. It seems like maybe more than just the cold is affecting him.

Gray eyes stare at me while he tremors and shakes from the adrenaline crash. He looks ripped open and raw, like I could reach into him and grab any part, no matter how deeply buried.

"I'm glad you were here, Silas."

I rub my hands up and down his arms on the pretense of warming him up, but really hoping it'll make him feel more grounded.

"Me too, Cade."

Something smashes into the wall of the trailer, making it shake. Cade flinches again.

It only takes a gentle tug from me to get him to lean over and bury his face in my neck. I turn so I can wrap my arms around him fully, even throwing one of my legs over his lap. I try to surround him with every inch of myself that I can, as if that were enough to make him feel warm and safe and not scared anymore.

Slowly, the shivering subsides.

But I'm not letting go until he makes me.

CHAPTER FIFTEEN

CADE

After what feels like hours, the engine of Dad's piece of shit car finally sputters and then roars to life. He screams out one last string of obscenities before pulling away, but the words all bleed together.

When someone has spent enough of your life attacking you with their words, they always bleed together. You hear their tone over everything else. I don't need to make out the individual words to know how much my father still hates me. He's always made that very clear.

It's fine. I hate him too.

I should feel calmer as I listen to the sound of his car tear down the driveway and away from us, but I don't. The fight-or-flight instinct ebbs, at least. But the feeling that it leaves behind is the opposite of calm.

If brittle were an emotional state, that's how I would describe myself right now. Dried out and spider-webbed with cracks, like the plaster on the ceiling.

Sometimes I wonder which one will last longer, me or this derelict trailer.

"Cade?"

Silas' voice is soft, and his breath is warm on my face when he speaks, pulling my thoughts back from the edge of whatever self-pitying rabbit hole I was about to dive down.

He's still got his arms wrapped around me, and it's selfish, but I don't want him to let me go. I'm an adult. I should be able to cope with the same shit that's been happening for years. But it's been a long time since Dad showed up looking that cracked out, and part of me had forgotten how bad it could be.

With my shitty but steady paycheck and the girls doing well, I'd gotten used to mom's occasional drinking, weeping and oxy binge being the worst thing that happens around here.

Clearly, it's made me weak.

And I don't know what I would have done if Silas hadn't been here to pull my soft ass out of the fire.

"He's gone, Cade. You should get dressed before you freeze."

I know I should, but the weak part of me wants to take comfort in him for just a little longer. Closing my eyes, I squeeze Silas to me as tight as I can for just a second. He stiffens a little, but doesn't resist. With my face buried in his neck and my eyes closed, I fill my nose with his warm, citrus scent and selfishly grasp for every shred of comfort I can take from him.

Then I school my face back to a less desperate expression, let go of him, and push myself shakily to my feet.

I hiss when my ribs twinge. The bruise there will heal, but it's going to be sore for a long time. Silas reaches for me, steadying me with one hand on my arm and the other on my waist, and I don't have the willpower not to lean into it.

For a million dollars and a pancake breakfast, I could not tell you the last time someone babied me like this. I want to curl into him like a cat.

I'm so fucking hungover. I was half-awake, lying in bed with a mouth like the Sahara as I regretted all my life choices and suppressed the urge to vomit, when Dad tore into the trailer on a mission. My body was up and moving on instinct before I knew what was happening, and everything after that was a haze of adrenaline.

Now the adrenaline is gone, but the hangover remains.

My hands are shaking, my stomach is cramping and my body is freezing cold even while uncomfortable waves of heat prickle over my skin. I'm sweaty and dizzy and hurt everywhere that Dad touched me.

Silas is here, though. He walks me to my bedroom, knocking and then speaking softly until Mom unlocks the door.

Everyone inside looks a little pale, but they're all strong. They know the score. Maddi and Sky launch themselves at me so hard that the pain in my ribs causes another wave of nausea to throb through me, and out of the corner of my eye I see Silas remind them to be gentle.

Reaching over their heads, I pull Mom into the hug as well. She holds herself stiff, but doesn't resist me. I know without looking that she still has the far-away, hollow look in her eye that she gets at times like this.

She's far from perfect. I give her plenty of shit for what she's done wrong, but sometimes I forget how much she's gone through as well.

"Are you okay?" My voice is pitched low enough that only she can hear me.

"I think I need a break."

She's completely flat and emotionless as she says it, which is what I was worried about. Pulling out of my arms, Mom turns away from all of us and goes out into the hallway. The girls are looking after her like they want to follow, but they know there's no point.

I can take drunk Mom that likes to get into bitchy fights, and I can take weepy Mom that needs to be babied. Functional Mom, although she's rare, is pretty cool. This is the only version of her I don't know how to deal with.

Zombie Mom. Which sounds more funny than it is. It's like the trauma gets too much for her and she just shuts down. Nothing gets through to her; not me, not the girls, nothing. She has a tendency to disappear for days on end and come back when she's dried out. Which is still better than when she stays here, slowly leeching the happiness around her.

This is the thing that I'm most afraid of when people tell me I can leave the girls alone with her. Even three-sheets to the wind, she'd never deliberately hurt them. In an emergency, she'd do her best. But like this, I've seen her walk out the door and not look back, no matter who or what she leaves behind.

The sound of the front door echoes down the hallway, telling me that this is one of those times. We'll see her when we see her, I guess.

I squeeze the girls as tight as I can while I rearrange my face into something less miserable, and when I pull back, I fake a smile. Two equally fake smiles shine back at me, because this is how it goes. Which makes this all even more sad.

"Okay, ladies. And Silas. How about I get dressed while you salvage whatever you can of your stuff from Tornado Asshole."

Of all the things to destroy, why did he have to start shredding his daughters' fucking homework in his search for hidden cash? The front room looks like it's covered in algebra-themed confetti. Maddi's face drops as I mention it, because she busts her ass at school and I know this is going to eat at her for a while. I push through.

"But then the four of us will get in Silas' truck and make him drive us aaaaaaall the way to Franklin, where they have that really nice Wendy's. Burgers and frosties for everyone. Then we can go to Walmart and replace any of your school shit that Dad destroyed. Deal?"

Both girls nod, sold on the idea. We don't have to drive for two hours to find a Walmart and let's be real, there's no such thing as a *nice* Wendy's, but it's about putting distance between us any and all blood relatives for the rest of the day.

"Perfect. Now everyone look at Silas with your most pathetic abused child face and say, 'Please will you drive us to Franklin because Cade is too hungover and needs to nap on the way?'." I stick my face next to theirs and give Silas the most charming grin my sallow face can manage.

Silas looks surprised by my brutal honesty, but that's what I was going for. If you have to go through the abuse, the very least you should get in return is getting to play the 'my dad's a violent asshole' card once in a while.

"Pleeeeeeeease, Silas," the girls say in unison. As if he was ever going to say no.

His gaze slides to me, and there's a hint of what I'm starting to think of as his *why is Cade like this* expression. I don't hate it, and when I smile back at him, it's a genuine smile.

"Of course." His voice is gruff, but there's the same softness to him that's been coming out more and more around the girls. "Go clean up your stuff and make a list of what you need replaced. Your brother has to shower before we leave. He's not getting in my truck smelling like a distillery."

I snort. I'm sure I smell like nothing but sweat and fear at this point, but whatever. He's not wrong about the shower.

The girls both slip out of my room. They're still subdued, but I think the cloud of imminent doom is gone. Everyone will definitely feel a lot better when we've put some miles between ourselves and Possum Hollow, hopefully getting back long after the old man has blown through town.

Hopefully.

Silas trails out after the girls and helps them clean while I take a quick shower. I feel a little more human afterwards, but all of my various aches and pains are also settling in. Pulling on clothes seems to take forever. My tank is running on empty, and the most I can manage is sweats, clean underwear and a baggy NOFX hoodie. It's two sizes too big and so faded it's more gray than black, but has holes in the sleeves that I've worried big enough to stick my thumbs through.

Tugging the sleeves all the way down to cover my hands makes me feel like a teenager again, but it's comforting. Going for broke, I pull the hood up over my wet hair as well.

When I finally throw myself down on the bed, I feel like a balloon with all the air let out. Lying flat on my back with my eyes closed is making the world spin, but the thought of moving is too much right now.

A few minutes later, something nudges my elbow.

"Here, drink this. You look like shit, man."

Opening my eyes leaves me staring straight at Silas' warm gaze. In the wintry morning light, his eyes are the color of melted caramel. The intensity of it is making me squirm.

"Thanks." I snort, accepting the glass and groaning as I sit up enough to drink from it. "In hindsight, I may have had too much to drink last night."

"Mmm, what was your first clue? Was it when you almost fell, getting off the barstool? Or was it when Wish had to basically carry you across the parking lot to her car?"

If looks could kill, I'd be stabbing him right now.

"The hangover and parental beating is punishment enough, thank you. I don't need a guilt trip on top of it."

A flush creeps up the back of Silas' neck as he looks at his feet, shifting his weight from side to side.

"I'm sorry."

Blowing out a long, deep breath, I rub my temples where a crippling headache is threatening to form. My throat is still aching where Dad grabbed me; and now I feel like a dick for snapping at Silas. He's literally the only person here trying to help.

There is no part of me that isn't squeezing with pain right now.

"I didn't mean it like that. And thank you for showing up unexpectedly and saving my ass. I thought you'd still be enjoying your hot date instead of jumping fists-first into my nightmare."

Silas avoids my eyes completely, but the thought of his night with Cassidy leaves a bitter taste in my mouth. I'm in too much pain to add self-reflection to the pile, so I don't push it.

The silence between us is awkward, and it makes me itch.

"Sit down, dude, you're looming."

It only takes a gentle tug at the hem of his t-shirt until he sits down heavily on the edge of the mattress next to me.

There's another silence before either of us speaks again, this one longer but less awkward.

"Does that happen a lot?"

"What, my piece of shit dad showing up like a special guest from Skid Row and tearing into our lives for no reason?" Silas nods solemnly. "It used to happen more. He and Mom were on again, off again for a long time, before he moved to Arkansas. She's been a lot better since he left. We all have. He's only shown up a couple of times since then, always for the same reason. Some bullshit, hallucinated idea that we owe him money. But it's been a while."

I laugh, although it sounds hollow, even to me. Silas looks at me with a twisted, concerned expression.

"I guess I'd almost let myself believe he was done fucking things up for us. I thought I was too old to be naïve anymore, but I was wrong. That's embarrassing."

Silas doesn't say anything. He doesn't have to. If anyone gets being constantly let down by someone and then hating yourself for letting it happen in the first place, it's him.

We're two peas in a very fucked-up pod.

Instead, he brings his hand to my back, rubbing it in slow circles that dial down the anxiety thrumming in my veins. We sit like that for a long time. The silence doesn't even bother me the way it usually does.

In the end, it's Silas that breaks it.

"Do you think he'll come back?"

CHAPTER SIXTEEN

SILAS

C ade shrugs, his gaze trained on the floor.

"Probably."

I've known Cade for a while now, not including watching him from a distance when we were kids, and I think I've gotten to know him pretty well. I've seen him happy, sad, angry. I've seen the way he gets playful and soft around his sisters. I've seen him talk with conviction about how much he hates toxic masculinity, but how he's still not immune to the instinct to straighten his shoulders and drop his voice around certain types of men. It's hard not to, when you grew up with fathers like ours.

I saw him be more gentle and empathetic than I knew how to deal with the night at the quarry. And I've seen him heartbroken, because let's face it, his life is not a picnic.

But I've never seen him look fragile.

Right now, he looks like bone china. Maybe it's the way the dark bruising stands out against his hangover-pallid flesh, or maybe it's the fact that he's sitting completely still for the first time since I've met him. Either way, it's really freaking me out.

The urge to fix it is all-consuming. I want to make him feel normal again more than I've ever wanted to win a stupid moto.

"And what happens if he comes back?"

Another shrug. "The same thing. It wasn't the first time, it won't be the last. He always tires himself out eventually and moves on."

Anger and adrenaline dump wholesale into my veins at the thought, and I have to clench my fists to keep from shaking.

"What if he hurts the girls?"

Cade shakes his head; the first thing he's done with any conviction. "I'd never let him. I'll swap my shifts so I can be here when they're not at school. Next weekend they can probably sleepover with my Aunt Jaz, as much as I hate to impose. Just until I'm sure he's left town. I'll be here to make sure they're safe."

"And when he hurts you again?"

Because it is a *when,* not an *if.* I've picked up that much.

Cade refuses to look at me and my anger is threatening to boil over.

I don't have it in me to keep quiet. "You can't just let this keep happening!"

When Cade looks up at me, his expression is sharp. I can see the tension running through every part of him.

"Yeah, and you can't keep living at your dad's house forever, bankrolling his drinking habit and letting him treat you like his emotional meat puppet, but it's a lot easier to say you'll fix something than to actually fix it, isn't it?"

There's a bite to the words and a challenge in his eyes. He's not wrong. Things with Dad have gotten worse and worse.

I used to think that all his strictness and his insane drive came from how much he cared about my success. If he was an asshole to me, it was because he wanted me to win more than he cared about being a decent father.

Now my career is over. No more training, no more trophies, no more excuses.

But his attitude towards me is worse than ever.

Maybe the shitty way he treated me was how he always wanted to treat me, and the racing just gave him an excuse.

I've given up trying to figure it out.

"You're right," I say. Cade's eyebrows shoot sky-high. I turn my body so I can look him in the eye. "You're right. He's getting worse, not better. We're circling each other in the same old toxic patterns and there isn't even an excuse for it anymore. I should get out."

Cade looks completely sideswept, and I'm not surprised. I'm kind of sideswept myself.

An idea occurs to me. It's dumb, but maybe it's also just what we need.

"What if I stay here? Just until your dad leaves town, to help hold down the fort. I know there's not a lot of space, but I'd get some distance from my own shitty dad, and I'd feel better knowing you guys were safe—"

"Yes!" Cade licks his lips nervously, looking a little taken aback by his own enthusiasm. "Yeah. I mean, that's a good idea." He blows out a breath and sags, his shoulder brushing against mine. "I'd feel better if you were here, too."

"Okay. Perfect." I lick my lips as well, suddenly nervous for no particular reason. "I'll go home and grab some stuff, and be back in half an hour, then we'll head out. Cool?"

Cade nods. His gaze hasn't left my face since we started this conversation. "Cool."

I don't move for a second. It feels like there's something else that needs to be said right now. There's something heavy in the air, but I can't figure out what it is.

Cade licks his lips again and leans incrementally further into the space between us. He's like a magnet, drawing me in as well, until there are only a few inches of charged air separating us. When I look Cade in the eye, I see his gaze flick down to my mouth and then back up.

My stomach bottoms out like I'm on a rollercoaster and there's a tingle in the tips of my fingers. The moment hangs between us, but no one moves. No one even breathes.

I have to break the tension before I do something insane. Focus on Dad. The fear of what he's about to do to me is an excellent distraction from whatever confusing shit just happened, so I grab onto it with my brain and don't let go. Leaning back, I push off Cade's mattress and walk to the door.

"Silas?"

"Yeah?"

"Thank you."

Now it's my turn to shrug.

"Hey, you're the one who did all the work and made us friends. This is what friends are for, right?"

A weird expression flits across his face, but it's gone before I can try to figure it out.

"Right."

The entire drive back to my house is a blur. I move on muscle memory, my focus turned inwards while I psyche myself up for whatever confrontation is coming. All the things I wouldn't dare to let myself think, let alone say out loud, are running through my head.

I'm an adult. You can't control me.

My career is over and we both need to move on.

I don't owe you anything.

You can't keep punishing me for what Mom did.

The words tumble through my head like a rototiller, but instead of getting me ready, it feels like they're carving off a little chunk of my confidence with every turn.

There's a reason I don't let myself think about these things. The longer I dwell on it all, the more images of Mom flit through my mind, sending everything off-kilter. I don't have many memories, and the ones I do are probably colored by Dad's rants from when he gets drunk and mouthy.

I remember how she used to wake me up in the middle of the night. She would be so panicked, convinced that something terrible had happened, but once she saw I was alright, the relief would wash over her. She'd pull me into her lap and cling to me. I thought it was normal at the time, because it was all I knew. Even now, two decades later, it feels weird to sleep through the night without being woken up. And even though I know it was a sign of how sick she was, I never felt more intensely loved than in those moments.

My fingers tighten on the steering wheel as I take the turn that leads into town, getting closer and closer to my house.

I don't have a lot of memories from Dad back then. It was only Mom. I don't think I went to school very often, either. Everything I remember is this long, hazy existence of the two of us in the house. Mom hated the bright sunlight, so she always kept the curtains drawn. She slept erratically, so I slept erratically, and days didn't pass the same way they do now. It was like we were suspended in time. Or maybe suspended just outside of time, hanging there, while the rest of the world continued their onward march in peace.

Being the center of her world was nice. I liked it, most of the time. But her anxiety was also our constant companion, and often competed for her attention. I think things got worse as I got older. I remember her crying a lot, and nervously pulling at her long, blonde hair until chunks of it were scattered around the house.

One of my earliest memories of Dad is when he came home from a race and noticed that I'd picked up the same habit. I'd started pulling out my hair when I got anxious, copying her. He was horrified. He yelled at her for a long time.

Then he shaved my head to break the habit. The feeling of his strong fingers digging into my skull to hold me still will be etched in my brain forever.

As I pull into my driveway, I realize that I've gotten so lost in the memory that I'm doing it now. I haven't worried about haircuts since my life imploded, and Dad has clearly been too preoccupied to think about it. My hair is still short, but longer than it's ever been since that first day he buzzed it off.

My fingers figured that out with no conscious effort on my part, resurrecting a habit I thought was long dead and buried. But the sting of my scalp as I tug at the strands feels good. It's grounding. It helps me claw my way out of this memory and back into the present.

I can worry about what that means some other time. Right now, I need to go inside. And Dad's truck is in the garage, so that confrontation really is coming.

I'm an adult. You can't control me. I don't owe you anything. I'm going to stay with Cade and people who care about me.

It runs through my head on a loop as I walk inside, pretending my hands aren't shaking.

It's not my fault she's dead.

By the time I get to the living room, I'm so flush with adrenaline that I feel like a bag of bees with a hollow chest. I expect to find him on the couch watching old race footage, as usual. Or maybe on the computer researching another one of his get-rich-quick 'investment' schemes.

If Cade can stand up to his father who hits him, I can stand up to the man who only ever attacks me with words. This will be good. This has been a long time coming.

But when I find Dad on the couch, fast asleep next to an empty bottle of whiskey, I'm not disappointed. I'm relieved. It makes me feel like a coward, but it's true. I don't know how, but Dad's always had this way of making everything seem so rational, like he's so right that it's all a foregone conclusion, and anyone who disagrees with him is acting crazy.

I was half-afraid that when I got here, he wouldn't get mad. He'd just tell me it wasn't happening, and I'd believe him. I can never trust my own mind when I'm around him.

Embracing the relief, I slink upstairs to pack my stuff. He doesn't wake up the entire time, and he's still snoring as I leave.

I can confront him whenever I get back. Right now, getting back to Cade is more important.

I'm not a coward. I just don't trust myself to know better.

CHAPTER SEVENTEEN

CADE

After the weekend I had, having the girls back in school and me being back at work feels blissfully normal.

It's pretty standard for an ambulance to be staffed with one paramedic and one EMT. Tristan spent years putting soldiers back together in active combat zones (he won't tell me where, I asked once; it did not go well). He went back to school afterwards for his paramedic license and practiced in the not-great part of Boston that spawned him and then gave up all that high-octane trauma medicine to come to Possum Hollow and narcan junkies behind dumpsters for a living. Because, according to him, "Trees are nice and possums are badass."

We've been friends for a year, and that's the sum total of biographical information I have on him. He's fucking cagey. But it's enough to know that he is the first, last and only person around here you want if there's a legitimate emergency.

Which makes me his bitch. I mean EMT. That's why right now he is sitting comfortably, counting back our drugs, while I'm scrubbing vomit out of the paneling. I've been doing this for six months though, after only four months of school, but I've been cleaning up junkie vomit since I was old enough to hold a sponge—thanks, Mom. This is an appropriate use of our respective skill sets.

Still sucks, though.

I distract myself by counting down the hours until our shift is over. It's been a very slow, very boring day and I'm ready to bounce. In the macro sense, I'm happy the people of this county aren't having severe medical emergencies, but I am not a fan of sitting still.

At least Silas is home today. Knowing he's there to watch the girls and keep them safe is such a fucking weight off my chest. It's like I didn't realize how heavy it was until Silas showed up and took it off me. It feels incredible.

It's not just that, though. Home has always been complicated for me. I love being with my sisters, and I wouldn't leave them for the world, but sometimes I think the threads of love and guilt and worry are all so knotted up that I'll never be able to untie them. Anytime I'm home, it's like I'm experiencing all those emotions at the same time. Dialed up to their maximum setting.

After all the chaos on Saturday and Mom bailing on us again, Silas was just *there*. He took us up to Franklin, and it barely took any time at all for the ghost of Dad's violence to fade into the past. We were normal people, eating greasy burgers and buying cheap school supplies. It felt like normal family shit.

Even when Mom showed up two days later—blitzed out of her mind and dragging the memory of misery with her before she disappeared again—it was easier to stay calm because Silas was there. He always has my back. It feels like we're a team.

I've been a team of me, myself and I since birth and I gotta say, this new way is pretty fucking cool.

Silas is pretty fucking cool.

Getting a front-row seat to watching him come out of his shell and learn to be happy? It's icing on the cake. Every day he's away from his dad, I swear his smile gets a little more carefree. No one could watch that without feeling like they're looking at a miracle.

I'm pretty sure I'm smiling to myself like a dope while I clean this vomit. It isn't until Tristan speaks that I snap out of my weird train of thought.

"So, I got called out to a bar fight on Saturday night. Treated some cuts and scrapes on a very belligerent guy who looks like an older, meth-ier version of you and shares the same last name. Anything you wanna talk about?"

I grimace. I try to keep the disaster part of my life separate from my job, where I pretend to be a somewhat put-together person. But it's a small town, and Tristan has lived here long enough. I'm not fooling anyone.

"Yeah, he likes to make an entrance whenever he comes back to town," I answer with a sigh.

Tristan keeps a carefully neutral expression. "Has he been around to see your mom? I can see you're sporting a nice new shiner and it ain't dirt bike season."

"It's fine. Silas was there. He helped me kick the old man's ass to the curb. It's all under control." A little smile teases my lips at the look of shock on Dad's face when Silas tackled him into the counter like a linebacker. If I had been breathing at the time, I would have fucking cheered.

"Ah. Silas." Tristan stares me down. "The infamous Silas."

There's a pause, and I can't figure out what Tristan is building up to saying. Calm green eyes take in every inch of me the same way he takes in a scene as soon as we arrive, and it makes me nervous.

"What?"

"I didn't say anything."

Tristan is my friend, but he's also a little scary sometimes. I've seen him in some of his less controlled moments and there's some real darkness behind his eyes. I get the feeling that his capacity for violence is a lot more extensive than he wants anyone to know.

Which is fine. Everybody deserves a fresh start. I don't need to pry, and I'm perfectly happy never pissing him off and finding out what happens when his control snaps.

But my patience is thin today. Silas is the one good thing that's happened to me in a long fucking time. If Tristan has something shitty to say about him, I want him to get it over with.

"Yeah, but you didn't not say anything, either. You've got that look on your face like you're about to tell me you're dying. Or ask me to help bury a body. I never know with you. I'm too tired and bruised to bullshit. Whatever you wanna say, just spill."

If he's surprised that I snapped at him, his face doesn't show it.

"You've been spending a lot of time with him, is all."

"Jealous, Tristan? You're still my work-husband, don't worry, boo. That relationship is carved in stone." I laugh it off, very determined to cover up how uncomfortable this conversation is making me.

"You know what I mean. He gets back to town, and first you're furious at him for some weird, made-up reason."

"It was not made up—"

"I'm not done. Then the next time I see you, you're friends. Not just friends, you're insta-besties."

I can't help but snort. Tristan is a good-looking guy, but he's also a big, very tough-looking guy. Like if Liam Hemsworth went to actual war and then got his nose broken a couple of times. I'm a big believer that there's no right or wrong way to 'be a man', but it's still surreal to see him use the phrase 'insta-besties'.

"And ever since, he's in every single story you tell. 'Me and Silas took the girls back-to-school shopping'. 'Silas has never played video games before, so I'm teaching him'. 'I need to finish my shift early so I can take Silas car shopping'. I'm glad you've made a new friend, but it all seems kind of co-dependent, don't you think?"

I stop, turning the thought over in my mind. Is it? Maybe from the outside it looks like that, but from my perspective, it's just Silas. Why wouldn't I want to spend more time with him? He's awesome.

The thought makes me laugh to myself.

"You don't get it because you don't know him," I explain. "He's impossible to get tired of. No one's given two shits about Silas since his mom died, if not longer. He's spent his entire life in a black hole of empathy, and managed to come out of it as this sweet, hilarious, generous guy. Now he's learning to enjoy his life for the first time, and I get to be the one to teach him. Who wouldn't want to be a part of that? And if I'm spoiling him with attention, so what? He fucking deserves it. He deserves everything I have to offer, so I'm not going to hold back because of whatever arbitrary decisions society has made about men needing to be independent. Fuck that and fuck you for suggesting it."

When I look up, I realize Tristan has completely stopped counting drugs and is looking at me with his eyebrows raised. He stares at me long enough that I feel like I'm going to explode, but before it gets to be too much, he speaks.

"Cade, are you guys involved?"

I freeze.

"What?"

His hands go up in the air while his voice stays low. "I'm not giving you shit, and this conversation stays between us. I know not everyone here would feel the same way. It's not a big deal. I'm just asking you, are you two involved? Because you're talking about him like he hung the fucking moon, and I've never seen you talk about anyone this way. Not even Wish."

The laugh that comes out of me sounds too loud and too high. It's weird.

"No, man. I'm not like, repressed or something." Tristan doesn't say anything, he just keeps staring at me, so my mouth continues to make sounds without permission from my brain. "My best friend is bi. I have multiple queer friends. I'm a thousand percent not homophobic. If I were into guys, I'd know by now, and fuck these assholes if they didn't like it. But full-ass adults don't wake up one day and change their sexual orientation. Not unless they grew up in some shitty situation that wouldn't let them figure it out sooner."

He doesn't cut off my rambling, but he does look kind of sad as he watches me talk.

135

"I'd know by now." The words sound weak, even as I say them. A squirrelly, vulnerable feeling takes root in my chest, and I have nothing to fight it with except anger. I don't even try to control my temper when it hits, and there's venom in my voice as I keep going. "I get enough of this shit from people about me and Wish being friends. I don't need you starting it with Silas as well. Close, platonic friendships exist, dude. If you haven't had any, maybe you're the problem."

It's a mean thing to say, and I can already glimpse the guilt that will take over once the flush of rage fades.

I flash back to the moment in my room the other day, after Dad left. Silas and I were sitting on my bed and I felt enveloped by this warm, safe, contained feeling I'd never encountered before. I wanted to...something. I don't know. I wanted more. And when he looked at me with that intense expression, I felt like he wanted more of it, too.

Now isn't the time to process that, though. I can sort those jumbled thoughts out when I'm not halfway through an argument with my coworker who I'm half friends with and half secretly scared of.

Tristan obviously didn't make it through whatever mystery combat zone by being a hot-head, so my pissy comment seems to roll right off him. He sighs, and continues to look at me with that too-knowing expression, tinged with sadness. When he speaks, I feel like he's treating me with kid gloves, which makes me want to lash out at him again.

"Look, Cade, I know you and I are more work friends than friend-friends, so I don't want to overstep. But I know what it's like to have to be an adult way too young. It probably doesn't seem like it, but you are still young. So young. You are allowed to still be figuring yourself out. Some people spend their whole lives figuring their shit out. If you're saying there's nothing romantic with you and Silas because you don't feel that way, fine. But if you're telling yourself there *can't* be anything between you two because twenty-two is too old to realize you might not be one hundred percent straight? That's fucking stupid."

I get squirmy.

"And either way, my co-dependent comment stands. Just think about it."

There are too many thoughts spinning in my head to pick one out, so I try to ignore the cacophony and turn my attention back to work.

"Oh, and Cade?"

I turn back to him one more time, still frustrated and annoyed. "What?"

"You've got puke in your hair. Might want to shower after your existential crisis is finished." And then he gives me the biggest, most shit-eating grin I've ever seen.

The man's a sadist.

This shift cannot be over fast enough.

CHAPTER EIGHTEEN

SILAS

Staying with Cade is weird. It's all chaos; between his mom being on a bender and the girls working through their trauma by fighting with Cade about everything. The trailer is messy and run-down, and there's nowhere near enough space for all of us.

Plus, there's the constant, looming threat that his dad will show up to kick the shit out of us. Which is why I'm still here. According to Cade's cousin, Kyle Waters still hasn't left town.

But it's also all very...domestic.

My house is bigger and has a lot more food in the fridge, but never felt half as welcoming to walk into. I love getting to come home to someone who is actually happy to see me. And I love getting to rest easy knowing that Cade is right in front of me, safe and sound.

We're still sharing his bed, because there's nowhere else for me to go. Folding both of us into a double bed is a tight squeeze, but it's better than trying to sleep in the bathtub.

And I can't deny I like having him close. In case he needs me.

I hate feeling like I'm in his way, though. I manage to be underfoot all night, constantly in the wrong place while he's trying to make food or go to the freaking bathroom. Doubt begins to creep in about how much good it's really doing for me to be here.

Maybe I'm just staying to make myself feel better and he's putting up with me to be nice, even if it's annoying. I've apologized so many times tonight that by the time we're climbing into bed, Cade looks like he wants to deck me. I only stop when he threatens to make me sleep on the porch if I don't shut up about it.

"If it makes you feel better, you can consider this repayment for me saving your drunk ass from drowning in the quarry. I rescue you, you rescue me, and every time we end up crammed into a teeny tiny bed together. It's the circle of life, apparently. So hakuna matata and go the fuck to sleep."

I laugh, making him grin even though his eyes are already closed. It eases some of that doubt that had been sitting in my chest like a lead weight.

He rolls over, putting his back to me. The trailer isn't great at keeping out the cold, but this room is small, so with both of us in here and the door closed, it heats up pretty fast. Which means we're both stripped down to our underwear, and Cade only has the blanket pulled up to his waist.

It's dark, but there's enough light for me to make out the long, smooth planes of his back. I've already gotten in the habit of mentally tracing the lines of his tattoos to lull myself to sleep, and I'm going to miss it when I eventually go home.

I wonder how relaxing it would be to reach out and trace them with my fingers.

Would his skin be soft, or could I feel the scarring of each tattoo if I closed my eyes?

What would he taste like if I traced them with my mouth? What would it be like to wrap myself around him, breathing him in and letting his hands touch every inch of me, so warm and reassuring?

Shut. Up.

I shove that part of my brain down as hard as I can and tear my gaze away from Cade's naked back. We never got the chance to talk after the bar on Friday, and I'm trying to table all these weird *what ifs* to deal with when Cade's not going through a crisis.

There's no reason to bother him with my confusing shit when he's got bigger things on his mind. Maybe it's normal. Maybe it's a side effect of the super-dramatic way we became friends. Maybe this is the kind of shit your brain likes to throw at you when you go through puberty, and for whatever reason, my brain is really, really late to the party.

I'll talk to him about it later.

And I'll come clean about not sleeping with Cassidy.

I will.

Cade is already asleep, his breath deep and rhythmic beside me. I don't let myself think about anything else, and I don't let myself stare at his tattoos. Instead, I listen to the sound of his breathing and remind myself that he's safe, and that's the only thing that matters.

It's my fourth night staying with Cade that he ends up tossing and turning, unable to sleep. The room is warm with our body heat and the bed is cramped, but that's always the case, so I don't know what's changed tonight.

Eventually, when he rolls over with an annoyed huff for what feels like the millionth time, my patience snaps.

"Cade, I know you don't like sitting still, but it's sleep time now. What the hell is going on?"

The silence that I get in response is a surprise. Cade is the chatty one. I'm the broody one. That's our dynamic. It makes me a little worried, but I wait for him to answer, and eventually he rolls onto his back with a sigh.

He's stripped down to his boxer-briefs, like every night, and the thin blanket is covering him up to his waist. But even through those two layers of fabric, even in the dark, I can see the bulge of the tent he's pitching down there. Reaching one hand down to cup his junk and squeeze, Cade takes a deep breath and sighs again.

"Sorry, man, I just... I haven't been able to get off in forever, and it's getting to me. I'm so fucking horny, it's driving me nuts."

He punctuates this by squeezing his junk again, and this time his hips lift a little off the mattress, and he lets out the faintest groan.

I wasn't hard before, but I am now. 0 to 60. Fully fucking erect. I'm lying on my side to face him, and I tilt my hips a little more towards the mattress so he can't see how much looking at him casually squeezing his boner is affecting me and realize how confused I really am.

"Could we just..." he keeps going, his gaze trained on the ceiling instead of me, his hand still on his junk, not moving even though he obviously wants to. The muscles and tendons in his neck are standing out from how tense his body is, and I watch a bead of sweat roll down over his jugular in the dim light.

I wonder what it would taste like if I licked it off.

God, what am I doing?

"Can I just get myself off so I can sleep and we can forget this happened? It doesn't have to be weird. I can't use the bathroom because the door doesn't close properly, and it's right next to the girls' room. If I have to traumatize someone, I'd rather traumatize you than my little sisters. Sorry. You know how often they barge in there without warning. It's why I gave up on jerking off in the shower a long time ago."

The words come out of his mouth all in a rush, and then he finally turns his head and looks at me.

I know I'm supposed to answer, but it's hard to think over the sound of blood rushing through my ears. I clear my throat and swallow past the boulder lodged there to buy myself some time.

"Yeah, uh, sure. Go for it. It's no big deal."

He blows out all the air from his lungs, and I realize he must have been holding his breath. I guess it is a weird thing to ask someone, but he's my best friend. I couldn't deny him anything. Even if I didn't have these weird, lusty thoughts about him.

But goddamn if it's not going to be hard to lie here and listen.

Rolling over onto my back so I won't be tempted to watch him, I hear the rustle as he reaches into his underwear and strokes himself. He lets out a long, shuddering sigh and my cock throbs in response.

For a minute or two we lie there, side by side, but not touching. The bed shakes gently with the movement of his hand and all I can hear are his soft, panting breaths and that roaring in my ears. My cock is so hard it hurts.

"Hey," he says, startling me. His voice is breathy and low, like I've never heard it before and would sell my soul to hear again. "You should do it too. I can see that you want to."

I make the mistake of glancing over at him while he talks. His hand is still moving, working over his cock, but his gaze is locked on mine. He nods his head towards where I'm tenting the sheet as he says it, but I'm distracted by the sight of him.

In the low light, his face is all shades of gray. Even so, I can see the flush that's climbing up his neck and cheeks. I can see the muscles in his arm flex and extend as he moves it rhythmically, the way his bicep bunches to look fucking huge, and I can see the way his mouth hangs open slightly, with his lower lip looking so thick and pouty I have the most inexplicable urge to bite it.

"Do it."

He looks at my erection again, and it's enough to snap me out of my trance. I look back at the ceiling and slowly, hesitantly, slide my hand into my boxers.

I will not look at him again while I do this.

Finally wrapping my fingers around my cock and giving it a gentle squeeze is such a fucking relief I groan. It feels like I've been hard for hours, even if it's only been a couple of minutes. I make a fist and start to jerk myself and it feels like heaven. At first, I wish I had lube, but all the filthy little sounds slipping from Cade's mouth are going straight to my dick, so the roughness of my palm ends up causing just enough discomfort to walk me back from the edge.

As soon as I joined him in the jerk-off session, he picked up the pace. Now I can hear the slap of flesh on flesh as he moves his hand, and his breathing is turning into ragged gasps. He sounds so desperate, and it's making me more turned on than I knew was physically possible.

God, it's barely been two minutes, but I'm ready to explode.

"Fuck," I bite out. "Fuck, I'm gonna come, Cade."

I don't know why I told him. It probably made it weird, but it slipped out.

"Do it," he says in that breathless fucking voice.

And that's all it takes. My balls draw up and my body tenses, then cum is spilling hot all over my hand. I hadn't pulled my dick out of my boxers, because I was being modest, so I've now filled them with jizz, but I don't care about that yet. I'm too distracted by the long, drawn-out feeling of euphoria that's flooding my body.

It's amplified when I hear him come beside me. He makes a choked noise and then groans, and then the bed is finally still.

Neither of us says anything or moves for a while. I'm completely drained, in a way that's good and bad at the same time. Eventually, Cade hands me a dirty t-shirt he picks up off the floor, and I use it to clean up as much as I can, but my underwear is still an uncomfortable mess.

Whatever. That's a problem for future Silas. Along with figuring out what any of the thoughts floating around my head mean. Right Now Silas wants to go to sleep in a post-orgasm haze.

"Goodnight."

It's the only thing he says to me before rolling over to go to sleep.

"Goodnight," I whisper to the ceiling.

It becomes our nightly ritual. Cade assures me, with that stupid, cocky grin of his, that it's not weird.

"Soldiers do this when they're bunking up during wars, you know. Or guys sharing a cell in prison. It just is what it is. You worry too much. Check your father's toxic masculinity at the door, remember?"

He grabs my shoulder with one big hand and gives it a squeeze as he says this. It makes me melt a little inside, but that doesn't make me worry any less. Would he still think this was fine if he knew about the thoughts I'd been having about him? Or what I'd been picturing the last time I jerked off at my house?

Every night it's the same. I bought lube, at least, which has vastly improved our collective quality of life, even though Cade laughed and called me Ritchie Rich, insisting that moisturizer is just as good. But come on, it was six fucking dollars.

If there's anything I've learned from my late-life sexual awakening, it's that life is too short to skimp on lube.

We lie on our backs next to each other, looking up at the ceiling as we do it. The bed shakes as we both jerk off, and the sound of Cade panting and grunting next to me sets my blood on fire. I still don't understand, but it's true. We've both been pulling our cocks out properly, because I'm not sleeping in any more wet underwear when it's too dark to see much, anyway.

I have not allowed myself to look at his cock. Not once. Not even out of morbid, self-destructive curiosity.

Last night, we ended up closer together than normal, and the two-inch no-man's-land between us suddenly wasn't there anymore. He's left-handed, and I'm right-handed, so our arms were grazing together as we both worked ourselves over.

I could feel how hot and sweat-slick his skin was, his firm muscle pressing against mine, and my orgasm hit me so suddenly I felt the cum on my hand almost before I realized I was coming.

The orgasm gripped my whole body, making my back bow off the bed, and the groan I let out was fucking obscene. I felt the motion of Cade turning his head to glance at me, just once, as I came. I heard the now-familiar choked sound that he makes, and knew he was coming, too.

After, instead of rolling over like he usually does, Cade lay on his back next to me. Our bodies were pressed together from our shoulders down to the backs of our hands, and his warmth beside me helped settle my nerves. We lay that way for a while before he passed me a tissue to clean up with.

He's my best friend. He keeps me safe. I keep him safe. This is just another part of that.

Neither of us has brought up the things that were different about our jerk-off session last night, and it's definitely not going to be me that does it.

CHAPTER NINETEEN

CADE

I t's the middle of Friday afternoon, and Aunt Jaz is picking the girls up from school to take them for the weekend, which I'm sure they're stoked about. It's been almost a week since Dad showed his face. Silas staying here has made all of us feel better, but I'm sure they could use a break.

Not to mention, the bender Mom's been on since Dad's little performance ripped the scab off all her trauma isn't fun to watch, whenever she shows her face. She knows better than to go around Jaz when she's like this. Technically, Jaz is her aunt, not mine, and she's the only one who can put her foot down around Mom and get away with it.

Today is going to be good. The girls get a couple days of relative normalcy, Mom's working overtime on a barroom floor somewhere, and me and Silas are both off work and have the whole place to ourselves.

One bright, shining tear in the time-space continuum. For one weekend we aren't brothers and sons and providers and protectors, but just two guys goofing off. It's fucking magical.

Right now, we're both lounging on the sofa, playing *Call of Duty* on my ancient PS4. I was right, and Silas didn't get to play a lot of video games as a kid, so I've been teaching him whenever we have downtime.

He deserves to play video games. There's something about the fact that it's totally, deliberately unproductive that feels so deliciously indulgent. I like watching him lean into that.

I get distracted watching him play. He gets so into it, just as focused on the game as he would be on the track. There's a flash of pink as he bites the tip of his tongue in concentration, and it pulls my focus from the game enough for me to get fucking destroyed.

"Fuuuuuuuuuuuuuck," I groan, throwing myself more heavily into the arm of the couch, stretching out one leg so I can prod his arm with my bare foot like a petulant child. "You're getting too good at this. I don't know if I wanna play with you if you're going to start kicking my ass."

I keep kicking him in the arm, smiling so he knows I'm kidding, and I get a half-smile, half-laugh out of him as he bats my bare foot away.

"You've always been a sore loser."

"I like to think of it as knowing my rightful place in the world. First place."

Silas tries to scowl at me, but it doesn't reach his eyes. He grabs my foot to keep me from kicking at him anymore, but instead of shoving it back towards my side of the couch, he drops it into his lap, bracing his arm on my shin as he picks up the controller again and turns his attention back to the TV.

Like it's no big deal.

Which it isn't.

Except it kind of is. Making him smile and laugh over something as stupid as a video game, or getting his touch-starved ass to be comfortable enough to physically lean on me just because he wants to, feels like everything.

Sometimes it feels like I was created specifically to undo every shitty thing that's ever been done to Silas. Every smile gives me a bigger sense of accomplishment than anything else in my life, and it's literally my job to save people's lives.

Maybe Tristan is right. Maybe me and Silas are too intense around each other and lack boundaries.

Of course, he said that without knowing about our exciting new bedtime activity. The one that is weird and confusing and so fucking hot that it eats boundaries for breakfast and spits out the bones.

Maybe I should talk to Silas about it. But I don't know what to say other than *I have no idea if any of this is normal friend shit, and it's confusing me.* I'm worried that any version of that sentence is going to sound like a rejection to him.

And it's not. I am the opposite of rejecting him. If I could hollow out the space inside my ribs and place him there for safekeeping, I would.

But that's a very weird thing to think about your friend.

So, my confusion persists.

Thinking about our midnight masturbation sessions was a bad idea, because once I start, I can't stop. It's clearly been too long since I hooked up with someone, because I forgot what it was like to listen to someone else be turned on. Silas and I aren't even doing anything together. We're just sharing space. Because of extenuating circumstances. But the sound of his hitched, heavy breathing puts fucking fire in my veins.

I'm normally too tired and stressed out to get off more than a couple times a week, especially considering how hard it is to carve out a little privacy in this house, even when I'm not sharing a bedroom. But ever since this started, it's like my dick has snapped to attention. Every night, I have to get off. And I need the sound and heat of him getting off next to me too, apparently.

I mean, I guess it makes sense. I'm a tactile person. I'm a social person. My dedication to solo sessions is due to circumstances, not preference. Jerking off with company seems like the perfect compromise to my weird-ass brain.

Of course, now that I let myself think about it, I'm horny as hell. Sitting on the couch with a hard-on in the middle of the afternoon like an animal. I'm surprised Silas hasn't wiped the floor with me yet in the game, because very little blood is flowing to my brain right now, so I look over at him.

Silas is wearing threadbare gray sweatpants that are fucking obscene. I mean it. They hug every curve of his muscled legs, and you can see a very detailed outline of his junk. Which is why I can see that he's having the exact same problem as me and is probably also not giving the game his full attention.

My foot is sitting in his lap, only inches away from his erection, and I don't know what to do.

As usual, I'm going with the flow. My flow is currently horny as hell, which is what I blame for my next decision.

"You got a problem there, stud?" I nudge his hard-on with my foot as I say it, and he hisses at the contact before bringing one hand protectively to his dick.

He looks over at me. I was hoping we could joke about this, but when I take in his face, he looks raw and vulnerable. It sobers me up, quick.

"Sorry, I'm not trying to be weird," he says. "I don't know why this keeps happening. I'm just fucking horny all the time. I feel like a fucking teenager."

He drops the controller and runs the hand that's not covering his erection through his hair, blowing out a frustrated breath. It sets off every single protective instinct I have, even if all I am protecting him from is being harsh with himself.

"Hey," I say softly, jostling his thigh with my foot. "It's fine. We said it's fine. We're stuck in each other's space right now, but we're making it work, right? You're here because you came to my fucking rescue. You can have as many awkward boners as you want."

I only get a half-smile to that, but he sits up straighter, and he seems to lighten.

Tugging my lip in between my teeth to chew at it for a second, I consider my options here.

"Hey, it's not like I'm not right there with you." I gesture towards my own embarrassing pants situation, and when Silas looks down at it, he blushes so red I can practically feel the heat from over here. I rub myself through my pants, just a little, because this conversation is doing nothing to cool me down. Fuck it. "There's no one home. It's a boner, not a vampire. It's not like there's a rule that you can only jerk it at night. You do you, man."

I lick my palm before slipping my hand into my waistband. Once I give myself a real, tight stroke, it feels so good I can't not lean my head back against the couch and sigh.

Silas' fingers dig in where his left hand still rests on my leg. The cuff of my sweats has rucked up, so his skin is on mine, and warmth is sinking into me everywhere he's touching.

"Should one of us....?" I catch his eye, and I can see the hesitance. If there's no one here, there's no reason for us to do this in the same room. But I'm stroking myself for real now, and his hand is warm on my leg, and I don't want either of us to move.

"Nah," I say. He licks his lips, and his mouth hangs slightly open as his breathing picks up. I don't think he's ever actually watched me during this before, and I don't hate it. I feel lust-drunk and pesky things like consequences are getting less important by the second. I throw my head back again, stretching out my body and finally pulling my cock out into the open air. "What's the point of having boundaries now?"

When I look at Silas again, his eyes are fixed on my cock. I wonder what he's thinking about, and if I just crossed some horrible line that I can never uncross and will ruin our friendship forever.

We will definitely have to have a conversation about what this means.

Later.

"You too, Silas."

Jogging him out of his stupor, he tears his gaze away from watching me work myself over and starts pushing at those damn sweats until his own cock is free.

I look. I fully look at it. It's as big as it looked through the sweats, straight and cut, thick enough that I wonder how heavy it feels in his hand. The tip is flushed the same bright pink his cheeks are when he's embarrassed, and there's already precum drooling from him, making his skin glisten in the light.

I've never thought a dick could look pretty, before. Never thought about dicks that much in general. But if there's such a thing as a pretty cock, Silas has got one. I'm kind of jealous.

It doesn't take long before the room is filled with the sounds of heavy breathing and slick skin. I have to close my eyes, because I look over and Silas is rolling his cockhead in his palm in a way that's mesmerizing me, and I don't have the capacity to figure out what that means right now. So I close my eyes, and focus on the feeling of my own hand strangling my dick, and the way Silas still has a chokehold on my leg. Like he's clinging to it.

"God, this feels good. Fuck, Silas. Fuck, I'm gonna come." I can't help but babble as I feel my orgasm brewing. I want him to come with me. The only thing that would be more awkward than this situation is figuring out where to put my eyeballs if he's still jerking off after I've finished. "Are you almost there?"

I crack open my eyes to see Silas looking completely debauched. His cheeks are flushed and his mouth is hanging open, his bottom lip swollen like he's been biting it. He looks at me with dark, lust-drunk eyes and nods.

It takes all my self-control to close my eyes again so I can't see either of us come. But I hear the sinful way he groans, and I know I'm making some obscene noises myself as my cock throbs and cum spills over my hand. My toes curl as Silas digs his fingers even harder into my leg while he groans.

I couldn't look. Because I couldn't explain why I wanted to look, and I still want to put that conversation off until I know what the hell I'm going to say.

We both float around in a kind of daze that night, blissed out from mutually phenomenal orgasms. Before bed, I ask Silas if he wants to smoke a little weed. I'm not a huge fan of getting high, because I don't enjoy feeling that out of control and I also don't enjoy looking into the mirror and seeing either of my parents.

But sometimes the anxiety hits, and there's nothing else that'll tackle it for me. Just a little to take the edge off and help us sleep, I tell him. Silas looks dubious, but tells me he trusts me. I think he still takes pleasure in these minor rebellions against his dad, even when his dad will never know. For me, I just need to turn my damn brain off. That's why I keep a little stashed around for emergencies.

Neither of us speaks much as we smoke. Silas coughs and sputters a little, but otherwise seems okay. Both of us get hazy and slow. It doesn't take much to get us ready to pour into bed, too tired to jerk off again. All we do is pull off our clothes and climb onto the mattress, both asleep as soon as our heads hit the pillow.

I sleep heavily and dream about Silas.

CHAPTER TWENTY

SILAS

When I wake up, I have to blink a few times because something is weird. It's not morning yet. It's still dark in here and I feel the kind of fuzziness that comes from only having slept a few hours. I only have to wonder what woke me up for a second before it becomes obvious.

"Cade?" My voice is croaky with sleep.

I don't think he's awake. He's plastered down the length of my body, bare-ass naked and pressing himself against me, and his hard cock is jutting into my hip. He has one arm thrown over my chest and his hand is on my pec, kneading it with his fingers in a way he's never done before, but is sending shivers of something through me, making me want more. His hips are moving rhythmically, thrusting against me, and his cock is gliding over my skin that's now slick with sweat and precum.

"Cade." I'm a little louder this time, still not sure if he's awake or asleep.

His eyes open, and he looks at me with this sleepy smile that makes me so happy I want to grab hold of him and never let go.

"Mmmm." He thrusts against my hip one more time.

"What are you doing?"

"Couldn't sleep. Horny again. I liked touching you earlier, made everything feel better." His hips are still rolling into me as he mumbles the words, and having his hard dick on my skin is making me just as hard. He's not looking, but he could, and then he'll see what he does to me. I don't know how that's going to make him feel. I still don't know how that makes me feel, other than worried.

"Okay, so you are awake. I wasn't sure."

I'm still lying on my back, not moving, because I have no idea if I'm supposed to be participating in this or not.

"Mmmm," he says again, but then he goes still. When he looks at me again, he blinks a few times, and I can tell the moment his brain comes fully back online.

"Fuck, I'm sorry. I didn't—I was dreaming, and you were there, and then I was hard and I wasn't sure if I was still dreaming, and I just... Fuck. I'm so sorry. I just like, assaulted you or something. Fuck."

Panic edges into his voice as he babbles and his eyes get way too wide. He shuffles away from me, but before he can roll back so he's not touching me anymore, my hand shoots out to grab his hip.

"Stop." My voice comes out as a growl. "Cade, breathe."

I continue to hold his hip tight, steadying him, and look him in the eye. He takes one shuddering breath and then another, staring at me with a quietly panicked expression. It's a weird role reversal for us, but all I can think about is how much I need him to be okay and to not run away from me.

He never, ever needs to run away from me.

"Shhh, it's okay." I use my hand on his hip to pull him in a little closer to me, but keep looking him in the eye. He always takes such good care of me. Why would he think I would want him to stop doing something that made him feel good? Especially when *he* makes me feel good.

"It's okay," I say it again, practically a whisper, before taking a deep breath and finally following my instincts. Letting go of his hip, I move that hand down to wrap my fingers gently around his cock. Despite his freak-out, it's still painfully hard and begging for friction, and I want to give it to him.

I look him in the eye, raising my eyebrows in a silent question as I stroke him once, slowly, from base to tip. Cade gives me this tiny, almost imperceptible nod, still wide-eyed, then lets his eyes sink close as he sighs in relief.

My hand has stopped moving, but his hips buck up until he's fucking my fist. I have a moment of fear that he's closed his eyes so he can pretend I'm someone else, but when he opens them again and pins me down with his stare, I know without a doubt that there's no one in his mind but me right now.

He's still fucking my fist, but I snap out of it and move, tightening my hand and moving with him. The skin over his cock feels velvet-soft and impossibly hot, and the weight of him in my hand is more reassuring than any other way we've ever touched.

Relishing in the heat of his hard cock against my skin is like the final card in my teetering, ridiculous logic that justifies what I feel, and what we've been doing, as normal best friend behavior. The alternative was too big and confusing to confront, so I wouldn't let myself consider it. It all comes crashing down after that.

But I'm happy about it. Because now I can stop lying to myself. And this feels like exactly where I belong.

I run my thumb over the wetness at the tip of his cock, pulling a moan out of him and making his eyes do that fluttery thing one more time. This time, when he opens them again, he shakes his head a little, and it makes me pause. I thought he was just as overwhelmed by desire as I am, but now I'm terrified about what's coming next.

"Fuck," he says, still staring at me the way he does. "We are so fucking stupid. No one is as stupid as we are. Fuck, we're dumb."

I don't have time to figure out what he means by that, because half a second later he launches himself at me and my lap and mouth is suddenly full of *Cade*.

For me, Cade has always taken up a disproportionate amount of space in the room. But right now, he's all-encompassing. I'm powerless to do anything other than melt into him, and it feels like my body was born to do this.

He's straddling my hips, the head of his cock dragging over my stomach where it hangs heavy with arousal. His hands seem like they're trying to touch me everywhere: running down my chest, gripping my biceps, running his fingers through my hair. I can't focus on it though, because of what he's doing with his mouth.

I've kissed girls before, and it's been nice. This is epic. This is all-consuming. It feels like we're trying to devour each other, and Cade is making these involuntary, animalistic little grunts as he pushes his tongue against mine. The sounds are making me so hard I can't stop myself from grinding my hips against his.

"Oh, fuck, Silas, yes," he mumbles into my mouth between kisses. I love it when he horny-babbles, and it's even better when I'm the direct cause of it, apparently.

It takes a few minutes for my brain to catch up to the fact that this is really happening. I've never allowed myself to imagine this. There was always too much teetering logic in the way. So, I don't know what we're supposed to do. But once I've allowed myself to accept that it's what I want, my hindbrain gives me a lot of suggestions.

Grabbing hold of him, I roll us over until he's on his back and I'm on top of him, bracketed between his legs. He looks a little surprised, but spreads his legs for me easily while I shimmy out of my boxers as quickly as humanly possible. The first time our cocks slide together, flesh on flesh, we're both watching each other as we moan.

The time for second-guessing myself is gone. I'm operating on instinct and desire now. And I desire all of him, wrapped around me until I can't touch or see or breathe anything that isn't him.

I rut against him to create more delicious friction, dragging his cock over mine again and again. Our faces are inches apart, and I can feel every one of his hot, panting breaths against my face, which only spurs me on.

"Fuck yes, Silas, that feels so fucking good. I always want you on top of me like this."

One of Cade's hands is on my back, his nails digging into the skin there so hard I think he could draw blood, and the other is wrapped around the back of my neck in a way that feels so possessive I want to dig a hole in his chest and never come out.

Looking at his face when he's this blissed out is too much. I bury my face in the crook of his neck, and finally, after all this time, I taste him. First, I run my tongue over his pulse point, savoring the salty musk of his skin. Then I bite down, just hard enough to make him groan.

The friction between us is good, but I don't have enough leverage. Propping myself up on one elbow, my other arm is free to come down and grab his round ass and pull him closer to me. My hand splays across his ass cheek, fingertips digging in and squeezing. I don't think about where I'm going until my fingers slip far enough to brush over his hole.

Cade hisses, and I freeze, wondering if I freaked him out. But one look at his face tells me otherwise.

"Yeah," he breathes. "Try it."

My hand goes back to his ass, where I think it should live forever now, and this time when I graze his hole, he makes a little pleased sound. I rub my finger over it for a few seconds, because I want to go slow, but the need to possess him is so fucking consuming I can't stand it.

"Fuck." I groan as I bury my face in his shoulder again and push the tip of one finger into him, just slightly. His body stretches to let me in, and then contracts around me like he wants to keep me inside of him forever, while his breath comes in harsh pants, right next to my ear.

That's it. I'm hooked. I need it.

I realize lube would probably help a fuck ton with this situation, but I'm so eager that I make a mess grabbing it and squirting it all over my fingers. By the time I'm touching him again there's lube smeared on my forearm, the bed and his thigh, as well as my whole hand, and Cade is laughing at me, but I don't fucking care.

When I bury my finger inside of him, he stops laughing and grabs my shoulders with both hands.

"Oh, fucking fucksticks, that feels weird but so good."

He tensed up initially, but I move my hand slowly, working inside him, testing out what seems to make him feel good and pulling filthy fucking sounds from his mouth. Gradually, he relaxes more and more. By the time I have three fingers in him, his hips are open and he's rocking down on my hand, fucking himself on my fingers like I once wondered if he did to himself.

His cock is stiff and leaking, leaving a trail of wetness where it's trapped between our stomachs, and I wonder if I could make him come just like this. When I find what can only be his prostate, his entire body shudders between me and he cries out.

"More," he croaks. "Fuck, Silas, more. More of you."

I don't say anything, and for a few seconds all I can hear is him panting and the wet sound of my fingers fucking into his hole, but then he says the thing that always gets me to do whatever he wants.

"Please."

I growl into his neck and pull out my fingers, making him whimper at the loss. Part of me knows everything is about to change, and I should be worried, but it all feels too good for me to care. Seeing him spread out underneath me, desperate and wanting like this, it's already changed me.

I've never needed something the way I need him right now.

"You want my cock?"

Cade bites his lip and nods, looking up at me with those stupid puppy-dog eyes.

"You want me to fuck you? To be inside you and fucking own you? Because I thought you were mine before, Cade, but this-"

My voice is a dry rasp. I push my fingers back into him, making him gasp.

"This is something else. This isn't something I can forget about."

"Do it." He sounds so sure. "Fuck me. Own me. You already do, I just didn't realize it."

It takes me about a second and a half to slather more lube on my cock. I squeeze the base, terrified that I'm going to come before I even get inside, but desperate to be inside him all the same. When I push the tip against his hole, I see him holding his breath and tensing up. I lean back enough that he can look me in the eye and I run my fingers under his jaw, letting him nuzzle into my hand.

"Breathe, Cade."

He lets out a big breath, his body relaxes, and the head of my cock sinks into his tight heat.

"Fuck, yes. Yes, Silas. Please."

I push in slowly, and he keeps babbling and clawing at me the whole time, arching his back and asking for more. I grab one of his thighs and push back until he's spread completely open and I can see exactly where we're joined. With one hand gripping his thigh and the other on his hip, I fuck the rest of my cock into him in a thrust.

The sound of his gasp will be trapped in my memory as the single hottest sound a person has ever made. His hole is clutching at me like he needs me there and for a second I have to fight a sudden hot pressure behind my eyes.

A lot of things are clicking into place that I didn't realize were out of place.

But I can't think about that now.

I blink the thought away, pull out, and then push back in again. Cade's hands are grabbing any part of me he can reach, and he's moaning low with every roll of my hips. I can't wait any longer.

Leaning over, I press our bodies together again in a long line, holding him as close to me as possible. I keep my thrusts shallow and gentle, careful not to hurt

159

him, but picking up the pace. My body feels like it's moving with a mind of its own and my brain is just along for the ride.

I pull Cade into a messy, open-mouthed kiss that we're both panting too hard to deepen.

"More," he moans into my mouth, clutching my shoulders. I shift my weight onto one arm so I can use the other to hitch his hips a little higher, changing the angle, feeling myself drag inside him with every slow thrust.

"Fuck, fuck, fuck," he chants, barely audible, still holding me close. I can't see his face, but I can hear the second he makes that familiar choked sound, then his cock twitches where it's pinned between us and my stomach is slick with his cum. His ass bears down on me like a vise.

"Fuck." The word leaves my mouth as a gasp. I'm so close. I press my forehead against his and hold him close, thrusting a few more times until my balls tighten and my orgasm hits, unloading into him. I shove my hips against him, some primal part of my brain telling me to stuff him so full of my cum that it never comes out, even though it doesn't make any sense.

When the last shuddering aftershock of my orgasm is finally done, I collapse on top of Cade and feel his arms tighten around my shoulders.

I have no idea how we got here, but I'm not going back to before. This feels too right.

When I lean back and pull out of Cade, he hisses in what looks like a mixture of pleasure and pain.

"Are you okay?" I rest my hand on his smooth, sweaty chest, like I need to feel his heart beating.

"Fuck, yeah, it's just weird. Good, but weird. And now sore. I don't know what the fuck you did to me, but when you made me come, it was like you punched a magic button with your dick. Like I was going to tear in half, but in a good way, if that makes sense. I swear, I came so hard I felt it in my toes." He laughs, making his chest vibrate under my hand.

Listening to him ramble makes me smile. It reassures me that he's still him, and I'm still me, and nothing has changed.

Of course, when I look between his legs to see how sore he really is, what I get is the sight of my own cum sliding out of his body. It makes me growl, and I know some things have definitely changed.

A part of him belongs to me, is the thought that flickers through my mind.

Without thinking, I use my fingers to push the cum back in. I want it to stay there. I'm gentle, but when I look up at Cade, he's watching me with heavy, lust-filled eyes, so I don't stop. I trust him to tell me if he wants me to stop.

"So messy," I mumble, watching my fingers disappear back inside him where they belong. "So fucking beautiful."

Leaning back, I pull Cade until his bottom half is in my lap, taking in the sight of him. His torso is shining with sweat, and there's cum smeared in the dark hair trailing down from his belly button. He looks fucking debauched.

He lets his legs fall open for me just as easily as he did the first time, and there's a lazy smile on his lips. Without getting rough, I go back to finger-fucking him like before, only this time I'm using my own mess to slick the way. I wish there was more of me in him, and the thought of it makes my dick give an interested twitch.

I keep the gentle pace, but explore different angles and ways of touching him and before long, I have him panting and begging for more. I figure out exactly where the spot is that makes him light up with pleasure when I stroke it. Watching him writhe on my fingers and beg like a slut is fucking phenomenal, and eventually I realize that I'm fucking hard again and leaking all over my lap.

Cade is half-hard and has been loosely jerking himself while I touch him, but that's not where his pleasure is coming from. Whenever I touch him just right, his hips buck. I keep going until he's fully hard again as well and has babbled so much that he's hoarse and barely making sense anymore.

"Please, baby, your cock, please."

Baby.

That feels way better than I ever would have guessed.

"Mm, no, I don't want to hurt you." He pouts, but I stroke him inside and the pout turns to a shiver. "Come for me like this, Cade. I know you can. You look so fucking beautiful like this."

My free hand is wrapped around his hip, holding him steady while I keep working him with my other. His hips are thrusting up into nothing and his breath is catching with every movement. The clench of his body around my fingers builds excruciatingly slowly, and by the time I push him over the edge, every muscle in his body is drawn tight.

When he comes the second time, it's this slow, drawn-out thing that seems to be pleasurable to the point of pain. His body trembles in my arms as his cock pulses weakly, and his hole clenches rhythmically for what seems like minutes.

As soon as he finally sags and my fingers slip out of him, I reach for my own cock. I'm so fucking aroused, it barely takes a half dozen pumps before I'm spilling my cum all over his thighs and sloppy hole. The sight of it grips my heart so tightly that for a second, I feel like I can't breathe.

We lie there for a long time after that. He continues to tremble for a while; I think from the adrenaline. I don't want to move him, so I clean us both up as well as I can with a pack of baby wipes I snag from the floor. Then I wrap him up in my arms and pull the blanket over us, even though it's warm in the room. When he buries his face in my chest I can feel wetness, but as soon as I try to pull back and check on it he clutches me closer.

"I'm not *crying* crying, I promise. I'm good. Shaky, but good." His voice is raw, but the way he clings to me makes me believe him. He speaks the words directly into my skin. "I just didn't realize it could be like this. This good."

I know what he means. A sudden rush of emotion pinches behind my eyes as well, but I push it back and press a kiss against his hair instead, holding him as tightly as I can. We're still like that when the early morning light starts to creep over the horizon. I nuzzle into him, taking in deep lungfuls of Cade with every breath.

My need to keep him safe has always been deep-seated, but now it threatens to overwhelm me.

CHAPTER TWENTY-ONE

CADE

S ilas is the first thing I see when I wake up.

Our legs are still tangled together, like they were when we fell asleep, until he woke up and slowly, gently put some distance between us.

"Hey." I hate that he's watching me with a guarded expression. He's not supposed to look like that with me, so I reach out and run my thumb across the arch of his cheekbone. His eyes flutter closed, and he pushes into the touch. Just a little. Just enough to let me know he needed it.

When he opens his eyes again, there's less fear in them.

"Hey," he says back.

He's waiting for me to freak out, I can tell.

I'm waiting for either of us to freak out, to be honest. Last night was a lot. But I wouldn't have done it if I didn't want to, and I think we can both admit it's been building for a while now, even if we were too brick-headed to recognize it.

I talk a lot. I know. But I'm not always good at actually saying stuff, and this seems like one of those times where actions are going to speak louder than words.

The sheets are warm and smell like both of us as I slide across the mattress towards him, inserting myself into his arms. My leg that was already between his pushes up closer, grazing against his groin, bypassing all the bestie double-speak we've been drowning in for way too long. I let myself luxuriate in the solidity of his body as I wrap my arms around his waist.

Everything about him is masculine. His chest is firm, covered in a light dusting of blonde hair. His shoulders are broad enough to bracket me in. It's all stuff that I never associated with comfort, let alone horniness, but now that the dam is broken I can't get enough. Silas hesitates for a second, but then puts his arm around my back and holds me close.

When our faces are only inches apart, the way they should be, I kiss him chastely on the lips and try again.

"Hey."

"Hey."

I'm worried I broke him.

But like last night, once he gets with the program, he fucking gets it. It took him a minute to adjust after I realized how fucking stupid we've been and crash-tackled him into the mattress, but barely fifteen minutes later he had me moaning his name into that mattress, and it looks like this is a gonna be a pattern with him.

He blinks a couple times and licks his lips, making me wonder if I taste like all the sweat I gleefully licked off his neck last night. Then he reels me back in and covers my mouth with his.

Silas doesn't kiss like someone who hasn't had a lot of sex. Silas kisses like someone who *fucks*. His tongue presses into my mouth, firm and sure, making me open up to him, while his hands explore my back and tug at my hair.

It doesn't take long before I'm writhing in his arms again, rocking my erection into his meaty thigh while he does the same thing to me.

"Fuck, Silas," I groan into his mouth before he swallows the words in another searing kiss.

I need to touch him. I need him to touch me.

Reaching down, I take hold of him, something I didn't get the chance to do last night. He's thick and heavy in my hand, just like I expected. As soon as I slide my hand down his length, Silas makes a strangled noise and drops his forehead against mine.

He takes me in hand as well, and it doesn't take long before we're both panting into each other's mouths. I come first, groaning his name as I spray cum between us, but he's quick to follow.

Neither of us pulls away this time. Our bodies are still pressed together as I hold Silas' eye, studying him. His expression is as serious as always, and I wish I could figure out what he was thinking.

It catches me by surprise when he reaches between us and swipes his fingers through the mess, then brings his fingers up and smears the still-warm cum across my lips.

I flick my tongue out to taste it, salty and bitter, while Silas watches me with more intensity than I knew was possible.

When he kisses me, it's deep and claiming. Our cum is pushed into both our mouths and it feels like the single most intimate experience of my life. Even after we break apart to catch our breath, it's a long time before I break the silence.

"I guess it's safe to say that last night wasn't a one-time thing."

Silas is making that face he makes when he can't find his words. Sometimes it's fun to tease him, but not today. I put him out of his misery. I kiss him one more time before pulling him with me as I get out of bed.

"Come on, let's brush our teeth and get some coffee before anything else earth-shattering happens and one of us ends up pregnant."

We both pull on sweats and shirts, because it's cold outside the fuck-cave that is my bedroom, and head to the kitchen. It's quiet as we putter around making coffee. Normally I hate the quiet, but this feels peaceful.

I know there are still a lot of unanswered questions, but for whatever reason, I'm not worried about the answers.

There's a hitch in my step that Silas notices. It's obvious he wants to say something, but isn't sure if he can.

"I'm fine, Silas. I'll admit, I may have gotten a little caught up in the horniness of it all and gone too hard for my virgin asshole. I'm pretty sore. But that's on me. I fucking begged you. All you did was dick me down better than I knew was possible." He blushes, so I keep talking to take the focus off him. "I mean, how have I gone twenty-two years without realizing I had a magic orgasm button inside me?"

Silas snorts. "You know, I always wondered if that was something that you were into or not. It seemed like the kind of thing you might do. Even if it was just on your own."

I arch an eyebrow at him. "You sat around wondering about whether I was into prostate play, but that didn't clue you in that there was some sexual tension between us? Wow, we're even stupider than I thought."

Silas shakes his head and shrugs like it's nothing, but his blush deepens and he focuses very hard on the coffeepot in front of him.

Interesting. Maybe he wasn't as clueless as I was.

When the heat finally fades from his cheeks, he looks at me again, his serious mask back in place.

"Are you sure you're okay?"

"I'll be fine. I just need an extremely thorough shower. And possibly to sit on an ice pack." I laugh, mostly joking, but kind of tempted. "I'm just sorry you lost your gay virginity in my shitty bedroom in my shitty trailer."

Silas frowns. "Does that matter?"

"I mean, no, but isn't your first time supposed to be all hearts and flowers with an R&B mix playing or something? Not whatever stupid dirty fuckhot shit we did last night."

He peers at me like he can't figure out if that was an insult, so I take the very gay bull by the even gayer horns and grab his hips, stepping up behind him to press a kiss into the back of his neck.

The scent of him is tangy and masculine, and it's kind of weird that he's as tall as me. But he shivers under my touch, and that feels fucking incredible.

I lean my forehead against his temple and close my eyes. I'm determined to let this wash over me and go with the flow.

"'Stupid dirty fuckhot' was a compliment, just fyi," I mumble into his warm skin.

"Noted." He takes a sip of coffee and looks out of the window for long enough I think the conversation might be dropped. "Was that what your first time was like? With a girl, I mean. Hearts and flowers and shit?"

"Mm, not so much." Silas turns around to face me, which gives me the perfect opportunity to loop my arms around his neck and kiss him. He's a little stiff, just like when I started hugging him way back when. But just like then, it only takes him a second to sink into the contact like he's dying for it. "I lost my virginity when I was fourteen, in the back of Leilani Dominguez's dad's Bronco, over in Mishicot, which has a population of 196, almost all of whom are on meth. We were both drunk, we didn't use a condom, and it wasn't even dark out. It was a real trailer park fairy tale."

Silas looks at me with exactly the expression that story deserves.

"Yeah, yeah, I know. It was a series of terrible choices. But thank fuck we were both innocent enough to not have any STDs yet, and we dodged the pregnancy bullet. Like two months later, my cousin Laiken, who was also fourteen, actually did get knocked up. And kept the baby, which is why I am an uncle to a fucking seven-year-old. And her baby daddy is a total scumbag, but we're all stuck dealing with him forever now. If that doesn't put you off risky sex for life, I don't know what will."

I didn't mean to tell him that whole very embarrassing story when I opened my mouth. But once I started, it kind of got away from me. It happens to me a lot. Most of the time, I think Silas thinks it's cute, or funny, or whatever. But right now he's looking at me with his head tilted like a lizard in the sun.

"What's wrong?"

"I didn't think about that."

"About what?"

"Last night, should we have... I mean, we can't get pregnant, but guys are still supposed to have safe sex, right? Sorry, I'm dumb about this stuff. Like I said, if it didn't have to do with motorcycles, it wasn't exactly something I was encouraged to learn about growing up, so I didn't think about it until now."

"Yeah, well I imagine neither of our fathers ever planned on sitting us down and talking us through the finer points of safe dick-in-ass sex." Silas grimaces at my choice of words, but it only makes me roll my eyes. "If you can't talk about it, you shouldn't be doing it, Silas," I say in a sing-song voice before biting my lip and looking up at him through my eyelashes.

Heat flashes behind his eyes and he immediately grabs my hips to pull me closer to him until we're firmly pressed together. The stiffness I feel tells me that I am so fucking good at gay flirting, which makes me smile more. Or maybe I'm just good at Silas flirting.

Who the fuck cares? He's the only one I'm flirting with, either way.

"My dude, you had your dick in my ass, and then you blew your load in my ass, and then you stared at your cum dripping out of my ass, said it was beautiful and finger-fucked me until I cried. This was like eight hours ago, Silas. I realize that a lot of shit has changed for us in a very short space of time, but I think you should be able to say the word 'condom' in front of me."

He's blushing so hard I'm worried he might burst into flames. Fuck, how is it this much fun to tease him?

169

My smile only gets wider. I don't see myself ever getting tired of this. I lean my whole body into him, pulling him into a slow, sensual kiss. I've had sex before, sure, and the occasional girlfriend, but this kind of soupy, lusty miasma? This feels like something new, and I want to swim around in it forever.

I grind against him, almost purring when one of his big hands grabs my hip, while the other runs up my back to tangle in my hair. He digs his fingers in, the tug and sting of it making me tingle until I almost forget what we were talking about.

It takes all my self-control to pull back from him before we get distracted and go for round two.

"Well, we both know I've had quite the dry spell recently, and my paranoia keeps me from slacking on getting tested. And you must be clean. I mean, you wore a condom when you fucked Cassidy, right?"

Silas' hand freezes, his fingers just under my waistband, and he looks like he just got caught with his hand in the cookie jar. I tense up because he tenses up, and a nervous energy invades our happy, post-sex bubble.

"Silas? Please tell me you did not have unprotected sex with a pit bunny a week and a half before you and I decided to discover the magical marvels of your dick being in my ass?"

"Dude, can you go three minutes without saying the words 'dick' or 'ass', please? I'm trying to have a serious conversation and every time you say the words, all I can think about is..."

"Your dick in my ass?" I'm so helpful.

"Dick." Silas scowls at me, leaning back far enough to punch me in the arm, just like Wish does. There's a moment where I think about how many normal friend things he's gotten used to, and it makes my heart do that squeezy thing.

But then I kiss him to get rid of the scowl, so I guess he's not really my friend anymore. Or at least not just my friend.

My mind snaps back to the matter at hand.

"Wait, focus. Was there a condom or not? Are you about to tell me that our first date is going to be at Planned Parenthood so we can both get our dicks swabbed? Because I'll do it if I have to, but I think I should be upfront that I definitely don't have a medical kink."

I know I'm trying too hard to be funny, but he's making me nervous.

"No, we don't need to do that." He sighs, but then his gaze flicks up to pin me down. "Wait, you want to go on a date with me?"

"Silas, not the point!"

"Sorry." The blush is back. "I actually didn't have sex with Cassidy. I just... I dunno. I couldn't do it. It felt weird, and I didn't like leaving you at the bar, but I couldn't figure out why. And I was going to tell you the next day, but then your dad showed up and things got crazy. I wanted to tell you that I didn't, but I didn't know how to without being able to tell you why I didn't, and I couldn't explain why. So...no. I didn't fuck her." He blows out a breath before adding as an afterthought, "And she's not a fucking pit bunny."

That's possibly the most words I've ever heard him say in one go. He's looking at me like he's worried I'll be mad at him or something, which is stupid as hell, and I want to wipe that expression off his face and never see it again.

"Hey," I take his face in my hands, pulling it up so he looks at me properly. "Hey, that's okay. I'm sorry. I shouldn't have pushed you so hard that night."

Taking a deep breath, something falls into place that I couldn't figure out before.

"I think... I think I was jealous. I didn't get it, but I was jealous of you giving her attention because I wanted all of your attention, but I knew I wasn't supposed to, so I pushed you towards her. And you were probably feeling something similar and confusing, so you went. So really, we're both idiots. As I pointed out last night."

I boop his nose with my finger, because there's no reason not to, and the sound of him laughing at me is so fucking pure I can't not kiss him.

171

CHAPTER TWENTY-TWO

SILAS

The smell of motor oil and the repetitive movement is normally something that grounds me. Focusing on the task at hand and drowning out everything else is what I'm good at.

But right now I couldn't focus if my life depended on it. Which isn't great.

I'm not exactly rushing into burning buildings for a living, but I am working with powerful machines that could hurt me, so I should probably try to focus a little.

At the exact moment the thought passes through my head, my hand grazes a hot engine and I snatch it back with a hiss.

Ford raises his eyes, looking at me from across the room where he's elbow deep in his current restoration project. An arched eyebrow is all he needs to ask if I'm okay.

"I'm fine." I hold up both palms to show him.

He doesn't move for another minute, still staring me down. Even though neither of us were looking for a chatty workplace, I was worried about being able to communicate with him whenever we didn't have the luxury of passing a phone back and forth. But he's pretty easy to read once you get to know him. And he can text me from wherever if he really needs to say something.

Right now, he doesn't need to text for me to know what he's saying.

I need to get my head out of my ass and pay attention to my work.

"I'm fine, I swear," I repeat.

If I say it enough, maybe we'll both believe it. It's enough for him to turn back to his own work, but I don't think he's convinced. I wish I could tell him the whole truth. He'd understand my inability to concentrate if he knew exactly how much my world has been flipped upside down in the past twenty-four hours.

It is physically impossible to think about mundane things like tire pressure and coolant levels when all I can picture is Cade's face. The face he made when I sank my cock into him for the first time last night. The face he made when he begged for more. Or his face when he came so hard he cried.

It was the most beautiful thing I've ever seen.

I don't understand how I've spent so much time watching him without letting myself admit how beautiful he is until now. But once it clicked, everything made sense.

He's mine. My job is to take care of him and keep him safe, like no one has before.

For the next couple of hours, I do my best to put all thoughts of Cade out of my mind. I'll see him tonight, after all. The girls aren't coming home until tomorrow night, which means I have one more night to wring as much noise out of his sexy, pouty mouth as I possibly can.

And I want to. More than anything.

It's insane to think I've spent my entire life not really caring about sex. Because the second Cade and I got our shit together, it became all-consuming. It wasn't just how much I care about him, although that's a huge part of it. But it's also this need to...have him. To own him, inside and out.

Seeing him marked up with my cum was like feeling a bunch of random puzzle pieces fall into place.

Does everyone feel this kind of possessiveness the first time they sleep with someone? Or every time? A part of me is worried that no one feels this way, and it's a hint that something much larger is broken inside me.

People aren't possessions. And I don't want to control him. I just have this irrepressible need to keep him close to me, so I know he's safe.

If his father tries to put his hands on *my* person again, I'll rip out his spine.

Picturing creative ways of disemboweling Kyle Waters helps keep me moving, and before I know it, I'm buzzing with enough anger that I've forgotten all about the other, more confusing thoughts. Even if I have to pretend not to notice the concerned glances that Ford has been sending my way.

I double-down on my attempts to focus on the disassembled motor mount in front of me, but it's only a few seconds later that my phone buzzes in my pocket. I can't not answer it. The chances of Cade's dad showing up are slim, but just in case. Holding the wrench in one hand, I pull out my phone with the other to check the incoming text from Cade.

> good news! my cousin texted me that dads back in arkansas so it looks like that black cloud of human misery is finally past us.

My first instinct is to breathe out a sigh of relief. As much as I'd love to get my hands on the asshole, the risk and stress to Cade's family wouldn't be worth it. I get back to work, trying to make up for all the time I've wasted day-dreaming this shift.

My next thought isn't so soothing, though.

Because I guess this means I have no more reason to stay with them.

It hits me like a bucket of ice water. We both said this was a temporary arrangement to keep everyone safe until their dad left. There's no other reason for Cade to share his teeny tiny living space with me.

I'm sure he'll ask me to pack up my stuff as soon as my shift is over. Not in a mean way, of course. It makes sense. He doesn't need me cramping his style.

It's not like we agreed we are anything to each other. Apart from two friends who have now fucked, which he probably saw as a form of stress relief.

It's fine. Everything will go back to the way it was before. He'll still be my best friend, I'll still have his family in my life, and I'm used to putting up with my dad's bullshit.

It's fine.

Everything will be fine.

I feel the sting in my palm before I realize the wrench has slipped, sending my hand jerking onto a dirty-ass screw that's sticking out of the motor mount. It chews through my skin like it's mulch.

Looking down, there's a lot more blood than I expected. I can see raw flesh where the screw tore into my palm, and blood is running down my forearm until it drips onto the floor. The sight of my blood soaking into the concrete makes the world tilt.

"Oh shit," I say, but my voice sounds like it's coming from far away, and it's muffled by blood rushing in my ears.

Obviously, Ford was right. I should have been paying more attention.

CHAPTER TWENTY-THREE

CADE

I've spent the whole day in a kind of pleasant daze. I probably look like a love-struck teenager, but I don't even care.

No one who's had the quality and quantity of orgasms that I've had this weekend should care about anything.

Dad is gone, hopefully for good this time. Or at least for a while. Mom answered the phone when I called to check in and sounded not-dead or dying; the girls are safe with Jaz and will be home tomorrow.

Silas works until 6pm today, and I don't start my next shift until 6am tomorrow. Which means we have twelve whole hours of privacy to continue to explore whatever my de-virginized little dirtbag wants to.

It would be physically impossible to bite back my smile. Why try?

It's only 4pm now, so I still have a couple of hours to kill until Silas gets home. Normally, I would spend it napping, but I'm too amped up to sit still. I move around the trailer, cleaning up whatever I can find to make it look a little nicer for him and the girls when they get back tomorrow.

I'm sprawled out, squeezing toothpaste into some of the smaller holes left by Dad's path of destruction, when I hear the door open. Confused, I push my chest off the kitchen floor to see who it is.

"Mom?"

"It's me." Silas' voice reaches me as he walks through the doorway. A flush of excitement surges through me, which is a new but not unwelcome development, and I scramble to my feet to go meet him. There are too many questions running through my head to get any answers.

Why is he home so early? Why does he sound weird and tense? And with this new thing between us, how am I supposed to greet him? I've spent all day here playing happy housewife and never thought about whether I'm supposed to kiss him when he walks in the door.

Do I want *to kiss him when he walks in the door?*

"What happened? You miss me so much you couldn't make it through a whole—" My words trail off when I see why he's home so early. "Silas, what the fuck happened?"

His gray hoody, the one that I love on him because it's so fucking soft to touch, is spattered with dried blood. He has the glassy-eyed look of someone who's still kind of shocky, and he's glancing around the room like he doesn't totally know what to do with himself.

The cause of all this, I'm assuming, is also why his hand is wrapped in several dirty fucking shop towels.

I grab his hand. He flinches, which makes me feel shitty, but I don't have time to baby him. Whatever's under here, it's clearly serious and getting dirtier by the second.

"What the actual shit happened? Did you drive yourself home like this?"

I get busy unknotting the rags to find the source of the bleeding while Silas mumbles his response.

"Ford dropped me off. I didn't wanna go to the hospital. It's fine, it's just a cut."

I try not to seethe. "You dumb bastard. Here, sit your ass down. I swear, if you get sepsis from Ford's grimy idea of first aid, I will murder you myself."

Silas doesn't respond, but he also doesn't put up a fight as I pull him over to the old laz-y-boy in the corner and deposit him into it. Kicking out the footstool, I get him to lie back and he closes his eyes while I work. He looks tired.

There's one towel still wrapped around his hand, but I want to grab my kit before I reveal whatever's underneath, in case he starts bleeding again.

"Do. Not. Move."

I can't tell who I'm more pissed at or why. I'm buzzing with adrenaline despite treating much more serious shit on a daily basis, and I have to force myself to shut the emotional part of my brain down for a second. Snapping into work mode, I distance myself from anger so I can focus.

It only takes a second for me to grab the med kit from under my bed and bring it out, unzipping all the pockets and sifting through until I find what I need. Saline to flush the shit out of the wound. Chlorhex to disinfect it. Skin glue if I have to, and bandage materials.

All of it's expired and ended up here as a detour on its way to the trash can at work. No antibiotics, unfortunately, because no one's going to fire me over some gauze, but I'm not losing my license for the sake of some bootlegged Augmentin.

I have suture shit, but that's way, way out of my wheelhouse as an EMT. I taught myself how to do proper suturing from YouTube, in case of dire emergencies. I've definitely advanced beyond the 'tie a knot and hope for the best' level. But it's his fucking hand. I'm not taking that risk. Not when one damaged nerve could fuck up his new livelihood just as he's falling in love with it. I'll eat the hospital bill for real stitches if it comes to that.

Or maybe Tristan will do them. Army medics have experience doing all sorts of fun shit civilians aren't allowed to even think about.

When I untie the last nasty rag from around Silas' hand, I feel my whole body sag in relief. It's not as bad as I was imagining.

The wound is messy, with a lot of torn edges where whatever he was using ripped through the flesh. It must hurt like shit, and I'm sure the amount of blood freaked them both out. But it seems more torn up at a surface level than any deep, significant damage.

Throwing a couple of chucks under his arm to absorb the mess, I pull on a pair of gloves and jab a needle into a bag of IV saline, squeezing it to make a strong enough spray to dislodge all that grime and grit. Silas winces at the sting, but other than that, he stays still and lets me work. He's facing the opposite direction and his eyes are still closed.

By the time the wound is flushed clean and I'm scrubbing it with antiseptic, Silas still hasn't moved or spoken. All my fear and anger have ebbed, and the silence in the room is threatening to choke me.

Screw it. It could stand to soak in the Chlorhex for a while, anyway.

Leaving the wet gauze on the wound to do its shit, I pull off my gloves and toss them to the side. I can clean up later.

I bring my hand up to take hold of Silas' chin, gently redirecting his face until he's looking at me for the first time since he walked in.

"Hey," I murmur. "What's going on?"

Silas swallows, and I can't help but watch the way his Adam's apple bobs with the movement. It reminds me of all the places on his neck I greedily sucked last night and how much I want to again.

Just above the collar of his hoodie, there's a bruise on his collarbone. I'm pretty sure it came from my mouth. I always thought hickeys were juvenile, but right now my cock is telling me screw the hand, screw the conversation; the most important thing is putting as many bruises as possible up and down Silas' neck to let everyone know whose mouth has been there.

"It was an accident. I was distracted and my hand slipped. It's no big deal."

I don't like how hollow his voice sounds at all. I don't like that he's not leaning into my touch the way he always has, even before he knew what I looked like naked.

"Yeah, tell me why I don't believe you." An invisible barrier seems to be building between us by the second, and I ignore my own growing anxiety to tear it down. Looking Silas in the eye, I repeat my question. "What's going on?"

Silas huffs out a breath like he's irritated, but his face doesn't quite make it there. He pulls his chin out of my grasp, but I don't let my hand go far, resting it on his chest instead.

"I told you, it was an accident. Don't worry, I'll get my stuff and you can give me a ride back to my truck once you're done playing doctor. I'll be out of your way soon."

There's a lot to unpack there.

Like in most situations, subtle is not how I roll. Silas looks upset, and he's talking about packing his shit. I could always un-upset him before by touching him, and after last night I opened up a giant bonus arsenal of touching to use on him, so this should be an easy fix.

He looks like a wide-eyed woodland creature when I climb up and straddle his lap, being careful not to mess with his hand.

Thank God this chair is big enough for both of us. I don't think I've ever sat in someone's lap before, but it's kind of doing it for me. There's something about the way he's looking up at me with his serious brown eyes that makes me feel powerful as shit. Having someone as strong as him underneath me—at my mercy—is a feeling I could get used to.

When I run both hands down his chest, he sucks in a harsh breath. That's all the encouragement I need to put my hands back on his face, tilt it up to me and kiss him.

It's soft. Gentle. But when I run my tongue along the seam of his lips, he opens for me easily, and we both sink into it.

"That's better," I say when we finally break apart. His half-hard cock is rubbing up against my ass where I'm straddling him, and it blows away any lingering insecurities I had that last night was a fluke for him. "Now, you seem upset. And I'm not letting you go home when you're upset. So, I'm going to finish patching up your hand. Then we're going to eat something, because you look a little pale. And then, if you're feeling up to it, I was really, really hoping to get laid tonight."

I punctuate this by rolling my hips into him, making him gasp and give an abortive half-thrust up into me.

"You don't want me to leave?" The vulnerability shining through in his eyes threatens to make me crack.

Of course he thought I was going to kick him out the second I didn't need him as a bodyguard anymore. I'm so used to looking at everything through the lens of my own abandonment issues, I guess now I need to factor Silas' in, too. Because I don't want to keep hurting him like this. Convincing him that I want him, not what he can do for me, is going to be a long, winding road. I have no idea how to do it. But things make a lot more sense now.

Taking a deep breath, I try to explain in a way that doesn't sound like a rejection.

"Silas, I don't think the two of us are ready to move in together in my teeny-tiny trailer with my batshit crazy family. But I'm not kicking you to the curb the second my dad leaves town, like I'm desperate to get rid of you. Besides, I thought we had stuff to figure out while we still have some privacy." I roll my hips again, grinding down harder onto his now fully-hard cock. "This stuff. If you want to, of course."

Silas bites his lip, his eyes clouding with lust.

"I want to."

"Perfect. Then be a good boy and let me finish with your hand, and we can move onto the fun stuff."

The way Silas' cheeks color at the words "good boy" is adorable, and for a second I think he's going to get all demure on me. But as I try to stand up, his good hand shoots out and grabs me by the back of the neck.

His grip on me is powerful, and he practically growls as he pulls me back down to him, claiming my mouth in a deep, dirty kiss that steals every last bit of air from my lungs until I'm drowning in him.

I may enjoy bossing Silas around in our regular lives, but our shiny new sex life has unlocked something growly and dominant in him. Something ferocious. The fact that I'm about to come in my pants tells me I don't hate it.

I really don't hate it later, when I'm on my knees with Silas' cock halfway down my throat.

Okay, that's an exaggeration. It's my first time giving a blow job, and Silas has a generously-sized dick. But what I lack in finesse I think I make up for in sloppy enthusiasm.

Just like the first time, once I decide to do something, I dive in at the deep end. I'd spent half the day thinking about what it would be like to taste him. As soon as the thought occurred to me, it was all-consuming.

After dinner and a shower, I pull him into my room, sit him on the edge of my mattress, and unwrap the towel from around his hips. He's tired, injured and emotionally wrung out, so I tell him to let me do the heavy lifting. But the hard, flushed cock that greets me tells me he definitely isn't too tired to fool around. It juts straight out from his hips, already leaking at the tip, practically inviting me to lean down and take a taste.

So I do. Pressing my tongue into the slit rewards me with a rich, salty flavor spreading through my mouth. I want to chase it.

Once I figure out the initial road bumps, I find a rhythm. Knowing that I'm the one to pull all those gasps and moans from him is heady, and only eggs me on. I love the feeling of my own spit mixing with his precum and smearing down my chin.

I love the way he looks at me, his pupils blown out with lust, like I'm beautiful. I love getting wrecked for him.

Now that I've been able to adjust to the weight of him on my tongue, I want to take him deeper. One of my hands is wrapped around the base of his cock to hold him steady, but the other is free. I shove my arm under his thigh, jerking his hips towards me and spreading his knees wider. It takes intense concentration to relax my jaw, but I can do it. It feels too good not to. I moan around him, drool spilling everywhere, as he sinks deeper into my mouth.

The muscles in his legs are twitching with the effort of holding back, and he's making bitten-off moans somewhere above my head. One hand threads fingers through my hair. He doesn't hold me down, but I can tell he wants to and *fuck me*, I kind of want him to as well.

Next time.

Silas is breathing fast, and when I look up at him, I can see every muscle tensed to breaking point. He's covered in a sheen of sweat, making his chest glisten, and the whole image is so erotic I can feel my own erection pressing uncomfortably hard against my zipper.

Pulling off, I take a second to gaze at him. The only sound in the room is our harsh breathing, and Silas is staring at me with dark, lust-blown eyes.

"Are you okay?"

"Don't hold back," I say, my voice already gravelly from the abuse. "I want to taste you. Feed me your cum."

As soon as the words fall from my lips, Silas moans so loudly his head falls back. I dive back on his cock like it's my last meal. I think I'm drunk on the feeling of power I have over him right now.

It only takes a few more seconds before his fingers are tightening in my hair as a warning.

"Cade," he says, in a voice so wrecked it barely sounds human. He grunts like a fucking caveman as he unloads into my mouth. Hot, salty liquid floods my tongue and I concentrate on swallowing as much as I can while the rest spills out, running down my chin.

Not that it matters. My face is already a mess. And from the way Silas is gazing at me like I'm something holy, it's working for him.

When he's finally finished, I let him slip from my mouth with a wet sound, so fucking turned on I think I could die. There's no time to fuck around. Standing up between his knees, I unzip my pants and shove them down so I can pull out my aching cock.

It barely takes a few strokes before I'm spurting all over his long, naked torso. My cum stripes over his chest hair in a way that's more satisfying than I ever would have expected, and the visual hits me hard. Silas, his body blushing for me, decorated with my cum, wrung out from what I did to him.

Fucking stunning.

Suddenly exhausted, I shove the rest of my clothes off before collapsing on top of Silas in a sweaty, sticky heap.

I don't know how much time passes before either of us speaks. His arms circle around me at some point, pulling me tighter into his side. I trace absent shapes over his skin with my fingers, my face buried in his shoulder.

There's a feeling of weight to his arms that I can't describe. It should be suffocating, but it's not. It's the opposite. It's like nothing I've ever experienced before. A tiny piece of my brain is screaming at me that this level of comfort can't possibly be sustained, and I should run before it can be ripped away from me in the most painful way possible.

The rest of me is too tired and blissed out to listen.

In the end, Silas is the one that breaks the silence.

"Thank you for taking care of me today. You're pretty good at that."

I laugh. "I've always been an underachiever, but apparently when it comes to gay sex, I can really throw down. Anal—check. Blow jobs—aced it. I'm basically a pro."

Silas snorts softly, squeezing me a little tighter and pressing a kiss into the top of my head, making my stomach flip-flop like a dying fish.

"That's not what I meant, asshole. I meant my hand and my weird meltdown. But the blow job was also... Mmm."

I lean back far enough to stare at him with a stern expression. "Mmm? Mmm?! If we're going to keep hooking up, I'm going to need you to get a thesaurus and work on your compliments, boo. My ego is fragile." Silas laughs, which almost makes me break, but I push through. "That blow job was not 'mmm'. It was spectacular. Incandescent. Life-altering. Phenomenal. Breath-taki-mph."

I'm cut off when Silas leans down and covers my mouth with a kiss that turns deep and filthy, very fucking quickly. By the time we come up for air, I'm a little tingly and his hands have roamed low enough that he's pinning us together at the hips. Both of us are definitely rallying for round two.

"Do you ever shut up?" Silas whispers into my mouth, still smiling.

"No. But you're stuck with me, anyway. No backsies." I grin.

There's a pause, and I can almost see the wheels turning while Silas tries to pull together the words for what he wants to say.

"Do you think we should keep this just between us for a while? Until we have a better idea of what it is?" He looks torn, and I know he's worried about hurting my feelings or something, but he shouldn't be. I'm just as overwhelmed as he is, enthusiastic dick-guzzling aside. "I don't know what my dad will think. It would be nice to have a little time to prepare."

Looking him dead in the eye, I nod. "Agreed. No jokes. I agree. It's new and scary and we deserve to figure our shit out before we have to explain ourselves to the masses. We'll take it slow. On that front, at least. It's probably too late to try to take it slow on the physical front."

I press a quick kiss to his lips so he knows I mean it, and he gives me a tense smile in return. "Deal."

Luckily, I'm a master at breaking the tension.

"I would also accept mind-boggling as a compliment. Or panty-melting. Dick-dazzling. You've been dickmatized, Rush."

Silas finally laughs again, and I know without a doubt that no matter what, I'll never get tired of that sound.

CHAPTER TWENTY-FOUR

SILAS

K eeping it a secret lasts less than three weeks.

It seemed like a good idea at the time. We're both still figuring out what all of it means: neither of us are used to dating, let alone dating another guy, and telling other people will only invite questions we aren't ready to answer. All we know is that we care about each other more than ever, and we are committed to making each other come in as many ways as possible.

We thought it would be easy to hide. What we didn't count on was the fact that Cade wears every single thought he has on his face, and I am apparently a terrible liar. I never had to do it much before.

Wish is the first one to figure it out. She finds a hickey while she's giving Cade a new tattoo. As soon as she interrogates him, he looks at me, which she notices, and then we both crack.

She is thrilled, and peppers us with difficult-to-answer questions until Cade finally agrees that she can give us matching tattoos on our hypothetical wedding day if she stops immediately. It is one of the most awkward moments of my entire life, and that's really saying something.

Wish stops pestering us, as agreed, but continues to be bubbly and enthused. I know she just wants her friend to be happy. Historically, that's not something that Cade is good at allowing himself.

I also catch her watching me warily when she thinks I'm looking the other way sometimes. Her enthusiasm may be genuine, but that doesn't mean she's doubt-free about the reality of this little venture.

Which is fair. If there's anything in life that I'm unprepared for, it's this.

Cade's mom finds out next, in a much, much more embarrassing way. We take the calculated risk of fooling around in his room while she's passed out cold on her sofa. I underestimate how addicted I am to the noises Cade makes when I have my mouth around his cock. What was supposed to be a quickie turns into the longest, messiest blow job I've given him yet, and we both fail to notice how loud he's gotten until his mom comes in to see what all the noise is about.

Kris and I get along fine. She never seems to have a problem with me being folded into the collection of 'children' hanging around that she loosely parents in between hangovers. But I never wanted her to see me naked.

And definitely not naked, on my knees, with my face buried in her son's crotch while he is spread-eagled on his mattress.

At least *he* is still wearing most of his clothes.

The saving grace of the situation—once we all get over the crippling, gut-churning mortification—is that she isn't pissed about it. Pissed that we didn't lock the door, yes. But not pissed that we're fooling around.

I've seen Cade go toe-to-toe with his mom in a thousand stupid arguments, because they're both ridiculous and love to fight. And I've seen them have each other's backs a thousand times as well, despite all the shit. But this is the first time I've seen him look scared around her.

His mom fails him a lot. It's never because she doesn't love him, though. We've talked about it before, and he knows logically that his mom isn't a homophobe and probably won't give a shit. But knowing something and facing it are very different. In that moment, while he's waiting for her reaction, it seems like the first time he is genuinely worried what might happen.

Instead, she rolls her eyes in that long-suffering way only parents can.

"If you guys are going to hump each other, can you at least lock the door? I may have created your testicles, once upon a time, but I don't wanna see 'em anymore. Especially not on Silas' pretty face."

That's it. She turns around and leaves us to it, Cade staring after her with wide eyes.

"And keep it down. If I wanted to feel like I was sleeping in a cathouse, I would work in one!"

The laughter that bubbles out of both of us is half-embarrassment, half-relief. When I kick the door shut again, tackle him to the bed and try my best to kiss that nervous look off his face, everything feels okay.

I keep waiting for some monumental cosmic shitfest to come down on us, but nothing has really changed.

We already hung out together all the time, anyway. Now I just sleep at the trailer more often. And with Dad spending more time out doing "business" that he always seems to come home shit-faced from, I'm happy to have the escape.

Until I walk into the trailer, stomping my boots from the thin layer of snow that's crusting the ground outside, and find myself in an alternate dimension.

"Yo!" Cade bounces over from where he has something bubbling on the stove. His eyes are bright and his cheeks are flushed with excitement, and there's cheap red tinsel wrapped around his neck. The rest of the tinsel is covering every inch of the trailer. He pulls me into a kiss that's a little too deep to be family-friendly, even though I'm sure the girls are home, and the stupid tinsel scratches at my face.

"Uh, what happened here?" I gesture to all the Christmas crap that's manifested since the last time I came over.

"Dude! Yes. Yes yes yes. I pulled out our decorations, and they were so depressing. But this is our first Christmas where I'm working a non-minimum wage job, so I thought we could celebrate. I went to the Dollar Tree and I may have gone a little overboard, but Christmas is Maddi's favorite holiday, so fuck it. Whatcha think?"

Words are failing me. The whole thing looks like a giant fire hazard.

"I feel like I'm living in Santa's ass."

Cade gasps and leans back, clutching at his chest like I've wounded him. "Oh snap, he makes jokes now. I've created a monster. Quick, bring back robot Silas. I can't handle new Silas with a sense of humor."

But he's so bright and happy, surrounded by all this cheap, mass-produced crap. I can't be grumpy about it for long. Snagging the front of his sweatshirt, I pull him back towards me for another kiss, determined to ignore the scratchy tinsel if it makes him this happy.

When his tongue slips into my mouth and his hips roll into mine, I realize I made the right choice.

"Ew." A voice interrupts us. "Cade, I thought we made a rule about not necking in the kitchen, where my innocent eyes can be traumatized."

Maddi walks past us, looking totally unperturbed despite what she says, and picks up stirring whatever Cade has forgotten about before it burns. She looks more like him than either Sky or his mom, with the same unruly dark hair and intense gray eyes, and the same delicate features. But where Cade exudes constant, buzzing energy, Maddi is calm. They're on opposite ends of the focus spectrum.

If I had to guess, I'd say she's the real reason this trailer hasn't burned to the ground.

"Hi, Maddi." I try not to get distracted by how much I love the sight of Cade's lips when they're slightly swollen and shiny with my spit, so I can remind myself there are other people in the world.

She gives me a small smile and goes back to stirring. Maddi and I have a mutual respect over being the only people in this trailer that don't need to voice every thought in our heads. It's gone a long way towards helping her accept me being around so much. She's a creature of habit, and was the one most likely to be disrupted by me invading their lives.

Sky is more like Cade. She's the star of her own show, so what other people do tends to roll off her as incidental.

"You'll be singing a different tune when you're the one getting caught necking in the kitchen." Cade sneaks up behind her, then snakes his arm around her waist and yanks her up in the air, spinning her around as he shouts, "Teenage-hood is upon you! The Waters house has been cursed a second time!"

Maddi wriggles and squeals at him to put her down, but she's laughing the whole time and so am I. The relationship they have might be unconventional, but it works for them. Anyone who walks in here can tell that the girls feel loved by Cade, and as safe as they can be, given the circumstances.

Snatching the spoon out of her hand, Cade smacks her playfully on the arm with it, leaving a smudge of sauce on her sleeve, before shooing her away from the stove.

"Go. Do homework. Or scrapbook with Taylor Swift lyrics. Whatever normal teenagers do. I can cook dinner."

Maddi grumbles as she wipes the sauce off, but she's still smiling. Cade calls over to her one more time before she disappears back down the hallway.

"Except what are the two things we absolutely do not do in this household?"

The long-suffering look she gives him in return seems well practiced. "Take meth or get pregnant."

"Exactly." The spoon is pointed at her for emphasis. "Now go."

He goes back to his stirring, and I take advantage of the brief moment of quiet to move over behind him, wrapping one arm around his waist and pressing a kiss against the back of his neck.

This is the stuff that makes me nervous. This is the stuff I have no idea if I'm supposed to do or not do or ask, or if it means we're more than we are, or what. But Cade is a fundamentally tactile person, and every time I do it, he sinks into me like a housecat, and the confusion seems worthwhile.

"I swear, Silas. A few more years and I'm gonna start leaving a fruit bowl full of condoms next to the door, where most people leave their keys. Just grab and go. Or maybe I can paint lamb's blood on the door like in the bible, and the puberty fairy will just skip us. The only thing that freaks me out more than the idea of *me* knocking someone up by accident is the idea of one of them getting knocked up while they're still kids. That shit keeps me up at night."

He shudders, his attention still on the pot of what looks like maybe chili.

It's tricky to follow his thought process when he's deep in ramble-mode. Something he said makes me pause, though. How much time does he still spend thinking about girls? Does he miss it? Does he think about going back to it?

These are all questions that I should probably ask him, but nothing comes out of my mouth. Instead, I keep leaning into his back, soaking up the warmth and feel of him for as long as I'm allowed.

Christmas morning, as soon as I wake up, I find myself thinking about the tinsel-covered trailer and wishing I were there. Instead, I'm still at home.

Dad and I never had our big confrontation after I got back from staying at the trailer that first week. He gave me shit for being out so much, but it was a lot less shit than I expected. He asked me for money, but also less than I expected.

Maybe he senses that we're building up to something, because he seems to be treading carefully these days. Still himself, but never pushing me hard enough that I snap and tell him I'm done being his piggy bank.

He's still my dad. And I do owe him. If he can keep his mouth shut and not ask me where I go at night, and we can manage a kind of detente in the house, maybe our relationship is still salvageable.

Christmas has never been a good day for us, even when Mom was still here. I think they fought a lot. Dad's always been a big believer that structure is the solution to everything. At the holidays he would be home more, and Mom's mood swings and bouts of malaise that I'd always considered normal seemed to get on his nerves more and more.

After she died, the whole thing felt like a joke. Dad started getting me motocross gear for presents with a single-minded intensity, and bikes became the only thing he'd talk about.

Until he'd get too drunk and start talking about Mom. But I learned pretty quickly that I didn't want to stick around for that part.

Right now, the atmosphere is more tense than it's been in years. We typically just exchange a couple of gifts and then move on with our lives, but it feels like this year we're circling each other, both on the precipice of change, waiting to see who shoves the other off the edge first.

We have breakfast together in silence, and then I tell him I'm going out. He raises an eyebrow, and I hold his gaze.

I dare you to ask me where I'm going on Christmas Day. Where I'd rather be than here. I want him to ask me, so I finally have a reason to say it.

All he does is shrug.

Feeling deflated, I take my plate to the sink and get ready to leave. Nothing else is said before I walk out of the door.

By the time I get to Cade's, they are already in the thick of their celebrations.

I let myself inside, braced for the sound of arguing because I know Cade and his mom, but pleasantly surprised. Instead, the only sound is the warm chatter of the girls floating from the back room, as well as Cade's voice talking excitedly with them about something.

If anything, there's even more tinsel than before, and I have to pick my way through a minefield to get down the hallway. But it's worth it for what I find at the end.

Sky is sitting on the floor, wrapped in so much tinsel I can barely see her under it. She's gleefully playing with some kind of paint-your-own-ceramic kit that I know Cade spent a long time agonizing over whether to buy her. If he asked me one more time whether I thought she would prefer dragons or dinosaurs, I was going to scream.

I don't know a lot about kids, but dragons are objectively cooler than dinosaurs. Judging from the rapturous look on Sky's face right now, I was right.

Cade and Maddi are sitting together on the floor, their backs against the couch, messing with some archery supplies she got.

The tree is a sickly-looking sapling that I helped Cade get a couple of days ago. We hacked it down with a hand ax, then shoved it in a bucket full of gravel to keep it upright. But with the amount of tinsel on it, even that looks festive.

Kris is on the couch. There's a large glass of wine in her hand that's definitely not her first, but the warm smile she gives me when I walk in tells me she's keeping it in check. And as she watches her kids mess around with wrapping paper and examine their presents, the whole scene seems like a pretty fucking normal Christmas.

Which is a first for me. At least since I was little. And probably hasn't happened for them very often either.

Warmth runs right through me and I sink down to the floor between Cade and Sky without waiting for an invitation. Cade's eyes light up as he watches me sit down and he leans over to kiss me hello, but before I can say anything, Sky is grabbing my arm to get my attention.

She's very insistent that I look at her present haul immediately, so Cade just smirks at me before turning back to his conversation with Maddi.

Twenty minutes later, I know way more than I ever needed to about both dragons and glitter. It's amazing. The sense of belonging is so thick in the room I can almost wrap it around myself like a blanket. It chases away the lingering guilt I have over leaving everything unresolved with my dad at the house, as well as the fractured memories of my mom.

There's only one thing tugging at my happiness. It's starting to feel weird that we're not talking about what this means. The more free we can be here, the weirder it feels when I see Cade outside the house and we have to pretend to be nothing more than friends. It feels like an itch I can't scratch.

Cade and I had agreed not to do presents this year. I provided most of the chocolate and booze for the day, which Cade said was much appreciated, and I wanted him to spend his money on the girls.

As we go to sleep later, overstuffed and fucked out, I can't stop thinking about next year. I don't see myself leaving Cade's life anytime soon. But I also don't know if I can keep this thing a secret for another year. I used to find it easy to mask my emotions, because I was already so numb to them.

Every day I spend with Cade makes me more vital and alive. My blood is pumping and my heart is full of something other than the weight of all that numbness. But it's making the mask harder to wear. Every day it becomes more ill-fitting, and I'm worried that if this goes on much longer, it will suffocate me.

Something has to change.

Whenever we're around Wish or his family, I can touch Cade however I want. Well, not however I want, we're not animals, but close enough. I don't have to put energy into stopping myself whenever I feel like reaching out or keeping track of the expressions I'm having. The longer it goes on, the more draining it is to pretend to be just good bros whenever we're in public. It's like I'm using that same fake smile-for-the-camera, pretend-to-be-normal publicity muscle that Dad worked so hard to strengthen, but it's even worse this time because I'm using it to hide something I'm not ashamed of. It hurts.

But the option of being more than just friends in public feels nebulous and confusing. I have no idea how people will react, or if they'll even care. But even if they don't care, they'll ask questions like *'Are you in a relationship?'* or *'Does this mean you're gay?'* that I don't know how to answer. I've looked at girls before and thought they were cute. I might have done the same thing with guys if I thought that was an option. I've never really been into anyone before, though. How do I tell a bunch of nosy strangers that Cade is the only person to ever make me feel this way?

Even if it gets out. Even if times have changed like I hope they have, and no one gives a fuck about two dudes getting naked together. Even if everyone minds their own business and doesn't ask me questions I can't answer. It will still get back to my dad. I don't know if he's specifically homophobic, but I don't have a good feeling about how he'll react.

It's all a good reason to keep things quiet. But not touching Cade whenever I see him is driving me fucking insane, especially whenever Cade goes on nights and we have to survive days and days between sleepovers.

I have no idea how I went twenty-two years without ever having sex, and only occasionally jerking off. The second I sunk my dick into Cade's warm, tight ass, I was a changed man. Now I'm hooked.

Waiting for him to pick me up from work today, I feel like an addict looking for their next fix. Against my better judgment, I have lent Dad my truck, because his is here getting work done. Work that I'm doing at cost, also against my better judgment. Cade is pissed about all of this and not keeping it a secret. The only upside is that I have an excuse to make him drive me around, so I see him twice a day.

When he pulls up, instead of getting in the car and going back to the trailer like a normal person, I lock up the shop, pull him over to where my bike is, lean him against it and unzip his pants.

I've never thought of myself as someone who gets hot and bothered over machinery. But something about Cade plus bikes really does it for me. I couldn't pass up the opportunity. I kiss him frantically while I stroke him to hardness, then undo my own pants and lean my weight against him.

He's pinned in between me and the bike, and as soon as I wrap my hand around both of us and stroke, he lets out a moan so goddamn filthy I almost choke.

For the next few minutes, the shop is filled with the sounds of skin on skin and wet, open-mouthed kisses while we rut against each other. Just me and Cade and the smell of motor oil and arousal. I want to suspend time so I can be in this moment forever.

Until I hear a door clicking open and heavy boots step inside. With Cade's tongue still in my mouth and both our dicks in my hand, I'm able to look out of the corner of my eye and see Ford stepping onto the shop floor. He's calm, but his eyebrows are raised and he makes a show of looking the two of us up and down.

A couple weeks ago, I found out that Ford is fluent in American Sign Language and used to communicate with his dad in ASL, which makes sense. It also means that he hadn't had a non-written conversation since his dad died. I felt a stab of empathy as soon as I realized it and downloaded an app to learn a few signs.

When I first showed him what I'd learned, the warm, unguarded smile I got in response fueled my good mood for days. It was awesome.

Right now, I kind of regret it. Because it means I have to hold eye contact with my boss while he looks at me and Cade—pants down and dicks out—points to me, then slowly and clearly makes the sign for *clean up,* then *when,* then *finished.* I feel like a busted teenager as I get one more pointed look. Then he turns around and sweeps back out of the garage.

Mortified is not a strong enough word. If blushes were an alternative fuel source, I could run my bike off how red my face is right now. Cade hasn't noticed, and his desperate noises are drawing my attention back to him.

There's time for my embarrassment to cripple me later, because I am never going to live this down.

CHAPTER TWENTY-FIVE

CADE

Since Christmas, there's been a tension between me and Silas that I can't quite put my finger on.

Or maybe it was since Ford caught us going at it in the back of the shop. Which wasn't as big a deal as I thought it would be, although he's really nailed the art of making fun of me with just a facial expression whenever I swing by.

But it's in the funny, *I caught you with your pants down,* teasing way that buddies do. Not the terrifying, homophobic way that I'm always low-key worried about. I asked Silas if he said anything weird about it, but Silas said he was cool. We've all laughed about it. So I don't know what kicked off Silas' downward spiral.

The more things I cross off my list, the more it looks like I might be the thing he's upset about. That thought makes me want to throw up, though, so I'm not facing it yet.

The only other explanation for his sullen mood is that his dad is pulling some shady shit behind the curtains. Which frustrates me. I know what Travis is capable of, but I can't stop it if Silas won't let me know what's happening. I still haven't even been to his house yet. He's so paranoid about potentially having me and his dad in the same space.

It makes me worry that maybe I don't know what Travis is capable of. That's the only rational reason Silas would hide things from me. We don't talk about his dad very often, but he's mentioned bits and pieces about his childhood. There's a lot that he knows I can infer from context, even if we're not putting it all out in the open. But if Travis is doing even worse shit than what we've already acknowledged, and that's what Silas is trying to hide from me, then we're going to have a serious problem.

Which is why I'm standing on his doorstep, waiting to see if Silas is going to answer my knock, or Travis, or no one.

This is a terrible idea, Cade.

I'm here now, so I might as well see it through.

I don't know what I'm trying to accomplish by surprising him. I don't know what I'm hoping to see. Nothing, I guess.

I have to know what's going on with him. Even if it turns out I am the one making him unhappy.

Wish was right about one thing, though. This house is a dump. I don't know why I thought he was so rich all through high school. As if there are mansions around here, anyway. Shoving my hands deeper in my pockets to ward off the cold, I stamp my feet and watch my breath curl around my face in the frigid air. Finally, the sounds of footsteps approach.

Please don't be Travis. I can't punch him in his stupid face and go to jail while the girls still need me.

Thank fuck it's Silas' face I see when the door swings open. Confused, but still gorgeous as ever. Even that little wrinkle he gets in his forehead when he frowns—which is all the time—that I always want to smooth out with my thumb.

"Cade?"

"Present. Is your dad home?" I don't wait for the answer before pushing my way into the house. I'm coming in either way, the only thing the answer will change is what I'm going to do once I'm in there.

Silas shuffles awkwardly out of my way and glances outside before he shuts the door, as if he's checking we're not being watched. "No, he's out. What are you doing here?"

Words are not important right now. Grabbing the front of his hoodie, I march him backwards until he hits the nearest wall hard enough to knock his breath loose before leaning in to steal it with a kiss.

"I want you to fuck me. That's what I'm doing here. It's been too long since I've felt you inside me." I mutter the words directly into his mouth, rewarded by the sight of his pupils dilating.

"Okay."

Okay. I guarantee in fifteen minutes the filthiest shit will be coming out of his mouth, but right now all he can manage is a wide-eyed "okay". Fuck, he makes me smile sometimes.

"Show me your bedroom."

My mind is a loud place. My life is also loud. Silas is the only thing in the world that can make it all go quiet.

Even if it's just for a little while.

I've been with girls before, and I like it. But I was always bigger and stronger, and it was always assumed that I would take the dominant role. It was fun, but it didn't do anything to turn off the barrage of thoughts and feelings that always seems to be cranked one setting too high inside my brain.

Everything is different when I'm with Silas. It's why I haven't asked him if he ever wants to switch. That, and because a tiny, paranoid part of my brain is scared that the question might shake loose some unspeakable trauma that he's not ready to face. I don't know what switches it flips in his brain to be on top and take possession of me, but it obviously works for him and I'm not complaining.

It works for me, too. More than I would ever have believed.

Right now, Silas has his big, powerful body draped down the length of my back, pinning me to the bed with his weight. His arm is wrapped around my chest, holding me tight, and he has one large hand wrapped possessively around my throat. He's not squeezing hard enough to cut off all my oxygen, but enough to let me know that he has me.

It feels like I'm split open on his fat fucking cock. He's tearing me in two, with his other hand holding my thigh open just enough to let him in, and all I can hear is the slap of his balls against my ass and the guttural, wild noises he's making in my ear.

None of these are things I ever imagined wanting. But something about all of them together, or maybe the fact that they're all coming from *him,* is turning me inside out and setting me on fire with pleasure.

"Yes, baby. Fuck me. Fuck me so good." My voice comes out rough as he squeezes my throat even tighter.

"Is that hitting the right spot?" Silas is practically growling in my ear, and he punctuates it by snapping his hips even harder, dragging his cock over my prostate and sending electricity sparking up my spine.

My cock is trapped between my body and the mattress, and he's thrusting so hard that the bed is rocking into the wall, so there's plenty of friction. But I don't even need it. I'm pretty sure I could get there just from the sensation of him pounding my prostate while he drowns me in his hot body.

He bites my earlobe hard, and switches his thrusts to slower but deeper, dragging an excruciating moan out of me.

"You know it is, asshole." My teeth are clenched so hard I'm scared I'm going to crack one.

"Are you gonna come for me?"

I can tell he's getting close by the strain in his voice, but he's holding back, focusing on hitting me at just the right angle. My face is being pushed into a mattress that's wet with my own drool. I'm so desperate to come I might cry.

"Please."

It's the only coherent word that I can get out right now.

"Your ass is mine, Cade," he says, sliding his hand possessively up from my thigh until he's digging his fingers into my ass cheek and then slipping them into my crack. His fingertips trace patterns over my skin and I swear he leaves trails of steam behind.

When he touches my hole, he's gentle. He rubs at the tender skin there, feeling how much I've stretched around him and how easily his thick shaft drags back and forth.

"Fuck," he grits out. He sounds like he's coming undone, and knowing that I'm the one who does that to him—that makes perfect robot Silas fall apart—makes me feel so powerful. Even if I'm the one getting torn apart right now.

"Your ass is mine, and so is your cum. I need you to give it to me. Give it up, Cade."

He picks up the pace again, and I can't catch my breath. I'm so close.

"Hand," I groan, reaching for my cock, but he slaps it away and grabs my balls instead.

"Give it to me. I can feel how full of cum you are. It's dying to spill out. Do you need me to fuck it out of you?"

The noises slipping out of me sound like a desperate animal. Words are beyond me.

Fuck, his hands are huge. He engulfs my balls, tugging and squeezing at them just hard enough to be on the good side of painful, and slams into me a few more times. It's all I need.

Groaning into the mattress, my cock throbs and flexes as I spill my cum everywhere, my body going tense. I feel like my brain whites out, but I don't have to think about anything other than riding out the pleasure. I'm vaguely aware of Silas keeping his firm grip on my balls and using it to hold me tight while he keeps thrusting into me a few more times until he loses it himself, and then I can feel him filling me up.

With one hand still kneading my throat and the other holding onto my balls like they're something precious, Silas' hips jerk against me as he unloads. I want to bear down and squeeze every last drop of cum out of him, and when I try, he groans and chokes me harder.

He nuzzles into me, the rasp of his stubble on my neck sending jolts of electricity through me as we both come down. I can feel his cock flex inside me one more time before he slips out, leaving a wet trail of cum down my crack to my thighs. It's cooling on my skin, the tactile marker of everywhere he claimed me.

I don't know how long we lie there. His chest is still pressed to my back and we both breathe heavy but in sync with each other. The sound of our matched, even breathing fills the room, complimenting the peaceful static that still fills my brain. At some point, he moves his hand from my throat to rest it gently on my chest, where it can rise and fall as well. He presses a soft kiss into the back of my neck, which makes a lazy smile spread across my face. I feel surrounded by him.

It isn't until the buzzing of my phone wakes me up I realize I fell asleep. Silas stirs but doesn't wake up, rolling over enough to wrap one beefy arm around me and pull me back into his chest.

I want to ignore the phone and snuggle as deep into Silas as possible, but it's annoying. I also need to figure out if I should sneak out of here before his dad gets back, so I try to blink some awareness back into my body and reach for the offensively bright screen.

MOM

She better not need a ride. I'm gonna be pissed if I have to crawl out of our little fucknest to pick her up. I should really let her go to voicemail so she can't talk me into doing any favors, but I've always been weak-willed when it comes to her.

Against my better judgment, I swipe to answer.

"What?"

The noise I get in response doesn't sound like words. It barely sounds human. But I recognize Mom's hysterical sobbing voice, and it pings my internal alarm system enough to have me sitting up and fully awake in an instant.

"Mom, what happened? Where are you?"

"Cade?" Silas grumbles next to me, but I ignore him.

Between sobs, the only words I can pick out are "I'm sorry", "accident" and "Sky". It's enough to get me moving. Panic grips me, but I shut it down fast. If the girls are hurt, I don't have time to freak out. Mom is clearly freaking out enough for the both of us.

"Baby, wake up. We've gotta go to the hospital." Calling him names like that is something I normally only do when we're naked and my guard is down, but in this moment, it feels right. I need a lot of things right now and one of them is him. All the confusing thoughts I've been having shut up in the face of that.

As soon as he hears me, he snaps to attention as well. Not bothering to ask me more questions while I'm still on the phone, he focuses on pulling on clothes and tossing me whatever comes to hand so I can get dressed as well, watching me with concern in his eyes. It's half the clothes I came in and half his shit, but I don't care. If anything, it's kind of comforting to pull on his stupid, boring gray hoodie.

Mom's still crying while we jog downstairs and out to the car, so I give up trying to get anything out of her and ask her to pass the phone to a nurse. She can't find a nurse, which is obviously not true, so I wait. By the time Silas is gunning the engine and peeling out of the driveway, Mom finds something better than a nurse.

She passes the phone to Maddi. Now, finally, I can find out what's going on. But as soon as she speaks, she sounds almost as hysterical as Mom.

"It's all my fault, Cade. I'm so sorry."

CHAPTER TWENTY-SIX

SILAS

It's a half hour drive to the hospital in Mission Flats, and the road runs through thick countryside, which means it's dark as fuck. I hate driving back roads at night. I've already swerved for like three raccoons, and if we make it to the hospital without being taken out by a rogue deer, it'll be a miracle.

Which also means my focus has to be on the road instead of on Cade, where it should be.

He's kept Maddi on the line the whole time. At first, their conversation was frantic. I could tell he was working hard to keep calm, asking her clear questions to get to the bottom of what happened. But now they've run through everything and they're trapped in a cycle of him telling her it's not her fault, which it sounds like she's not accepting.

Every time he says it, there's more and more heartbreak in his voice. I hate it.

From what I can piece together, Maddi and Sky were cooking dinner together while Kris was passed out in the back room. The skillet they were using caught fire. Maddi didn't realize you can't put out a grease fire with water, so she made it worse. The girls got the fire out eventually, but Sky got pretty badly burned in the process.

Maddi called the ambulance herself, and Kris didn't wake up until they were on their way. The fact that she was at least up and conscious when they arrived is probably the only reason she's not in jail right now, facing child endangerment charges.

Now Sky is being treated for the burns, Maddi is blaming herself, and there's no way they're getting out of that hospital without a CPS interview. The guilt settling over Cade is like a physical weight, making the whole truck feel heavier by the second.

The road gets busier, with a few more signs of life when we hit the edge of town. When we're a couple of minutes out from the hospital, Cade tells Maddi we're almost there and hangs up the phone. The way he throws his head back against the seat, with his eyes closed and tension etched in every inch of his expression, makes me ache. I want to fix it, but there's nothing I can do.

It's completely silent in the truck. With Cade sitting next to me, that feels unnatural, and for once I'm the one rushing to fill the void.

"It's not your fault. I know it probably feels like it, but you can't be with them every second of every day." I take a deep breath, spilling more words into the air in the absence of a response from him. "Accidents happen, even in the best, richest families in the world. You take such good care of them. Please, Cade. Please don't tear yourself apart over this."

My voice is wrecked, because I can already see how much this is hurting him. He seems like he's a million miles away, and no amount of reaching out is bringing him any closer. The wall of his guilt and anger is sitting between us, and it might as well be made of concrete.

"Thanks for driving me," he says. I glance at him, and his eyes are open again, although he's looking out at the road ahead. His voice is flat. "It really helps that you're here."

Throwing me a small smile, Cade reaches over and grabs my knee, pressing his thumb into the notch on the outside like he's using it to cling to me. It gives me a spark of hope that he isn't completely falling apart.

We can deal with this. This will be okay. I can be here for him. I don't know how to, but I'll figure it out.

He deserves that.

Silence settles over us again while we pull into the hospital, quickly finding a place to park. As soon as we get out of the truck, I take his hand and intertwine our fingers, squeezing it like I've wanted to do for the entire freaking drive. He clutches at me, and we walk close enough for our shoulders to brush all the way up to the entrance of the ER. I feel solid and purposeful. He can lean on me.

Stepping from the dark lot into the too-bright halogens and sterile white walls of the ER is dizzying. It makes me want to hold Cade closer, but that's the moment he pulls away.

The second we're in there, he's cutting through the noise and chaos to speak to the nurse behind the front desk. They exchange wan, tense smiles and seem so familiar with each other, which is when it hits me.

This is basically where Cade works. He operates out of the station, sure. But this is the closest hospital, and he probably brings patients here multiple times a shift. These nurses and doctors are his coworkers.

Which is nice, because it means that Sky is in good hands and he can trust them to talk to him, but it also means that he's about to go through one of the shittiest, most exposing experiences of his life in front of people that are supposed to see him as a professional.

He's going to hate that. And I can't help but worry that me being here is only making things more complicated.

If someone asks who I am, what do I say? I can't out him to his coworkers. But standing this far away from him while he's hurting is already killing me.

Fuck. I need an adult to tell me what I'm supposed to do. I've never felt less like an adult than right now. Cade walks back to me after talking with the nurse.

He doesn't say anything, but he leads me through the winding, curtain-lined ER hallways with purpose until we get to the elevators that take us to the general inpatient unit.

It's not a large hospital, so there's no pediatrics wing, apparently. If she were more seriously injured, they would have airlifted her to a specialist, but according to the nurses, the burns aren't that severe. They admitted her for treatment and want to keep her overnight for observation and some IV pain management, but she can go home tomorrow.

By the time we get to the room, Sky's already asleep. They gave her pretty heavy pain meds while they cleaned the wounds, and she's got bandages covering huge chunks of her arms. Her face is peaceful, and I have no doubt she's medicated enough not to feel a thing, but it all makes her look so small.

Sky is always larger than life. Her energy and personality take up ten times as much space as her body, just like Cade. Right now, she seems fragile.

And as Cade rushes in to kneel on the floor next to her, silently brushing the hair out of her face, so does he.

Maddi is slumped in a chair, leaning over her sister on the opposite side of the bed. She's pale, highlighting the bags under her eyes, and the sheer weariness rolling off her makes her seem closer to thirty than thirteen.

As soon as Cade walks in, though, she brightens. She runs over to him, letting him scoop her up for a tight hug. There's only a few seconds where she returns it before she starts crying into his shoulder, babbling the same endless, guilt-stricken apologies I heard pouring out of the phone on the drive over. Cade eventually takes her seat, pulling her into his lap and cradling her like a little kid.

She goes willingly, and it doesn't take long for him to get her settled. No amount of guilt or anguish can stop her natural, practical personality from coming out, and as soon as Cade asks her questions about where Kris is, Maddi swipes her tears away and puts her game face back on.

"She's with the social worker," Maddi says. The tension in her voice tells me she trusts CPS about as much as Cade does. "I already had my interview, but I didn't tell her anything. I just said Mom was asleep, and there was a fire. They can't prove anything. It was an accident!"

"It *was* an accident," Cade whispers, looking her pointedly in the eye as he tucks a lock of dark hair behind her ear.

They seem to realize they've hit an impasse, so they both drop the conversation and we all sink back into silence. Maddi huddles deeper into Cade's chest while he strokes his hand lazily up and down her back. I hover beside them, my hands shoved in my pockets. I feel awkward, but also like I couldn't physically move away from them if I tried.

Eventually, a doctor walks by the open door and tosses her head at Cade to join her in the hallway. Nodding, he tries to stand up, but Maddi squeezes him tighter and makes a whimpering sound that's fucking heartbreaking.

She is the strongest, most level-headed kid I think I've ever met. Seeing her torn apart like this, acting like a little kid desperate for comfort, is hard to watch.

"Silas?" His voice is soft, and he only has to look at me for me to know what he means.

I lean over them both, scooping Maddi up and pulling her to me. She sniffs again, but shifts to burrow into my chest the same way she did to Cade without protest. It feels strange, in a way. A few months ago, these girls were strangers to me, and it's not like I have any experience being around kids.

But what's stranger is how easy it's been to feel like a brother to them. Between the amount of time I spend at the trailer, and the incredible example Cade sets, it just fits. I've never experienced having siblings. I've never experienced having a family that I'm close to. But if the fierce protectiveness that's running through me right now is any indication, I'm probably getting there.

Maddi is so hard-working, and she doesn't ask for shit. If she wants to sit in my lap and cry and snot on my hoodie for the rest of the night, she fucking deserves that.

Cade slips out of the chair, pausing briefly to look at the two of us with an unreadable expression. Then we switch places as I sink down into the chair, holding Maddi close, and he goes into the hallway to talk to the doctor in hushed tones. He's out there for a while, but I don't eavesdrop. He'll tell me what he wants me to know. Maddi isn't crying anymore, although her breathing is still ragged, so I try to copy the soothing way that Cade was stroking her back until she settles further into me.

A hesitant calm settles over us, so I close my eyes, letting my mind go blank. I don't know how much time passes, but when I open them again, Cade is back in the room. He's standing just inside the doorway, leaning against the wall and staring at me with dark, intense eyes.

I want to say something. I want to ask him how he's feeling, or tell him I'm here for him. I want to tell him it's okay to be upset, but that this isn't his fault.

Before I can get any words out, we're interrupted.

Kris comes shuffling back into the room. Her body is bowed and hunched in on itself, making her look even more frail than usual, and a pang of sympathy for her runs through me. I'm angry at her, too, but I'm also realistic.

There are no winners here. Everybody's hurting. Everybody seems to be piling enough guilt on themselves without it being added to.

From the look on Cade's face, he isn't thinking the same thing. Anger flashes in his eyes, and he's already opening his mouth to unleash what I can only imagine will be a tirade of nastiness when someone walks into the room behind Kris.

It's a middle-aged woman with dark hair in a long braid, a sensible but soft-looking sweater, and a clipboard in her hands.

Every inch of her screams *social worker.*

Cade's mouth snaps shut on whatever he was about to say. The woman introduces herself as Rosemary and is apparently the hospital social worker, not from CPS. Kris gave consent to let her interview everyone, because Kris is so dazed she'd agree to anything right now.

Rosemary emphasizes that this is all standard procedure for when a child gets injured and no one is getting blamed, but none of us are buying it. She turns to me next, thinking I'm Cade. When I shake my head and Cade steps in front of her, a series of micro-expressions flits over her face.

Surprise, then adjusting and turning her attention to Cade, then back to me. I can see the wheels turning as she tries to figure out why there's an unrelated adult man with a thirteen-year-old girl huddled in his arms, and her analytical gaze makes me want to cower away, even though I haven't done anything wrong.

Maybe I am overstepping by being here. Uncertainty sinks its claws into my chest and refuses to let go. But Cade asked me. Maddi needs me, too. I thought I was becoming part of their family, but this stranger's stare is making me feel like I'm the outsider here, not her.

"And you are?"

"Silas," I croak, my voice rough with disuse after all this quiet. "Silas Rush."

She jots something down on her clipboard. Her tone isn't accusatory or suspicious, but I'm very aware that I'm being studied. Maddi hasn't moved, comfortable where she is, although she's glaring up at the social worker from where she lies against my shoulder.

She's made it very clear where her allegiance lies.

"And what's your relationship to the family?" Her pen is poised in the air like a weapon.

"I'm, uh.." Every word in the English language chooses that moment to fall out of my head. And because I'm hesitating over what should be a simple question, whatever I end up saying is going to look like a lie.

Time seems to stretch out infinitely before me while I continue not answering and Rosemary becomes justifiably confused by my silence.

"He's my fucking boyfriend, okay?" Cade's voice is like a whip crack through the tension. "He stays with us half the time, and he's here because he's part of the fucking family. But I work here, so I'd rather you didn't spread my personal shit all over this hospital. If you want to interview me, let's get it over with. The girls will be safe with Silas."

It goes unsaid that he doesn't consider them safe with their mother. Cade heads for the door without waiting for an answer, anger and tension obvious in every movement he makes.

Rosemary, at least, seems to get it. Once the pieces fall into place, she gives me an understanding nod and a smile that isn't forced. A few more scribbles go into her clipboard, and when she speaks to me before leaving, there's a lot more warmth in her voice than before.

"Of course. Thank you, Silas."

Following Cade out, I'm left alone with a silent Maddi, a quietly crying Kris, a sleeping Sky, and the fact that Cade just called me his boyfriend for the first time. I have no idea how to feel about any of it. It would have been less confusing if he hadn't spit the word out in anger, but that might be too much to ask, given the circumstances.

CHAPTER TWENTY-SEVEN

CADE

My interview probably didn't last more than fifteen minutes, but by the time I'm done, I feel like I ran a marathon. The amount of stress and fear and shame running through me has wrung my body dry.

A report has already been filed with Child Protective Services. At some point in the next forty-eight hours, we'll have a home inspection and more interviews for what she called a 'Family Assessment'. Rosemary assured me multiple times that no one is being accused of anything, and CPS doesn't actually want to take kids away from their homes. They just want to give us extra support if we need it.

Yeah, right. I'll believe that never. But I can figure out how to deal with that mountain of bullshit tomorrow.

Tonight, I just need to make sure my family is okay.

It feels like everything has spun out of control so quickly. Just walking back into Sky's room and seeing everyone in one place, more or less in one piece, makes me sag in relief. Silas is still in the chair, holding Maddi in his arms just like I left him. He looks at me as soon as I step inside, and I have to force myself not to run across the room and fling myself into his lap as well.

I just outed us to this entire hospital, and I didn't even ask him first. He would have every right to be pissed at me. Seeing the way he slid into that role so easily was confusing. He feels like family. Him being here makes me feel like I'm not dealing with this alone.

That's really fucking scary.

I've survived all these years by expecting to be disappointed by everyone. My parents, the cops, social services; all of them. I don't expect them to help me, so it's not a let down whenever they fuck up. But Silas is so strong and steady and *there*. It makes me want to trust him, and I'm afraid it's already too late. If he let me down, it would fucking hurt. It could be enough to break me.

I can't think about that right now, though. I nod at Silas, but don't let myself reach out for him the way I really want. Leaning against the door frame lets me wrap my arms around myself and maintain the illusion that I can still handle this alone.

Not that I've been doing such a bang-up job. Maddi has been so heartbroken ever since I first spoke to her on the phone. She took every ounce of blame, as if a child could be held responsible for another child's safety, because a whole-ass adult didn't feel like being awake.

I know I've leaned on Maddi's practical personality to help around the house. She cooks and cleans and helps keep the rest of us focused on our shit. But I thought I'd at least taken the emotional burden of being responsible for us. I didn't want her to ever have to feel like she was the parent when she's barely double-digits herself.

That's exactly what I didn't want for her, and somehow it happened anyway. I let myself get so wrapped up in Silas and dirt bikes and finally having a job I didn't hate; I let too much slip through the cracks at home.

That has to change. Which is just another reason I can't let myself rely on Silas more than I already do. He's spent his entire life being neglected by his dad. He doesn't deserve to be neglected by me as well. Even if my sisters need me more.

"I can hear you thinking from here." Silas keeps his voice a whisper so Maddi doesn't wake up.

I give him a wan smile in response, trying to pick the right words to explain how I feel.

Hold me. Promise you'll never leave me. Be my family and let me be yours. I can only breathe because you're still here.

"I'm just tired." Silas nods and gives me a sympathetic look.

My heart is pounding so hard in my chest, I'm worried he can hear it. If he pushes me, I'll crack. I know it. I'll spill my guts out and he'll see what a disaster-human he's shackled himself to, and then he really will leave.

I wouldn't blame him, but that doesn't make it any less terrifying.

Anything would feel better than this wild, uncontrollable panic galloping through my chest. I try to force myself to stay calm, but it has the opposite effect. My breathing gets faster and harsher, and the sound of it seems to echo around the small room.

Silas notices, looking at me with a frown. But before he has the chance to ask me what's wrong, Mom stirs. She's been huddled in the other armchair, pushed so deep into the corner I almost forgot she was here. As soon as she's awake and looking at me, I remind myself whose fault this is.

All of my anger from earlier comes rushing back, chasing the anxiety and panic and insecurity from my chest. It feels fucking fantastic. Anger makes my blood rush and my spine straighten. There's a wild animal inside me, throwing itself against the bars, and I want nothing more than to open the cage door and set it free until I forget I ever knew the meaning of the word fear.

"What did you tell the social worker?" she asks me. The fucking audacity.

My voice is cold when I reply. I don't want to yell and disturb the girls, so I keep it quiet, but you can practically hear the venom dripping off the words. I want her to be scared, like I was scared. I want her to hurt, like I hurt.

"I told her that this is my fault. If I'd followed my gut and filed for custody the day I turned eighteen, none of this would have happened. Instead, I trusted you when you said you'd change, and this is where it got us."

I'm quivering with barely contained rage and I can feel the way shock ripples through the room at my words.

Mom isn't shocked, though. She looks at me dead-eyed. I thought she'd fight back, but she's more resigned than anything.

"Accidents happen, Cade. I do my best, and you know exactly how much I've suffered to protect you kids. Or at least you do whenever you're not wrapping yourself up in this self-righteous bullshit. They're my kids, not yours. You use me to feel better about yourself. As if bringing home a paycheck and talking down to me somehow proves you're nothing like us. Like you're not just as angry and unpredictable as your father."

I punch the table, startling everyone in the room with the sound. Only Sky sleeps through it. Maddi and Silas are looking at me with something close to fear in their eyes, while Mom is arching an eyebrow at me like I somehow proved her point.

"Cade, please stop," Maddi begs, with tears in her eyes.

Sucking in a breath through my nose, I'm able to shove my anger down a little. I love it when it chases away the fear and weakness, but not when it becomes uncontrollable. My stomach clenches with the effort.

Maybe she's right. Maybe I am just like him. A wave of self-loathing hits me, but I file it away to process later.

Swallowing the lump of rage in my throat, I keep my voice as even as I can.

"Silas, can you please take Kris and Maddi home and stay with them? If Mom wants to prove she's not a complete liability, she can focus on cleaning every inch of that trailer and herself before CPS shows up for their inspection. Maddi can get some sleep, and she will not be left alone with Mom for one single, solitary second."

The air still hums with tension, but everyone slowly stands and gets ready to go. Maddi looks exhausted, Mom looks pissed, and Silas is staring at me like he has something to say. Whatever it is, I hope he doesn't say it. I'm not sure I can handle any kindness right now. I definitely don't deserve any.

I give Maddi a hug goodbye. Silas hovers awkwardly for a second, but when his hand comes up I flinch, so he drops it. I didn't mean to, and the look of hurt that flashes across the face makes me sick, even if he's quick to mask it.

"Call me in the morning when she gets discharged?" He stares at me, like he can somehow hug me with his gaze if I won't let him actually hug me.

I nod. Mom doesn't even try to touch me, thank fuck, but I catch her arm before she can go past me. Leaning in close, I whisper low enough that only she and Silas can hear me.

"If there are any drugs in that trailer when I get home, I will take the girls and leave forever, custody or no custody. Understood?"

The stare I get in response is so hard I almost crack. I love her. She loves me. We fight, but I've never been cruel to her.

I've also never been this scared and angry before. I have to put it somewhere or I'll collapse in on myself like a dying star.

Silas and I nod at each other one more time, and I pretend not to notice the long, lingering look he gives me as they walk down the hall.

When it's just me and my sleeping baby sister left in the room, I slump into the armchair. All my anger left the room with mom, leaving behind someone with the structural integrity of a wet napkin. My face is hot and tears are pricking at my eyes, but I don't let myself cry.

If I cry, I'll sob. And once I start, I don't know when I'll be able to stop.

Instead, I focus on breathing slowly and steadily through my nose. I stare at Sky's sleeping face and try to match her respiratory rate. I let the darkness and the quiet sink into me, and every time a thought cycles through my brain, I bat it away.

No more thinking tonight.

I don't sleep, but it puts me into a sort of meditative state for a while, deep enough that I jump the next time a nurse comes in.

It's a guy in his mid-twenties that I recognize from when I work night shifts. He nods at me politely before quietly going about his business, checking vitals and hanging a bag of IV antibiotics.

I've noticed him before because he's one of those guys that seems to wear his sexuality without a hint of a question mark. The way he walks, the way he talks, even the dainty rainbow drawstring on his scrub pants. There's no hiding his queerness to anyone he shares space with.

That shit seems brave to me. The idea of taking this intimate part of yourself that you know some people hate and putting it on display 24/7. I can't imagine how much bigoted shit he's had to deal with in his life, and it makes me feel like a fraud.

Silas and I have this incredible thing between us. But we're so scared of what people might think that we've only told our closest friends, at least until tonight when my hand was forced. And we both still walk around like living, breathing, macho dirt bike stereotypes.

I wonder if this guy would think I'm a coward. If he had someone as incredible as Silas, I'm sure he wouldn't hide how he felt.

"You're Tristan's partner, right?" He interrupts my weird shame-spiral, whispering across the room while he charts on the computer in the corner. The screen is the only light source in the room, casting an eerie glow over his face.

"Yeah. Cade." I sit up a little and try to remember what facial expressions people make when they're not having an existential crisis. "I thought I usually saw you in ER, not inpatient."

He shrugs. "My name's Micah. I don't think we've officially met. They floated me tonight. Short-staffed. I guess it's a break from the drama." He keeps typing, but I catch him sneaking a look at me out of the corner of his eye, as if he's scoping me out for something. "Although you seem to have plenty of your own drama in here tonight."

I snort. "You could say that. I can't tell you how much fun it is for everyone I work with to watch me fight with my drunk mother and get interrogated by social services. It feels very professional. I can't wait to be back here in a few days, dropping off patients to you guys."

Micah shrugs again, looking unperturbed. "Hey, it's emergency med. We're all fuck-ups and chaos junkies. Show me an ER nurse who doesn't have some kind of trauma in their past and I'll show you a liar. How else do you learn to be the only calm person in the room when the world is on fire?" He smiles to himself, but it's a weird smile. Almost vicious. "At least your friend was here to help. He seems nice. And oh-so-handsome, if you're into men who glower."

My lips lift in the closest approximation of a smile I've made tonight. Silas does love to glower, and he looks damn fine doing it.

But this conversation feels like fate. A few seconds ago, I was wondering if I was a coward for not being open about Silas. Everyone we've told is because they caught us or we had to. Never just because.

It doesn't matter if I correct this random stranger in the grand scheme of things. And the thought of having to constantly correct everyone I meet for the rest of my life when they call Silas my friend is already exhausting. Even if that's getting way ahead of myself.

But in this moment, I want to correct him. Because Silas is fucking awesome, and everyone should know. Taking a deep breath, I look Micah in the eye while I say the words. It feels important.

"He's my boyfriend. And yeah, he's the best."

It shouldn't feel good. It's not even the first time I've said it tonight. But something about saying it because I want to, not because I have to, makes me feel like a weight has been lifted off my chest. Like my lungs can fill with air a little more. I have a sudden prickling sensation behind my eyes, but that's ridiculous, so I push it down.

Micah just smiles at me softly. He hums, and for a second I feel like I've passed some sort of test. "Like I said, yummy. Good for you." There's a pause while he gathers his stuff back up and looks me up and down. "You should get some sleep. She'll be out all night, and I'll be in to check her vitals every hour. I'll wake you up if anything changes. Your family needs you rested, too."

He sweeps out of the room without waiting for an answer, but leaves me feeling a little more settled in his wake. I sink back into the chair, determined to sleep.

CHAPTER TWENTY-EIGHT

SILAS

The cold is making my hands stick to the metal frame of the patio chair. My breath fogs in front of me, and I can't stop shivering as the first tendrils of sunlight snake over the horizon. It's not even 6am yet. But I can't bring myself to go back inside.

It took the three of us a while to get the trailer looking presentable, in case CPS decided to show up at an ungodly hour. Then, while Maddi was in the shower, Kris handed over her small stash of prescription pills to me with a defiant expression.

I threw them down the garbage disposal, along with the scribbles of weed I knew Cade kept stashed in his bedroom.

After everyone was showered and settled, I couldn't get to sleep. Cade's tiny room still felt huge and hollow without him in it. I slunk outside to pace on the porch like an alley cat instead, waiting for him to call and ask me to come pick him and Sky up from the hospital.

He hasn't texted. Which is fine. Hopefully, he's sleeping, and then I'm sure there will be paperwork and other bullshit to get through when she's discharged.

At least Sky's nurse had the foresight to grab us as we left last night, asking Kris to sign a form that would let Sky leave in Cade's custody in the morning so she didn't have to go all the way back in and cause more family drama in front of everyone.

Logically, I know there are a million reasons Cade hasn't texted. But none of that has stopped my mind from spinning out, playing through endless scenarios that all spell disaster.

It caught me by surprise just how right it felt when Cade called me his boyfriend to the social worker. He said I was part of the family, and I felt it. For one bright, shining moment. Then he locked up and pulled himself away from me more than he ever has since the day he saved me at the quarry.

I'm trying to rationalize it. I'm trying not to feel hurt. But I have no idea what it all means.

Cade saying the words out loud made me realize I want to be part of his family more than anything. I already feel like part of his family. But based on how much he withdrew as soon as he said it, I'm scared that it made him realize the exact opposite.

Maybe he realized that he misses girls, and this is all a pit-stop on the way to the real, normal family of his own that he'll have one day. Just the thought of it makes my stomach churn.

The deepest, darkest part of my paranoid brain keeps spinning an insane narrative for me. One where his extreme need for physical intimacy combined with his pathological fear of knocking someone up by accident, creating very specific extenuating circumstances where the only solution was to sleep with a man. Even if it was something he'd never normally do.

Nothing makes sense right now.

I keep staring at my phone, holding a mug of cold, untouched coffee in my hands and listening to the birds wake up around me. My fingers are gripping the mug so tightly my knuckles are white, but I couldn't unclench my body if I tried.

The sound of an engine breaks me out of my intrusive thoughts. Gravel crunches under wheels, and I look up to see a car pulling up the long, bumpy driveway.

It's some kind of vintage Mustang. Huge, ostentatious and probably worth a lot of money, even though it's not in the best shape. Powder blue, with a black racing stripe running down the middle.

The kind of thing that car nerds probably cream themselves over, and it couldn't possibly look more out of place out here in the woods at the ass crack of dawn. I'm not even surprised when I look through the windshield and see Tristan behind the wheel. Of course, this is what he drives. He's such a drama queen.

But I do feel a pang of something like jealousy when I see Cade and Sky in the car. I was supposed to go get him; I was waiting for his call. That's what he said last night. Instead, he left me sitting here all morning like a chump, while he woke up his work buddy to collect them both at ass 'o clock.

That's my job. I'm his family. Or at least I thought I was.

The car shudders to an uneasy stop. Cade gets out first, then opens the door to the back seat and pulls Sky out and straight up into his arms. Shoving my hands in my pockets, I hurry to meet them. They both look sleepy and rumpled, giving me the urge to wrap them up tight, but I don't know where we stand right now, and it feels like it's tearing me in two.

Sky is resting her head on Cade's shoulder, her eyelids at half-mast and her face pale. I smile at her and she smiles back, but it's small. Cade isn't smiling. He's barely looking at me. His face is vacant in a way that terrifies me, reminding me too much of how Kris looked right before she left us to drink herself half to death for a week. And while Cade won't look at me, Tristan is studying us both with an intensity that makes me squirm.

The tension mounts between us, and I'm desperate to find the right words to dispel it, but the only thing that comes out of my mouth is silence. Cade ends up speaking first.

225

"Thanks, bro. Go get some sleep."

Tristan nods from inside the car, giving me one last long, appraising look before shifting into reverse and turning around to leave.

Once the sounds of his metal beast are finally gone, the woods seem unnaturally quiet. I'm staring at Cade, willing him to talk to me, but that vacant expression is still in place. Eventually, he murmurs something about putting Sky to bed, and I can only nod.

It isn't clear whether he expected me to follow, so I linger on the porch. This is it, basically. This is my life right now. One foot in his world, one foot out, with the thought of if I'm welcome constantly shifting like sand beneath me, making it impossible to find my footing and just exist for a minute.

Seconds tick by, then minutes, then more. I can't bring myself to go in without an invitation. A voice inside my head is warning me that this could be the moment it all comes crashing down around me. If he tells me to get out, I'll crumble. I know it.

But my indecision is rewarded when Cade eventually stumbles out of the house and rejoins me, pulling the other chair until it's flush with mine and then collapsing into it with a sigh.

"Thank you for cleaning," he says, after a silence that stretches on long enough to make me scratch nervously at my scalp.

I nod, not looking him in the eye. Words are hard sometimes.

"This family assessment is going to be a fucking nightmare. Strangers coming in here, poking around to tell us everything we're doing wrong with our lives, so they have an excuse to take the girls away. I can't..." He blinks furiously, looking away from me for a minute. "I can't stand the thought of it. It's been running through my head all night. At the hospital, I felt like everyone was watching me, waiting for me to do the wrong thing and fuck up. But all I do is fuck up."

"Hey," I whisper, reaching out to tilt his face back towards mine. It's the first time I've touched him all day, and it makes me feel so much more real. He's not crying, but his eyes are red and his skin is blotchy, like the threat of it is lurking.

"No one wants to take the girls away. I know you have this thing about social services, and I get it. You've heard a million horror stories from your mom. But I'm sure an under-funded government agency doesn't really want to take kids away from homes if they don't have to. That's gotta be way more paperwork. They just need to do their checks and fix things they think need to be fixed. Hell, maybe this will be a good thing. Maybe this'll be the final kick in the ass that gets Kris to go to rehab."

Cade snorts, but he doesn't tear his face out of my hand, so I take it as a good sign.

"I don't know how I would have gotten through last night without you, Silas."

My heart stops beating for a few seconds. When it starts again, I feel the faint spark of hope for the first time all morning.

"Really?"

His lips are parted slightly, and his eyes are locked onto mine. "Of course, baby. You're my rock. I was waiting for you to run screaming from the room any minute, but you never did."

"What?" Whatever confused expression I make at him makes him laugh, the sound warding off the chill that's been seeping into me all morning. After a brief moment of happiness, Cade looks at me again with a somber face.

"Come on, Silas. I don't know a lot of guys who want to be saddled with an insta-family at twenty-two. Especially ones who already missed out on the oat-sowing portion of their teenage years. Having you with me for this stuff means more than I can put into words, but I don't want to rely on it too much. I know this can't be it for you."

I feel like I've been poured out and I'm now a puddle of melted butter around Cade's feet. But I can't explain that to him, so instead I scrabble at his hands, pulling him as close to me as possible and doing my best to explain to him how fucking wrong he is about everything.

"Fuck your oats, Cade. I want this. I was going crazy at the hospital, not being able to touch you or be there for you like I wanted. The whole time I just wanted to wrap you up and tell everybody else to fuck off. I feel like that all the time. But I don't want to freak you out, or move too fast, so I've been trying to be normal. And I think you'd be the first person to admit that's not where I excel."

Cade snorts a little, even as his eyes shine with emotion. "Yeah, baby, that's not your area."

"You know I'm not great at reading people. But I want to be here for you all the time. So you have to tell me what you need. If you want me to touch you and be there for you, just let me. If you need space, tell me and I'll give you space. But you can't...go away. In your head. Like you have for the past twelve hours. Because I can't figure out what you're thinking, and my fucked-up brain is always, always, always going to assume the worst. Deal?"

He blinks at me, his gray eyes pale in the early morning light, shining with all the tears I'm sure he hasn't let himself shed tonight. He looks hopeful, for once. The wind blows a stray curl of dark hair into his face, so I push it back where it belongs while I wait for his answer.

"Deal," he finally says, sealing it with a kiss.

CHAPTER TWENTY-NINE

CADE

The sounds of heavy breathing echo through the room, intensifying like it's feeding off itself, until we finally collapse in a sweaty heap.

Silas' lonely mattress on the floor of his childhood bedroom is depressing. More depressing, somehow, than the ramshackle poverty-cage I call home. But he's here, and that's all it takes for me to follow, apparently.

There's been a shift between us since the hospital. We haven't talked about it in more depth, but everything has felt more real. More settled. It's like a lot of our unspoken insecurities have been put to bed and we're both coming to terms with the fact that whatever we're doing together isn't going to blink out of existence at the slightest provocation.

I wrap the thought around me and snuggle into it, the same way I snuggle deeper into the reassuring cage of Silas' arms. They're both equally comforting.

We agreed we wouldn't make an effort to tell people we're together, because all the important people in our lives already know. But we're not hiding it, either. Travis is the last real question mark. I may have been pushing that envelope a little by spending more time over here at *Casa de Rush,* hoping he'll stumble in on us and we can finally put all the wondering behind us.

If he's going to flip out and try to take Silas away from me, I'd rather face it sooner than later. It might as well be now. I'm still simmering in anger that I can't take out on my own shitty parents. There's plenty to go around. My dad is gone and my mom has actually been *trying* since the accident. Travis can come at me.

I have crippling childhood attachment issues, and I've officially gone emotionally all-in with Silas. Travis can pry him out of my cold, dead hands.

It's not like he's around much these days. Whenever I ask Silas, he says his dad's been real cagey and insists he's "working on something big", whatever that means. As long as he's not asking Silas for money, and whatever it is distracts him from fucking with my baby's head, I'm okay with it.

The thought makes me press my face deeper into the crook of Silas' neck. His skin is warm, still flushed and sweat-damp, and the smell of us is so thick in the room I feel like it's trying to drug me into a calm sleep. Silas' breath ghosts over my skin, warm and even, and I let myself be lulled by the rise and fall of his chest under my shoulder.

"Don't fall asleep, sweetheart," he says, his own voice sticky with sleep before he presses a kiss to the top of my head. Trust Silas to be watching out for me, even when he's halfway to passed out. He knows I won't sleep anywhere but the trailer anymore. No matter how much Mom cleans up her act, I can't do it. I shouldn't have done it in the first place.

Rolling back a few inches, I tilt my head to look at him and arch into a stretch like a cat.

"Mmm, not sleeping. Jus' comfy."

He snorts. His eyes look dark in the low light; a deep, earthy brown color that always makes me feel rooted in place. He watches me stretch, using it as an excuse to rub more of my sweaty, naked body against him, and the naked affection in his eyes makes my heart do a weird *thump-squeeze* thing.

"That's what you always say. Then you start sawing logs. Then I wake you up and you paw at me like it's my fault you can't keep your eyes open."

"It is your fault," I say, shutting my eyes. "You fucked my brains right outta me. How am I supposed to stay awake after that? Let alone get up and walk to my truck?"

I can't see his face with my eyes closed, but I catch the softest sound, like an exhalation of air, that tells me exactly what expression he's making.

"Do you need me to carry you? Like a baby?"

"Yes." I roll over, flopping my entire body on top of him and making him grunt. He wraps his arms around me again anyway, and the almost imperceptible squeeze he gives me tells me he doesn't want me to leave anymore than I want to.

"How's your mom?"

He already knows, but this has also become a new habit of ours. Buying time with small talk, dragging out the minutes before we have to separate with inane conversation.

"She's doing pretty good. CPS has her on a tight leash. They put her on a whole drug and alcohol performance safety improvement something something. I dunno what it's called. There's a fuckton of paperwork, but the social worker isn't that bad. Doesn't buy mom's crap for a second. Makes her go to AA and NA and parenting classes and all the rest of it. So far, she's trying. Now that the motocross season's here, I'll take all the help I can get, I guess. Sometimes I think I should just quit riding and pick up extra shifts or whatever, but I know I'd miss it."

"Nah, you can't quit. You love it. I wish you could see yourself when you're out there, the way you light up. You look so beautiful."

My forehead creases. I don't think anyone's ever called me beautiful before, and it's creating a tight, squirrely feeling in my chest. Must deflect.

"Yeah, well you know how it feels. It's like freedom, handed right to you."

Silas doesn't say anything for a long time. I press my ear to his chest, still blanketing his body with mine, and listen to the loud staccato of his heartbeat. Maybe I shouldn't have said that. Riding has always been the only simple thing in my life. I guess for him it's the opposite.

His fingers trace the edges of a scar on my forearm, one that I covered up with a tattoo of a motorcycle tread. It was my first tattoo, and the only one I have that wasn't done by Wish. I broke the bone when I flipped over my handlebars doing a jump that I had no business attempting, and I didn't get the follow-up care that I should have, so it never quite healed right. The nerves are still a little funky there, so the drag of his fingertips makes pins and needles light up across my skin in inconsistent little waves.

"This is from the time you broke your arm, right?"

I hum and kiss the skin over his heart. I'd forgotten he was there that day. My own fingers are trailing over his ribs, tracing every notch and groove until I can memorize the planes of his body. If I know him well enough, he'll become a part of me, and then no one can truly take him away.

My fingertips find a knot of scar tissue high up over his ribs, to the side of his pec. I've wondered about it before, but never had the courage to ask.

This time, he doesn't wait for me to ask.

"My lung collapsed. I crashed and broke my collarbone two years ago. The bone punctured my lung, and they had to cut a hole in my chest to let it inflate again."

Fear, dark and unctuous, leaches into me at the thought. Which is stupid, because it was a long time ago. I don't speak, settling for digging my fingertips into his skin and clinging to him even more tightly. News of the accident made it here at the time. I never realized how much they downplayed it, though. It felt like he was back racing barely a week later.

I'm sure I have Travis to blame for that, but I don't ask, because confirmation will only make it harder to contain my rage. All I can do is focus on the Silas I have here in front of me, and keeping him safe.

His heartbeat continues to thump, quick but steady, under my ear.

"Cade?" His voice is a whisper, but it sounds loud, like it's echoed by all the things we're both not saying right now. "Do you remember Anthony Turner?"

It's been years since I heard that name, and it makes my gut twist. I freeze, my muscles caught in a trap and held there by the memory.

"Yeah," I say. "I was at his funeral. I think everybody was. You were there, right? With your dad?"

He hums his confirmation. "A lot of it is a blur. I remember thinking his coffin was so little."

"Me too," I say, swallowing down my nausea at the thought. Something about a child-sized coffin seemed profoundly wrong to me, even though I was still a teenager myself.

"Were you at the track when it happened?" There's a hollow, far-off quality to his voice that I recognize. It's never a good sign.

"No." I don't want to ask. "Were you?"

He doesn't answer for a while, but the roughness of his breathing tells me before he speaks the words. "Yeah. It was bad. You could see right where his neck had broken. It happened in an instant, and he was just gone. There was nothing anyone could do."

"I bet." I kiss his chest again, and this time there's a smudge of wetness where all the nameless emotions I'm shoving down spilled over and leaked out of my eyes.

Silas' fingers are tangled in my hair the way he likes, rubbing at my scalp and tugging at the strands.

"Do you ever get scared, Cade?"

His chest shudders beneath my face as he takes in a deep, slow breath. It's such an off-the-wall question, I wish I could peel back the layers of his mind and see what's making him think about this shit. Especially considering I can feel his fear in the way he breathes underneath me, but I can't hear it in his voice.

233

He has moments like this. Not often, but occasionally. Where the Silas I can touch and the Silas trapped in his head are two completely different beasts, and the one spinning out in his mind is dealing with a version of reality that I can't quite perceive.

It scares the shit out of me, but there's nothing I can do about it except continue to be here. As long as he needs it, I'll be as steady as a maladjusted adrenaline junkie from Possum Hollow can be.

"Sometimes, baby. Sometimes." Pressing my skin to his, I squeeze my eyes shut and try to stop the leaking. I don't know where it's even coming from. His fingers continue their ministrations as he takes one slow, shuddering breath after another, and his heartbeat continues to race beneath my cheek.

I think Silas and I are scared of very different things. But we're both scared. The silence goes on for too long, and eventually I have to break it before something else snaps.

"Are you nervous about tomorrow? Is that what this is about?"

His fingers stop moving over my scalp. "Why would I be nervous?"

"It's your first time riding since the suspension was made permanent."

Silas huffs like I'm being ridiculous, as if he isn't the one who just dragged out the greatest hits of all our dirt bike-related trauma. "It's just another race. I'm sure Dad will crawl out of whatever hole he's hiding in to come yell at me, like always. It'll be like any other race, even if it's not at a national level."

Like everything to do with Travis Rush, the words spark my temper, and I have to fight to keep my voice even.

"I don't know why that asshole thinks he has the right to yell at you about anything. He's the one who was responsible for your bike. You were banned for whatever additives they found in your fuel tank. If you didn't put them in there, they sure as hell didn't climb in there on their own. Process of elimination tells us exactly who should get his ass handed to him here, and it's not you."

Rant over, I go back to seething quietly. I keep holding him tight to me, as if I can hold him tight enough to shield him from things that have already happened.

"I told you, Cade, it was an accident." His voice is resigned. He's said this to me so many times, I can't tell if he really believes it or if he's just given up caring. "These things happen. Fuels get mixed up. You use the bike for other things. A tiny fraction of something left in a tank from a different event can set off the sensors. I'm not the first person it's happened to, and I won't be the last. Honestly, they were waiting for a chance to get rid of us. Between Dad's constant fights and sketchy shit and my 'personality' problems, we weren't marketable anymore. The league had an opening, and they took it. Dad's an asshole, but that doesn't make it his fault."

It makes sense. If I had to work with Travis Rush year after year, I'd find an excuse to have him banned as well. But it still doesn't seem like the whole truth. At least Silas isn't talking about old accidents anymore. That was a weird detour down memory lane, and I still don't feel comfortable leaving him in the wake of it.

I don't have a choice, though. The girls need me, and I'll see Silas at the track tomorrow.

"Okay, I gotta take off before he shows up, because I really don't want to see him. Get some sleep. Don't think I'm gonna take it easy on you tomorrow just because you dicked me down so good tonight."

I kiss him one more time before I crawl up out of his crappy floor mattress and look around for my clothes, and the sound of his laughter warms me all the way down to my truck. Maybe I was worried about nothing.

235

This place is buzzing with excitement. It's the start of the season, so everything's still ramping up and the crowd is small, but the riders are all eager to hit the track and the energy is pulsing.

There's been one event in the season so far, but it was AML-sponsored, so Silas wasn't able to enter. I thought it would bum him out more than it did. His license being revoked meant he wasn't allowed to ride, but there wasn't anything stopping him from attending as my own personal pit crew, and he actually seemed to get a kick out of it.

He'd been in a great mood the whole time, going over my bike like a pro, then setting me up at the gate with a warm smile

Not to mention, his ass looks fucking delectable in a jumpsuit. Like a peach.

The whole time, he looked like a wet dream. I even got him to wear my battered old pink ball cap for good luck. He's gotten a deep, golden tan from spending time outdoors without wearing a motocross jersey, and he was all stubbly and grease-smeared. His compulsively short, neat hair has grown out long enough on top to get a little messy, and now I see why he's so obsessed with raking his fingers through mine. It's sun-kissed with just a hint of a curl, and I want to touch it all the time. It's not as long—or as pretty—as mine, but it still feels like a physical reflection of all the ways he's let himself be free.

Which he gets the credit for. He did the work. But I know I played a role in it, and that fills me with a possessive kind of joy that I've never experienced before.

Getting back on my bike with Silas watching me felt like coming home. I only came in third, so the prize money was shit, but I didn't care. At the end of the race, my little robot was grinning like I'd won the world championship.

Being out in the open with him has caused less drama than I expected, but I still wasn't going to make out with him in the middle of the Mission Flats Raceway. For all the progress the world has made, there are still shitty people around, and I didn't want those outliers to beat the shit out of us in the parking lot later. I was more than happy to get off my bike and jump into his arms though, smearing him with dirt and nearly knocking both of us to the ground in the process.

I don't know if he'd been putting on a brave face to not distract me, or if he genuinely wasn't upset, but the whole day his smile didn't waver. I've never seen him so happy. It was almost enough to make me think depressed robot Silas was a thing of the past.

Today, I was excited to see that bright, happy version of Silas race for the first time.

Which is why it hits me like a ton of bricks when he shows up, wearing an expression that fills me with a sense of despair.

To most people, he probably looks as serious as he always does. Maybe a little more pissed off than usual. But I know all his faces, and this isn't him just being focused or robotic.

He looks hollow. He looks like he did when I found him at the quarry, teetering over the edge, talking about how it might feel to fly.

"Hey," I say, rushing over to him and pulling his face until he's looking at me. "What's up? What's wrong?"

He shrugs and shakes his head, but his eyes shift as he avoids my gaze. A hand comes up to scrub through his hair, tugging at the longer strands.

"Nothing."

"Bullshit. Did your dad do something? Where is that asshole?"

Silas huffs out a laugh that sounds almost pained.

"No, Cade, he didn't do anything. I haven't even seen him."

"What?"

"He's not here. He never came home last night, and he's not at the grounds. I texted him and he replied to tell me he's not coming, and nothing else." There's a pause as he looks off into the distance and I realize I have no idea what to say. I think it's a good thing his asshole sperm donor isn't here to treat him like shit, honestly, but not if it's going to make Silas look this vacant.

"Hey," I repeat, pulling his gaze back to mine. "I'm here. I care about you a thousand times more than he ever did. I'm in your corner. It's going to be fine."

I can almost see the moment his expression shutters into nothingness. His voice is completely flat when he speaks.

"Really, it's fine. Racing was what he always showed up for. I lost my career, so it makes sense that I've lost him too. It was the only thing he ever wanted from me."

I don't think twice before reaching to pull him into my arms, but he takes a step back out of my reach and shoots me a glare.

"I thought we agreed we wouldn't do that here."

I'm so shocked I think my brain blue-screens. It feels like someone's twisting my guts tighter and tighter, and something's about to snap. Touching Silas has always been my sure-fire way to soothe him. His anxieties are a minefield that I will never be able to understand, but as long as I can touch him, I know I can help.

If he takes that away from me, what else do I have to offer?

"We agreed not to suck face in front of the sons of the confederacy, not to avoid all physical contact. Friends can hug, dude. This town is conservative; it's not Saudi fucking Arabia," I say. My heart is racing. It's from fear, not anger, but anger is what my body knows, so my words come out sharp.

He's not even looking at me. The twist in my gut gets even worse.

"We should get to the gate. We're starting soon."

Grabbing his bike, he takes off before I have the chance to reply.

For three months, I've been waiting for the other shoe to drop, while telling myself it's just my abandonment issues talking and everything is fine.

For once, I owe my abandonment issues an apology. Everything is obviously not fucking fine.

Chapter Thirty

SILAS

The race was a blur. I'm good at shutting everything else out, but this was more extreme than usual. I know Cade thinks I should be grateful to be ditched by my dad, but he doesn't get it. I'm not sure I really get it.

It just hurts. Dad is a piece of shit, but until Cade showed up, he was the only person who ever cared if I lived or died. He asked me for one thing in return, and I couldn't give it to him.

If I couldn't keep an asshole like my dad happy, how can I possibly be good enough for someone like Cade?

Half of my brain is screaming at me to run before my own poisoned existence bleeds into his, while the other half is endlessly spinning, trying to think of how I can be worthy of him. If I can convince him I can take care of him, maybe that will be enough. Maybe he'll stick around.

We need our own place, one that our parents' chaos and misery can't bleed into. Cade won't leave his sisters, and neither will I, so it needs to be big enough for the four of us. Which means I need money.

I'm not telling Cade about my plan until I have everything figured out. He's done so much for me and everyone else in his life, I have to show him that he doesn't always have to be the adult.

Then he'll keep me around.

Maybe.

Dad used to drink *around* races instead of at them. Without them, it seems like he's lost his own structure to cling to. I see him less and less, and he's messy more often than not. The last time I saw him was four days ago, and he hugged me for the first time in years. Before that, it was last week, and he told me he wished he'd let me die with Mom.

It wasn't the first time Dad had said something like that, but this time was sticking with me more than normal. Images of him and Mom and poor little Anthony Turner's corpse are filling my head to a point where it might burst. More and more, I've been dreaming about the day Anthony died, but my mind replaces his body with Cade's.

Night after night, I watch Cade break his neck on the track while I'm helpless to stop it. I know it's just a dream. I know I shouldn't let it get to me. But I can't help wondering if it's an omen.

There's so much dark crap shoving itself in my brain that the space for rational thought is already occupied.

I did my best to shut all that out and focus on the race, and I felt like a fucking machine as I tore up the track. Lap after lap, analyzing every corner and every jump, letting my instinct take over and all that emotion and doubt get left behind.

When I won, my first instinct was to look for Dad's smiling face, and when I remembered he didn't show up today, it was like a gut punch all over again.

The winning doesn't matter; I reminded myself. I just need the money.

I was so out of it I didn't even see Cade finish, and by the time I look around for him, I'm swept up in the small crowd of people trying to congratulate me. Winning the money means nothing if I don't have him. Realistically, I know he's here somewhere, but the fact that I can't see him makes a weird, indistinct fear lodge in my throat.

Losing Cade somehow seems like an ever-present threat that I can't escape. It's a sword hanging over me, waiting to fall. I just need to find him, so I can reassure myself that he's okay and walk back the irrational rush of panic that's threatening to take over my brain.

I swipe my gaze methodically over every inch of the space until I spot that stupid hot pink jersey in the throng.

When I see who he's standing next to, my pulse spikes. There's no thought of whether I'm being rude as I push away from the people talking at me to rush over to him. I'm shoving through the crowd dramatically enough that both he and Tristan look startled at my approach.

"What is it? What happened?"

There's no disguising the panic in my voice. Cade and Tristan are friends, sure, but there's no way he would have skipped seeing me at the finish unless he went to Tristan for an injury.

Tristan's wide eyes quickly narrow as he takes me in. We've only met a few times and I've never gotten the impression that he likes me that much. There's always been a coolness there. He's a little taller than me and just as broad-shouldered, but with about a thousand times more real-world toughness. Whenever he squares up to me, I get a distinct vibe that he wouldn't mind murdering me if he had the right motivation.

It has taken all my self-control not to obsess over the idea that he's secretly in love with Cade. Because there could be a million reasons not to like me. I'm not that likable. I have a lifetime of evidence for that. It could have nothing to do with Cade.

But the way he subtly shifts his body towards his friend as he looks me up and down, making me feel like a lunatic with the dramatic way I just burst through the crowd so hard I'm still out of breath, makes me feel like I'm something he just stepped in.

Like I'm something dangerous that he needs to protect Cade from.

Or maybe I've finally become unhinged, and all of this is in my head.

"Good ride, baby," Cade says, and both his voice and the rare public use of the endearment pull my attention back to him. He's perched on a stack of beer crates, and reaches out with his right hand to grab my jersey sleeve and tug me into his side. I move closer and he slides that arm around my waist, splaying his hand over my hip.

It's intimate and possessive and mollifies me a little. Even if it's a lot more intimate than we'd normally be in this setting. The fear I felt when he reached for me before the race is gone; burnt out by the irrational worst-case scenarios that have been throbbing through my consciousness like a fever-dream for the last ten minutes.

Cade's movement also draws my attention to his left hand, which is propped up on the edge of the crate. Tristan is slowly wrapping tape around two of his fingers.

"What happened?" I want to snatch his hand away from Tristan, but I have enough self-control not to act completely crazy. Mostly.

The medic, of course, is watching the whole interaction with that piercing gaze of his. Like he knows every embarrassing impulse I've ever had and isn't impressed that I manage to suppress some of them. Cade's the one that answers my question, while Tristan continues to glower.

"It's fine. I jammed it into the hand guard when I landed weird and I think it's sprained. I just wanted to get it taped before it started to swell. I'll be all patched up and ready to go in a couple of minutes."

His fingers dig into my side, grounding me, even though I feel my brain spiraling with an unnecessary series of worst-case scenarios.

The conversation we had last night comes screaming back into my mind. This is a dangerous sport. What if Cade got hurt and I was too busy with my own race to notice? Or worse, what if I caused an accident that hurt him?

I'm trying to breathe, but it feels like the air keeps getting stuck in my throat.

That was what he accused me of that first race, after all. Being reckless and putting him in danger. Dad always said I liked to drag people down with me. Maybe being around me is dangerous for Cade in more ways than one.

"Silas?"

His voice and the bite of his fingers into my side brings me back into the present. Soft gray eyes are looking into mine, and I feel more raw and exposed than I want to. A choked feeling threatens to overtake me, and I know it's rude not to say anything, but all the possible words are like a messy spiral and I can't pick out the right ones to force out of my mouth.

Cade catches my eye again and speaks a little more forcefully. "Hey, do you think you could load up my bike for me while I finish up here? And I'll meet you at Ford's?"

Ford lets us store our bikes there as well as work on them now. Which is really fucking nice of him and makes it significantly less likely that any of our blood relatives will steal them in the middle of the night.

I nod, swallowing around the inexplicable lump in my throat. At least that's a task I can focus on and accomplish.

God, why do I feel so fucking scattered?

Everything is fine.

All I need is a few more wins, and then I can ask Cade to move in with me. In our own place. With both our incomes and no parents skimming off the top. We can stop racing for good and I won't have to worry about either of us breaking our necks on the tracks.

Then I can also stop running around like a crazy person and Tristan can keep his dirty looks to himself.

"He's a big boy. He'll be fine without you," Tristan says, not trying to hide the edge to his tone.

Yeah, the sooner we can get into our own place, the sooner all these other problems and all my consuming thoughts will go away. Simple.

By the time Cade gets to the shop, I've already got my bike unloaded and put away. I was able to shower most of the grime off myself back at the track, so I'm more-or-less clean, dressed in sweats and a t-shirt, pacing across the shop floor as I wait for him.

Today was fine. Dad didn't show up, but that's something I should get used to.

I won the race and got more money for the house deposit fund.

Cade got hurt, but it wasn't anything serious, and his friend was there to patch him up.

Now we have the rest of the day to spend together.

There's absolutely nothing wrong. There's no reason for this mounting sense of dread that's spreading through me, sinking its fingers into my rib cage and threatening to shake me until I scream.

Something terrible is going to happen. I just don't know what it is yet.

The clatter of the roller door opening snaps my attention back to reality. Cade is standing there, also dressed in soft sweats and a hoodie. His hair is still wet from the shower and he's got a gentle smile on his face—a smile just for me—that eases some of the tension that was threatening to choke me earlier. Behind him, the sunset spreads across the horizon like a bloodstain.

I blink against the red-tinged glare, making Cade's silhouette fragment and multiply until it's superimposed over everything else.

"Hey," he says. "Help me with my bike."

We don't talk much as I unload it for him, but my gaze keeps straying to the tape on his fingers and I know he clocks it. He's watching me with a soft expression, but there's concern there. Which only confirms that I'm acting as weird and spun out as I feel.

Once everything's put away, I expect Cade to try to drag an explanation out of me. What I don't expect is for him to grab my shirt front and march me backwards until my back hits the wall hard enough to knock the wind out of me.

I barely catch my breath before he's kissing me deep and dirty enough to take it away again.

When we finally break for air, our bodies are pressed flush, with all of his weight leaning me into the wall and his half-hard cock digging into my hip. He only pulls back a couple of inches from me, enough so we're still sharing breath and there's nowhere for me to escape his gaze as he pins me under it.

"What was going on today? In your head?"

I could play dumb, but there would be no point. Cade and I both know that my behavior was weirder than usual.

"I don't know. I don't know what's wrong with me."

There's a pause as Cade takes a deep breath, in and out, and the silence feels like it's crushing both of us. Cade never stops staring at me, and I hold on to that like a lifeline.

"Were you upset that your dad didn't show up?"

"No."

It's not technically a lie. Upset isn't the word I'd use, anyway.

Cade squints, and I feel like a puzzle he's trying to solve.

"Were you jealous of Tristan?"

Now I squirm, because that's much more embarrassing, and closer to the truth.

"I don't know," I say. "I don't like it when you're hurt. But I also don't like it when he touches you. It's not about how hot he is, it's just about him being not me. It all ties together and makes me feel...something. It's hard to pick apart how much of it is rational and how much of it isn't."

245

Cade hums like that makes sense, even though it very obviously doesn't.

"I know we don't talk a lot about whatever *this* is." I try not to hold my breath, as a tiny voice in my brain tells me this is it, this is the moment that Cade tells me I'm too crazy and he's over it. "But you know I'm yours, right?"

Fuck. I did not know that.

"I like that you're protective of me. It's new for me. I might actually like it too much." He chuckles to himself, continuing to advance on me like I'm a meal he's about to devour. "But there's no reason for you to be jealous, okay?"

As he speaks, his hand moves to cover my crotch. Just the proximity of him had been sending my blood rushing south, and it doesn't take long before I'm fully hard in his hand.

Cade sinks to his knees, using his uninjured hand to pull down my sweats and free my cock. Which only reminds me he's hurt, and whether or not I'm horny for him should be the last thing he's worried about.

"Cade, your hand. Don't-"

"Shh," he interrupts me, leaning forward to lick the crown and pulling an involuntary shudder out of me. "I don't need my hand for you to use my mouth. Show me who I belong to, baby."

His eyes are wide and his cheeks are flushed as he looks up at me. The sight of him on his knees for me, so open and trusting, does something to me that I can't describe. One of my hands cups the back of his head to hold him in place, my thumb stroking over the soft skin of his cheek. I start out slow, pushing between his lips into the wet, welcoming heat of his mouth, biting back a groan at the sensation.

Cade's tongue runs over my shaft as I move, as if he's desperate to taste every inch of me. His fingers, except for the injured ones that stick awkwardly to the side, dig into my thighs. Desperation is rolling off him in waves, and it's feeding into my own desperation in an endless loop.

My breath is heavy, and before I even realize it, I've gone from gently sliding in and out of his mouth to thrusting. I'm pushing in hard enough that the head of my cock is nudging the back of his throat with every thrust, and it's drawing these choked sounds out of him that make my balls draw up. I can feel my heartbeat in my throat. It feels like every inch of me is being buried into Cade's mouth right now, and I only want more.

The room is filled with the sick sounds of it: my heavy grunts over his wet choking. Tears are streaming down his face and there's spit and precum hanging from his chin in strings that should repulse me. Instead, I reach out with my free hand and smear that spit across his face, making his red, blotchy skin shine with it.

His fingers are still gripping onto my thighs for dear life. Every point of contact between us, however small, feels electric. It's the only reason I notice when one of his hands slips off my leg, reaching down to his own crotch. I can see a fucking wet patch over his hard cock—screaming evidence of how turned on he is right now—and it makes me feel feral.

This is where we belong. This is because he belongs to me. Covered in me. Filled with me. Tasting and smelling and drowning in me until we're so tightly woven together that no one can break through that connection to hurt either of us ever again.

Cade groans, his body tensing, and the wet patch between his legs darkens and spreads.

I lose control.

With a growl, I thread my fingers through his hair and hold him tight, shoving myself deeper into his throat than I thought was possible. His throat spasms and constricts around me like he's begging me to stay there, and the sound of his choking reaches a fever pitch. I fall over the edge with him, unloading down his throat, watching his face darken as he struggles for air.

There's a moment where I feel so sated I could collapse. All that restless anxiety that's been pulling me around today finally quiets. Knowing that Cade is going to be walking around coated with me, inside and out, sets me at ease.

But then reality sets in.

I jerk back, pulling my still-hard cock out of his mouth so quickly I wince as I catch a snag of teeth. But he needs fucking oxygen.

Cade takes huge, gulping breaths. His chest rises and falls, the air moving in and out with a wet sound that set my blood on fire a second ago, but now turns my stomach.

I can't believe I just had the best orgasm of my entire life by choking Cade half to death. He looks fucking destroyed, and even now, the sight of his wrecked, spit-and-cum slick face and swollen lips is making my cock twitch.

He can't even talk. He's still trying to catch his breath, swaying on his knees, looking up at me with heavy-lidded eyes.

All because I needed to... To what? To claim him?

Maybe I really am toxic.

The thought hits my stomach like a stone, and for once I welcome the numbness as it spreads through my mind.

CHAPTER THIRTY-ONE

CADE

When Silas steps back and his cock slips from my mouth, I sway like I'm fucking drunk on him. He's everywhere; the taste of him, the scent of him, the heat of him. All of it surrounds me like a warm blanket and I feel like I could float away.

I take my time, catching my breath and letting the world come back into focus as my blood refuels with oxygen. That was intense, but in the best possible way. Something about the contrast between the gentle hold he kept on my neck with the ferocious way he fucked my throat had me lit up from the inside, and if I could have talked, I would have begged and screamed for more.

He was surrounding me, possessing me so completely I felt like I ceased to exist. It was the most freeing thing I've ever experienced. I was floating there, wrapped around him, and Silas was my one tether to the Earth.

Now that I'm coming back down, sensation and reality are trickling back into my body. My knees ache from kneeling on the cold concrete floor, my sprained finger throbs because I was not delicate once I started scrabbling at Silas' meaty quads for balance, and my throat feels like I swallowed broken glass.

But it was totally worth it. My veins are effervescing with arousal and something more intense than just affection for this man who's come to own me, inside and out.

I look down, and realize from the wet patch on my sweatpants that I barely even noticed rubbing one out as I let him use me, I was so fucking turned on.

"That's it," I say, ignoring the dreamy, far-away tone of my voice that contrasts with how rough it is from the abuse my throat just took. Silas looks down at me sharply. "No one has ever done sex as good as we do sex. We sex the best. Sex champions."

Okay, I may be a little dickmatized, but I'm alright with that. It was incredible.

Silas doesn't laugh, though. Instead, he gives me more of the intense, worried looks he's been giving me all afternoon, and I hate it. Reaching down, he grabs me by both arms to pull me to my feet, and I take the opportunity to smooth out that ever-present furrow between his eyebrows. He's still breathing hard, even though he's not the one that just got choked out. In fact, his breathing seems to be getting faster since we finished, instead of catching his breath and coming down like you'd expect.

"Why are you frowning, robot boy? Nothing's wrong."

Silas doesn't say anything, and the first flicker of doubt creeps in, invading the wave of bliss that I was riding. Obviously, something is wrong, and he's just not telling me.

But he takes my face in both hands, like he always does, and kisses me like I'm something soft and precious and delicate. The effervescence returns in full-force, and I'm tempted to fall back down on my knees to show how much I adore this weird, awkward guy that has ended up in my life.

Nah, nothing's wrong.

He'd tell me if something was wrong.

"So, did you enjoy your spanking last night?"

I turn to Tristan, my confusion clearly written on my face. He's driving us on the way to our next call—low priority, so no lights or sirens—and the streetlamps are casting deep shadows over his face that make him look even more menacing than usual.

"What the fuck?"

"I can only assume that after that little display at the race, your *daddy* turned you over his knee and spanked you for being in contact with a man without his permission. That's what all his glaring was about, no? He looked at me like he wanted to relieve me of my spleen."

I don't know whether to laugh or smack him upside the head, so I settle on neither.

"No, dude. And please don't overreact. I have enough of that in my life."

"I wonder who from."

"Can it." I'm snapping at him, but I don't care. "He had a bad day, and he got upset when he realized I was hurt. Emotional regulation isn't always easy for him and sometimes he overreacts, but there are no spankings or weird control issues, if that's what you're implying."

Tristan sighs. The severity of his expression almost makes me wish he'd go back to the mortifying 'daddy' jokes, because I don't think I'm going to like whatever he's about to say.

"I'm not implying anything. I'm saying straight up that you two have gotten really close, really fast, and it doesn't always seem like a good thing. Five minutes ago, you were swearing on your life that you were straight and you guys were just friends. And I'm happy you figured that out, honestly. But the second you admitted you were into each other, it was like boom—married. Your life has become his life."

"Yeah, because his life fucking sucked. Have some compassion, man. He was all alone for so long."

Tristan softens, which is already unlike him, and his words come out almost painfully empathetic. He is clearly using his entire year's supply of empathy on this conversation, which makes me feel very fucking concerned.

"That's what I'm saying, Cade. He jumped from whatever shitty situation he was in to completely throwing himself into your life with zero in-between. Doesn't that worry you? You're a medical professional. Please do me the courtesy of not lying and saying he doesn't have glaring signs of mental health issues. That shit doesn't just go away because you fall in love."

I twitch at his use of the "L" word, because it feels like something that's way too close and way too far away at the same time.

It's not something we've brought up, and I'll be damned if I do it first. We haven't even officially said if we're boyfriends or whatever. Because boyfriends makes me feel like I'm back in grade school.

"I take your silence to mean you know I'm right, as usual, but you don't want to admit it. Also, as usual."

Something about the way he's ping-ponging between compassion and snark really pisses me off. Since when did it become open season on the ins and outs of my love life? I grit my teeth as the familiar surge of anger and adrenaline threatens to take me over, tightening its grip on my chest until it can wield me like a puppet.

I can't stop myself from arguing back. "I mean, he's got problems, sure. But who doesn't around here? I do. You sure as shit do, Captain PTSD, and I don't see you going to therapy on your days off."

The look Tristan gives me makes me feel like a piece of shit, and a lot of that anger fizzles out as quickly as it flared up. That was such a shitty thing to say.

"I'm sorry, I shouldn't-"

"First of all, it's Sergeant PTSD, fuck you very much. And second of all, don't pretend you can tear yourself away from Dirt Bike Ken and his magic dick long enough to know what I do on my days off."

We continue to stare at each other, the pain and offense hanging between us like a live wire. I still feel like a piece of shit.

"I'm sorry, Tristan. That was a shitty thing to say." This time he at least lets me get all the words out. He nods in acknowledgement and considers what he wants to say next.

"It was. And it still didn't throw me off your scent. I think you know me well enough to trust that I've seen a lot of shit, and I know how insidious said shit can be. Especially when you hinge your happiness on the idea that one job or one relationship or one whatever is the thing that will let you brush all that shit under the rug. If you care about him as much as the fucking heart eyes you're always giving him say you do, then I want you guys to be happy. So, all I'm saying is don't get so wrapped up in the fun parts that you both forget to sort out your shit. Separately. Or this weird jealousy is only going to get worse."

He takes a deep breath and studies me a while, his eyes flicking between me and the road. I get the feeling he's not finished with whatever wisdom he's doling out, and I've been bratty enough so far, so I keep my mouth shut.

Eventually, he continues. "Even before you got together, he looked at you like you were the only thing in the room. That kind of attention can go to your head. Especially for someone who's always been shortchanged in that department. That feeling can get addictive. But there's a fine line between being intense and being toxic, and you guys seem intent on fucking all the way over it."

More silence. What the fuck am I supposed to say to that? I love that Silas looks at me like he's desperate to keep me close all the time. I'm pretty sure if he didn't, I'd be spinning out all the time, wallowing in my own insecurities.

Maybe that's toxic. Or maybe that's just all our psychological damage complimenting each other.

I chew on my lip, turning his words over in his mind as we pull up to our destination. I switch on the lights to make ourselves known and hop out of the cab. What Tristan said bothered me enough that there's probably a lot of truth to it, but I don't have time for introspection right now.

All thoughts of Silas get shoved to the back of my brain as I pull down the shutter and switch my brain into work mode.

"He's over here." Rolla is already walking out of the front to meet us, with a pissy expression on her face.

"Are you the one who called it in?" Tristan asks.

"Yeah, I called. He's been here every night this week, drinking himself into the ground, but he can normally drag himself out of here. Tonight he made it as far as the parking lot and now he refuses to get up. I didn't wanna call the cops on him, though."

As she talks, she leads us around the one story building that houses the bar and pool hall, The Last Glass, which is popular among the residents of Possum Hollow mostly because it's the only bar you can go to without having to leave town. I don't need to be led, and neither does Tristan, because we've been called out here for bar fights and overdoses on more than one occasion, but Rolla is polite and I love that about her.

What we find in the back is what I expected; a figure slumped against the dumpster, semi-conscious and sitting in a puddle of his own vomit.

What I am surprised to see is that it's Travis Rush.

"Shit," I mutter under my breath, pulling Tristan's attention to me as he keeps walking over. All he does is raise his eyebrows, and I know I have to spill. Silas will be embarrassed, but he's going to find out eventually, so I might as well save us the time so we can focus on his care. "It's Silas' dad."

Tristan's eyebrows shoot sky-high, but he doesn't say anything about it as he crouches next to him to take vitals.

I kneel down in front, getting in Travis' face and checking to see how conscious he is.

"Sir, can you hear me? Do you know your name?"

"Travis." His eyes stay closed and his voice is rough, but at least he got that right.

"That's right, Travis. Do you know where you are?"

"The bar." Bloodshot eyes open and take me in, slowly but steadily focusing on my face. "I know you," he slurs.

"Yeah you do, good job. Can you remember my name?"

Although I've avoided him since he came back to town, and as far as I know, he's still in the dark about what me and Silas really mean to each other, he has seen me a couple of times in passing.

Tristan continues to take vitals and jot everything down while I ask him questions and keep him focused.

"You're the Waters boy. Your daddy's a scumbag."

Pot, kettle, but sure. Whatever.

"I won't argue with you on that, sir. How much have you had to drink tonight?"

He waves me off, and it's a weird, terrifying echo of how Silas looked when I was trying to patch up his hand while he was upset with me. I never really realized how similar they look. Mostly because I avoid looking at Travis so I don't get overwhelmed with seething hatred, but there are more similarities than I thought.

One of the only things Silas has said about his mom is that he looks like her, not Travis. Right now, taking in his wiry build and pale blue eyes, that sounds about right. But there are little things that connect them. Silas has the same nose as him, narrow and straight with a little dusting of freckles across the bridge. He also has the exact same set to his jaw when he's being stubborn.

"You're pretty dehydrated, Mr. Rush, how would you feel about coming with us to the hospital for some fluids?"

Tristan's voice makes me realize how long I must have paused for, lost in my thoughts.

"Pssht, I'm not going to a hospital. I'm fine." He struggles to his feet, unsteady but at least not blacking out. Tristan and I manage to get him back to the ground, but he snatches his arms away from us as soon as he's seated.

We go back and forth for a few minutes, but the old man isn't budging on the hospital front, and the more we talk, the more coherent he seems. I pull Tristan away for a sidebar.

"What do you think?"

"He's definitely shit-faced, but he's alert and oriented, so we can't take him involuntarily. If he wants to AMA out, he can. I just don't want him to try to drive. Or wander down the highway until he meets a big rig, face first. Do you think your boy would come get him?"

I hate the idea of waking Silas up to come deal with his dad in this state, but it might be the best option. Ubers don't exactly hang around these parts in the middle of the night.

"Yeah, let's try."

We have him sign that he's staying here against medical advice and I send Rolla back inside, telling her to make sure no one serves him again tonight, which makes her snort. I also make sure she has his car keys tucked safely behind the bar so he doesn't get any dumb ideas while he's waiting for his ride.

"Can I call Silas to come give you a ride, Travis?" I ask once everything else is settled.

I expect a lazy nod or possibly more childish defiance. I don't expect the raw anguish that takes over his face.

"Silas is a ghost. You can't call the dead."

Tristan and I are left gawking at each other.

"Cade, do you know what he's talking about?"

"I have no fucking idea."

Drunk people say a lot of shit, but this is weirder than anything I've heard before. I try to gently prompt him a couple more times, but all it does is make him more and more agitated, spilling incoherent things about Silas and ghosts and death, over and over. The fact that I spoke with Silas a few hours ago, before he went to sleep, is the only thing allowing me to stay rational and not worry that something fucking unthinkable has happened tonight.

It doesn't stop the pit of *what if* from weighing down my stomach, though. If something happened to Silas, I wouldn't be called. I'm not his family. I shove the thought away, along with all the other troubling shit that's invaded my mind tonight, and focus on the task at hand.

I don't know what Travis is talking about, but it's clear that if Silas shows up right now, he's going to lose his shit and make everything a hell of a lot worse. And possibly say some shit to Silas that will haunt his nightmares forever.

"Fuck." I run my hands through my hair, trying to think, before eventually turning to Tristan. "Okay, it's almost midnight. Let's go back to the station, leave him here with Rolla, and then when we clock out, I'll come back as a civilian and drag him home in my truck. Professionally my hands are tied, but as his son's very pissed-off...whatever—" Tristan smirks when I equivocate over what word to use. "I have no issue hog-tying him in the back of my truck and dragging his ass back to town. Hopefully, he'll pass out on the drive so we can get through the whole thing without waking Silas up and pulling him into this shit."

Tristan nods. His arms are crossed over his chest, drawing attention to how fucking wide he is, and there's a hint of a murderous expression in his eyes. Tristan's always been a question mark in my life. There's a lot I don't know about him or what he's capable of. But times like this make me damn glad that he has my back.

"I'll come with you, in case he puts up a fight."

I want to object, but to be honest, I probably need the help. I just want to get through this without Silas knowing. So instead, I sag with gratitude.

"Thank you."

He claps me on the shoulder with one strong hand. "Thank me by thinking about what I said before. I also accept sports cars."

CHAPTER THIRTY-TWO

SILAS

I'm woken up by the sound of a crash downstairs, followed by muffled cursing. At first, I assume it's Dad finally dragging himself home, until I hear a familiar voice.

Cade?

Hauling myself off my mattress and rubbing the sleep from my eyes, I rush downstairs to see what's going on. I'm only wearing sweats, but if someone's breaking in, they can murder me shirtless.

It's still dark downstairs, but there's enough light coming in from the porch to show Cade and a slightly bulkier figure—Tristan, if I had to guess—dragging a third person into the entryway.

"Dad?"

Cade and Tristan both look up at me, but Dad remains slumped between them. The naked pity on both of their faces is something I'd love to never, ever see again.

"Hey, baby," Cade says in that soft voice he uses when he's worried about me. I don't know why he's being so delicate with me, but the use of the endearment has me flushing crimson, anyway. Hopefully, it's too dark for Tristan to notice.

"What happened?"

"He got a little too sauced out at The Last Glass, but he wouldn't let us take him to the hospital," Tristan says, still in professional mode while Cade watches me with sad eyes. "Cade said you had work in the morning so we thought we could pick him up when our shift finished and bring him home, save him from waking you up to get a ride."

It makes sense, but there's a shifty energy between them that makes me think that's not the whole story.

Knowing Dad, it never is.

Numbness sinks into me as I walk down the stairs, my steps heavy, and help them drag him in and deposit him on the couch. I turn to face them both, awkwardness hovering over the room like a cloud.

"Thanks, guys. I appreciate it. You should go home and get some sleep."

Cade looks at me, with his head cocked to the side like a German Shepherd. I know I'm being weird and formal with him right now, but I can't let him come any closer. I feel like if I do, I'll crumble.

When he speaks, his tone is low and intimate, and he's stepping towards me. It sets off every warning bell I have. I want him to get away from Dad as quickly as possible, as if the Rush-family bad luck could rub off on him just by standing too close.

"Silas, I can stay and help. You don't need to deal with this shit alone."

I take a step back, out of his reach, and pretend I don't see his face fall. Tristan is watching the whole exchange with his eagle eye, and for a fraction of a second, I want to punch him in his stupid, expressionless face.

"It's fine. He'll sleep for the rest of the night, no big deal. And you're right, I have to get up early. You should go home and check on the girls."

My voice sounds distant and tinny to my ears. The world is kaleidoscoping in and out of focus. I'm trying to maintain the mask of being normal, but it feels like all the cracks in that mask are showing and my crazy is leaking out of them.

It only makes me shut down even more. I'm sure Cade would say I was peak-robot right now, if his feelings weren't so hurt.

That's a problem for future Silas.

"Okay," he says, shrinking away. "Call me if you need me, I guess."

He and Tristan exchange a meaningful look before they turn to go, but I can't figure out what it means because I'm too busy focusing on how to breathe.

In and out. Stand up straight. Normal, neutral expression.

It feels like my blood has been replaced with motor oil, thick and sludgy, dragging all my limbs down to the ground.

I walk them to the door, and Cade kisses me briefly before they go. Even though I kiss him back, it does nothing to wipe the concern from his face.

He's so worried about me. He's so fucking good, down to his bones. I could live a thousand lives and I would never deserve someone as good and vibrant and alive as he is.

When the door closes, there's an air of finality to it, and I can breathe again. In here, it may be dank and miserable, but at least I know what to expect.

I go through the motions of taking care of Dad. I prop him up on his side with a pillow so he doesn't choke on his own vomit in his sleep, putting a bucket near him in the hope that he'll find it. I leave water and aspirin within his reach.

I'm about to head back to my room when I hear him moving. As I turn around, the moon illuminates Dad's face in a cold white light. He looks like a hunter crouched among the bushes, watching me with the same predatory intensity he used to save for race days.

Usually, the drunker he gets, the louder he gets. This is the kind of focused quiet that steals the breath from my lungs in the worst possible way. I freeze, like a rabbit in his sight line.

"Come here." He's quiet, but his voice seems to boom across the room to reach me, anyway.

The obedience he's carved into me moves my arms and legs without my consent, and before I know it, I'm sitting on the carpet in front of him. My knees are tucked up in front of me like a child, and I feel smaller and more fragile than ever as he looks me over.

When his fingers reach out to rest on my knee, I manage not to flinch. I don't know why I want to, anyway. It's not like he's ever truly hurt me.

"I don't want you to worry, Silas," he says, as if I have any idea what he's talking about. "I know this has been bad for you. You're too much like your mother. I won't let you keep rattling around this house, getting crazier and crazier."

He pauses, and I don't know what to say. There are a million things. I want to ask him why it always sounds like he blames Mom for how she was whenever he talks about it, as if it was something she could control. But thinking about it brings back these fragments of memories that make me feel like a scared little kid again, which makes me want to beg him to keep protecting me and never stop.

Instead, I don't say anything. Like always.

His rough fingers wrap around my wrist, squeezing it tight enough to burn, and the sensation makes my throat feel thick. I swallow hard, but still can't find the right words. When I force myself to look him in the eye, I can see tears there, waiting to fall.

In these rare moments of honesty, it feels like I have at least one of my parents back, and I want to cling to it.

"I promised I would protect you, remember? I'll take you far away again, where she can't get to you," he says. His words are a slur, and his fingers are clumsy as he brings them up to jab at the side of my head. As if Mom is somehow pulling the strings in my fucked-up brain from beyond the grave. "It'll be just like before. I only need a little more time. I know you don't always like me, but I've kept you safe. I won't let her ruin your life like she ruined mine."

Like she ruined mine.

The words echo through me like a pulse. I know he's cracked when he talks about how being here is making me more like her. That's drunken hyperbole, and I ignore it, as usual.

But he's not wrong about the fact that I'm like her. Probably in more ways than I know. I have no idea what he sees when he looks at me, and the thought makes me shudder.

What's worse is the image of Cade in twenty years, lying on this couch in my dad's place, mourning a life wasted spent trying to love someone who's too fucked-up to be loved. Poisoning yourself in the process, until both of you wither on the vine and die.

At least Dad's disaster of a life isn't my fault. I did my best to live up to what he wanted for me, and to pay him back for everything he sacrificed to keep me alive. I may have let him down a lot, but I've tried.

It's not too late for Cade to dodge that bullet.

"I know, Dad." I let myself lay my head on his hand where he still clutches at me. I wait for the usual numbness to take me over, but this time the numbness is outpaced by despair. My stomach twists and my skin feels cold and clammy, like a corpse. Every cell in my body throbs in pain at the thought of losing Cade, but I can't deny what's right in front of my eyes. I can't let Cade suffer through all of this.

I'm able to blink back most of the tears, but one escapes and rolls down Dad's weathered skin where it presses against my face. "Thank you," I say. I really mean it.

"You were so small," he whispers, his voice trailing off as sleep tugs at him. "You weren't even crying. Like a little corpse. You never cried after, either. Silas, my little ghost."

He finally drifts off. I want to cry properly, to prove him wrong. I want to scream and wail and let out the pulsing knot of emotion that's lodged in my throat, until I can figure out what I did to deserve this. But apart from that one tear, nothing else comes out.

His words have eaten through my insides, leaving a husk behind. I sit there for a long time, listening to him breathe.

Of all the memories that have been clambering through my consciousness the past few days, there are some I've kept locked up. The edges of those memories are scratching at my brain now. They're begging to be let in.

Maybe I should let them in. I tried to move on from the past, and the past continued to chase me, making me feel crazy and causing chaos in Cade's life. Maybe if I give into it, whatever is going to happen will finally happen. Losing Cade might kill me, even if it's for the best.

At least it'll be over with.

CHAPTER THIRTY-THREE

CADE

Everything that happened yesterday has fucking haunted me. I couldn't sleep, thinking about how Silas looked as he helped us haul his dad's limp body into the living room.

Which makes me wonder how many times his dad has said the nasty, surreal shit he said to us earlier to Silas' face. I wonder if that's what taught him how to shut down.

He's always had ups and downs, but he's never felt so completely out of my reach before. Not even before we were so close. I could always get through to him with a touch or the right word, but last night it was like talking to a brick wall, and that's fucking terrifying.

And it's not like this was the only time. He was already shut down the day of the race, when his dad didn't show. I've been too caught up in the CPS Family Assessment and keeping a closer eye on the girls. Silas has been around, but I'm suddenly realizing I haven't really paid attention to him. It's possible a fuck ton of warning signs have been slipping through the cracks.

Tristan was right. There's more wrong than I realized, and as much as it fucking kills me to admit, maybe my loving Silas isn't enough to make all his pain go away.

Oh yeah, because that's the other thing I realized.

Somewhere around the fifth hour of lying in bed, obsessing about how to help Silas and playing out all these different hypothetical situations, I realized something. I kept thinking of everything in terms of *our lives*.

Together. Like the fact that we would deal with these things together was a given.

I was looking up how much therapy costs and thinking about how to convince him to go. I was planning contingencies for if he got worse and worse and needed legitimate medical help. I was trying to figure out how health insurance actually works and if we could get it. All of it was turning over and over in my mind, the same as if it were Maddi or Sky with the problem.

He's my family. I love him and I'm not going anywhere.

So his shit is my shit, and that means it's time to deal with it.

Together.

This revelation gave me a new burst of energy. Combine that with way too much caffeine, and I am now cracked out but ready to tackle the day. More importantly, I have a plan.

First, get Silas as far away from his toxic sperm donor as possible.

Second, evaluate how he is when he's not being dragged down by that asshole every day, and talk about options for addressing it.

Third, tell him I love him.

Today, we're only dealing with step one. And thank fuck, because step three is way scarier than it should be.

"Mom, can I talk to you?"

She's awake at a reasonable hour, smoking a cigarette while she puts on makeup for her shift slinging burgers at DQ. It's a new job, and she has to drive nearly two hours to Franklin because she's burned most of her bridges around here, but so far she seems to be taking it seriously, which is more than I could have hoped for.

I agreed to compromise on the smoking inside thing because she's been following the rest of the CPS safety plan to a T. She's been going to NA and AA like she's supposed to. I've seen no sign of drugs in this trailer, despite turning it upside down at least once a week, and even though I'm not convinced she's totally sober all the time, she's at least keeping it under control enough to be functional and present.

Which is more than I've ever gotten from her before.

"Sure, hun, what's up?"

Part of me wants to deliberately not ask permission. To prove that I'm in charge here and she fucked up too many times to deserve a vote. But I think the hospital was a wake-up call for her. She's never going to act like a real mom if I don't treat her like one sometimes.

"How would you feel if I asked Silas to move in with me? Here?"

She freezes, mascara wand in mid-air, and eyes me in the mirror.

"That's a big step. You sure you're ready for that?"

I nod, something settling in me as I do it. I'm used to bullshitting my way through a lot of situations, but in this case, it's not bullshit. This thing with Silas isn't going anywhere. I want to do whatever I can to make it work.

"Yep. I know there's not a lot of space, but he's gotta get away from his dad. And between the three of us, we could probably start saving up to move someplace that isn't thirty percent toothpaste, y'know? I... I love him. He belongs here with me."

She looks at me. I feel like she wants to say something, but she's holding back to not piss me off. That's another thing that's new with her, although it's the one new thing I'm not crazy about.

"Well, I think we both know I gave up the right to boss you around a long time ago, even if I don't always act like it. I never protected you like I should have when you were little; I was always too busy trying to make it to the next day in one piece." She sighs, looking me over one more time. "Maybe now's the time to make up for that. You do what you gotta do, and I'll back your play. Deal?"

"Thanks, Mom." I feel more emotional than I expected to, and I can tell from the shine in her eyes that she does, too. We're both comfortable with big, loud emotions like anger and grief, but this kind of quiet support feels unfamiliar. It's like an ill-fitting second skin, but it's not something I want to shrug off yet. When she reaches out to touch my face, I get a glimpse of some alternate reality where all the pain and trauma of her childhood didn't boil over and leak into mine, and we were happy.

Not that this is so bad. It was rough getting here, but right now I'm pretty happy with what I've got. And I think I'm doing a damn good job of giving Maddi and Sky a better chance at normalcy than me or Silas ever had.

"Thanks, Mom." I'm repeating myself, but I need her to know I really mean it.

"Of course, hun. I'll see you after work, okay?"

She leaves.

Now I just have to get Silas on board.

I decided to hold off on asking the girls how they felt about it until after I ask Silas, just in case he says no.

Not that I think he will. Even though there has been some tension between us lately, I know we're on the same page. That tension is coming from how miserable he is, and that misery is coming from Travis fucking Rush and his bullshit emotional abuse.

This will fix everything.

I know it.

When I approach Silas' house, I don't see Travis' truck out front, which I take as a good omen. Silas isn't expecting to see me until tomorrow night. I know this could wait, but I feel like I'll burst if I don't talk to him about it now.

Plus, the radio silence I've been getting from him via text is starting to freak me out.

Pulling into the driveway, I try not to trip over my own feet with nerves as I park, hop out of the cab and jog up to the front door. There's a long enough pause after I ring the doorbell that I think maybe Silas has gone out, but his truck is sitting in front of the garage and this isn't a 'go for a walk' kind of neighborhood.

Maybe he's napping.

I buzz again and give him a minute.

When the door finally opens, Silas looks worse than I had feared. His movements are sluggish, like I did just wake him up in the middle of the afternoon, and his eyes are dim. He looks at me like he's not sure if he's dreaming still.

"Cade? Did I know you were coming over?"

I had a plan. I was going to go in and then I had a whole speech sketched out with pros and cons and a long lead-in about why he should consider moving in with me, but how I wouldn't pressure him if he wasn't ready.

As soon as I see him looking so drawn and exhausted, my anxiety gets the better of me and the rational plan goes out the window. Instead, I word-vomit on him, right there on his doorstep.

"Move in with me."

He freezes, the look of shock on his face the only sign that he heard me.

"What?"

"Move in with me. Leave your dad and this fucking house behind. It's killing you, and watching it happen is killing me. I know the trailer is a shithole and comes with a lot of noise and drama attached, but I want you there. So do the girls. The first time you stayed there was to take care of me, and I was so grateful. Now I'm begging you to move back in so I can take care of you."

I want to tell him the rest of it, too. That this is meant to be the start of our life together. That we belong together, no matter who is taking care of who. That we're a family.

But those words are a lot harder to get out.

I expect him to look shocked, or maybe confused, but as I step closer to him and take his face in my hands, his expression crumbles into something closer to heartbroken.

It's only for a second, though. He pulls his neutral robot mask back in place before I have the chance to kiss the misery off his face.

"Cade, I can't."

"Don't say that. Whatever it is, we'll figure it out. I promise. You don't owe your dad shit. Please, baby, you belong with me. With us."

He takes my hands in his and gently pulls them away from his face.

"Cade, I'm leaving." I don't hear him. My breath hitches in my chest while my stomach bottoms out because Silas' words came at me too garbled to make sense. "I'm leaving town to restart my career. In Canada. Dad arranged everything with some friend that owes him a favor or something. He tried to tell me last night when he was drunk, but he wasn't making sense. Today he explained it for real. He wants to leave tomorrow."

"But we have plans tomorrow..." I say, like a dumbass. Like someone whose heart isn't tearing apart in their chest.

Silas exhales, and his body sags so much that for a second, I think he might collapse to the ground. When he looks back at me, his eyes are vacant. His mouth keeps moving as he speaks, but his voice is toneless and dead. It's like he's not even in there anymore. Like I'm looking at the husk that used to hold Silas, but the essence of him is gone.

"I'm sorry, Cade. I was going to tell you. Dad says we don't have much time."

Stepping into the doorway, I grab his shoulders hard enough to send him back a step. I want to shake him. I want to scream. I want to do anything that gets him to snap out of it and look like himself again, instead of this hollowed-out version that's about to blindly follow his dad to Canada and leave me alone forever.

"Silas, stop. This isn't what you want. You don't have to do anything he says, you can just stay here. Stay with me. Tell him no. I will help you tell him no. All he's ever done is make things harder for you and force you to do shit that you don't want to." I'm trying to stay calm, but his eyes are still glazed over and I can tell my words aren't penetrating whatever shell of numbness is wrapped around his brain right now.

I pull him into a hug, squeezing tight enough to hurt. When I speak again, the words come out in a sob. "Baby, please. Don't go. I can fix everything, as long as you stay. Don't leave me."

Silas pulls back and untangles himself from my arms. I can feel tears on my face, but I'm so far past caring about my dignity. All I need is for him to listen to me.

When he looks at me this time, I see a glimmer of the real Silas underneath all that blankness, and it almost gives me hope. Until he speaks.

"Look at me, Cade. You look after everyone in your life. You deserve so much more than getting saddled with me, too. Dad can—" He swallows hard, and I can see the blood rush to his face, like he's fighting off a surge of real emotion. "Dad knows how to handle me. You shouldn't have to."

I'm speechless. Of all the twisted up logic in the world, I don't understand how he convinced himself this is what I deserve.

I don't deserve to be abandoned by the person I would fucking die for.

My mouth opens to tell him as much, again and again until it gets through his thick skull, when we're interrupted. Travis is home, after all.

"What's going on, Silas?"

270

His voice makes my blood rush with anger, and adrenaline dumps into me so abruptly my fingers tingle with it. I see him saunter over, calm as anything, as if he isn't about to ruin his own son's life for the chance to squeeze a little more money out of him.

"You selfish, sadistic piece of shit," I hiss. "What the fuck did you say to him?"

Travis looks shocked, but not afraid of me, which is his first mistake. He comes to a stop a few feet away, looking both of us over, clearly taking in the sight of my tears and Silas' quiet distress.

"Silas, what does Kyle Waters' son want from you?"

Silas' eyes dart between us, but he stays silent. This would have been a difficult conversation under the best circumstances, let alone like this.

I don't care, though. I don't care about Silas wanting to keep things calm. I don't care about whatever sick sense of loyalty he still has to his father. All I care about is getting him as far away from Travis as I can.

Looking at him right now, I know that if he goes back to racing and being alone, he'll end up dead. Maybe it'll seem like an accident. Maybe he'll even think it's an accident when it happens. But he'll get more and more shut down until he's so detached from his life that he can't even protect it anymore. And I won't be there to stop him.

Anguish rushes through me in a searing wave as I accept the inevitability of it all. I cover my face in my hand for just a second while I bite back a sob. I have no control here. It's all fluttering just out of my reach, and no matter how fast I run, I can't catch up.

When my hand comes away from my face, the anguish is replaced by rage. If I can't stop this from happening, then anger is the only thing I have left. Before I realize what's happening, I've crossed the distance over to Travis, grabbed him by the shirt, and slammed him into the wall.

His breath comes out in a satisfying *whoosh*. He's caught so off-guard, he barely puts up a fight, and the animal in me is ready to pound him until his face is nothing but blood and gore.

I only get one punch in before Silas pulls me off him. I have all the physical advantages when it comes to fighting Travis, but Silas will always be stronger than me. He pins my arms to my side with his bulk, dragging me away from his dad while I kick and curse at him like a maniac.

"Cade, stop!" Silas pushes me a few feet away, putting himself between me and Travis, his arms outstretched. I can see Travis rubbing at his jaw, so I know I made contact. It's satisfying, but it's so much less than he deserves.

"Silas, please. Don't listen to him. He's the reason you can't go to a race without having a fucking panic attack. He's the one who got you banned in the first place. I'll leave him alone. Let's just go, please. You don't have to see him anymore. I'll take care of you. I promise. Please, Silas."

I'm begging. I'm begging and on the verge of crying again, but I don't care. I'll get down on my knees if I have to. I'll promise him anything if he lets me protect him from this.

But Silas' robotic, impassive mask is back in place. He won't even look at me when he speaks again, continuing to stand between me and his father.

"I need you to leave, Cade. Forget you ever knew me and go."

My heart wrenches as I turn around, but I'm out of options. Silas has been torn between his old life and the one I'm offering him for a while now, and he finally made his choice.

And I'm not it.

CHAPTER THIRTY-FOUR

SILAS

The devastation on Cade's face as he turns and runs away from me feels like the final nail in my coffin.

I always thought it was a fight between Dad and Cade for where my loyalties lie. But the last twenty-four hours have shown me that the only thing I'll ever be loyal to is my own fucked-up insecurities.

Knowing that doesn't change anything. Just because I know that there's something wrong with my brain doesn't mean I'm not right. All I do is cause problems for Cade and force him to clean up my messes. It's better that we get a clean break before he wastes any more of his energy trying to save me.

My old self—the self that excels at being numb and emotionless—takes over. I move around the house in a daze, mechanically packing up the house. It's not like we ever bothered to buy more furniture, so everything we own will still fit into Dad's truck. The numbness fills my head with white noise, helping me ignore the sound of Dad calling Cade and his family names while he ices his jaw.

He keeps up his running commentary all night, and I keep ignoring him. Instead of sleeping, I spend my last night in this house staring at the same water stain as always. It feels like I should have something profound to say. Maybe I should say goodbye to Mom. I'm too tired to think of anything good, though, so I stay quiet.

In the morning, I take a final look around the house that I grew up in while I wait for Dad to pull himself together. Hopefully, this time we won't come back. I don't think I could bear it.

Home. This is the place I've come closest to death. The idea of having a 'home' is almost laughable.

My family was fucked from the beginning. Dad was a hotshot rider and Mom was just another pit bunny. When they experienced Cade's worst nightmare and found out they were having me, they had a shotgun wedding and he set her up in the house he inherited from his own miserable, dead parents. Mom's parents were churchy. They didn't approve of her life to begin with, and apparently marrying a coked-out dirt bike rider was the last straw. I don't think she ever heard from them again.

Dad knocked her up, married her, and then left her here alone. She wasn't even from this state, so she didn't have any friends. It was just an empty house and a baby on the way that she didn't know how to take care of. All while he was off living his dream.

Even after I was born, he was barely around. It took him a long time to notice she was sick, I think. He calls it "baby blues" to this day, which is a very cute name for something that sounds like it destroys your mind from the inside out. When they first got together, she was the life of the party, according to Dad. She was non-stop energy and chaos. His wistful, liquor-fueled descriptions of her in those days kind of remind me of Cade.

Then I was born, and she just stopped. He told himself that all she needed was more time to adjust and went back on his tour.

Every time he came home, she would be more depressed, and he would tell her to pull herself together. Then her behavior became erratic. He's never given me the details, but I can fill in the blanks.

Still, he went back on tour.

After one road trip, he walked into the house and thought both of us were dead. It turned out we were both close, but still hanging on. He got us to the hospital, and then used his money and influence to make the whole thing go down on paper as a horrible accident.

That was what got him to stop touring and stay with us. Six years later, Mom finished what she started and took her own life, but Dad's presence is probably the only reason she didn't take me with her.

He's been making me pay for it ever since.

I should be more grateful. He saved my life once, and then he gave up his career to protect me. But after twenty years of constant reminders, he's made it feel less like gratitude and more like a punishment. He can't punish a dead woman, but I'm right in front of him.

My life has always been a bargaining chip to him. I'm used to it. It's not like he's the one who tried to kill me.

In my cursed family, love never entered into the equation.

All of that lives in this house. I was beginning to hope I could make new memories here with Cade, but that was a pipe dream. My family's shitty luck is too strong. All I can do is run as far away from him as possible before it smears over his life as well.

"Silas!"

Dad's trying to get my attention, obviously, which makes sense because I didn't even realize he was standing next to me.

"Yeah?"

His eyes are bright and clear. This is the first time I've seen him sober in a while, and the first time he's seemed happy in even longer than that. It should make me feel better about choosing to go with him, but I'm still too numb to feel anything.

Digging up so many old memories has woken up the child that cowers inside me; the one who is still frightened and alone and desperate for affection. That's dangerous. Filling myself with numbness is the only way to escape.

He keeps talking, oblivious to my growing internal void. "How much do you think your creepy boss would give you for your truck? There's no point in paying for twice the amount of gas all the way to Canada, and we need the cash. My buddy is confident he can fast track your Canadian motocross license application, but it still might be a minute before we've got winnings coming in."

"Um..."

I think about the intense feeling of pride and warmth and *home* that I felt the day Cade and I picked out that truck. I think about taking Cassidy home in it, and how it put things in perspective and showed me how I felt about Cade. I remember taking him and the girls into the city after their dad tore through town. Cade was bruised and hungover and slept the whole way there, while the girls slowly relaxed the farther we got from the trailer, until it all felt like it was just a bad dream.

I love that truck.

Maybe it is best if we sell it. My head is spinning, and the cleaner the break, the easier it'll be to keep myself from crawling back to Cade and begging him to forgive me.

I love him. That's why I'm leaving, and that's what I need to keep reminding myself. I'm doing this for him.

"I'll ask, Dad," I answer, as he's still staring at me.

"Good. We've got the money from last weekend-" he continues to mutter to himself, working out how much cash he can squeeze out of everything I've earned in the past few months.

I had a decent amount saved for a house deposit. The Silas that saved that money was embarrassingly naïve, looking back now.

Pulling out my phone, I tell myself it doesn't sting that I don't have any missed calls or texts from Cade. This is exactly what I wanted.

A clean break.

CHAPTER THIRTY-FIVE

CADE

I don't know how many hours it's been since someone came out here to talk to me, but I thought they'd finally taken the hint. There's nothing to talk about. I want to be left alone. The sound of the screen door closing tells me that my brief window of solitude is drawing shut again.

Another empty soda can topples to the ground with a satisfying *ping*. I keep doing what I've been doing since yesterday: letting the sensations ground me, focusing on the tiny details of the present to keep a leash on my brain and not let myself think about how my life just fell apart.

The grass itches at my elbows, my skin prickling with irritation because I've been lying here too long. There's a glare reflecting off my remaining line of cans, letting me know that the sun is well and truly up for the day. The breeze carries the smell of the forest over to me, reminding me that I'm at home, and the weapon in my hand—pathetic as it is—is the one thing I can control.

Ping. Another can goes down.

Dirt and gravel crunches underfoot as whoever it is comes to a stop a few feet behind me.

"I thought you got rid of all the guns in the house after your dad left the first time?"

Wish. Mom must have called in reinforcements.

Ping. There are only two cans left, but I still don't feel any better so I'll have to scrounge up some more. There's a bottle of whiskey sitting next to me that's been burning a hole in my awareness for nearly twenty-four hours, and if I run out of things to shoot, there's nothing left to distract me from opening it.

"I did," I say, refusing to turn around and look at her. "I'm not a moron. This is just a BB gun. It can barely knock these cans over, let alone hurt someone." It's designed to look like a rifle, and pushing the stock into my shoulder while I squeeze the trigger brings back some of the only happy memories I have of spending time with my dad as a kid. The thought of getting rid of it hurt more than I want to admit.

I don't say any of that out loud, though.

There's a long pause while Wish works out what angle she's going to take, but I ignore her. I don't have the energy to fight with her about this.

"Kris called me. She said something about you asking Silas to move in, and now Silas isn't answering the phone and apparently you've been out here all night with a bottle of rotgut, popping cans and doing your finest impression of your father. She said you wouldn't even talk to the girls, Cade. She's really freaked out."

Still not looking at her, I pick up the bottle sitting beside me and wave it in the air.

"I haven't even cracked the seal. You can call off the hounds. I'm not hurting anyone."

With a deep sigh, Wish sinks down to take a seat next to me. She folds her legs underneath her, sitting close enough that I can feel her body heat, but not enough to touch me. Carefully, she picks up the bottle and moves it a little further away from me. As if that's any kind of deterrent.

"What happened?" she asks.

"I don't want to talk about it." *Ping.*

"Tough. It's either me, or I track Silas down and drag the answer out of him."

The idea of her looking for him and seeing his empty house makes my stomach cramp. All the hurt that I've been walling up inside my brain surges back, and I finally twist to look at her.

"Good luck. He's in fucking Canada. His dad decided they were moving, so they left. And I don't like that the only things I can think of to do right now are shoot and drink, but I didn't exactly have stellar role models in that department. I decided the fucking BB gun was the lesser of two evils, so I'm going to lie here and shoot cans until I don't want the fucking whiskey anymore, and if anyone mentions how much I look like Dad while I do it one more time, I'm going to fucking lose it, I swear to God." My breath is heaving by the time my rant comes to an end, and Wish is staring at me with wide eyes. It takes more effort than it ever has before to keep myself calm when I continue. "I'm fucking trying. Okay?"

Thinking about it, she eventually nods. Wish tears apart strands of grass while she stares into the distance, letting the silence settle over both of us as my anger ebbs.

Every time the wave of anger recedes, something like grief tries to push its way in, but I refuse to let it. I fight off both feelings with whatever numbness I can muster without chemical assistance, and turn my attention back to the last can.

Ping.

It stopped being satisfying a while ago.

Eventually, I'm the one that breaks the silence.

"I really thought we had a chance, Wish. I thought we were going to rise above all the shit we were born with and not turn into our parents." I laugh, but there's no humor in it. "And look at us now. I'm here, doing the same shit as Dad, and he's with Travis, doing the same shit as him. We were never going to be different. This is in our blood."

"The full bottle of whiskey here says otherwise, Cade," she says. "You're right. You are trying. It took a lot of strength to not drink yourself into a coma last night when you had every opportunity." Wish reaches out, running her fingers through my hair and pulling my attention to her eyes. "It probably doesn't feel like it, but I bet Silas is trying, too. After a lifetime of watching your mom, you know how impossible it can be to get away from someone who convinces you that their abuse is what you deserve. Anyone can see how much he loves you, just like we can see how his dad fucks with his head. Don't count him out just because he lost this one fight. Let him keep trying."

"From Canada?" I arch an eyebrow at her. This situation feels so closed, it might as well be welded shut.

Wish shakes her head at me, looking exasperated. "You have a phone, dollface. I know your heart is broken, but if he's the one still trapped in hell, isn't it worth rising above all that to remind him he's still loved?"

"Yeah, maybe." I start tearing out chunks of grass as well, turning away from her so she won't see whatever tortured expression I must be making at the thought. If I could rip Silas away from his old man, I would do it in a heartbeat. But he won't let me.

Wish stays for a while longer, sitting in silence. It's not normal for either of us, but this is the one time we've both run out of things to say. When she leaves, she kisses me on the head and takes the whiskey with her.

I'm grateful, because I was running out of reasons not to open it.

Pulling out my phone, I spend another half hour debating whether to send him a message, and then fuck-knows how long writing it. After I hit *send,* I try to picture his face as he reads it.

If I can't save him from Travis, at least I can leave him with a reminder that I want to. I can remind him that as far as I'm concerned, he deserves to be saved.

CHAPTER THIRTY-SIX

SILAS

We've barely driven past Mishicot, and the weight of everything that's happened already feels like it's crushing me into the passenger seat.

I thought we'd at least make it out of the county, if not the state, before I totally crumbled. But I can practically feel the will to live draining out of me like dirty bathwater. Looking out of the window, I stare at the remains of the high school that used to serve this district. They closed it because of a population drop in the nineties, I think, when they were saving money by merging some of the school districts together.

Which happened around the same time everyone and their mom started batch-cooking meth for a living. It doesn't take a high school diploma to figure out why the empty structure partially burned down soon after it was boarded up.

I guess the money it would take to clean it up is better spent elsewhere, because it's been sitting here on the edge of town for as long as I can remember. An old building, gutted by looters and half-charred, left to crumble slowly over the years until it falls back into the dirt. Like everything else around here.

The sound of Dad's voice droning on and on about Canada is an obnoxious buzz in my ear. I'm trying to shut it out, but it's persistent. I think going cold turkey is getting to him, because he's been sweaty and anxious for the last hour and will not shut the fuck up. My tongue feels thick, like my mouth is full of cotton, and my eyelids are heavy. Even the act of moving my eyeballs to look at the school seems to take a herculean effort, and by the time it's out of sight, I'm even more exhausted than before.

There's a more insistent buzz layered over Dad's voice, and the accompanying vibration draws my attention downwards. My phone's in my hand, the screen glowing with a notification.

CADE: New Message

My thumb shakes too hard for me to swipe properly, so it takes me a few tries. I don't know why.

> Silas. Don't let that asshole convince you that you're a burden. You're not. I know I joke around about saving you at the quarry, but you're the one that saved me. You're the strong one. My life was never better than it was with you in it. You're my hero, and I love you. Never forget it.

A complicated knot of emotions wraps itself around my heart, squeezing until there's no more space for it to beat. Time stands still, while the words sink into my numb brain. I've shut myself down to keep out all the memories of Mom and Dad and everything else I want to forget, but it's also kept out thoughts of Cade, and now they're worming their way back in.

I already miss the way he laughs at his own jokes, or gets way too excited about an idea that we'll never be able to actually do. I miss the quiet, knowing looks

283

that Maddi and I sometimes share when Cade and Sky are egging each other on in their ridiculousness. I miss the way everything in me settles when he falls asleep with his head on my chest.

Maybe this is a mistake.

"See, this is my point. Snap out of it." Dad's voice breaks through my thoughts, only because he also reaches across the center console to grab my shoulder and shake it. I snap my head to the side to see what he wants. "This is why you need to be on the road. All this lying around moping is no good; you're already halfway-catatonic. You're too much goddamn like her. That's why you need to win. It keeps you focused. If that fucking official I paid off had kept his word and not tested you, none of this would have happened. I'm not pulling you out of a bathtub full of blood, Silas. I fucking refuse."

The words spill out of his mouth like an oil slick, heavy and toxic. There's too much buried within them for me to pull out any one thing, so I settle for gawking at him, hoping he'll explain.

He doesn't, though. Instead, he pats my cheek in some rough approximation of parental affection. His eyes are red-rimmed, although I can't tell if it's from emotion, detox, or both.

"Everything's going to be just fine." I don't know who he's trying to convince, me or himself.

I turn it all over in my mind, one sentence at a time, until I figure out the question I want to ask.

"What do you mean, you paid someone off?"

Dad sighs, making the same face he does whenever he thinks I'm being childish or naïve. I've always hated it, and right now I feel like I might puke.

"It's fine. Everyone does it. You were having a bad run and I could see how down you were getting. I thought you needed a little boost, is all. If he hadn't tested your fucking fuel tank like he promised, none of this would have happened. You're a winner, like me. You just need a nudge once in a while to help you get out of your own head."

Cade was right. It really was all his fault, and I'm the idiot who gave him the benefit of the doubt. Closing my eyes, I try to ward off the throbbing in my temples, but it doesn't work. He just dumped too much information into my lap and my head feels like it's going to explode.

"You're telling me you actually cheated, because you think it was losing races that was making me depressed?"

His eyes dart between me and the road, then he shrugs, like it's no big deal. "It's not cheating! It was just a nudge. I told you I'd always take care of you, didn't I? I won't let you end up like her. I promised."

The throbbing intensifies. His logic is so twisted I have to fight the urge to choke him with it.

"So you cheated, because I needed to win, because if I didn't win I would get depressed and ultimately kill myself? Because I'm just like her. It's in my blood. And you're just the good man in the storm, holding back the tide of all that crazy with your bare hands, trying to save your family."

He blinks, looking confused. "We shouldn't talk about this. It's all in the past."

Ignoring him, I keep going. "And it had nothing to do with you wanting money or fame or a repeat of your own shitty career?"

"Silas," he growls a warning, clearly out of patience for the topic. I'm on a roll, though. He's shocked the numbness right out of me, and now I'm fucking pissed. I haven't felt this angry in a long time, and it feels fantastic. I can see why Cade is so intoxicated by this.

"Did you ever consider that I could be depressed *because* I was on the road all the time? I think most people would tell you that having no friends and no family and nothing but work is pretty fucking depressing. Probably more of a determining factor than whatever broken brain chemistry I inherited from Mom."

He looks shocked. I've never spoken to him like this in my life, and it's obvious he doesn't know what to do with it.

"I'm your family, Silas. You had me."

Closing my eyes, I take a deep breath in through my nose, while the pain in my head continues to throb in time with my pulse.

"Stop the car."

"What?"

Now I'm the one who's growling. "Stop the fucking car before I throw you out of it."

Cursing under his breath, Dad pulls the truck onto the dirt shoulder of the long stretch of blacktop we're on. Thankfully, it's the middle of nowhere, so there's no one to see our abrupt, mid-highway stop.

Once the truck comes to a rest, the only sounds I hear are the tick of the cooling engine and both of us breathing heavily, while Dad stares at me with wild eyes.

"Silas, what is going on?"

I look him in the eye and keep my voice steady, so he knows I'm serious. "I'm not coming."

"What? Where?"

"To Canada. You should go and start fresh. You have friends there, like you said. But I'm not coming. I'm staying in Possum Hollow. In fact, you can go wherever the fuck you want, but I want Possum Hollow to myself."

"Silas, you can't—"

"I can." I cut him off before he can spew whatever bullshit he's about to. "I know you mean well, but I'm an adult and I can take care of myself. Keep my bike, keep my money. All I want is the house and Possum Hollow."

There's a long pause while he keeps looking at me like he can't figure out if I'm kidding, and the reality of the situation breaks in. I fucking hate him. But he's still my dad. He saved my life, once.

My whole body sags, and I look at him with whatever scrap of affection that still exists between us written on my face. "Please, Dad. I know you hate it there, just like you hate babysitting me. You should be able to start over. So should I. Let's just finally let it go, okay?"

He swallows. His eyes are more red-rimmed than before, and I can see him warring with himself on how to handle this. I'm sure a huge part of him wants to do what he always does and tell me to obey. But I can also see how tired he is.

"This is really what you want?"

"Yeah, Dad. Take the money and start over. I'll be fine."

In the moment where he makes up his mind, he softens, and he seems to age right in front of me. I pull my duffel bag out of the back seat, not wanting to drag this out any longer than I have to in case he changes his mind.

"You sure you don't want to take the bike? You love that thing," he says softly, still looking shocked.

"No, you love that thing. I think I'm actually done." I nod as I say it, and it feels true. A hint of a smile tugs at the corner of my mouth.

I open the door, clambering down from the cab into the dirt. My backpack is slung over my shoulder and I have a duffel bag full of my clothes. Everything else in that truck belongs to him. I don't need any of it.

"How are you going to get back?" he asks before I can close the door.

"I'll get a ride."

We look at each other. Neither of us moves until I finally let the door close with a soft *snick*. He sits there for a few more minutes, and I can see him going back and forth over something in his head.

In the end, he gives me one last look, then puts the truck in drive and pulls back onto the highway. I stand there by myself, watching him disappear. My bike on the back gets smaller and smaller until it's just a black dot that vanishes over the horizon.

Once the adrenaline and emotion have finally run their course, I let myself pull out my phone to make the call. I only hope he answers, or I'm fucked.

Chapter Thirty-Seven

CADE

My fingers have kept up an anxious staccato on the steering wheel for the entire drive here. I keep forcing myself to unclench the muscles in my jaw and neck, as if physically relaxing will somehow make this moment less precarious. Thank God I managed to keep my hands off the whiskey, or it would be Wish driving me right now and I'd have even less to distract myself with.

I don't know what I'm expecting to find when I get to the pin that Silas dropped for me. I assumed he must have had an insane fight with his dad to leave him literally on the side of the highway, so when I finally see him and he's not bloody or bruised, relief flows through me. Throwing the truck onto the shoulder, my first instinct is to dive out of it and run towards him.

Something stops me. I climb out of the cab slowly, watching Silas as he stands up and waits for me to move closer. He seems so small out here by himself with just a couple of bags, surrounded by endless, stretching nothingness. His eyes are warm as he takes me in, but he doesn't say anything or move closer.

It's not too late for the rug to be pulled out from under me again. Life has taught me that, and it makes me cautious as I approach.

"Are you okay? Where's Travis?"

Silas sniffs. When I come to a stop a few feet away from him, he leans back, wrapping his arms around himself like he's cold, despite the midday heat.

"He's gone," Silas says. "I told him to go. You were right; I didn't want to leave. Cade, I'm so sor—"

He takes a step towards me with his hand outstretched, but I move out of reach. Now it's my turn to wrap my arms around myself, until we look like two little kids, huddled into ourselves, staring across the three feet of air between us that feels like it's as wide as the Grand Canyon.

Chewing on my bottom lip, I try to figure out what it is that I want to say to him.

"You're staying? For real?"

He nods. "For real. Even if you can't forgive me for running away, I'll still be here."

My heart breaks a little, watching him stand there all alone, apologizing to me for something that he should never have had to deal with in the first place. It's enough to shut down the last of my defenses and make me close the distance between us.

"Fuck, baby, I'm not mad," I say, wrapping my arms around him. He stays rigid for a few seconds and then melts into my chest with a tremor as I talk. "It's not your fault. I was never mad; I was just hurt and scared for you."

He nods, his face smushed into my chest, as his arms snake around my waist and squeeze. "I'm sorry anyway," he says, although it's muffled by my shirt.

Pulling back enough to look him in the eye, I take his face in my hands and hold him steady. I try to pour the sensation of how much I love him into his skin, whether he feels it or not. I want to say the words as well, but they stick in my throat. Everything feels too raw and open, standing here on the side of the road.

"Let's go home," I say.

He nods, looking exhausted, and follows me like a shadow as I lead him to the truck.

We head for Possum Hollow, and I keep Silas' fingers laced with mine in between us for the entire drive. I want to ask him more about what happened, but I don't know where to start. I keep expecting him to speak, but he never does. Instead, he leans against the window and stares at the countryside, slowly retreating into himself in the way that I've come to fear so much.

My mind spins through every possibility. I don't really care what happened between him and Travis, as long as Travis is gone. What I care about is where his head is at, and whether the blankness I've seen consume him over the past few days is about to get better or worse.

Worst-case scenarios present themselves in vivid technicolor in my head, no matter what I try to focus on. Letting Travis take Silas away from me was hard enough. The thought of actually having Silas—getting to love him the way I want and still watching him slip through my fingers because of something in his own mind—is fucking terrifying.

I don't know if it's something I could come back from.

With one hand on the wheel and the other gripping Silas', the only part of me that's free to fidget is my brain. And it goes wild. When we hit the edge of town, my lungs feel heavy and there's a steady panic creeping through my veins.

I take us to his house instead of the trailer. Whatever this conversation is about to turn into, we don't need an audience for it.

By the time I pull into the driveway and kill the engine, Silas looks half-asleep. I feel like I'm about to tear into little pieces and scatter myself over the driveway like anxiety confetti. He reaches to open the passenger door, but I pull him towards me.

"Silas, I meant it when I said you are the best thing in my life. I..." My tongue struggles to get the words out as I feel raw and vulnerable, but I push through. "I love you so much it scares me. You scare me sometimes. I'm all in, but you have to tell me what we're up against. This thing..." I cast around for the right word while Silas stares at me. "This depression. Did you get it from your mom? Is it because of how your dad treats you? I'm here, no matter what, but right now I'm so fucking scared imagining the worst possible things. I need you to tell me anything you can so I know what to watch out for."

I'm panting, because all the pent-up anxiety from the last hour has just poured into the space between us like a poison fog. Silas didn't flinch or react to the words, though. Maybe he was expecting it.

Eventually, he gives my hand a reassuring squeeze and answers.

"Before I got out of the truck today, Dad was rambling. He's been kind of a mess since he stopped drinking so suddenly, and he was saying so much shit, it was hard to pick out what he meant by all of it. You were right, by the way, he was trying to cheat when they found the fuel additives that caused my suspension."

I'm too distracted to gloat, but I definitely knew it.

"He said, 'I refuse to pull you out of a blood-filled bathtub'. It was part of the twisted justification for all his bullshit, but it stood out to me. So much of what he was saying came back to his obsession with the idea that I was just like Mom, and unless he kept me constantly distracted with work, I would end up killing myself. I never really thought about it before, but that's a lot of paranoia to carry around for twenty years. I always figured he brushed it off so easily because he didn't care, but maybe I didn't look hard enough. Everything he saw must have stuck with him."

Silas looks unnaturally calm as he says it, but all he's doing is making me more anxious. I have tried so hard not to pry, but if this is really going to be *our* life from now on, I have to know.

"Baby, what happened?" I whisper.

Instead of answering, he turns to open the door and gets out of the truck. I follow, and together we unlock the silent house and head inside. Once his bags are on the floor, Silas takes my hand again and leads me to the bedroom that used to be Travis'.

He points to a spot in the corner, a few inches of worn carpet between the bathroom door and the wall.

"This is where Dad found me, the time he thought I was dead. I was less than a year old, and he said I was wrapped up in sheets like she'd tried to strangle me. I was cold when he touched me. 'Like meat.' That's how he described it."

My eyes are glassy, but I focus my attention on *my* Silas, here in front of me. My brain is screaming at me to claw my way through time and save him from all of this, because it never should have fucking happened. It's all I want. It's impossible, though, so the least I can do is set aside my own emotions to give the present-day version of him my full attention.

We move into the bathroom, and he points at the floor by the toilet.

"She was here. She'd taken pills, but she was still alive as well. He took us both to the hospital, and once we came home, he quit touring and convinced himself that everything was going to be fine. Six years later, she killed herself in that bathtub." He gestures towards it absently, and I'm rocked by a wave of nausea in response. "By cutting her wrists. I was with her, but I don't remember. I always used to wonder why she wanted to take me with her the first time, but not the second. I guess I'll never know."

Silas swipes at his face, even though it's bone dry. His fingers reach up to tug at his hair out of habit, but I don't think I can watch any more of this. Moving closer, I pluck his fingers from his hair to wrap his hand up in mine again instead.

When I press my face into the side of his forehead, we both take a deep breath at the same time. Our combined exhalation seems to scatter the remnants of memories from the room until it's just us again. The way it was meant to be.

"It's been a big day, baby," I say to him. "Let's go to your room and sleep for a little while. We have the rest of our lives to deal with this shit."

Silas doesn't answer, but he rolls his head until there's barely an inch between his lips and mine, and our breath is mingled in the space between us. Nodding slowly as he keeps pressing into me, Silas lets his body sag into mine, and I'm there to catch him.

We stay huddled together as we head upstairs, our movements sludgy with exhaustion. I'm about to dump him onto his mattress because I'm well past giving a fuck about putting sheets on it, but Silas stops me.

"Can I take a shower first? I feel..." No words come out to finish that sentence, but I can fill in the blanks. It's a gross kind of day.

"Of course." I press a kiss against his lips, but break away before we have the chance to get distracted. "I'll see if I can find some sheets or something, then we'll rest for a while."

The smile that takes over Silas' face is small but genuine, which makes my heart seem to swell to the point of bursting.

"You don't have to go to work today?" he asks.

I shake my head. "Tristan's covering for me. He says you owe him for that, by the way, and I have no idea what he's going to want in return. I hope you think me and Possum Hollow are worth it, because he definitely might ask you to help him bury a body. Who the fuck knows."

A warm chuckle spills out of Silas before he kisses me again. This time is a little deeper, his tongue tracing the seam of my lips, but I still don't let us get derailed.

"Go. Shower," I say, swatting him on the ass. "I promise I'll still be here when you get out."

He sways as he turns to go, nearly drunk with exhaustion, but he's still smiling. The tendrils of hope that have been steadily wrapping around my heart finally outnumber all the anxious ones, and I can breathe again.

Right: sheets. Bed. *Silas.*

CHAPTER THIRTY-EIGHT

SILAS

By the time I step out of the shower and towel off, my mind feels like a battlefield.

The familiar, almost comforting tug of numbness is there, telling me to wall off my brain and go to sleep. But for once, there are too many other thoughts and emotions vying for my attention. Part of me wants to melt into Cade's arms and cling to him, convinced that everything will work out as long as we're together. Part of me is buzzing with happiness that I finally made a decision for myself and went after what I really wanted. And part of me is already wrapped around the laundry list of practical things I need to deal with in order to survive, like begging for my job and truck back from Ford.

Meanwhile, the small, lurking voice of fear is still asking me if I made a mistake, and if this isn't the first step I've taken towards ruining Cade's life by hitching his wagon to my broken one.

And the smallest, most child-like part of my mind is wishing Dad were here. It's like I'm mourning the death of some potential future-Dad who woke up one day and suddenly said and did all the right things, and cared about me the way I wanted him to. I know that was never going to happen, but now that he's gone, there really isn't a chance.

"You okay?"

Cade's voice brings my attention back to the present. I'm standing in my room with a towel wrapped around my waist, but not moving towards the mattress.

The mattress which has sheets on now, I notice. Because Cade went and found some for me. This is probably the kind of thing that most people's family do for them all the time. It's tiny, really. But something about it is taking root in my heart and not letting go. There's a burning pressure behind my eyes, and I don't cry, but it's the closest I've come all day.

Over fucking sheets.

"Silas?" He moves closer to me, concern obvious in his eyes.

I want to thank him for taking care of everything today, and apologize for being such a mess.

"I love you," is what I say instead.

Cade's head tilts, like a different angle will help him figure out the deeper meaning of it all. Then a slow smile spreads across his face and he reaches for me, pulling me towards him and relieving me of the towel in one movement.

"I love you too," he murmurs, his lips so close to mine I can barely hear the words. I don't need to hear them though, because when he kisses me, it's all right there. I can feel that he means it in every way he touches me and pulls us closer together.

Somehow, we collapse to the mattress together. I'm already naked, and it doesn't take long for Cade to strip his clothes off item by item, in between kisses. We're warm and tangled together, but even though we're both turned on, there isn't the desperate urgency we usually get when we're together. Neither of us makes a move to do anything other than kiss, and for once I'm content to lie here and luxuriate in it.

After a while, my eyelids grow heavy but my mind is just as loud and chaotic as it was in the shower. Cade pulls away, studying my face for a second before he speaks.

"Do you wanna sleep? You look exhausted."

I sigh. "I can't seem to turn my brain off. I'm normally so good at that. Shutting down is my go to. But it's like everything is on a loop in there and it won't shut the fuck up."

"Welcome to my life," Cade says, smiling. "I know exactly what you mean. All the lights are on but nothing makes any sense, 24/7, right?"

I huff a laugh at the mental image. "Pretty much. So what do you do? How do you turn down the volume?"

"Well, there's a lot of unhealthy ways that I don't recommend, but the most effective way I've found is letting you rail me into blissful oblivion. Your magic dick shuts my brain right the fuck up. All those endorphins, baby," he says, grinning at me like an idiot and tracing his fingers over my semi-hard cock as he says it.

I know he's being playful, but I'd never really thought about it like that before. It puts everything that I was worried about before in a totally different light.

"You mean that doesn't scare you?" I ask.

Cade frowns at me. "What?"

"When I lose control and get rough with you? You never said anything, but I was always worried you didn't want to hurt my feelings, or whatever."

There's a long pause while Cade squints at me, and I can almost see the wheels turning in his brain as he figures out how to phrase whatever he wants to say.

"You mean I never said anything other than good stuff? Like 'that was awesome' or 'God, we're so good at sex we should start filming ourselves'."

"I mean," I squirm, trying to figure out what I really do mean. "Yes? No? I can't always tell when you're joking or being polite or trying to placate me or what. I know you'd tell me if you wanted me to stop doing something, but I don't know how much you put up with for my sake, not because you really want to." Panic is creeping into my voice. I can see how serious this conversation has become from his face, but I'm not sure where I went wrong.

I'm never sure where I went wrong when it comes to this stuff. All I do is flounder and wait for things to fall apart.

Maybe *that's* where I'm going wrong.

"Oh, Silas," Cade says softly, rubbing his hand over his eyes before reaching out to cup my face. "Our communication skills are a fucking dumpster fire. I can't believe you've been worried about this the whole time. I'm so sorry."

The right words to answer with are there, but whenever I reach for them, they duck out of reach. Silence stretches between us while we both come to terms with the idea that we have more to work on than we thought.

"Silas, I know we were both raised on bread crumbs of affection and emotional stability, so this stuff feels like speaking in code sometimes," he says. "But I need you to promise me that you'll at least try to talk to me about it. Whenever something's bothering you or you can't figure out how I feel, you have to say something. Otherwise, I won't be able to help you. It's the only way we'll be able to make things work when we have the combined emotional intelligence of a celery stick, okay?"

Nodding, the tension is already relaxing its grip on my body at the knowledge that Cade isn't really angry with me. If he sees this as something we can learn to cope with, then maybe we can.

He kisses me quickly, slotting one of his legs in between mine and pulling me closer to him before he continues.

"There's one more thing I need you to promise me. We don't need to start today, because things have been crazy, but promise me that you will see a doctor about your mental health stuff. We can figure out the money. I can save on every ER bill by putting you back together with duct tape and superglue; I'll do the same thing with my bike, but I don't have emotional duct tape and I don't know the first place to start, so I need you to see someone for real. Please."

The vulnerability and fear in his eyes is unnerving. His fingertips dig into my skin everywhere he's clutching at me, and I can feel his sincerity dripping off of every word.

"Yeah, Cade. I can do that, if you want." I wrap my fingers around his hip and give it a reassuring squeeze. "I never thought about it before because it wasn't an option, but I guess there's nothing stopping us now. If it'll make you feel better, I'll do anything. I don't want you to end up like my dad, feeling like you have to watch over me. I didn't come back to burden you like that."

Cade nods, and his breathing slows down as the panic spiral that was trying to take hold of him seems to dissipate.

There's still a dark intensity in his eyes as he looks at me. I hate it. Thinking about what he said before, I realize I have the perfect way to get his brain to go offline.

"Like you said," I inch towards him until our faces are nearly touching, "we can work on all of this later. The important thing is that we're here, and no one is going anywhere. Now why don't you let me shut your brain up for a while, if you're interested."

Cade's mouth opens underneath mine and he kisses me back greedily. Soft, hungry noises fill the air around us as we devour each other and the rest of the world stops spinning. This time, his cock hardens quickly where it's digging into my hip, and I'm already stiff and aching. My body wants nothing more than to bury myself inside him and reclaim him until he's covered in the taste and scent and feel of me.

Dragging the head of my swollen cock against his skin pulls a groan from me. Wetness trails after, and my hand moves from palming his ass to tracing the line of his crease.

Cade sighs when my fingertips graze his hole. We've done this enough times that it's become a routine, and both of our bodies know the steps well enough to pour through them like molten metal. My brain is already buzzing with happiness when Cade abruptly breaks off our kiss to look me over.

"Not that I don't like where this is headed," he purrs. "But in the spirit of our shiny new communication skills..." He trails off, and doubt creeps back into my mind as I wonder where he could possibly be going with this.

"Tell me," I say, reining in the thrum of fear in my veins.

"Why have you never bottomed? I didn't want to ask in case it cracked open some horrific pandora's box of trauma that you weren't ready to talk about, but I think we just established that tiptoeing around each other's feelings is causing us nothing but problems." He sucks his bottom lip into his mouth, chewing on it absently before rushing to add, "It's okay! I'm not complaining, to be clear. I think we can agree that since we unleashed it, my inner power-bottom has been fucking unstoppable. That bitch does not quit. I just wanted to see if there was a reason, or if you wanted to try but were too shy to ask, or if I was missing something."

It takes me a while to answer, mostly because I'm not sure what the answer is.

"There's no specific reason, I guess," I say, watching the relief spread over Cade's face. "I never really thought about it. From the first time we hooked up and I saw what you looked like spread out underneath me, I was hooked. I wish you could see yourself like that, Cade. It's unbelievable."

"Sloppy and desperate?" He asks, but there's a teasing lilt to his voice.

"No, dumbass. You look free. You're totally uninhibited, and it's like I get to be the thing that wraps around you and keeps you safe. I don't know, that probably sounds stupid," I say, stumbling over my words as I realize that half of them don't make sense.

"No, it's not stupid at all." His fingers are tracing patterns over my ribs, setting off little sparks of electricity that draw my attention back to my needy erection. "That's actually what it feels like. I don't want to stop you from experiencing that as well, though, just because I love it."

I exhale, shaking my head. "I don't think I contain that kind of wanton, uncomplicated happiness. But helping you feel that way makes me happy, so it shakes out in the end, right?"

Cade's face is still twisted up, like he's not convinced. Then something sparks in his eyes, and the corner of his mouth curls into a smile.

"Well, if you don't want to try bottoming—although I think you should because my dick is stupendous, but we can come back to that later—I have another idea of how to get you out of your head. There's something I've been wanting to try since the first time you bent over in front of me while wearing a jumpsuit." He punctuates his words by squeezing my ass hard enough to make me jump, and then lays a loud smack across my flank. "On your stomach, robot boy."

I could ask questions, but I know what he's like once he gets an idea in his head. And honestly, I don't care what we do next. Whatever he wants to try is fine with me, as long as it makes him happy and I get to keep him close.

Rolling over, I make myself comfortable and focus on unclenching my muscles one by one, releasing the knots and snarls of tension. Cade climbs up to straddle my hips. The weight of his body sinks me into the mattress, relaxing me even more, and suddenly his hands and mouth are on every part of me they can reach.

His fingertips dig into my sides and trace the curve of my hips. His mouth trails wet, sucking kisses down my spine until he reaches my ass and bites down. It's a shock of pain, but he soothes it by reaching under me to stroke my cock at the same time, and I almost choke on the groan that comes out of me.

There was no warning before the bite, and there's also no warning before Cade's fingers tease my cheeks apart to run his warm, wet tongue over my hole. It's unlike anything I've experienced before, and apart from a sharp intake of breath, my body goes still.

Cade runs his nose along my skin. His fingers are pressing into me and his torso is draped over my legs, and I feel surrounded by his warmth, which holds me steady. When he licks me again, I'm not as shocked and have the chance to actually feel it, alongside the scrape of his stubble on my skin. He doesn't stop, pressing his mouth against the sensitive flesh and licking into me like he's worshiping me. All the nerve endings I never knew were there light up in the process. It feels like my body is switching back on, cell by cell, after being shut down by my traitorous brain for too long.

My hole clenches and relaxes as he works, and before I know it my hips are rocking into the mattress. I'm fully hard and leaking more than ever, searching for any kind of friction on my cock for some release. Soft moans are spilling out of me. Every sound and move I make seems to spur Cade on until his face is buried in me.

It's incredible, but there's something about the sheer intimacy of it that's building the drumbeat of desire taking over my body.

I don't know how long I lie there for, slowly become one with the mattress. At some point, Cade slips a finger into my softening entrance. The pressure adds to every throb of pleasure, and I continue to float on wave after wave of sensation until I become nothing more than the thing wrapped around Cade's tongue and fingers.

When he eventually stops, I whine in protest, but whole words are beyond me. Cade rolls me over and I take in the sight of him. His face is flushed and streaked with saliva, his hair is wild, and his own cock is rigid with need.

This would normally be the moment when I throw him down and fuck him until he screams, but I feel too loose. He looks as beautiful as ever, though.

It turns out that I don't need to do anything. Moving with the frantic speed of a man who needs his hole filled, Cade straddles my hips as soon as I've rolled over and then leans over to the side. He's rummaging for something, and as soon as he straightens up, there's a tube in his hand and the familiar click of a cap that tells me he found lube earlier and kept it to hand. Thank God he was prepared.

With sloppy movements, Cade smears his fingers and then reaches behind to prep himself. I normally love the feeling of him slowly stretching and softening around me, but right now, just watching him is tantamount to ecstasy. I put my hands on his hips to brace him, holding him upright as he fucks into himself more roughly than I ever would.

His mouth is open and the relief on his face is rapturous. As soon as he's ready, he lubes my cock before bringing me to his entrance. I want to hold him tight and push into him slowly, but he doesn't give me the chance.

Cade has made it clear that he's in charge right now, and he uses that power to swallow my cock to the hilt in one smooth movement.

As soon as I'm inside him, the edge of desperation leaves his movements. Cade relaxes, leaning back and rocking his hips, grinding himself down my length while I'm powerless to do anything but hold his hips and take whatever he gives me.

After so much buildup, neither of us can wait much longer. It isn't long before Cade leans forward to brace himself on my chest, riding me hard enough to make me curse and groan, while his heavy cock bounces between us, leaking a long trail of precum onto my chest.

"Fuck, baby," is all he says when I move my hand to wrap it around his length. He comes so suddenly it catches us both by surprise. I see his stomach tense, and then there's cum arcing out of him, splashing across my abs and chest. He lets out a raw noise of surrender as I stroke him through it, milking everything I can from him.

His rhythm stutters while he comes, but his hole clenches around my cock and throbs, pushing me to the edge. When I'm satisfied I've drained Cade's cock completely, I grab his hips tight and fuck up into him. It only takes a few thrusts before I'm pulsing my own release, and I keep hold of him throughout so I can bury it as deep inside his body as possible.

When the last waves finally fade, a haze of satisfaction settles over both of us. Cade is giving me a sloppy grin, all the love that neither of us can articulate written clearly on his face. I can't see myself, but it's easy to know I look the same.

He collapses on top of me. Our bodies are sticky with sweat and cum, but it only makes this feel more real. When my cum starts to leak out of Cade and down his thigh, I drag my fingers through it to smear across his skin.

I want him to be so dirty with me that it can never wash off.

There's still a million things to talk about. We have a whole future to plan, and a lot of stuff neither of us is equipped to deal with. But for now, Cade is here, and both our brains are finally quiet.

It's a start. We can deal with the rest after we sleep.

EPILOGUE

Three Months Later

CADE

"Hurry up dude, the bus will drop off any second," I say, fighting to catch my breath between words. Silas' mouth is full, but I swear I can *feel* him smirk around my cock.

I'm propped on the edge of the bathroom counter, because this was meant to be a shower quickie, but things got way out of hand. His fingers pump lazily into my hole, slick with the load he just filled me with, refusing to let any of it leak out. A fuck-ton of things have changed in our lives since we first hooked up, but that never has. Silas has never wavered in his need to have me coated in him, inside and out.

And I've never wavered in how much I love it.

Normally, I would have exploded in his mouth as soon as he pulled out and knelt for me, but he's been teasing me and drawing it out with agonizing patience. I'm right on the edge, and this would be infuriating even if we weren't on a tight schedule.

"You motherfucker," I say through gritted teeth, as he laves his tongue over the crown of my cock but refuses to take me deeper. "If I don't finish before they get here, I swear I will cut you off for a week."

It's a lie, and we both know it. He plays along anyway.

I hear a distant rumble, and hope it's not a bus engine. All my attention stays focused on Silas, and how incredible he looks on his knees for me. My eyes trace the long lines of his back muscles. They flex as he moves suddenly, swallowing me to the hilt and sending fireworks up my spine in the process.

With a gasp, I finally release and empty myself into his mouth. He swallows like the greedy bitch he is sometimes, muscles still flexing and beautiful in the soft light. All I can do is lie back and admire the view while my orgasm continues to rock through me.

When Silas finally pulls off, he shoots to his feet and smashes our mouth together with a feral intensity. I swear, one day he's going to break my nose. I kiss him back just as fiercely, pushing my tongue into his mouth so I can taste myself on him.

The sound of someone knocking on the door is what finally makes us tear apart.

Maddi and Sky both have a key to Silas' house—*our* house—for emergencies, but they know better than to use it if they don't have to. That was the deal we all made. Mom tries to parent, Maddi and Sky try to be regular kids for once, and Silas and I try to have a life of our own that doesn't revolve around disaster management. Which means this house is only PG-13 when we have an appropriate amount of heads up.

"Fuck," I hiss. "I told you we didn't have time for this." I cast around, looking for any clothes I can pull on, and find some mismatch of mine and Silas' on the floor that will do for now.

Silas gives me a smug smile. Cocky is a new look for him, but it's delicious. It makes me want to devour every inch of him. But that's what made us late in the first place.

"I think they've survived worse than waiting on the doorstep for thirty seconds to be let in. Come on, the more time you spend whining, the longer they wait," he says.

306

Silas also pulls on some clothes as we move, and by the time we get to the front door, we look more or less respectable. As soon as the latch clicks, Maddi and Sky walk in and dump their bags on the ground, giving us a rushed hello on their way to raid the fridge.

They treat this place like it's theirs, because it basically is. Mom has continued to work with CPS to keep custody, and so far she's doing a good job. The trailer is where they live. But whenever she's at work and they're not in school, they come here, so I know they're safe.

And even though I'm proud of Mom for how much she's changed recently, I've been figuring out how to keep the kind of paper trail I might need if I ever had to apply for custody in the future.

I hope it never comes to that, but until recently, hope hasn't been on my side.

SILAS

Once the girls have loaded up with an unfathomable amount of snack food, they clamber into their regular seats at the table and pull out their homework. I take a seat next to them, with my own little stack of worksheets in front of me.

Cade calls it 'homework club', which he thinks is hilarious, but also makes him happier than he'd ever admit. Maddi and Sky are learning how to have structure in their lives, I can help them with their work if they need it, and I also have time to do the mountains of paperwork that come with being in therapy.

I didn't know what to expect when we finally figured out how the fuck the healthcare system works. No wonder no one goes to the doctor, because even if you have health insurance, that shit is a nightmare of bureaucracy guaranteed to give you new mental health issues before you can even treat the ones you have.

There were about a hundred times I was ready to give up. I'd lived with my off-kilter brain my entire life, I was convinced that if I just loved Cade enough, I could keep pushing through. All I needed was him.

Unfortunately, it turns out that's not how shit works. The longer we were 'happy', with a house and jobs and no dads around to tear us down, the more frustrating it got that I didn't automatically feel and act normal.

It was better, sure. But I was still fucked. I still had bouts of intense melancholy or paranoia, and the nightmares about Cade dying only got worse.

Cade breaking his neck on the track instead of Anthony Turner. Cade dying in the bathtub instead of my mother. Cade burning to death in the trailer when his mom falls asleep with a cigarette.

I was doing well enough that I was completely aware of how fucked up and worthless these nightmares were, but nothing made them any better. So, I let Cade keep pushing me until we figured out the healthcare bullshit enough to get a doctor and a therapist.

Which has somehow ended up with me having endless piles of homework. Around the table, Sky is doing some kind of quiz on verbs, Maddi is writing an essay on American history, and I am filling in a worksheet about 'distress tolerance'.

All under Cade's soft, happy gaze.

Honestly, even if it weren't helping, I'd do the stupid therapy just to make him happy. But it does help, so I try to keep my bitching to a minimum.

The first time I saw Cade after I moved back, I remember thinking that I would slit my wrists to be able to have a little bit of the sunshine he carries around with him. It might have been a sign that my brain chose to phrase it that way.

It turns out, all I have to do is the opposite. I'll do anything to protect Cade and the girls. Even if that means I have to go against all my twisted instincts and protect myself first.

X THE END X

Up Next

68 Whiskey, Possum Hollow Book 2

Out Now

Tristan & Ford

Ӿ

Running Feral, Possum Hollow Book 3

Coming November 29th 2024

Tobias & Gunnar

Available for Pre-Order Now

Ӿ

Possum Hollow Book 4

Release 2025

The second half of Silas & Cade's love story

Ӿ

Possum Hollow Book 4.5

Release TBD

Rebecca & Wish Novella

Savage, Sins of the Banna Book 1

Available now as a serial on REAM along with other subscriber benefits and Possum Hollow bonus content.

Micah & Savage

Will be published on Amazon once complete in early 2025

68 Whiskey Teaser

TRISTAN

The Egg McMuffin I'm shoveling into my mouth is at least two hours old. It's a stone-cold mess of congealed and cheese, but it's still the best goddamn thing I've put in my mouth all week.

As depressing as that is.

Eight years in the military living off MREs and chow hall slop really gives you an appreciation for any food that doesn't come out of a vacuum pack. On top of that, this has been a grueling fucking shift. It's one of those sweltering summer nights, the kind where it feels like the humidity is trying to drown you, and there's no reprieve from the heat. Even at 2a.m., I was sweating out my body weight and it's only gotten warmer since then. I'm dehydrated and I'm fucking hungry.

Possum Hollow is a teeny, tiny little town in the middle of nowhere, Missouri. It's stereotypical rural poor, so working on an ambulance I see a decent amount of action with bar brawls, overdoses, and diabetes complications, but not a lot else. Most days, the shifts feel like a breath of fresh air compared to all the lives I've lived before.

Tonight was an exception. There was a multi-car pile-up, which is not something we see that often. My partner Cade—the EMT to my paramedic—had to pop his solo-CPR cherry because there were too many casualties to triage while we waited for other ambulances to be routed from nearby counties.

He handled it, though, and I'm pretty damn proud of him. Not that I'll say so. He's been on the job a little over a year, and this is when his ego needs to be kept in check before he gets over-confident and accidentally kills someone.

I'm not judging. He'll fuck up and kill someone eventually; it's a rite of passage for emergency med. But as the person who sucked him into this messy-ass job by convincing him to go to EMT school, I feel obligated to try to shield him from the worst of it as long as I can.

Right now, he's sitting still for once in his life; his head tipped back in the passenger's seat and his eyes closed. Cade normally has the energy of a golden retriever puppy trying not to trip over his own paws. Instead, with blood and vomit on his shirt and a fresh trauma running through his mind, the atmosphere in the cab feels heavy.

"Eat," I say, throwing his own gelatinous egg sandwich into his lap.

The grimace I get in response tells me he's not feeling it, but I'm not taking no for an answer.

"Trust me. You're going to feel like shit either way, and your body needs the fuel. The shift ain't over yet. The last thing you want is for us to get called to another fucking job and you start feeling faint half-way through."

Begrudgingly, Cade reaches for the sandwich and peels back the wrapper. He looks pale, and it's weird not to see the normal current of energy running through him. I fight back the paternal sense of worry that automatically builds in me.

More and more, I'm forced to remind myself that he's not my kid to take care of. I moved here to put distance between myself and the rest of the world, not adopt every waif and stray that runs across my path. Just because his own parents couldn't give two shits about him and he's the spitting image of my little brother...

I have to get a grip.

Beep beep beep.

Of course, the sound of our motherfucking tones interrupts us.

Shoving the rest of my breakfast in my mouth like a chipmunk, I confirm our response and then listen to dispatch rattle off the address as I try to chew through the wad of cold food as quickly as possible. The call is for a 22yo male who's been stabbed, which is a lot spicier than most of our calls. I have a vague idea of where the address is, but I've only lived here for a couple of years, so I don't have the same internal GPS that Cade does.

Which is why I look across the cab to see if he recognizes the location. Instead of a normal response, I find him staring at me wide-eyed, all the blood drained from his face, looking like he's about to hurl his single bite of food onto the dash.

"That's Ford's garage." His voice quavers as he speaks.

"Fuck."

I don't bother with other questions. My hand flicks the switch for full lights and sirens. I slam-reverse out of the space we were in and gun it to the highway.

I've never been to the garage. The only thing I know about it is that Cade's buddy Ford owns it, and his boyfriend Silas works there. The love-of-his-life, borderline-adorable-borderline-codependent, all-consuming, he-hurts-I-hurt boyfriend that he *just* settled down with.

This is not good. My stomach lurches at the thought of how many ways the next hour could play out for my partner.

I know better than anyone that the worst day of your life is never something you see coming.

Red tendrils of dawn are licking over the horizon as I careen across town in record time. The good thing about Possum Hollow is that it's fucking small. I can make it there in six or seven minutes if I disregard all safety protocols, and fuck safety protocols right now.

There's one corner that I take hard enough for the inside wheels to lift a little, but apart from that, the drive is clean.

As I'm pulling up to the auto shop, I debate whether to call for back up right away. I don't know how objective or functional Cade is going to be once we get inside. The kid's had a fucked-up life, and he's generally pretty good at compartmentalizing, but he's been all kinds of soft for Silas since the day they met.

There's no one else on duty right now, so I'd have to get someone from a different station, which is why I ultimately decide to take a wait-and-see approach.

We both clamber out of the ambulance at full speed. I switch my brain to maximum work mode, and I can see by the set of Cade's jaw that he's trying to do the same.

"Are you gonna be able to do this, kid?" I ask, my voice nearly drowned out by the sound of our feet crunching across the gravel parking lot.

"If you try to make me sit outside, I'll deck you. I swear to God."

Cade doesn't get serious very often, but he has a dark side buried in there. I haven't seen it a lot, but he can be ferocious when he needs to be. Blame my own lifetime of trauma, but the fact that he's getting pissed instead of weepy gives me more confidence in him.

"I'll assess the scene. You will do every single thing I say, exactly as I say, or I will bench you and deal with this myself. Understood?"

I don't get an agreement, which makes my inner sergeant chafe at the disrespect, but I also don't get a "fuck you", so I'll take it.

There's a police cruiser in the lot with its lights still flashing, but the roller door at the front of the garage is pulled down, so we can't see the situation inside. I had let myself be optimistic and didn't bother with a stretcher until we get the lay of the land. Cade walks us in through the side door like he's been here

315

a million times, which I guess he has, and my brain immediately starts breaking down everything that's going on inside.

Silas is sitting down, holding a questionably clean towel against his ribs over what I'm assuming is his injury. He looks bright and alert, though, even if he's in pain, which is a good start. Cade is thundering over to him before I get the chance to say anything, of course.

"I'm totally fine." Silas heads us both off at the pass. "The knife glanced off my ribs, it's barely a graze. Please don't freak out."

His words do nothing to eat at the worry rolling off Cade in waves, but it settles me a little. Silas is stoic, but he's rational. At least about things that aren't to do with Cade. Confident that he's probably not dying, I'm happy to let Cade handle it and turn my attention to the chaos unfolding on the other side of the shop floor.

"Full head-to-toe, make sure there aren't any injuries the adrenaline isn't letting him feel. You've got this," I call out to Cade as I walk past the pair of them.

Because my attention is on the same thing as the cops are focused on, which is the other person in the building. The two patrolmen have him penned into the corner, and the energy coming from them is that kind of crackling tension that spells trouble. He's in handcuffs and he's bleeding from a small head laceration, but the fact that he's not already in the back of their cruiser makes it unclear whether he's the perpetrator.

"What's going on?" I'm vaguely familiar with both officers. I can't remember their names, but they both look like they walked straight out of central casting for small town cops with a grudge and a power trip. "Is this the suspect?"

"He's my fucking boss!" Silas yells from across the room. I don't think I've ever seen him raise his voice before. He's normally pretty shy, but right now he looks pissed. Cade pulls his focus back to the exam, but Silas jerks away to keep yelling. "These assholes put him in cuffs because they're morons. He doesn't fucking talk. If he's cuffed, he can't type or sign, so how can he give a statement?

They made shitty assumptions as soon as they walked in the door and haven't listened to a word I'm saying."

"That's enough attitude out of you, son," Officer Asshole Number One says. "We know it's Ford's shop, but he's acting erratic, and we just want to keep everyone safe while we ascertain the truth of the situation."

"The truth of the situation is that I got stabbed by a fucking meth head who was trying to rob us. I called the cops and because he's upset that his shop was trashed, you called him 'aggressive' and treated him like a criminal," Silas calls out.

The tension in the room is rising, but I narrow my focus on the man in question.

I've heard of Ford Novack, but we've never actually met. Apparently, he has a reputation in this town for violence, although according to Cade, it's outdated.

I can see why he would put people on the defensive. The man is ferocity in human form. I'm fucking tall at 6'3", and he's got at least an inch on me, plus a lot of muscle and bulk. Long, dark hair that was probably tied back earlier, but has come loose and is flying around his bloodied face adds drama to the image, and underneath the blood and beard I'm pretty sure I can see a big-ass scar running down one cheek. His pale skin makes all that blood and hair pop, so he looks like something out of a graphic novel.

The thing that really gets me is his eyes. He has husky eyes. Light blue and totally fucking crazed. I love it. Something about that raw, feral intensity sparks my own crazy in response.

I don't generally trust cops any more than I have to. I've seen too many who are so shit-scared in their suburban neighborhood that they can't exercise a little self-control and not open fire at random. Compared to the nineteen-year-old kids who get thrown into literal open warfare and still manage to adhere to the rules of engagement.

But even if I was going to side with the cops, crazy husky eyes here would have changed my mind.

This situation is rapidly deteriorating, and I'm too exhausted and hungry not to take charge.

"Well, if he didn't commit a crime, I'm gonna need you to remove the cuffs so I can give him medical attention. If you're too piss-scared of a random law-abiding citizen just because he's taller than you, then give me the keys and wait in your cruiser while the grown-ups work."

Watching the cop's face turn red is deeply satisfying. I'm not going to lie.

"Hey, I don't know how things work on the east coast, but around here, the law is in charge."

Jesus fucking Christ, he even talks like he walked out of a bad cop movie.

"Bitch, I wouldn't trust you to police your way out of a traffic jam. Unlock the cuffs now, or I'll be filing a report with your department for unlawful detention. You may think you're hot shit, but this is middle America and a lot of people are willing to listen to a war veteran first responder over some small-town schlub on a permanent power-trip."

Apparently, that's enough to close the issue. The cop looks pissed as hell, but he takes the cuffs off Ford before walking away. I know making enemies in a small town isn't a great idea, but I'm from South Boston. If there's anything I know how to do, it's hold a grudge.

Both cops retreat to take a statement from Silas, leaving me and Ford in a tentative little bubble of peace. The amount of tension running through his body is palpable, even from three feet away. In deference to the cops, Ford does look like he wants to crush someone's skull in his giant canned-ham hands. I still think I could take him if I had to.

"Can I take a look at your head, man? You're bleeding pretty good."

I watch as he forces his muscles to unclench, one by one. The anger slips out of his body and is replaced by a profound level of weariness. As he nods his consent, he seems to sway on his feet.

"Let's sit down." I place a hand on his elbow, which makes him scowl, but he lets me guide him gently until he's sitting on some kind of toolbox. I crouch down in front of him to take a look. I try to place my fingers on his chin to tilt his face towards me, but this time he jerks out of my grasp completely.

This guy seems like he's pretty self-contained. And if you don't talk, I imagine most people find you difficult to read. But I make my living looking at people's bodies for clues. Which means I clock that his pulse immediately starts to speed up, to the point that I can see his vein fluttering over his throat. I see his jaw clench as his nostrils flare and his eyes widen, all while he pulls away from me.

That's not anger. That's fear.

Oh, he's just getting more interesting by the minute.

I need to grab a Telfa pad from my jump bag anyway, so I turn away as slowly as I can, using the moment to give him a second to breathe. When I turn back around, his chin is tilted in a little protectively, so I take a different tack.

"You're still bleeding, so I'm gonna hold pressure for a couple of minutes, okay?"

I get the smallest possible nod, those bright blue eyes watching me with the hyper intensity of someone who's known more bad touch than good. I'm an expert at keeping patient interactions surface-level, but something about his expression hits me deep.

Avoiding touching him anywhere else, I press the pad against his forehead. From a cursory glance it doesn't look terrible, but foreheads are vascular as fuck, so I need to stop the bleeding before I can do anything else with it.

"What happened?"

Huffing, Ford shakes his head and rolls his eyes so hard it almost dislodges my hand. His hands come up in front of him, clutching uselessly at the air, and I put two and two together. He doesn't have his phone, and Silas said that's how he generally communicates.

"You sign, right? Go ahead, I know ASL."

This time when he jerks away from my hands, it's in shock, not fear. Our gazes collide, and he looks at me for longer than I expect, his expression guarded.

Intensity hangs between us like the spit-trail after a really dirty kiss.

Eventually, his hands move. Slowly at first, but with more confidence as I nod to confirm that I'm following what he's saying. My hand is still pressing the gauze to his forehead, which limits his ability to raise his eyebrows, basically hamstringing him from signing properly, but there are enough context clues for him to get his meaning across. If I miss anything, it's my fault for getting distracted by how nimble he manages to be despite the obvious strength in his hands.

"We don't usually open until later," he signs. "But Silas has a side project he wanted help with, so we came in early. When we got here, three guys were inside, ransacking the place. Meth heads, grabbing shit and breaking shit at random. I grabbed one, but his buddy got Silas with a knife, so I let him go to help. They all ended up running out before I could catch any of them, but one of them hit me with a fucking wrench in the process. Then Silas called 911 and everything just got worse."

He looks around briefly at the shop, which is definitely trashed, and the heartbreak is clearly written on his face. Then he turns back to me. Narrowed eyes tell me he still isn't convinced I understand, so I switch out my hand for his holding the pad and sign back at him instead of talking.

"My little brother was deaf. I'm a little rusty, but I understand you." I lean in to whisper the next part, "Don't tell Thing One and Thing Two over there, though, because they're nosy and I don't like to talk about it."

He fingerspells "OK" softly, like an afterthought, still holding my gaze.

The laser focus that I normally carry into a scene stutters for a second. It's been a long night, followed by a weird end-of-night call, and saying anything personal about myself always sets me on edge. I feel like all the wheels and cogs inside my work-brain are catching slightly off, and I have to concentrate to bring my attention away from Ford's haunting, anguished eyes back to the scene.

"Cade, how's your boy?" I yell across the open space once I've rejoined the living.

"He's stable; single shallow lac, but we're taking him to hospital to get him double-checked by a trauma doc if I have to fucking sedate him to get him there."

I bite back a smile. Cade may be a golden retriever most of the time, but he's a bulldog when he's in protective mode, and it's one of the things that cemented our friendship.

"Fair," I say, turning back to Ford. He's still staring at me with an inscrutable kind of intensity. "What about you? Feel like a field trip to the ER? I can make sure you're stable, but I'd feel a lot better about your head if you got a CT."

As the words came out of my mouth, I knew the answer would be a hard *no*. Ford's face shutters. In the short time I've been there, he's been constantly expressive: despairing about the shop, angry at the cops, fearful of me, shocked that I understood him... But this is nothing. This is totally shut down, in a way that seems familiar to him.

I inhale and exhale through my nose, long and slow, weighing the pros and cons of arguing with him. In the end, I decide against it. We've built a fragile peace after he seemed ready to tear those cops apart, and it's not worth ruining that over a fight I won't win, anyway.

Instead, I let the silence fall over us. I take his vitals, checking he's okay before I touch him each time. I go through concussion protocol to see if I have cause to bring him in against his will. He sits through the whole thing like a rock, and he's as stable as I'd hoped. The head lac has stopped bleeding, so he lets me give it a rough-and-ready cleanup and a quick butterfly bandage before his patience runs out.

I go through my spiel about why he shouldn't be skipping the CT and signs of a concussion to look out for. I tell him to have someone monitor him, though I know he won't, and pull out my iPad for him to sign that he's staying Against Medical Advice.

Leaving him alone feels wrong, but I know there's no kind of logic or cajoling that's going to work against his brick wall of obstinance. By the time I'm done, Cade and Silas are out in the ambulance, ready to go.

With a last look, I watch him sit there in silence, surrounded by the trashed shop that he obviously loves, staring at the floor and already pretending I don't exist.

About the Author

Erin Russell is a queer writer living in Los Angeles. They write hurt/comfort queer romance novels with the occasional horror story thrown in the mix.

Connect with Erin on social media or through their newsletter, and check out the Stupid Dirty *playlist on Spotify using the QR code below.*

Printed in Great Britain
by Amazon